Runaway Heart

Leslie McKelvey

ISBN 978-1-936556-78-6

Published 2016

Published by Black Velvet Seductions Publishing

Runaway Heart Copyright 2016 Leslie McKelvey
Cover design Copyright 2016 R. J. Savage

Published 2016
Printed by Black Velvet Seductions Publishing
A division of Savage Publications

Visit us at:
www.blackvelvetseductions.com

To three amazing women in my life....

First, my cousin, Barbara D'Souza, I so appreciate your support and feedback! I wish you the best of luck with your writing endeavors and know that you, too, will achieve your dream of becoming a published author. Believe in yourself; I do!

Second, my very dear friend, Barbara Martoncik, I am so glad to have met you! You are kind, sweet, and generous, and I cannot thank you enough for believing in and supporting my books. You are an amazing woman and a kick-ass PA, and Maryann is lucky to have you. (By the way, Bear is MINE!)

Last, but definitely not least, Jennifer Beard. We haven't known each other for years, but it feels like we have. We clicked from the get-go and I am deeply grateful for your friendship, support, and advice. The only thing I would change about our relationship is the distance between us, so we could spend more time together.

Love you all!

Chapter One

Lindsay Davenport peered through the dirty windows of the abandoned building, a throb pounding at the base of her skull as her heart climbed into her throat. The almost overwhelming urge to flee started the flow of adrenaline, and it took her several deep breaths to pull in her galloping pulse. *Relax, Lindsay. You can do this. You have to do this.*

The street was clear, for the moment. She'd been careful, but she still expected Roger, her husband's bodyguard, to pull up in the black Navigator and drag her home. Behind her, Peebo put the finishing touches on her new documents. A new work history and personal history were already done and printed out so she could memorize the particulars. His fingers moved rapidly over the keyboard, and the sound reminded her of machine gun fire. She grimaced and moved back to his side.

"How much longer?" she asked in a low voice as she listened for the drone of the Lincoln's engine.

Peebo smiled, his dark eyes focused on his computer. "You've waited six years for this, Lindsay. A few more minutes ain't gonna kill you."

Lindsay shuddered and wrapped her arms around herself, a chill worming through her. "Yeah, but Roger and his associates might."

He looked up in alarm, perspiration beaded on his brow. "You weren't followed, were you?"

She shook her head and went back to the window. "No, but I keep expecting them to show up anyway." She gave Peebo a weary smile and took a deep breath. "I guess I just can't believe it will all be over soon."

His full lips widened in a smile, making him almost pleasant to look at. "No fear, chica. Once I'm finished you can disappear and no one, including your husband, will ever find you if you don't want them to."

Tears stung and she sank down onto a chair. Peebo went back to work, the printer and scanner humming, his eyes dancing as he continued. She ran a hand over her face and took a shaky breath.

Seven years ago she'd thought herself the luckiest woman alive as she strolled down the aisle with Lucas Davenport, heir to one of the nation's largest private pharmaceutical companies. Their chance meeting outside her stepdad's cafe had gone from casual "boy bumps into girl" to "boy asks girl out" to "girl falls in head-over-heels in love." She'd thought herself a modern-day Cinderella, minus the evil stepmother and stepsisters, and Lucas Davenport was her Prince Charming. To go from a waitress in a rural Texas diner to the bride of a multi-millionaire and the man touted as "a rising star shooting straight for the State Senate," was more than she'd ever hoped for. How quickly her dream had turned into a nightmare.

Her husband was the pride of Dallas society, and a favorite among the ladies. At first his handsome looks had charmed her and she'd felt proud to be on his arm. His hair was a rich, dark brown that begged to be touched, his eyes a vivid hazel that could warm her, or chill her, depending on his mood. While not physically imposing he was tall and athletically built, but his presence was bigger than he was. He exuded confidence from every meticulously cleaned pore and his smile could charm a snake. What she'd found beneath that pleasing, designer clad exterior, however, had killed the love she'd felt for him. A monster in Armani was still a monster.

"Lindsay? Lindsay!"

She jumped and came back to the present. The worn bricks of the building came slowly back into focus, sunlight turned dingy brown as it filtered through the dirt-smeared windows. She looked at Peebo and got to her feet. "Yeah, what?"

Peebo grinned and handed her a manila envelope. "You're ready, baby. Everything you'll ever need is in there. You've got a social security card, driver's license, birth certificate and passport. There are letters of recommendation from previous employers, so you should have no trouble getting a job. And I even threw in a valid credit card with a $5,000 limit. The Witness Protection Program should be so thorough."

Her hands shook as she took the envelope and her eyes stung. Slowly, reverently, she opened the package and pulled out her new birth certificate. "Lacey Jamison," she said softly. She glanced at Peebo. "Pretty name. Thank you." She thought Peebo blushed, but with his swarthy skin it was hard to tell.

"Well, it had to fit the owner," he said. "And it's not too far from

Lindsay, so it should be easy to adopt."

Lindsay put the paper away, a contradictory mix of hope and fear churning inside her abdomen. The conflicting warmth and cold made her feel mildly nauseous. "Make sure you destroy everything that has to do with this." Her voice was hushed. "Anything that would show I was here, or that you did this for me, get rid of it." She stood in front of him and gave him a pointed look. "I mean it, Peebo. *Everything.* Make sure there is nothing to link you to me, nothing."

Peebo stood and smiled at her. "Chiquita, I've done this long enough to know how to take care of myself. It's been a while, but I still remember the important stuff. Trust me, if your husband's goons come here looking for something, all they'll find is an empty building." He started to put his equipment away. "One job, one location, no paper trail."

She swallowed hard. "I can't thank you enough for helping me."

"You paid me, remember? Quite well, I might add."

She stared at the envelope and shook her head. "No amount of money is worth the danger involved here."

Peebo scowled. "Lindsay, you are the reason my family didn't starve when your husband fired me." His expression turned pensive and he studied her face briefly. "You're also the reason we didn't lose our house, or have to pull the boys out of that private school my wife loves so much, and you kept me from having to return to my prior life of crime." A meaty hand came up onto her shoulder and squeezed lightly. "I know your husband is a monster, and you've been unhappy for a long time." With a shrug he released her and continued to pack. "I wanted to give you back some of what you gave us."

Lindsay looked at his back. "What's that?"

He paused and looked at her over his shoulder, his expression solemn. "*Hope.*"

***

As the sun began its descent into the western sky, the bus wound its way toward downtown Dallas. Lindsay waited until it pulled up at the huge shopping mall. A glance down the long aisle of parking spots near the bus stop showed her little BMW Z8 coupe right where she'd parked it a few hours earlier before taking the bus to meet Peebo. The bright red sports car stood out like a beacon amongst the sedans, trucks, and minivans. After looking around carefully she disembarked and followed the throng inside the air-conditioned mecca.

She clutched her bag, her precious paperwork inside. Nervous shivers fanned over her skin and she felt chilled in spite of the afternoon heat. As casually as she could, she made her way to Neiman Marcus, eyes alert. Pausing at the cosmetics counter, she listened absently as the salesgirl explained the virtues of their newest skin care line.

Her mouth was dry and her palms clammy as she looked around, half-expecting her husband's security chief to appear. Roger would be easy to spot as his blonde head would tower over the crowd. After purchasing some perfume, she meandered through the store, appearing nonchalant but ever watchful. She bought several new outfits without even trying them on, thankful for her standard size 8 figure. After only half an hour in the store she had an armload of packages. If anyone decided to check on her whereabouts, as her husband often did, she hoped she'd purchased enough to convince them she'd spent the past several hours shopping rather than planning her escape in an abandoned warehouse.

For authenticity's sake she wandered through the mall to Macy's, running up even more charges on Lucas's credit card. A flash of guilt hit her and she stamped it down. The money she spent was small recompense for what she'd been through in the last seven years.

She thought briefly of the cash she had stashed away, and wondered if it would be enough to keep her until she could stop running and find a job. For the past five years she'd taken most of the cash Lucas had given her and hidden it, because she'd known when she gathered the courage to leave she would need it. As her departure grew imminent, however, she found herself assailed by doubts, and more than a little fear. To leave Lucas was to take her life in her hands, but she knew it was time. She was tired of being Lucas Davenport's pretty, quiet little wife and favorite punching bag.

Strolling toward the exit, Lindsay paused near the center escalator where a shelter for women and children had set up a small booth. Two young ladies, one blonde, one brunette, sat at the folding table calling out to passing shoppers. They were raffling off a "romantic dinner for two" at a high-end restaurant in downtown Dallas to raise money for new playground equipment. Judging by their discouraged expressions, it didn't appear as if they had many takers. The tickets were $5, quite a deal for what the prize was worth. Lindsay thought about it for a moment, and a moment was all it took. She walked over to the table.

"Dinner for two?" the brunette asked hopefully.

A slow smile spread over Lindsay's face. "Not anymore," she assured the girl. "Not anymore." Lindsay pulled out all the cash she had, several hundred dollars, and handed it to the dark-haired woman. It was money she could use, but the irony was more satisfying. The girl looked up in surprise and her mouth dropped open as she stared at the wad of bills. Before the young lady could say a word, Lindsay turned on her heel and continued toward the exit, her steps far more lively than when she had entered the shopping center.

She bought a dozen Mrs. Field's Milk Chocolate Chip Cookie Bites on the way out of the mall and strolled toward her car. She loved the red sports coupe, and frowned when she remembered when and why Lucas had purchased it. He'd presented it to her at the hospital, but she'd been unable to drive because of her broken arm. She popped a cookie into her mouth and pulled out her keys.

Lindsay opened the trunk, put her packages inside, and jumped when she felt a hand clamp down on her shoulder. Fear surged through her in an icy wave. Her bag of cookies fell to the ground as she spun and looked up into Roger's face.

He glanced at the bags in the trunk then turned a cold eye on her as he slammed the lid shut. "Lucas has been wondering where you've been."

His voice sent a chill up her spine. She swallowed hard and forced herself to meet his gaze. "I think you can see where I've been," she replied, keeping her voice neutral. "If Lucas was looking for me, he could've called. My cell phone is on."

Roger frowned. "I didn't say he was *looking* for you. I said he was wondering where you've been." He leaned forward. "Your husband is interested in how you spend your time."

Lindsay's chin tipped up and she returned his baleful gaze in kind. "Then perhaps he should ask me. I'd be more than happy to give him an accounting of my day."

"Perhaps he's afraid you won't be entirely honest."

A hot spurt of anger burned through the fear and the words fell out before she could stop them. "As if Lucas Davenport would know *anything* about honesty."

Roger studied her silently then his face broke into a cold smile. "You know, I thought he'd have crushed you by now." He tucked a lock of hair behind her ear, and chuckled when she jerked away from him. "But you've still got some fight left in you. I wonder how much longer that will last, and what it'll take to break it."

Her eyes narrowed, his words like breath on coals. "It'll take more than him...or *you*." He laughed as she picked up her bag of cookies, stepped around him, slid behind the wheel, and slammed the door shut. She fastened her seatbelt, opened the window, and looked at him over her shoulder. "In case you're wondering, I'm going to spend the next half hour driving home, but after that I'll be improvising." Without waiting for a reply, she turned the engine over and sped away.

***

Lindsay stroked the horse's nose as the bay gelding stood quietly in the stall. It was late and the chirp of crickets and the creaking of the barn were all that broke the stillness. She felt like a cat on a hotplate - all bunched nerves, taut muscles and jumpy. Since she'd finally procured her paperwork from Peebo her gut had been telling her to *run*, to drop everything and *flee*. Thankfully, she'd fought that base instinct. She had to behave in a normal fashion, act as she usually did, or Lucas would know something was off. Had she taken off in the bright light of day Roger would no doubt have already tracked her down and dragged her back, literally. No, she'd been smart to stick to her original plan of leaving in the dead of night. That way Roger would be asleep and Lucas would be occupied elsewhere, giving her the head start she'd need to get away.

At the moment Lucas was in the house with several executives from the company. The men had come for drinks and dinner, and she had played the entertaining, dutiful hostess as she usually did. *Behaving normally*. When the liquor was gone and the meal was over Lucas had dismissed her with a wave of his hand. Relieved, she'd smiled at their inebriated guests and left without a word.

As minutes ticked by her anxiety level went up, the tranquility of the evening directly contradicting her emotions. Her stomach knotted and twisted in her belly, and her throat went tight. The horse seemed to sense her distress and butted up against her with his nose, whickering softly. Unbidden, she smiled. A chuckle escaped her as she scratched the animal's ears and patted his neck.

"I'm going to miss you, Midnight," she whispered. "But don't worry. Lucas will take good care of you. He thinks *you're* worth something."

She knew if she didn't return to the house soon Lucas would send Roger to look for her, so she left the barn and strolled slowly across the broad lawn. She gazed at the imposing structure. It looked like it had been transplanted straight from *Gone With The Wind* with its tall columns gleaming in the moonlight. Huge magnolias lined the drive, their branches heavy with blossoms. She mounted the wide, flat steps, and inhaled their fragrance.

Pausing on the veranda, her eyes slid to her right toward the northern wing of the house where Roger had a suite of rooms. The lighted windows told her he was still awake. Uneasiness skittered coldly up her spine and goose bumps peppered her arms. If anyone would wreck her plans it would be Roger. Lucas paid the enormous man very well for his allegiance and he took his job *very* seriously. A large shadow briefly darkened the curtained glass and moments later the lights went out. The fact he was heading to bed did *nothing* to lessen her anxiety. Swallowing hard, Lindsay forced her feet to move.

Careful not to disturb Lucas and his colleagues, she entered through the kitchen and made her way up a back staircase to the master suite. She dressed for bed and turned out the lights, staring at the ceiling as the minutes ticked by. It was nearly midnight when Lucas's associates left, and it didn't surprise her when he didn't come to bed. Outside she heard the Porsche roar to life. No doubt he was going to visit Amelia, his latest mistress.

It didn't bother her anymore that he was unfaithful on a regular basis. In fact, it was a relief. With all his girlfriends to satisfy his carnal appetites, he rarely bothered her, choosing more warm and willing partners. Sending a silent prayer heavenward, she asked for Amelia to keep him all night. That would give her a better head start.

Her watch alarm went off at 3:45 a.m. She was still awake, but her throat closed up and her breathing hitched at the soft beeping. Lucas hadn't come home and she thought of sending Amelia a thank you note. She got up quietly and donned black jeans, a black sweater and tennis shoes. Once dressed, she retrieved the manila envelope from where she'd hidden it, taped to the underside of a drawer in the closet. Using a pocket flashlight she double checked that all her documents were still there. She heaved a sigh of relief, put the envelope in the waistband of her jeans, and pulled her sweater over them.

She left the bedroom and closed the door silently behind her. Holding her breath, she paused, listening for anything out of the ordinary. All she heard was the house settling and the ticking of the grandfather clock in the downstairs foyer, and she jumped when the chimes for the hour echoed off the walls. Her heart started to race and she took a shaky breath. She waited a few seconds and then made her way down the servants' staircase. When she entered the darkened kitchen her eyes jumped to the glowing keypad near the back door and she quickly crossed the room. After punching in the deactivation code for the security system she slipped outside and reset the alarm. She closed her eyes briefly and exhaled. *Almost there.*

The garage was next to the house, connected by a covered breeze way dripping with wisteria. The dense vines hid her quite well, but she wasn't worried about being seen at this hour. Lucas trusted technology more than people so, aside from Roger, prying eyes weren't a concern. After unlocking the garage door, she stepped inside.

It was even darker here than outside and she paused, letting her eyes adjust before she moved. The last thing she wanted was to knock something over and wake Roger. Her heart knocked loudly against her sternum at the thought. Sweat dripped between her breasts and she wiped an arm over her brow as she waited. When her eyes had adjusted to the dimly lit interior of the garage she moved. Now came the tricky part; getting out of the garage and down the driveway without waking anyone.

The remote for the garage door opener was clipped to the visor, and she held her breath as she pressed the button. Her lungs started to burn as the door slid up silently, and she thanked God that Lucas demanded the best of everything, including garage doors. Her knees went weak and she sagged against the car. It was several moments before she could move again.

She opened the car's door and put the coupe in neutral, then released the emergency brake. Thankfully the Z8 was small and light and she started pushing, amazed at how easily it moved. The tires whispered as they moved over the cement, the sound turning crunchy when they hit gravel. It didn't matter now if anyone woke up, and her fear slowly turned into elation as the coupe picked up speed. Excitement started to warm her belly, expanding outward from the deepest part of her, but she pushed until she reached the end of the long driveway. With one last look at the house, she got in and started the engine.

Lindsay kept a close eye on her rear-view mirror as she headed west. About ten miles down the road, she turned onto the now familiar dirt lane on the edge of the Davenport property and doused her headlights.

There was enough moonlight to illuminate her path and she slowed to a crawl. Three miles later she stopped in front of a ramshackle building, nothing more than the skeleton of an old house that had probably been here just as long as the dirt on the ground. She turned the engine off and got out. After opening the trunk, she made her way carefully across the rotted porch.

In a corner of the main room, Lindsay knelt on the rickety floor and pulled up several of the boards in front of her. She reached in and pulled out two large canvas bags filled with clothes, flinching when a large spider crawled up her arm. She grimaced and shook it off, then searched for the strongbox that contained her precious cash store.

She sat back on her heels and blew the dust off the lid. She sneezed once, then slowly opened it and stared at the stacks of bills. There was almost $75,000 inside. Her fingers trembled as she closed the box and locked the latch. She hefted the canvas bags over her shoulders then took them and the strongbox out to the car.

Twenty minutes later, she was back on the main road and headed west again. The sky behind her brightened with the approaching dawn, and she estimated how much time she had before the alarm would sound. If Lucas stayed true to form, he would go straight to his office in Dallas from Amelia's condo. That would leave Roger to discover she was missing, which wouldn't happen until he decided to come looking for her, or noticed her car was gone. Conservatively, she had until about 10 a.m. before the proverbial hounds were released.

She hit the interstate and drove east, pulling off on the outskirts of a small town as the clock read nine a.m. An old, deserted service station was her first stop. Lindsay pulled behind the building to don a red-haired wig, blue contact lenses and some heavier makeup. It took her only minutes to put on her disguise, but even she was surprised at the difference when she was finished. Grinning at her new self in the rearview mirror, she started the engine and pulled out of the station.

After driving up the main drag, she found an empty parking lot in which to leave the Z8. She emptied her purse, getting rid of all her ID, family pictures and credit cards. A snapshot of her with her mom and stepdad slipped from her fingers. Her heart dropped and thumped uncomfortably as she bent to pick it up. Her eyes stung and she ran a finger over her mother's image.

"I'm sorry, momma," she whispered. "I should have listened to you."

Lindsay pressed her lips to the photo and then she put it in an envelope with everything else that would connect her to this life and stuffed it under the seat. Her new ID and documents took the place of the old ones. When that was done she got out of the car and locked it. Then she opened the trunk and strongbox, pulled out several bundles of bills and stuffed them in her purse.

There was a bus station up the street a couple blocks and she forced herself to walk calmly toward it. She purchased a ticket to the closest large town, and ran to catch the departing bus. Several hours later she got off in Texarkana, and the woman at the counter was kind enough to direct her to the nearest car lot.

Again, she found her way to a service station where the red wig and contact lenses ended up in the restroom trash can. She then put in green contacts and stripped off her sweater. She reached into her purse, pulled out a t-shirt and a second wig, and quickly put them on. A baseball cap completed the ensemble. With the long, black wig firmly in place she left the restroom and continued on to the car lot.

It didn't take her long to choose an older Jeep Grand Cherokee. Where she was going she'd need something with four-wheel drive, and the salesman was only too happy to let her take a test drive. After driving around for a bit she went back to the lot. She looked at the $10,500 price tag and smiled inwardly. She'd done her homework, and she knew what she would and wouldn't pay. And $10,500 was more than she was going to pay. Cash transactions more than $9,999 drew attention; attention she didn't want. Besides, the Cherokee wasn't worth that.

"So, what do you think?" the salesman asked after she'd parked the Jeep.

Lindsay looked at him, indifferent. "I'll give you $8,500 cash for it."

The man's jaw dropped then he snapped it shut. "I have to get my manager's approval."

If there was one thing she had learned from Lucas, it was how to read people and get what she needed from them. She pulled out a wad of bills. "Okay, but the dealer down the street already told me he'd be happy to bargain." She glanced at the Jeep. "And *his* is a newer model."

The salesman's eyes bulged when he saw the cash. He licked his lips. "I - I'll be right back." The man ran to the office and returned in less than three minutes. He was out of breath when he stopped in front of her. "With tax, license and reg, make it $9,000. Deal?"

Lindsay studied him for a moment then nodded. After following him back to the office she filled out the necessary papers and counted out the cash.

"All right," he began, his fingers tapping on the keyboard, "now if I could get a home address Miss...Jamison...we'll be all done."

Lindsay's pulse jumped and she faltered. "I...um...I don't have one. I'm in between residences right now." The salesman looked at her strangely and she lowered her eyes. "Messy divorce. My husband got everything, including the house, and the car." She glanced up and nearly sighed in relief when the man gave her a sympathetic look and nodded.

After printing out the documents, the salesman spun the bill of sale on the top of the desk, pushed it toward her, and handed her a pen. Lindsay gulped, put the pen to paper, and started to sign. Once the "L" was done she hesitated. *This is it. This is the moment Lindsay Davenport officially dies. This is the day I die and become someone else.* She blinked several times, took a deep breath, and finished Lacey Jamison's signature. *And with a stroke of a pen, I've been reborn. I'm free.* A strange elation welled up inside her as she handed the pen back to the salesman, and she could barely contain her excitement as the man gave her the keys. She fought the urge to throw her arms around him in a celebratory hug. Instead she shook his hand and left the office.

Lindsay had to concentrate to keep from skipping to the Cherokee, but she did turn and give the salesman a jaunty salute as she slid behind the wheel. He smiled and waved, then turned and went back inside without a second glance. Lindsay took a breath, smiled at her reflection in the rearview, and started the engine.

When she hit the outskirts of town she spun around and headed west, stopping for a blonde wig, dark brown contacts and a bite to eat. By the time she got back to the lot where she'd left the coupe it was nearly dark. Apparently the sidewalks here rolled up shortly after sunset, and an almost preternatural quiet hung over the town. She drove around the block several times, her hands tightened on the wheel with each pass. Finally, when she was convinced no one was watching the Z8 she parked the Cherokee in an alley behind the parking lot, out of view. Ever alert, she transferred her bags from the sports car to the Cherokee. She moved slowly and quietly, watching for anything out of the ordinary, her breathing shallow and palms clammy. Thankfully, there were no lights in the lot, so she was able to do her work under cover of near darkness. The strongbox came last, stowed beneath the front passenger seat. Then she made sure the coupe was locked, leaving all her keys, and her wedding ring, on the front seat in plain view. With one last lingering look at the sporty Z8, she got into her vehicle and drove away.

Hopefully, Lucas would think she'd gone to visit her parents, as she'd insinuated the previous evening she wanted to do. That way, when he realized she wasn't out shopping or visiting *friends*, he'd head south to her folks' place and start his search there. For a brief moment, she thought of calling and letting him know where he could find the coupe, but she knew there would soon be an APB out for her and the car, if there wasn't one already. Let the police find it and return it to him. That would give her an even bigger lead.

Once she reached the interstate she turned into the setting sun. A strange, intense feeling welled up inside her, and she imagined it was a sensation similar to what the pioneers had felt when they first struck out. Scared to death, and euphoric, she couldn't help but smile. With each passing mile, Peebo's gift grew until her heart fairly burst with it. *Hope.*

Chapter Two

"You open yet, Ross?" The familiar voice of Sheriff Edward "Boomer" Madison traveled through the bar and Ross smiled. "Hey, Ross!"

"In back, Boomer," he called back. "And you know we're not open yet, but since you're already here..."

Ross strode into the main bar toting three cases of beer as Boomer kicked the snow off his boots, stepped inside, and shut the door behind him. The sheriff took off his hat and scarf and hung them on the coat rack then did the same with his heavy parka.

"Hey, did you hear? Fanny finally sold old man Tinker's place." Boomer sat down on his favorite stool and swiveled to face Ross. When Boomer saw him loaded down with beer Boomer rushed to help, took two cases, and put them on the counter as Ross slid the third alongside the others. Boomer leaned an elbow on the carton with *Budweiser* printed across the top. "Did you hear what I said?"

Ross tossed him a glance then went to work stocking the cooler. It was a Friday night, and they were always his busiest nights. "Yeah, I heard. So who broke down and bought that isolated piece of property?" Ross paused when he saw the gleam in Boomer's eye.

"Don't know, *she's* not from around here."

Ross saw the bait, and feigned interest. "She?"

Boomer nodded, his brown eyes shining. "Yeah, and from what Fanny says, she's a right pretty thing." He paused for effect and twirled one end of his moustache. "Paid cash."

Ross's head snapped up. "Cash?" He tried to wrap his brain around that and failed. "Must be nice. What was the asking price on that cabin, $45,000, $50,000?" With a shake of his head and a low whistle, he went back to stocking the cooler.

Boomer sat his considerable girth back on the bar stool, his leather utility belt squeaking as he shifted. "Seems strange, don't you think?"

Boomer narrowed his eyes. "I mean, an attractive woman wanting to live way out at the end of that lonely road, paying cash for the place. Fanny says she tried to get the woman to talk, but she was awful skittish."

Ross paused and raised one dark brow. "I think you're bored and looking for a mystery to solve. Face it, Boomer, Cooper's Ridge is not the place for a natural detective like you. Just leave the woman alone. It's obviously what she wants."

Boomer immediately perked up. "Oh, that reminds me. She asked Fanny about a job and Fanny told her you were looking for a waitress." He smiled. "You still are, aren't you?"

Ross stopped what he was doing and stared at the large man. "The last thing I need in here is an attractive woman. You know what this place is like, especially on the weekends."

Boomer only grinned and turned to look out the front windows as an older Jeep Cherokee pulled to a stop. Ross followed the direction of his gaze and groaned when a woman got out and made her way toward the door, her steps hesitant. The sign said closed, and he scrutinized her as she read it then checked her watch.

She was pretty, but he'd seen prettier. Her hair came to just past her shoulder blades, dark blonde corkscrews framing an oval face. He guessed she was about 5'7", but with her heavy coat on he couldn't tell anything about her figure. If she wanted to work here he hoped she was sturdy, and not too curvaceous.

He knew she saw them, but instead of knocking she got back into her Cherokee, a plume of vapors rising from the tailpipe as she let the engine run, obviously to keep the car's heater going. He realized she was going to wait until they opened. Ross placed his hands on the bar and glared at Boomer, who only grinned in return.

"I've got one piece of advice for you," Ross said, irritation swirling hotly in his belly, "stick to being sheriff and quit trying to play Cupid."

His cell phone rang then, and Ross pulled it out of his pocket to glance at the display. *Suzanne. Great, just what I need.* Growling softly, he silenced the ringer and put the phone back in his pocket, tossing another scowl at Boomer as he did so.

With a frustrated sigh he walked to the door and opened it. The sub-zero temperature hardly fazed him and he waved at her, gesturing for her to come inside. He watched as she got out of the vehicle and walked toward him. She halted in her tracks a few feet away and looked at him uncertainly. A few moments passed and she didn't speak, so he did.

"Being timid is no way to get a job, miss," he said softly. "We don't do timid in Alaska."

She glanced toward the street. "I wasn't being timid, I was being polite." Her eyes swiveled back to him. "Or, don't you do polite in Alaska?"

Ross raised his brows but didn't reply, and she didn't hold his gaze. He held the door open as she preceded him inside. He noted the graceful way in which she walked and the almost regal air. She wasn't arrogant, just...*genteel.* He already knew the Northern Lights Saloon was *not* the place for her, and silently cursed Boomer for putting him in this position. He hoped she wouldn't resort to tears when he told her she couldn't work here.

She took off her coat and hung it next to Boomer's parka, then removed her gloves and stuffed them in a pocket. Her fingers were long and slender, with short, neatly trimmed nails. He saw her hair, which had at first appeared dark blonde, was actually many colors, from palest blonde to light brown, and every shade in between. All the colors of autumn. As she removed her scarf he let his eyes rove over her, and frowned. She filled out her jeans exceptionally well, and he could see the nicely rounded, ample breasts beneath the heavy wool sweater. He glanced at Boomer and saw the sheriff, too, appreciated the woman's shape. When Boomer saw Ross's mutinous expression, he immediately stepped forward and extended his hand.

"Well, hello. I'm glad we finally have a chance to meet. My wife, Fanny, sold you that cabin out in the middle of nowhere, and she's taken a real shine to you. I'm Sheriff Madison, but round here everyone calls me Boomer."

Ross watched the exchange with interest, noting the flash of trepidation in her eyes before she took Boomer's hand and shook it firmly.

"Lacey Jamison," she said. Then she smiled and continued. "But you probably already knew that. It's a pleasure to meet you after all your wife has told me."

Boomer turned and grinned at him. "And this here unsociable creature is Ross Devlin, our local libations engineer."

She turned to Ross and he found himself looking into eyes of caramel brown, the color of expensive whiskey, lined with thick, dark lashes. Again he saw the flash of apprehension and wondered at it, then shook her hand. Her grip was firm, her skin smooth beneath his fingers.

"Hello," she said. "Fanny told me you were looking for a waitress."

After releasing her fingers, he put his hands on his hips and scowled. "Have you ever waitressed before?"

A small smile curved her mouth and she nodded. "It's been a while, but I think it will come back to me. I grew up waiting tables at my Pop's cafe."

He wasn't moved. "Have you ever worked a bar before? Have you ever had to fend off drunks and still maintain a smile? Have you ever had to be polite to people you really didn't care for and serve them as you would your own family?"

Her eyes narrowed a fraction and it seemed she was remembering something, and then she looked at him directly. "No, yes, and yes."

Ross felt something shift inside him, and wasn't sure whether he liked it or not. Her candor was refreshing, and her lack of elaboration was even more refreshing. In his business, he learned far too much about far too many people. He was often tempted to remind some of his customers he was a bartender, not a priest.

He was too stubborn to give in just yet, however. Despite her firm answers she looked soft, too soft for a place where the Sheriff was frequently called in to break up the fights. The loggers could be a rough lot, and the last thing he wanted was a skittish female who bolted at the first sign of unpleasantness.

"How are you in a fight?"

She thought about it for a moment and glanced at Boomer absently. The sheriff sat on the nearest bar stool, watching this exchange with far too much interest and amusement for Ross's taste. He glowered at Boomer before turning his gaze back to Miss Lacey Jamison. He studied her intently, seeing the hard swallow and the tipping of her chin.

"Let's just say if I wasn't a fighter, I wouldn't be here now," she said.

He contemplated that remark, and set his face in stone. Her gaze wavered slightly and she looked down at the ground, scuffing the toe of her boot against the well worn hardwood floor.

"Look," she began, "I really need a job. I'm not going to burden you with my life story, but I'm not afraid of hard work." She looked up at him then, and he saw a myriad of emotions reflected in her eyes; fear, uncertainty, and, strangest of all, determination. "All I ask for is a chance."

"C'mon, Ross. You know you need a waitress. Why don't you give the lady a try?" Ross glared at Boomer, and decided to have a talk with the barrel-chested sheriff as soon as they were alone. Boomer seemed to read his thoughts and his smile widened. "She'd sure dress up the place."

Ross rolled his eyes.

"Let me work tonight," she suggested. "If you don't think I can handle it, you don't have to pay me and I won't bother you again."

He turned his gaze to her. Her request had been more like a proposition than a plea, and as he looked at her she raised her chin another notch. She really was pretty, he decided, and wondered where that thought had come from. She had a generous mouth, with full, ripe curves and a pronounced cupid's bow. Her nose was straight and tilted up slightly, her eyes large and wide set. Sensing there was much more to Lacey Jamison than what he could see, he decided it might be interesting to find out what else there was. He kept his expression impassive, however, and gave her a short nod.

"All right. Be here by 5:30 and you'd better wear something cooler than that sweater. It can get a mite warm in here when the place is full up."

She watched him carefully for a moment, as if she was uncertain whether she should believe him or not. When he didn't retract his offer, she gave him a small smile. "Thank you. See you tonight." She extended her hand and they shook again, then she donned her coat and strode out the door into the snow.

Ross stood there, hands on hips, watching as she drove away. A strange niggling sensation started at the base of his spine. He shook his head and then went back to the cooler. "I've got a feeling, Boomer. That one's trouble."

Boomer laughed. "For who? You? I didn't think you were affected by big brown eyes and a well rounded backside. You worried the boys might start a fight over new meat and break up the furniture?"

Ross rested his hands on the bar gazing in the direction the Cherokee had gone. "No, it's not that, because *that's* almost guaranteed. I don't know what it is. Call it...a gut feeling."

"Well, your gut's not usually wrong, but I can't see how a bit of fluff like Miss Jamison could be trouble. At least, not any trouble you can't handle."

After a few moments Ross shrugged the feeling off and shook his head. "We'll just have to wait and see, won't we?"

Boomer gave him an impish grin. "That we will, Ross. That we will."

***

Lacey added a couple of logs to the fire, knelt before the blaze, and extended her hands. A knock sounded on the door and she jumped, nearly falling over. Her heart rapped sharply against the inside of her chest. Cautious, she retrieved a pistol from a drawer on the credenza and approached the door of the cabin.

"Who is it?" she called.

"Name's Jack Calhoun. Fanny sent me out to take a look at the roof. Said it needed some fixing."

Lacey heaved a sigh of relief and put the gun away. Fanny had called earlier to tell her of Mr. Calhoun's impending visit. She opened the door and stepped onto the porch.

The source of the voice stood on the top step, hands stuffed in the pockets of his jeans. He was tall, probably six feet or just above and nicely built. Sandy brown hair peeked out from underneath his ball cap, framing a ruggedly handsome face. His eyes were deep brown and the corners crinkled as he smiled at her. The man took his hat off and twisted it in his hands.

"So," he said, extending his hand, "you're the mystery woman everyone is talking about." He paused. "You can call me Jack." She shook his hand briefly but said nothing, and he shifted on the step uncomfortably. "Well, I'll go up and take a look at the roof. Shouldn't be anything serious, 'cause Ol' man Tinker knew how to build things. Probably a loose shingle."

Lacey nodded and wrapped her arms around herself. Jack Calhoun was obviously used to this weather, dressed only in jeans, boots, a turtleneck sweater and a flannel shirt. He gave her another boyish smile before he walked back to his truck and unloaded a ladder. Lacey watched him for a moment and then went back inside.

The cabin was a simple place with only one bedroom, one bathroom, and a large main room that served as living room, dining room and kitchen all in one. There was a large couch in front of the fireplace, the cushions well worn and comfortable, two chairs, two end tables and a coffee table. The furniture looked as if it had all been made by Ol' man Tinker, and Lacey remembered the small workshop out back. It was full of saws and woodworking tools. Maybe when she settled in and got to know a few people she could get someone to show her how to use those tools, perhaps Ross Devlin.

She stutter-stepped and wondered why that thought had entered her head. Shaking herself, she moved to the hearth and sat cross-legged on the floor in front of the fire. Her heart rate picked up as she remembered him: tall, dark, intense, and brooding. He was certainly handsome, but not in a pretty-boy way like Lucas. His face was as harsh and forbidding as the Alaskan wilderness. He had a Roman profile with a long straight nose that ended above a pair of nicely shaped lips, lips made for kissing. At that thought her mouth dropped open and she ran a hand over her eyes.

Try as she might she couldn't get his image out of her head. He was taller than Jack Calhoun and powerfully built, and his presence was formidable, at least to her. Piercing, deep-set blue eyes had stared hard at her from beneath dark, slashing brows, the square jaw with its neatly trimmed beard clenched as if in anger. It had been an effort just to maintain his gaze. Try as she had, she knew she'd been, for the most part, unsuccessful. Truth be told, the man frightened her in more ways than one. When he scowled it felt like a physical blow, and even now she felt a bit bruised.

Shaking off the feeling, Lacey got to her feet, walked into the bedroom, and went into the cedar-lined closet. Her clothes, what few there were, already hung inside the heavenly smelling cubicle. She reached for a denim button-up shirt and donned it, then sat down on the large, four-poster bed and ran her fingers over the handmade quilt. There was a smaller fireplace in here, but the hearth remained empty for now. With a sigh she knelt on the floor and pulled the strongbox from under the mattress. She opened it and started to count.

She'd paid $45,000 for the cabin, broken up into chunks to avoid any undue attention. A chuckle escaped her as she remembered the shocked look on Fanny's face when she had said she'd pay cash. Another $9,000 had paid for the Cherokee, so after traveling and various other expenses she had about ten grand left. It would suffice until she started bringing in some money. She glanced at the clock on the night stand and shot off the bed. It was 4:45 p.m. If she didn't hurry she'd miss her first shift at the bar.

She hurried into the living room then threw on her jacket and scarf, pulling on gloves as she rushed through the cabin, checking the locks.

After grabbing her purse from the side table she stepped onto the porch and locked the door. When she turned, she bumped right into Jack Calhoun. He grasped her arms to steady her.

"Whoa! You sure are in a hurry."

She twisted away from him and he released her. She stepped back and pressed up against the cabin door, her breath catching in her chest. His sudden appearance sent her pulse skyrocketing and it was several moments before she could pull air into her spasming lungs. After she finally managed to inhale she pushed away from the door and straightened her jacket.

"I have to be at work in half an hour," she said at last in a shaky voice. "It's my first night and I don't want to be late."

Jack smiled. "Right. Fanny said you were looking for a job. So, where you working?"

Lacey wondered if the entire town was aware of her comings and goings, then remembered that in a small town like this, everybody probably knew everybody else's business. That was something she was going to have to be careful about, like it or not. She took a deep breath and cleared her throat softly.

"The Northern Lights," she answered. Jack's brows shot up and he gaped at her, but Lacey ignored him. "I'd love to chat, but I have to go." She stepped around him, then stopped in her tracks and turned. "I'm sorry. The roof?"

Jack nodded. "Just some loose shingles and bad plywood. If it's okay with you I'll be back out tomorrow afternoon. I'll have her fixed up in no time."

She gave him an apologetic smile and nodded. "Okay. Tomorrow afternoon." She paused. "Thank you."

He smiled at her, a winsome smile that made him even better looking than he already was. "No problem. See you tomorrow."

Lacey walked through the front doors of the Northern Lights at a 5:15 p.m. Ross sat at the bar, counting out the cash drawer. He looked up when the bell on the door jingled and, seeing her, got to his feet.

"C'mon. I'll show you where you can put your stuff and get you an apron. You're going to need it. You can park behind the building and come in the back way if you want, it's easier."

He gave her the grand tour, such as it was. He showed her the small, tidy kitchen, the store room, his office which was nothing more than a glorified broom closet. Within five minutes they were done.

Lacey paused at the bottom of a narrow staircase. "Forgive me for being curious, but what's up there?"

Ross glanced at the stairs then proceeded to walk around the bar, flipping on neon beer signs as he went. "My apartment. The entire top floor is mine."

"Oh."

"Now, come on. Your first duty will be to get the tables wiped down and the snack bowls filled. The first customers should be arriving within the next half hour, and they like peanuts with their beer."

Lacey nodded, hating the way her pulse quickened when he was close. She could smell his cologne, a subtle, spicy scent that made her want to get closer. At that thought she gulped, turned, and walked away from him.

After gathering the bowls from the kitchen, she put them on the bar and retrieved a large container of peanuts from the store room. The jar was heavy, and when he moved to help her she pulled away.

"Thank you, but I'm perfectly capable of handling a jar of peanuts," she said.

His brows rose, but he said nothing as he raised his hands and stepped back.

One of the things Lucas had insisted on was that she work out regularly, and he'd hired a personal trainer to make sure she did so. She'd hated the man, called him a bulldog behind his back, but he'd helped her become stronger physically. In truth, she had him to thank for her decision to leave. Self-esteem and confidence were powerful motivators.

"After that wipe down all the chairs and get ready for the coming storm." She looked at him quizzically, and one corner of his mouth lifted in a smile. "My last waitress was named Hilda, and she fit whatever images that conjures up. Most of the customers were afraid of her. You on the other hand..." He grinned when she lifted her chin. "We'll see how much of that bravado you have left at the end of the night."

He stepped behind the bar and double-checked all the bottles, making sure they were full and he had extras on hand. Lacey filled the bowls with peanuts and put them on the tables, taking a cloth wet with disinfectant and wiping the tables and chairs as she went. She felt him watching her, and was determined to do the best job possible. Granted, she was qualified for more than a job as a waitress, but she figured she'd draw the least amount of attention here. She doubted Ross Devlin was going to do a background check for a waitress, especially if she could pull her weight tonight. Not that she couldn't withstand the scrutiny. Peebo did good work, but the fewer people who pried into her past, the better.

Finished with the task at hand, she tossed the cloth back into the bucket of disinfectant and looked for something else to do. Seeing a stack of freshly washed glasses on a dish-drainer next to the sink behind the bar, she grabbed a towel and started to dry them, hanging them in the overhead rack as she went. Once that was done she checked the ice bins, and headed into the kitchen where the ice maker was. She picked up a bucket, filled it with ice, then lifted it and carried it back to the bar.

Ross Devlin watched her with guarded interest, and his gaze was as tangible as if he were touching her. She tried to ignore him and filled the ice bins. Truth be told, she enjoyed honest work. She'd done this very thing at her stepfather's café when she was a teenager, more times than she could count. Once the bins were filled she checked the various juices for the more exotic drinks, restocked the napkin holders and the fruit trays where cherries, olives, onions, lemon and lime wedges waited. After wiping her hands on her apron she looked around, and nodded in satisfaction.

"I'm impressed," Ross Devlin said quietly. Lacey glanced up. She'd almost forgotten he was there. When their eyes met, the look he gave her felt like a caress and her cheeks went hot. He chuckled. "If you do as well the rest of the night, you've got yourself a job."

She licked her lips self-consciously and his eyes narrowed a bit. Unable to hold his gaze she looked down at her hands. "Don't worry," she said. "A bunch of rowdy truckers can't be much different from the people you get in here." She glanced at him as a wry smile curved his mouth, and she saw the spark of amusement in his eyes.

"The ratio of men to women in Alaska is nearly two to one. They're going to look at you as fresh meat, pardon the expression." He went back to counting the drawer, finished and slipped it inside the register. "I doubt the truckers in California are bothered with a shortage of women, like the men here are."

Flattening her hands on the cool surface of the bar she blinked, and a cold swirl of dread started to curl in her belly. "May I ask what I'm to do if someone gets...out of hand, Mr. Devlin?"

He glanced at her then leaned against the counter, well muscled arms crossed over his chest. "You do what you have to, short of killing someone," he replied. "They may be a rough lot, but they know when they deserve an ass-kicking. And I can handle anyone you can't."

She nodded slowly and pushed away from the bar, the walls starting to close in. "Mr. Devlin, I think I'm going to step outside for a minute, if you don't mind?" He only nodded, but she felt his eyes on her as she walked down the narrow hall past the bathrooms.

Once outside Lacey was wrapped in frigid air and welcomed it. She took a shaky breath and wondered if she could pull this off. Lucas's abuse made her wary of men and the thought of having a large group of them pawing at her made her stomach roll dangerously.

She'd chosen this town because of its size and location; close enough to civilization should she need it, but far enough away and small enough to go relatively unnoticed. Cooper's Ridge had a population of just over two thousand.

Her breath turned into fluffy clouds of vapor in front of her as she tried to calm herself. She was so involved in her own thoughts that she didn't hear the door open.

"Miss Jamison, you okay?"

She started violently and whirled, coming face to chest with Ross Devlin. Summoning the courage that had enabled her to leave her husband, she squared her shoulders and forced her gaze upward. "I - I'm fine, and please, call me Lacey." He studied her for a moment, the directness of his gaze quite unnerving.

"Only if you'll call me Ross. They call my *father* Mr. Devlin."

She smiled at that and nodded. "Okay, Ross, what else needs to be done before the crowd arrives?"

He raised one dark brow and lifted the corner of his mouth in a half smile. "I think you've covered it. Why don't you pop some coins in the jukebox, get it warmed up?"

He held open the door for her and she walked past him, her shoulder brushing his chest. She paused, held out her hand, and Ross dropped several slugs into her palm. Though the contact with his body was brief, its effect on her lasted several more minutes, and goose bumps prickled over her arms.

With country music filtering through the wall-mounted speakers, the clock read 6:04 as the first customers walked in. It was a group of about ten men, and they took up residence in the large booth in the back corner of the bar, all eyes trained on her. Forcing herself to remain nonchalant, she approached them.

"Hi, gentlemen, what can I get you?" she asked.

"A sister, if you've got one," one of the men said.

Lacey turned a sweet smile his way. "I don't. Now if you want something to drink, *that* I can help you with."

"Honey, you can help me anytime."

Looking at the man directly, she raised one blonde brow. "I'm not a psychiatrist, I'm a waitress. Now, do you guys want something to drink or not? I can always come back if you need some time to decide." The bell on the door rang and Lacey glanced over her shoulder. She recognized Boomer, who smiled and nodded at her before sitting at the bar across from Ross.

An older man in the rear of the booth took pity on her. "Three pitchers of beer."

Lacey gave him a grateful smile and strode back to the bar.

The place filled rapidly, and Lacey had the distinct feeling most of the people had come to see her; the new meat, as Ross had put it. She was acutely aware of the muttered comments and lusty glances sent her way, but she ignored them, her old waitressing skills coming back as if she'd never left the profession. With her tray balanced easily in one hand, she maneuvered her way through the throng, avoiding sprawled legs and searching fingers with practiced ease.

She recalled the many parties Lucas had thrown, remembering all too well the drunks she'd had to smile at and be nice to. It had become almost second nature, so it wasn't hard to draw on that this evening. While Ross was busy at the bar, she knew he was keeping a close eye on her, and didn't know whether to appreciate that or not.

When closing time finally arrived, most of the customers were more than ready to head home. Ross gave the signal for last call and Lacey sent up a silent thank you. She was exhausted, and couldn't believe she'd forgotten how hard on the feet waitressing was. As she put a tray full of beers on a table, one of the men sitting there grabbed her around the waist and pulled her onto his lap. The mugs clinked together and beer sloshed over the rims, pooling on the tray as it dropped onto the table.

"Hey, sweetie, how's about a kiss with that beer?"

Lacey tried to disentangle herself gracefully, but the logger would have none of that. In her periphery she saw a man at the bar tap Ross on the arm and nod his head in her direction. As Ross came around the end of the counter, Lacey took one of the large mugs and poured it over the man's head, drenching herself in the process. The man howled and immediately released her. She scrambled to her feet and backed away, her heart knocking violently against her sternum. He came out of his chair, but his buddies held him back, forcing him to sit while they laughed.

"C'mon, Frank, settle down," one of the guys said. "You deserved that. Besides, Ross is headed this way."

Lacey stood absolutely still as Ross strode over, his face an expressionless mask. The man named Frank also stayed put and looked up, his expression contrite, as Ross interposed himself between the two.

"You okay?" he asked her. She swallowed hard and nodded.

"I didn't mean no harm, Ross," Frank protested. "I was just havin' a little fun."

Ross turned a stony eye on the man. "What do you say I call Helen and have her come down and pick you up, Frank? You want to explain to your wife why you're drenched in beer, or should I let Lacey do the talking?" The man's eyes widened and Ross continued. "Now you apologize to Miss Jamison here, and I'll let your buddies take you home, okay?" He stepped back so Frank could see her.

Frank gave her a sheepish look and ducked his head. "Sorry."

"That's okay," Lacey said, "this time. In the future, let's just be friends." She smiled at him and extended her hand.

He shook it and gave her a wry grin. "You're okay, even if you ain't from around here."

Lacey glanced at Ross, surprised by the look of approval in his piercing eyes. His gaze then circled the room. The other patrons remained quiet as they watched this little exchange.

"All right everyone," he said, "drink up. I, for one, am ready to call it a night."

The noise resumed and Lacey made her way around the bar, picking up empty glasses and bottles until her tray was full. The knowledge the evening would soon be over buoyed her spirits, and she was unable to keep the smile off her face as many of the people she'd met that evening stopped before leaving to call out their goodbyes. Before she realized it, Ross had shut the door and flipped over the closed sign.

He turned toward her, leaned against the doors and watched as she finished clearing the tables. Lacey felt his gaze on her and the sensation sent a shiver up her spine. Once the tables were cleared, she set about washing the glasses as Ross moved slowly to the register and pulled out the cash drawer. He had to squeeze past her as he did so and his hips brushed against her backside. Lacey faltered a bit, but kept her face averted. She scooted forward when he passed by her again, and he took up a seat at the end of the bar so he could run the night's numbers.

After finishing the glasses, she grabbed a wet cloth and wiped down all the tables and chairs, then got a broom from the supply closet and started sweeping. The work helped keep her mind off the fact that Ross was watching her as he counted the till.

"Do you always work this hard?" he asked at last, his deep, rough voice carrying through the room like a shout.

Lacey gulped and glanced at him, then resumed sweeping. "This *was* a job interview, wasn't it?" He chuckled and she leaned her arm on the top of the broom handle as she looked at him. Brushing the hair from her damp forehead, she waited.

Ross put down his pen and spun around to face her. "We're closed Sundays and Mondays, I pay minimum wage, and your tips are your own."

She opened her mouth, and then snapped it shut. Forcing herself to return his gaze she fought a smile. "Thank you." Her hand dipped into the pocket of her apron where a sizeable wad of bills and coins lay.

"Be here by 5:30, we go until 2:00 a.m., and then we're done at whatever time after that it takes to set the place to rights." She nodded and resumed her sweeping, pausing when he said, "Hey, Lacey, you did well."

When she straightened she felt an inch taller. She gave him a sidelong glance as a proud flush warmed her cheeks. "That's the nicest thing anyone's said to me in a very long time." Humming, she dumped the contents of the dust pan, unable to keep the grin from her face.

Chapter Three

Lacey poured some Epsom salts into the basin of hot water and put it on the floor before the fire. After pulling up a chair she sat down and eased her feet into the water, sighing softly as she leaned back. She'd showered and changed into a pair of pajamas, the smell of beer and cigarettes had been replaced with the aroma of shampoo and body lotion. Running a hand over her damp hair, she took a deep breath and exhaled slowly.

She positioned a TV tray over her legs, dumped her tips onto it, and started counting. She didn't bother with the change. The coins went into a large Mason jar. Leafing through the bills she grinned; $283.00. She closed her eyes as she pressed the money to her nose and inhaled its unique scent. Euphoria started to spin in the pit of her stomach and expanded outward until she felt like she was flying. Perhaps everything was going to work out after all.

Looking around the quaint cabin she sighed, content. While it was nothing compared to the grandeur of the house she'd shared with Lucas, it was hers, and she loved the rustic charm. The roof needed some minor repair but Jack Calhoun would help with that, thanks to Fanny. Lacey wrapped the stack of bills with rubber bands, put it aside, and moved the TV tray as she stretched. She felt good, she felt free, and it was intoxicating. She dried her feet and carried the pan into the kitchen, then poured the water down the drain. After double-checking the locks, she made her way to the bedroom. Yawning loudly, she crawled beneath the covers and fell into an exhausted sleep.

***

Ross rolled out of bed just shy of ten a.m. and rubbed the sleep from his eyes. His stomach grumbled and he ran a hand over his hair then walked blindly toward the bathroom. He turned the water to near scalding, undressed and stepped into the steaming shower. As he scrubbed himself, his thoughts drifted to the seemingly shy and quiet

Lacey Jamison. He had to admit she'd handled herself well. He chuckled as he remembered the look on Frank's face when she'd poured that beer over his head. Even Hilda had never done anything like that. Then again, no one had ever tried to kiss Hilda.

Then there was that remark at the end of the night. *That's the nicest thing anyone's said to me in a very long time.* What was that about? It wasn't as if he'd given her a standing ovation. Nevertheless, he'd seen the pride in her eyes, as if she'd accomplished something worthy of an Olympic gold medal by making it through one night at Lights. He wondered what kind of life she'd had that surviving one shift was an accomplishment. Worry scratched his spine again but he brushed it aside.

After getting out of the shower, he dressed and made his way to the café across the street. Annie, the waitress who'd been there since the day the place opened twenty years ago, smiled when she saw him. In her late forties, Annie had a head full of red curls worn in a tight bun, snapping blue eyes and a welcoming grin for all who entered the café. She put a steaming cup of coffee in front of him as he sat down at the counter. Ross was the only customer in the place.

"The usual?" she asked. He only nodded, never fully awake until he'd had his first cup of coffee. Annie put in his order and stood in front of him. "So, I hear that new girl worked out pretty well last night." Ross looked up at her and she shrugged. "I've waited on her a couple times. Good tipper. She stayed at the River Front Hotel until the deal on the cabin closed. I was surprised when Boomer told me she'd be working for you. Seems kinda sweet and quiet for a joint like Lights."

He didn't know why he was surprised that Annie already had the scoop on the latest gossip. In this town nothing was secret, at least not for long, and especially not for Annie who probably heard it *all* while filling coffee cups and hovering over tables. Taking a drink of coffee, he closed his eyes as the liquid burned its way to his stomach. He finished his cup and put the mug down as he looked at her.

"Yeah, well, she held her own."

Annie smiled. "Frank was in here this morning and told me all about what happened. If you ask me, she should've brought the *glass* down over his head, not the *beer.*"

Ross laughed as she refilled his cup. "I'm glad she didn't. Helen would've been banging on my door this morning wanting to know why her husband was unconscious and bleeding."

A smug smile curved Annie's mouth. "Yeah, well if *Sue* saw your new waitress, *you'd* be the one unconscious and bleeding. Renee, on the other hand, probably wouldn't consider Miss Jamison competition. Have you heard from either of them since they moved?"

As if to answer the woman's question, Ross's cell phone rang. He glanced at the display, rolled his eyes, and silenced the phone.

"Renee? Nope," Ross replied. "I imagine she's working on becoming the next anchorwoman for that news station in Juneau. And Sue? I heard from her less when she lived here. I wish she'd lose my number."

"You are a hard one, Ross Devlin," Annie said with a wry twist of her lips. "Don't you miss either of them?"

Ross shrugged and took another drink. "Well, Renee was all right. She understood we were just friends and she was fine with that. Sue, on the other hand..."

"I gotcha," Annie said with a nod. "She always was the clingy type." The cook growled and Annie turned. She picked up Ross's food and put the plate in front of him. "So, what's the new girl like? She's a looker, I'll give her that. I wish I had her hair."

Ross smiled and scooped up some eggs. "You have great hair, Annie, and I don't know what she's like. She seems nice enough, but something about her strikes me as odd."

"She's running from something, or someone," the waitress said. Ross's head snapped up and Annie nodded. "You can see it in her eyes. Every now and then there's a shadow, a flicker of something from her past. She seems...*haunted.*" Annie rolled her eyes and leaned her elbows on the counter. "There's probably a man responsible for that."

Ross raised one brow. "And you guessed all this from waiting on her a few times? Boy, you're the most intuitive person I think I've ever met. I should tell Boomer he needs to hire you as his new deputy. Put an end to this crime wave we have going in Cooper's Ridge."

Annie gave him an indignant look. "Scoff if you must, but mark my words. There's more to Lacey Jamison than meets the eye." Another customer entered and she walked away with a sniff.

Ross had just finished his meal when someone sat next to him. He turned and nodded briefly at Jack Calhoun. The man looked bothered by something, but Ross wasn't interested in why Jack looked bothered. In fact, Ross wasn't interested in Jack at all. The younger man was brash and had more mouth than backbone or sense. Thankfully, Ross rarely had to spend more than a few minutes at a time with the local lothario because Jack chose not to frequent Lights; a fact for which Ross was extremely grateful. He had no desire to hear Jack boast about his latest conquest, and that seemed to be all Jack ever talked about. After tossing a bill on the counter, Ross waved at Annie and got out of his seat.

"So, Lacey's working for you."

It was more a statement than a question and Ross paused. He hadn't been aware Lacey and Jack even knew each other. "Yeah, she is."

"What do you think of her?" Jack asked, a muscle twitching in his cheek.

Ross shrugged. "I *don't* think of her, other than in the respect that she's a good waitress."

"You don't find her attractive?"

Ross felt the frown. *What are you fishing for, Calhoun?* Ross *did* find Lacey attractive, but he wasn't about to give Jack that information. He studied the younger man for a moment. "She's pretty enough I suppose. She'll definitely make good tips." Jack scowled and Ross responded. "You have a problem with that?"

Jack shook his head. "No problem. She just seems a little meek for a place like Lights."

Irritation bubbled in his gut and he fought the urge to come to Lacey's defense. Those saying Lacey was timid hadn't seen her dump a full mug of beer over Frank's head. She was quiet, perhaps a little gun-shy, but faint-hearted? No. He pulled in a long, slow breath. "And how did you reach that conclusion?" Ross asked.

Jack smiled at Annie, who placed a cup of coffee in front of him and retreated.

"Well," Jack said, "I just met her yesterday, but she was awful skittish. Didn't say more than two words to me."

"She didn't fall all over herself drooling on you, you mean," Ross said. In Cooper's Ridge it was well known that Calhoun was a womanizer who notched his bedpost on a regular basis, the fact that men outnumbered women notwithstanding. Jack scowled but didn't reply. Ross's respect for Lacey grew and he continued. "Other than Fanny, I'm the only other person in town who's spent any amount of time with her, and—"

Jack's head snapped around. "You call working the bar one night spending time with her?"

Ross gaped at him. Jack had always been a hothead, but this seemed a little over the top, even for him. "Have *you* spent time with her?" Ross snorted. "Trust me on this one, Calhoun, Lacey Jamison is out of your league. From what I can tell she has class and she has brains. Those two things *alone* set her out of your reach."

Jack's eyes flashed angrily. He jumped to his feet and got in Ross's face. "And I suppose she's well within *your* reach? Because you went to college and lived in New York for a couple years, you think you're better than the rest of us." A sneer twisted his lips. "You're a man of the world, a man of *sophistication.*" Jack's gaze raked over him. "Well, if you're so great why haven't you dated anyone since Renee and Sue left town?" He took a step back and stared at Ross through narrowed eyes. "Six months is a long time to go without female companionship." A scornful laugh escaped him. "Maybe you don't really like girls."

"You're right, Jack," Ross said, his voice laced with disdain, "I don't like girls." He gave the younger man a small smile meant to unequivocally convey how little Ross cared about him or his opinion. "I like *women.* And most *women* don't think of sex as a sport you win by having the most partners." Jack stared hard at him and Ross returned his gaze in kind, unmoved by the younger man's bravado. "See you tomorrow, Annie."

"Have a good one, Ross," the woman replied.

Ross gave Jack a nod as he turned and strolled out of the café, whistling.

***

Roger fought the smile as his employer's eyes glittered angrily and his face turned a deep scarlet. *Better watch the blood pressure, boss.*

"What do you mean, you can't find her?" Lucas Davenport raged, looking at the telephone receiver as if it had suddenly turned into cow dung in his hand.

Roger sat nearby, fingers laced over his stomach, watching Lucas as the man continued his tirade.

"How can one timid woman outsmart the best P.I. in Dallas?" Lucas ran a hand over his face. "I don't want any more excuses, Dillon. *Find her!*" He slammed the phone down.

"At least you got the car back, and the ring," Roger pointed out, keeping his voice carefully neutral. Lucas could be more volatile than nitro-glycerine when provoked, and Roger enjoyed his job too much to risk his employer's petulant wrath. "Why don't you let it go? Divorce her, and let it go. She didn't take anything of value."

Lucas's eyes widened and he turned, his expression incredulous. "You don't think my *pride* is valuable?" he asked. "You don't think my *reputation* is valuable? If I were simply planning to run this company I might consider your suggestion, but I have bigger plans, and you know that. The public doesn't look favorably upon a politician whose wife has left him. It leaves too much open for speculation. Why did she leave? Did he force her to leave? What kind of man drives his wife to leave him?"

Roger smiled, already bored with this conversation. "Perhaps she left because she was seeing another man. She left so she could carry on with her lover, and now her husband is heartbroken, unable to fathom why the wife he adored and doted on would betray and hurt him so deeply."

Lucas rolled his eyes. "The people who know me and Lindsay will never buy that."

"Yes, but what percentage of the voting population do *they* make up?" Roger steepled his fingers and touched them to the end of his nose. "Besides, there are others who can be persuaded to support my version, or at least refute anyone else's, if the price is right."

"And where do the payments stop?" Lucas asked. He leveled his gaze on Roger, his expression hostile. "First you pay them to corroborate your story, then you have to keep paying them so they don't go public and say it was all a lie in the first place." His fingers drummed on the large, mahogany desk, eyes narrowing on some distant point. "No, I want her back. She promised to love, honor and obey me, and by God, she's going to fulfill those vows, until death do us part."

***

Lacey stared at the tall trees surrounding the house, a pad of paper on her lap and a box of charcoal pencils sitting next to her on the top porch step. Her fingers were covered in the sooty stuff and she imagined she probably had some on her face as well. She didn't care. Her art was one thing Lucas had never been able to take away from her. He could take away her self-esteem and her pride, but her love of drawing and sketching had been hidden in a place he could not touch – her heart.

She moved the pencil over the paper, lifting her eyes when she heard the sound of a vehicle approaching. Instinct told her to run and get her pistol, but she stayed put, and relief flooded her when she saw Jack Calhoun's truck. He pulled to a stop next to her Cherokee and got out, all smiles.

"Afternoon," he called. "How was your first night at Lights?"

"Fine," she replied casually. "A little rowdier than I'm used to, but then Alaska is not something I'm used to. It's an adjustment all around."

He took a ladder, propped it against the side of the house, then walked back to get his tools. "Alaska is a big adjustment for anyone not born or raised here. Where you from?"

She hoped being vague would be enough for the attractive handyman. "California."

"I hear that's a nice place," he said as he hefted his tool box. "Where in California?"

Well, that didn't work. Lacey turned her eyes to her paper, making wide swaths with the pencil. "I don't mean to be rude, Mr. Calhoun—"

"Jack."

She glanced at him and went back to her sketch, her stomach knotting. "Jack. I don't mean to be rude, but are you here to interrogate me or fix the roof?"

He seemed unaffected by her reluctance to answer and smiled. "Just being neighborly."

Frustration started to bubble. She didn't want to be discourteous, but she also didn't feel like dealing with overly curious strangers. Unfortunately, it seemed Jack Calhoun was the type who required straightforward bluntness. "Well, I appreciate the sentiment, but I don't have any neighbors, in case you hadn't noticed."

He chuckled and his smile widened to a grin. "An artist in seclusion?"

Apparently, as long as she was outside he would continue to end every sentence with a question mark, and she was done answering questions. "Exactly." After gathering her supplies, she stood. "Let me know when you're done and I'll pay you. I assume cash will be okay?"

His expression never faltered and he nodded. "The greener the better."

She knew he was trying to be charming, and with anyone else he probably would've been successful. But she wasn't anyone else, and she had no desire to be charmed by Jack Calhoun, no matter how cute he was. She opened the door and stepped inside, but his voice stopped her.

"Lacey?"

His voice made her chest tighten and she clenched her jaw. She took a deep breath, slowly turned, and he took a step toward her.

"May I call you Lacey?" Her eyes narrowed on him for a moment, but she pursed her lips and inclined her head slightly. He smiled. "Welcome to Cooper's Ridge. If you need anything, anything at all, I'm your man."

Boy, being new meat really sucks. She understood his inquisitiveness, she'd probably feel the same were positions reversed, but she wished he'd just get on with his work and leave her alone. His interest was starting to abrade her nerves, and reminded her vaguely of Roger. She nodded and forced herself to return his smile. "Thank you, Jack. I'll remember that."

The phone rang just as the door closed behind her. Frowning, she put her paper and pencils down and picked up the receiver. "Hello?"

"Lacey! Hello, it's Fanny. I'm calling to see if you're settling in all right."

Lacey leaned against the sideboard and smiled. In the short time she'd been here, she'd grown to like the petite woman. Fanny's warm manner and exuberant personality were two of her most endearing qualities. She was pretty and pleasantly plump, with a gentle Southern drawl and an energy that captivated all those around her.

"I'm settling in wonderfully, thank you."

"And Jack," Fanny continued, "is he taking care of that roof?"

A hammer started banging over her head and Lacey chuckled. "As we speak."

"Oh, good. Now, Jack's a charmer, so watch yourself. He'll probably lay it on extra thick with you because—"

"I know, I'm new meat." She chuckled. "Don't worry, Fanny. Ross warned me about that last night. I'm going to be a novelty for a while." Fanny laughed, and it was a warm sound that reminded Lacey of her mother. The thought sent a shaft of pain through the center of her chest and her eyes stung.

"Y'know," Fanny said, "I like you Lacey. How'd you like to come to dinner tomorrow night? Boomer is awfully taken with you."

Lacey swallowed hard. "Thank you, Fanny, but I don't think so."

The line was silent for a moment, and when Fanny spoke again her voice had taken on a serious tone. "Can I give you some advice, hon?"

She hesitated. "Um, sure, I guess."

"The more you keep to yourself, the more attention you're going to draw, and I get the feeling that's not something you want."

For a few seconds Lacey's heart stopped and her lungs refused to draw air.

There was a pause and Fanny sighed. "I'm not inviting you over so I can *interrogate* you. I'm inviting you over because I *like* you. And in Cooper's Ridge, it's common to have the people you like over for dinner. I promise...no questions, only food and good conversation of the most benign sort."

The stinging in her eyes intensified and in spite of her uncertainty she smiled. Kindness wasn't something she had seen much of in the recent past, and she couldn't refuse the invitation. "Okay. What time?"

"Six o'clock and I hope you like meatloaf."

"I *love* meatloaf, just make sure there are plenty of mashed potatoes."

Fanny chuckled. "You got it. See you tomorrow."

"Okay, and, Fanny?"

"Yes, hon?"

Lacey paused, unable to find her voice. She cleared her throat softly and said, "Thank you."

"You bet, honey. Bye now."

Lacey hung up the phone and stared at it. Fanny was right, of course. Having come from a small town herself, she knew those who cut themselves off from the locals only drew the sort of attention they sought to avoid. That was the last thing she wanted.

She heard Jack moving around on the roof, so she returned to the porch, sat down and picked up her drawing where she'd left off. The road to the cabin was lined with thick forest on both sides. Set back from the main thoroughfare, the property was indeed isolated, the narrow lane covered with gravel and curving until it disappeared from view. Above, the sky was filled with thick clouds and Lacey inhaled deeply of the crisp air. She wondered if it would snow, and hoped it would. As a native of California and then southern Texas before her move to Dallas, snow wasn't something she had seen a lot of. Granted, there was a lot of snow on the ground here, but it had been here when she arrived. She wanted to see it falling, to look up and feel the cold flakes dusting her cheeks.

Several hours later she had three sketches finished, each a different view of the landscape. She was signing the last one when Jack came down from the roof. He put his tools and ladder away then approached her.

"All finished. You'll be as snug as a bug in a rug." She smiled at him and got to her feet. As she did so his eyes caught sight of her drawings.

He reached out and picked one up before she could stop him. "Wow. These are really good."

Lacey was tempted to grab the paper, but didn't, and extended her hand instead. "Thanks. Now, if you'll give that back to me I'll get your money."

"You could sell these," he commented as he returned the sketch.

She gave him a benevolent smile and put the drawing inside the leather portfolio. "Thanks, but it's just a hobby. How much do I owe you?" He told her and she went inside the cabin briefly to get the money.

After paying him, she turned to go inside and he blocked her path. She took a step back, startled. He moved away from her and looked at the ground with a sheepish smile.

"I – I'm sorry. I don't mean to invade your space, but I was wondering...would you like to catch a movie with me some night?" He stuffed his hands in his pockets and dared a quick glance at her. "I'm really not a bad guy, once you get to know me."

Her heart did an uncomfortable flip. "Thank you for the offer, Jack," she began, her voice low, "but I don't think so. Dating isn't really something I'm interested in right now."

"It doesn't have to be a date. I mean, *friends* go to movies together, don't they?" He searched her face. "We could even go dutch, if that would make you feel better."

She contemplated him for a few moments then dropped her chin to her chest. "Give me some time to settle in, okay?" When she looked up, she smiled at his hopeful expression. "Maybe once I've adjusted a little to life in Alaska, I'll feel more sociable."

"So, that's not a no, right?"

Lacey shifted her gaze and chuckled. "It's more like a...let's wait and see."

Jack nodded. "Well, that's definitely better than no." He tucked a stray curl behind her ear and she jerked back, but he seemed not to notice. "I have to go. Maybe I'll see you later?"

"I'm working later, remember?"

Jack shrugged and gave her that boyish grin. "I go to Lights every now and then."

She tried to keep her disbelief hidden, but when he chuckled she knew she'd been unsuccessful.

He walked down the steps. "Hey, it's a Saturday night."

She remained silent.

He opened the door to his truck and said, "Just don't be surprised if I show up."

Crossing her arms over her chest she watched as he drove away. With a shake of her head, she picked up her art supplies and went inside the cabin.

***

Lacey had just put the snack bowl on the last table when Ross appeared, his boots like drumbeats on the stairs. When he saw her already there and working he gave her a rueful smile. His hair was damp and he looked quite handsome, the blue flannel shirt bringing out the color of his eyes. His jeans hugged him and Lacey gulped when she realized she'd been checking out his backside with more than a little feminine appreciation. Fortunately for her, he'd missed that.

"Sorry I'm late. Looks like you've got things well under control though."

She gave him a smile and a nod, her cheeks warming. He pulled out the cash drawer and counted it, but Lacey felt him watching her in the mirrors that hung behind the bar. After a few minutes of his scrutiny she turned to him. "What? Am I doing something wrong?"

He pursed his lips and shook his head. "No. Why?"

"You're staring."

A sheepish smile curved his mouth and he chuckled. "Sorry. I guess I'm not used to having such efficient employees. I had to threaten Hilda to get her to do anything other than wait tables."

She put the jar of peanuts away, then moved behind the bar and started hanging glasses in the overhead rack. "I told you. I'm not afraid of hard work."

An amused twinkle glinted in his eyes. "I realize that. It's just strange, seeing a society dame like yourself pouring peanuts into cheap wooden bowls."

Her head snapped up. She stared at him and a brandy snifter almost slipped from her fingers. "Wh - what do you mean by that?" she asked, her stomach rolling.

Ross's brows drew together and he frowned. "Relax, Lacey. It was a figure of speech." He tipped his head to the side. "It's just the first time I met you, I thought of you as, well...*elegant*. It'd be easier to imagine you in a frilly dress at an afternoon tea party than working a rowdy, smoke-filled bar."

Lacey averted her face, her eyes closed, as she took a deep breath and tried to rein in her galloping pulse. Leaning her hands on the bar, she swallowed hard. "Sorry." She glanced at him cautiously. "I'm overly sensitive sometimes. It won't happen again." Taking another breath, she turned and walked away.

Ross watched her in silence as she disappeared into the kitchen, and wondered at the stark terror he'd read in her eyes. His remark had been harmless enough, but the color had drained from her face so quickly it had startled him. Annie was right. She was definitely running from something, or someone.

When Lacey re-entered the bar area she appeared totally composed, though she was still a little pale. It was on the tip of his tongue to tell her she looked pretty, but he kept that thought to himself, afraid it would bring on hysterics or worse. For some reason he wanted to reassure her, to tell her she had nothing to fear here. Then again, he didn't know if that was true or not.

Their first customers entered, the same early birds from the night before, and he saw her shoulders square before she went to their table. Finished with the drawer, he slipped behind the bar and slid it into the register. By the time she returned with their order, he already had the pitchers filled. He gave her a warm smile. She hesitated for a second before returning it.

The night wore on, the place even fuller than the night before. Jack Calhoun and some of his friends came in around ten o'clock, the younger man's eyes glued to Lacey as she moved easily around the room. Strangely enough, his scrutiny bothered Ross, though he was at a loss to explain why. When Lacey walked up to the waitress station he leaned forward slightly.

"It looks like you've made a friend," he commented with a covert shift of the eyes toward the table where Jack sat.

Lacey didn't even look. "Guess so. Gin and tonic, vodka rocks, and three beers." She pushed a stray curl from her forehead and pursed her lips. "He told me he'd show up tonight."

"You like him?"

The question was casual but Lacey glanced up, her expression guarded. "I don't know him well enough to like him." She placed the drinks on the tray and paid for them, waiting as Ross got her change.

"He fixed my roof and asked me out."

"Did you say yes?"

Frowning, she hefted the tray and turned her back to him. "What do you think?"

Ross grinned. Apparently, she had a saucy side he would never have guessed existed. With a shake of his head he moved back down the bar, making sure everyone had plenty to drink.

"She certainly adds something to this place," a familiar voice said.

Ross fought the eye roll. "She does brighten it up a bit, doesn't she?" He glanced at Jack out of the corner of his eye and saw the younger man was still watching Lacey.

"We're going out, you know." Jack turned to him, his eyes red and glassy. It was almost midnight, and in the two hours he'd been here Lacey had been to his table frequently. He grinned and waved a hand. "Not right away of course. She wants to get settled in first. But then, I'm going to take her out and show her the best night of her life."

Ross couldn't help himself. "Good for you, Jack. Let's hope Lacey enjoys herself as much as you think she will."

His mind fuzzy from the alcohol, Jack didn't recognize the sarcasm and turned to Ross with a smile. "Thanks, Ross." His eyes narrowed and he leaned forward. "Sorry about this afternoon at the café." He clapped Ross on the shoulder. "You're all right." With that he turned and staggered back to his table. Ross was amazed he made it without falling over.

As last call drew closer the crowd started to thin, but the men made a point of saying good night to Lacey before they left. Ross had a feeling all the attention was getting to her, and her smile grew more and more strained as the night wore on. Obviously, she wasn't a woman accustomed to so much masculine regard, and that surprised him. She was pretty, after all, and he imagined she would turn more than her fair share of heads.

Jack Calhoun was the last to leave. Lacey planted a hand on his chest and forced him gently out the door as Ross watched, amused. After closing the door in Jack's face she quickly flipped the latch and closed the blinds, effectively shutting him out. Ross couldn't help but chuckle and Lacey heaved a sigh as she leaned against the door and ran a hand over her face.

"I take it you're not accustomed to all this attention," Ross commented as he emptied the ashtrays from the bar. "You don't like it?"

With a roll of her eyes she started to clean up. "Not particularly."

He put his elbows on the bar and watched her. "Now, that strikes me as odd." She stopped gathering the snack bowls to gape at him, and he held up his hands. "I'm only saying that most women would enjoy being the center of attention."

She planted her hands on her hips and stared at him, her expression stony. "I guess that should tell you I'm not most women."

His eyes narrowed and he fought a grin. "*That*, Miss Jamison, I already knew."

Chapter Four

Lacey pulled in front of Boomer and Fanny's house at quarter of six. Situated on the outskirts of town, it was a cozy two-story home, smoke curling lazily from the chimney, the driveway and the walks neatly shoveled. She smiled as she looked at the white picket fence. The place suited the older woman perfectly. It was pretty, welcoming, and charming, like Fanny.

After parking the Cherokee she got out and grabbed a loaf of banana bread she'd made earlier. It was still warm, but as the cold air hit her she knew it wouldn't stay that way. She walked to the front porch and was just raising her hand to knock when the door swung inward.

"Hello there," Boomer greeted her, a broad smile on his weathered face. "C'mon in." Lacey returned his smile and stepped into the house as Fanny appeared at her husband's side.

"There she is. And what is that?" Fanny asked as she gestured to the foil wrapped loaf.

Lacey smiled and handed the bread to her. "Banana bread. I had some bananas I had to use." Boomer helped her out of her coat and Lacey gave him a murmured thank you. "I'm not much of a cook, but I do have a few dishes I'm good at, and banana bread is one of them."

Fanny held the bread to her nose. "Mmm, smells wonderful. How did you know banana bread is Boomer's favorite?" Lacey glanced at Boomer who nodded emphatically, took the bread from his wife, and walked away with it. Fanny called after him. "Now, Boomer, dinner will be ready soon, so don't eat all of it." The woman shook her head, laughed and turned to her with a smile. "Come on, I'll show you around."

Fanny took her on a tour of the four-bedroom dwelling, a wistful expression coming into her eyes as she stood in the doorway to her youngest son's room. "He left for college last fall." She gave a shaky laugh and wiped a tear away. "My goodness, it's hard to believe he's been gone a year." Looking at Lacey, she squared her shoulders. "I'm sorry, Lacey. Someday, when you have children of your own, you'll understand."

Lacey patted the woman's arm. "I don't have to have children to know how it feels to miss your family." She averted her face briefly and swallowed the lump lodged in her throat. It had been nearly six years since she'd seen her family. Lucas had made sure of that.

Fanny, seeming to sense her distress, grabbed her hand and gave it a squeeze. "I know, dear. Let's go downstairs and I'll get you a mug of spiced cider. It's a perfect night for cider."

Lacey glanced at her and nodded. She followed Fanny into the kitchen, which was separated from the large living room by a long, tiled counter. Boomer stood near the sink, a buttered piece of banana bread partially in his mouth. A guilty flush crept into his cheeks when he saw his wife. He tried to hide the half-eaten loaf, and shrugged his shoulders when Fanny glowered at him.

"Good thtuff," he said from behind one hand.

Fanny rolled her eyes and gave Lacey a grin. "That means he likes it. Now, why don't you go sit by the fire and I'll get you that cider."

Lacey walked into the living room and sat on the large stone hearth, a blaze crackling merrily at her back. She leaned her elbows on her knees and gazed about the homey residence, then took the mug from Fanny's outstretched hand.

"Here you go, dear."

"Is there anything I can do to help?" Lacey asked.

Fanny shook her head and bustled back into the kitchen, slapping Boomer's hand when he reached again for the banana bread. Lacey chuckled and sipped the cider slowly. Suddenly the front door opened.

"Hey, *Lucy*, I'm *home!*" a familiar voice called from the foyer.

What the heck? Lacey sat straight up, listening to the sound of someone removing their coat, and a moment later Ross appeared in the doorway. His blue eyes met hers, and he paused briefly on the landing before descending the three steps into the living area.

"Hi," he said.

"Hi." Lacey mentally kicked herself for the lack of vigor in her voice. She glanced toward the kitchen and saw Boomer watching her with a twinkle in his eyes as Fanny saw to the mashed potatoes with an amused smile twitching about her mouth. *Odd that you didn't mention anyone else would be joining us.* Her eyes narrowed slightly and she looked back at Ross, who watched her, his hands on his hips.

Ross saw the shadow in Lacey's eyes and realized his appearance was a complete surprise to her. He looked toward the kitchen, but neither Fanny nor Boomer returned his gaze, both of them focusing on the mashed potatoes. *So, you're playing matchmaker again, eh Fanny?* He smiled. *Fine, I'll humor you.*

"Fanny," he called, his eyes swiveling back to Lacey, "your manners are slipping. Are you going to introduce me to your lovely visitor, or am I supposed to guess her name?"

Fanny gasped in mock surprise. "You two haven't *met*? Oh, dear. Do forgive me."

Ross looked at her and his smile widened when she gave the potato masher to Boomer and wiped her hands on her apron before walking into the room. She approached him, took his hand, and led him across the floor.

"Ross Devlin, this is Lacey Jamison. Lacey, this is Ross Devlin."

Ross extended his hand. For a few seconds Lacey looked perplexed, and then he saw the light bulb go on. A smile started to twitch about her mouth. When his fingers closed around hers a blush brightened her cheeks and she rolled her eyes.

"It's a pleasure to meet you," he said. He inclined his head, his hand still clasping hers firmly. "I understand you've just moved to our lovely little town."

Lacey gently disentangled her hand from his. "Why, yes," she replied in a low voice. She cleared her throat softly. "And I find I like it, very much. The people are so..." She glanced at Fanny, "...friendly."

Fanny smiled warmly, a mischievous glint in her eyes. "I *love* meeting new people, don't you?" Before either of them could reply she continued. "Well, I have to get dinner finished or we'll never eat. Why don't you two get acquainted in the meantime?"

She retrieved a mug of cider for him then went back to the stove, speaking with Boomer in hushed tones. Ross shook his head and sat down on the couch opposite Lacey.

"Fanny. You've gotta love her," he said, eyeing the woman fondly.

Lacey chuckled. "Yeah, she's great."

He nodded. "Indeed she is." He paused and studied her for a few seconds. "What are you doing in Cooper's Ridge?" Her brows shot up and he shrugged. "She said get acquainted, and I couldn't think of any better way than to just ask what's on everyone's mind."

She blinked. "You cut right to the chase don't you?"

He fought a grin. "Beating around the bush only postpones the inevitable," he said.

She stared at him for a bit then focused on her cider. "I needed a change of scenery."

He knew she was being deliberately vague, and it intrigued him. "That's it?"

Lacey nodded and sipped her drink, averting her gaze. "That's it."

Ross leaned back against the cushions. He wished she'd open up a bit, relax, but he could tell she wasn't entirely comfortable with him. "Why Cooper's Ridge?" he asked.

Holding the mug between her hands, Lacey studied the amber liquid with a small smile. "I got out a map, closed my eyes, turned in a circle three times, and pointed."

He laughed. *Well, an evasive answer said with humor is better than no answer at all, I suppose.* "*Three* times?" he said. "Not two, or four, but three?"

Her flush deepened a shade and she nodded, as if she knew how ridiculous it sounded. "Of course three," she affirmed, squaring her shoulders. "Don't you know? It doesn't work if you don't turn exactly three times."

"I did not know that," Ross said with a short nod. "Thank you for filling me in."

"You're welcome."

The conversation ended there, and after a few silent moments Lacey realized she didn't *want* it to end. Neither Lucas nor Roger had been much for conversation, not that she would have had anything to say to either of them. Ross, on the other hand, she *wanted* to talk to. She watched him, hoping for another question, hoping for another reason to converse, but he just sipped his cider, his gaze warm.

As they stared at each other, it struck her again how attractive she found him. She liked his eyes, the way they crinkled at the corners when he smiled, the way the blue lit up and sparkled when he laughed. The flannel shirt emphasized the width of his shoulders and the jeans showed off the tight, roundness of his backside. After her years with Lucas, she'd thought she'd never find another man appealing. Apparently, her heart knew something her head didn't.

"So, why are *you* in Cooper's Ridge?" she asked at last, breaking the quiet.

He looked at her over the top of his mug. "Quid pro quo?"

She tipped her head to the side and nodded.

He grinned and arched one dark brow. "Born and raised here. That's the only excuse most of us have." His eyes probed hers. "Not many people from outside come here. That's why our population has steadily declined over the years. More people want *out* than *in*."

Lacey was surprised. "Why? It seems like a great place to live and raise a family."

"It is, but for young, single people it's boring, suffocating." He looked into the fire. "There's no vibrant nightlife, no club scene. Everyone knows everyone else, there's *nothing* secret here, and meeting other single people can be quite a chore." He narrowed his eyes on her. "That's one of the reasons *you're* so popular."

She rolled her eyes. "That will pass. Pretty soon I'll be old news."

"Not until every single man in town has made a play for you."

Lacey pursed her lips and gave him a wry look. "Do you include yourself in that group?" When she saw his expression she wished she could retract the words, and looked away. "I'm sorry. I'm assuming you're single." A flush crept into her cheeks and she glanced up when she heard him chuckle.

"I am, and I would include myself, but I'm more than one of the single guys. I'm your boss, and I don't think either of us would be comfortable in that situation."

Lacey didn't know why, but for some reason that disappointed her, and she averted her eyes before her feelings could reflect there. "Of course. I was only kidding."

"I wasn't."

She felt him watching her, and wished he wouldn't. When he spoke again, his voice was low, for her ears only.

"You're a very attractive woman, Lacey, but I have the feeling you'd bolt if I even looked at you sideways."

She got to her feet. "Well, you're probably right about that." She glanced up, very aware of those penetrating eyes. "I'm going to see if Fanny needs any help."

"Dinner!"

Lacey smiled sheepishly. "Or not."

Ross chuckled and got to his feet. "We can help by eating the meal."

He cupped her elbow and she tried not to jump, but she knew he'd felt her tense.

"Relax, Lacey. I'm being a gentleman."

She swallowed hard and looked up. He was so close, and she smelled the faint scent of his cologne, saw the corners of his eyes crinkling as he grinned at her.

"Ladies first."

Boomer sat at one end of the table, Fanny opposite him. To her surprise, Lacey felt completely at ease with Fanny and her sheriff husband. The conversation remained light and lively, as Fanny had promised. Even more surprising was the fact Lacey felt comfortable with Ross sitting across from her, his blue gaze always there when she looked up. It was obvious the three were old friends, and Lacey enjoyed their teasing banter.

"You know, Ross here is one of the most sought after bachelors in Cooper's Ridge," Fanny announced. Ross rolled his eyes and looked at the older woman in annoyance. Fanny only chuckled. "Don't you roll your eyes at me, Ross Devlin. You know it's true."

Ross snorted. "In a town where the men outnumber the women by two to one, being asked out once by a woman makes a man sought after." He tossed Lacey a harassed look. "Because I went to the movies last week with Annie from the café, Fanny now thinks I'm *in demand*."

Lacey stifled a giggle. "Well, I can certainly see why you would be. I imagine a tall, dark, handsome, independent businessman like you would be considered quite a catch." Something in Ross's expression changed and Lacey took a drink of her wine as she glanced at Fanny.

The woman's eyes twinkled and she gave Lacey a wink. "He's a stubborn one though," Fanny said as she looked at Ross with open affection. "I've tried to set him up a number of times, but he simply *refuses* to cooperate."

"Until tonight," Boomer interjected. Everyone at the table, including his wife, turned wide eyes to him. His fork stopped in mid-air. "What?" he asked.

"Edward Boomer Madison!" Fanny gasped.

Boomer put the forkful of mashed potatoes into his mouth and frowned. "Oh, come on, Fanny. Is it simply a coincidence you called Ross and asked him to come over tonight instead of Monday night?"

Fanny's mouth opened and closed several times, making her look like a fish out of water. Lacey wanted to laugh, but the reality of what Boomer had said was sinking in. Color stained Fanny's cheeks. The woman got to her feet abruptly and started to clear the dishes.

"I must apologize for my husband," she said stiffly. "He's never been known for his *tact.*" After giving Boomer a pointed look, she took the handful of plates into the kitchen. Lacey glanced at Ross who returned her gaze forthrightly, then they turned their eyes to Boomer who seemed suddenly uncomfortable. He wiped his mouth, pushed his chair back, and stood up.

"If you'll excuse me for a minute, I think I have some apologizing to do."

When Boomer had disappeared through the swinging door Lacey and Ross looked at each other, then burst into laughter. Not wanting Fanny to hear, Lacey covered her mouth with her hands and tried to still her giggles.

Ross took a long drink of his wine and shook his head. "Those two. If ever there was a perfect couple, it'd be them."

"Fanny's not really upset, is she?" Lacey asked.

Ross pursed his lips. "I don't think so, though I wager she'd have preferred we find out about this setup over dessert."

Lacey put her napkin over her plate. "I must admit, I had a feeling something was going on when you came through the door." She propped her chin in her hand and smiled. "Like you said, you've gotta love her."

"Please don't say you would've preferred Jack Calhoun."

She frowned. He watched her intently and she had the feeling she was being tested, though for what she couldn't imagine. "I don't think so."

"Good." A smile curved his mouth as he toyed with the stem of his wineglass. "I have to say, I was a little taken aback when Jack told me you two were dating, or at least you would be once you got settled in."

Lacey blinked. "He said *what?*"

Ross's expression turned serious. "You heard me."

A spurt of anger burned hot in her chest, but she pushed it aside and took a deep, steadying breath. She stared at the lighted candles on the table and shook her head, disbelieving.

"The arrogance of some men," she said under her breath. "Does it know no bounds?" Blinking again, she looked up. "Rest assured, we are *not* dating, nor will we be."

"I'm sorry, Lacey," Ross said, his tone apologetic. "It's none of my business."

She looked down at her hands, and was surprised to see they were shaking. She fisted them in her lap and forced herself to look at him. "No, I'm glad you told me. I've spent far too much time being...I mean, he has no right to go around talking like that. If he told you, who else has he told?" Instead of abating, her fury only grew. Frustration simmered hotly, starting angry tears behind her eyes. "Excuse me." She got abruptly to her feet and practically ran down the hall into the bathroom, locking the door behind her.

Ross watched her go. He wanted to stop her but knew better than to try. He'd seen the shadow in her eyes when he'd told her what Jack had said, and Annie's words came back to him. *She's running from something, or someone.*

He'd been surprised when he'd seen her sitting on the hearth, the firelight haloing her hair around her face. Thinking back, he realized he should have suspected something. Fanny was a person who was set in her ways, and changed them only if she had ulterior motives. For the past fifteen years he'd dined at their house on Monday night, never once deviating. At least not until tonight; until Lacey Jamison had come to town.

However begrudgingly, Ross had to admit he liked Lacey. She was quiet and soft-spoken, but there was an inner strength he sensed in her; a band of flexible steel that ran the length of her spine. He had the distinct feeling she would bend, but she wouldn't be broken.

Then there was the fact she was pleasing to look at. *That* took no inner debate. He wondered what her hair would feel like in his hands, or how her lips would taste, or if her body was as appealing as it looked. He shook his head at the thought and took a deep breath.

"Where's Lacey?" Fanny asked as she put a delicious looking chocolate layer cake in the center of the table. She planted her hands on her hips and glared at him. "Ross Devlin, what did you say to her?"

Ross opened his mouth to speak, but was interrupted before he could.

"He didn't say anything," Lacey said from behind Fanny. "I went to the bathroom. Oh, wow, that cake looks *amazing*."

After dessert and coffee, the four of them went into the basement, better known as Boomer's Man-Cave. Along one wall was a fully stocked bar, and a pool table dominated the rest of the room. A fireplace stood in one corner, and this was where the women sat as the men played nine ball. Fanny and Lacey nursed mugs of cider and watched Ross and Boomer play as they chatted.

"I'm sorry about all this, Lacey," Fanny said as she shot a glare at her husband's back. "I guess I'm a romantic at heart. Ross is such a good guy, and you're such a nice person I figured you two would go well together."

Lacey smiled and patted Fanny's hand. "It's okay, Fanny. And Ross and I do get along well, but he's my boss, remember?" She looked down at her mug and ran her finger over the rim, fighting the swell of disappointment. "Besides, I'm not looking for a man."

Fanny gaped at her. "Then why on earth are you *here?*" she asked. "That's the only reason I can think of for any woman with a lick of sense to come to Alaska."

She stared at the older woman. "Is that why *you* came here?"

"Of course," Fanny replied with an emphatic nod of her head. "My friends and I came from Tennessee. After three months they chickened out and went back, but not me. I was determined." This time the look she turned on Boomer was anything but a glare. "I've never regretted coming here. Boomer's one of the finest men I've ever known."

"Quit staring at me, Fanny," Boomer called out, even though he was sighting down a shot and not even looking their direction. "I might think you've got something on your mind other than entertaining our guests. Perhaps you're thinking about entertaining *me* a little bit."

Lacey stifled a laugh and Fanny smirked.

"You should know better, honey. Entertaining *you* is the last thing on my mind. Why, I've got a dozen other things I'd think about before that."

Boomer sank the ball and looked at his wife over his shoulder, eyes twinkling in amusement. "Yeah, like how to get me alone."

"Yeah, so I could *leave* you alone." Fanny pretended to buff her nails, apparently disinterested in this conversation, but Lacey saw the gleam in her eyes.

Boomer straightened and turned to Ross. "Think long and hard before getting married, Ross. You know the saying that once the vows are said the sex is gone?" He waited until Ross nodded, then he sighed. "It's a lie. Once the vows are said, the wife expects it morning, noon and night, twenty-four, seven." He sighed melodramatically. "I'm surprised this old body of mine holds up with all the abuse I take."

Fanny snorted and rolled her eyes. "*Take* being the operative word."

Lacey nearly choked and Ross laughed heartily, leaning on his pool cue. He looked at her then, his gaze warm, and Lacey felt her heartbeat jump as their eyes locked. Heat crept into her cheeks and she glanced at her watch self-consciously.

"Oh, wow...it's almost ten o'clock." She saw that Ross was surprised, as he, too, glanced at his watch. She got to her feet and smiled warmly at Fanny. "Thank you so much for your hospitality, but I really do have to get going."

"That makes two of us," Ross added, shaking his head. "I'll walk you out."

Lacey could find no good reason to protest, so she merely nodded. Fanny and Boomer walked them to the front door, and, after thanking them again, Ross cupped her elbow and walked her to her car.

"I didn't realize it was so late," he said.

Lacey looked at him out of the corner of her eye. "I thought you were a night owl. For a man who is up 'til four a.m. most nights of the week, I would think ten would be early."

They stood by her Jeep and Ross gave her a wry smile. "Well, if I didn't have a second job, it would be."

Lacey frowned. "A second job?"

"Yeah," he said, nodding. "There's a lodge up north that caters mostly to the wealthy and business people. When one of their guests gets a hankering for a more true to life wilderness experience, the lodge calls me and I escort them into the woods."

She was surprised. "You're a wilderness guide?"

"Yes, I am." He gave her a sheepish look. "It's nothing big, really. You get some New York types who want a close up look at the wildlife, and I take them for an overnight stint to see if we can find some."

"So, you've got an appointment tomorrow with some suits who want to rough it for a night?" Again, he looked embarrassed, but Lacey was fascinated. "Sounds like fun."

"Yeah, well, it's nice to get out for a bit, even if it is only overnight. Alaska is the last frontier, so they say, and there's some really gorgeous country up that way."

She opened her door and slid behind the wheel, then rolled the window down. "Remind me to ask you to show me around sometime," she said, immediately wondering where those words had come from. The surprise on his face sent heat into her cheeks. "I mean...oh, forget I said anything."

"You could go with me tomorrow." Her head snapped up and she blinked at him. He smiled. "It's just an overnighter, and one of the guys canceled at the last minute so I have an open spot."

"I don't think..."

"If you're going to live in Alaska you need to know the place, at least a little bit." Leaning on the window frame he gave her a tentative smile. "This isn't a date or anything, so don't look so spooked. Consider this a...welcome tour. As long as you can carry your own pack, you'll do fine." Again she hesitated and he continued. "Look, I've taken Fanny and Boomer, and even Jack Calhoun. Why put off until tomorrow what you can do today?"

At that phrase Lacey was transported back in time. Her husband's former lawyer was looking at her over a tray of pasta in a trendy Dallas restaurant, a sheaf of papers in his hand.

"I know you want this, Lindsay," Frank Milligan said. "You said he'd sign anything you put in front of him without even reading it. They're working on the new stable, so tell him it's an electrician's contract for the barn. Tell him anything you want."

"I - I can't..."

"Never put off until tomorrow what you can do today." Frank took her hand and pressed the papers into it. "Once he signs these, you're free..." The last line echoed in her head and she took the papers.

"What's this?" Lucas asked. Lindsay licked her lips and spread the sheet wide on the desk, rubbing her hands over the page to flatten it.

"A contract for the electrical work in the barn." She picked up a pen and held it out to Lucas over the top of the paper he was reading. "The man said you need to sign here, and here."

Annoyed, Lucas flung the newspaper aside and grabbed the pen, smirking when she flinched. "Where?" She pointed, and true to form, Lucas signed with a flourish, never once reading the heading or any of the fine print. "There. Now go away and stop pestering me." She took the outstretched pen and put it back in its holder as Lucas huffed. "Damn, I'll be glad when all that construction is finished. Half the time I don't know what I'm signing there's so much paperwork floating around here." Lindsay murmured in agreement and picked up the papers, starting when Lucas grabbed her wrist and held her fast. "You *did* have them put in writing about the hard-wiring to the stable office for the new computers?"

Heart in her throat, she nodded, her eyes wide. Knowing he liked her fear more than anything, she let herself tremble, instead of fighting it as every instinct told her to.

Lucas grinned and patted her cheek. "Good girl."

"Lacey, you okay?" Ross asked.

Lacey came back to reality with a start and blinked rapidly several times before focusing on his face. "Um, yeah, I'm fine." Swallowing hard, she forced herself to look Ross in the face. "What time do we leave?"

Chapter Five

Five thirty a.m. came early for Lacey, but her excitement banished any weariness she might have felt. She'd already packed a change of clothes and, with the sharp bite of winter in the air, extra socks and long underwear. After dressing, she braided her hair, then took her bag and locked up the cabin. With a whistle on her lips, she got into the Cherokee and headed into town.

She met Ross in the airport parking lot, smiling as she got out of the Jeep and pulled her small bag with her. After locking the car doors, she followed him onto the tarmac and to the pier, which was hardly more than a narrow finger of wooden planks jutting into the river. A pontoon plane was waiting.

"You look awfully chipper," he commented as he tossed her bag into the rear of the Piper Cub. "Have you had any coffee yet?"

She shook her head. "Nope, didn't need any." She closed her eyes and inhaled deeply. "This was all it took to wake me up."

He chuckled. "Well, I need more than cold air. Let's go get a cup before we take off."

Lacey felt like a schoolgirl going on a field trip for the first time. Excitement bubbled up in her and she couldn't help but smile as they walked across the tarmac to the small terminal.

Ross looked at her with bleary eyes. "All right, I have to ask. Are you always so happy in the morning?"

"No," she replied with a shake of her head. "I'm excited. I've always wanted to visit strange and exotic places, and I can't think of any place more exotic than right here."

"And it's in your own backyard," he added wryly.

She grinned. "That makes it even better. I could spend the next decade exploring Alaska, and still not see all of it, wouldn't you agree?" She laughed softly and spread her arms wide.

Ross lifted one brow. "Okay, Miss Energizer. Temper that excitement until I wake up a little, or I'll have to remove your batteries."

Lacey tried to look contrite and Ross laughed. He ruffled her hair and turned away, missing the surprised look she gave him.

By 7:15 they were airborne. Lacey peered through the window as the ground below raced by. Once the plane reached cruising altitude she turned to him.

"When you said we were going to fly up to the lodge, I didn't think you meant *you'd* be flying us." She tried to hide how impressed she was. "You're a pilot, a wilderness tour guide, bar owner, and bouncer all in one. What other talents do you possess?"

He gave her a sly grin. "*That* you'll have to discover for yourself."

Lacey lifted one brow. "Is that a challenge?"

"You bet."

They bantered back and forth, Ross flying the plane with relaxed self-assurance. He pointed out various landmarks and points of interest along the way. She gasped in wonder when he flew over a herd of caribou and the magnificent beasts took off at a dead run. Later, a pair of bald eagles took up flight near them, as if pacing the airplane.

"They're beautiful," she said in awe.

Ross nodded. "Did you know eagles mate for life?"

Lacey nodded, staring at the graceful winged creatures. After a while, the eagles lost interest and returned to wherever they'd come from. She watched them until they disappeared.

"I feel like I've entered an entirely new world," she said. "Everything is so different here." She turned to Ross and smiled. "I like it."

He smiled back as the plane cleared a mountainous ridge. "There she is. The Gateway Lodge."

Lacey looked across the lake nestled in between snow-covered crags and her eyes widened. Butted up against the mountain on the only sizeable piece of flat land was a huge, three-story log building. Smoke curled from the many chimneys and hung like cobwebs in the still air. A large deck encircled the entire first floor and a pier extended from the bottom of a long staircase into the clear waters of the lake. Giant pines and huge boulders outlined the perimeter of the property and the water's edge, giving the place a forbidding, primitive air. She had never seen a more intimidating yet beautiful building in her life. It sat on the shore of the mountainous, volcanic lake with a presence and air of grandeur that made it look as much a part of the landscape as the rocky, white-crusted peaks that embraced it.

Ross circled the lake once then prepared to land the plane on the placid surface. For the first time since taking off, Lacey felt butterflies swirl in her stomach, and stuffed her hands into the pockets of her thick, down coat. As they drew nearer to the water she wanted to shut her eyes, but she forced herself to keep them open.

"It's okay, Lacey," Ross assured her, giving her a sidelong glance. "I've done this a thousand times. It's a bit bumpy, but it will be over before you know it."

Lacey nodded. "Sorry. I've never been in a plane like this before." She didn't mention the times she'd been in Lucas's private jet, or the many times he'd deliberately tried to scare her when she'd flown with him. Those thoughts she would keep to herself.

When the plane first touched down it jolted and shuddered, but Ross's self-confidence was reassuring, so she managed to maintain a cool façade despite her rapidly thumping heart. The plane settled into the water and he taxied toward the dock where a man waited to help secure the craft. Once the engine was shut off, the man opened Lacey's door and helped her out, Ross following behind with the bags.

"Hey, Ross," the man said as the two shook hands. "Long time no see." Then his glance swiveled her way. "Who's your friend?"

Ross sat the bags on the dock. "Brad, this is Lacey. Lacey, this is Brad Thornton. He's kind of like the jack of all trades around here. He manages the lodge, plays bartender, bellhop, waiter, whatever."

Lacey smiled and extended her hand, and Brad shook it firmly. He was tall, an inch or so taller than Ross, with black hair and dark brown eyes set in a pleasantly featured face. As he looked at her, Lacey wondered silently if all the men in Alaska were ruggedly handsome.

"Pleased to meet you," she said warmly. "I must say, this is quite an impressive place. It looks absolutely imposing, even from the air."

He grinned and picked up one of the bags. "To stand out against the Alaskan wilderness, it has to be imposing." His gaze lingered on her face for a moment, and then he started walking toward the lodge. "Come on. I'll show you around."

"Are my clients up and about yet?" Ross asked.

Brad laughed and shook his head. "No. Jason was up until two waiting on them, and they went through three bottles of my best scotch."

Chuckling, Ross shook his head. "Great. I'm going to have a bunch of hungover businessmen trekking through the forest. Wonderful."

They mounted the long staircase and Lacey looked up at the grandiose facade of the lodge, astounded at its size. She and Ross followed Brad inside, and the men dropped the bags in a small room off the front desk area. With wide eyes she turned in a circle, taking in the full scope of the vaulted ceilings, the rustic décor; the idyllic feel of the place. A huge stone hearth dominated one wall of the central room, and Lacey guessed she'd be able to stand inside it without having to stoop. She wasn't surprised to see the racks of antlers adorning the walls, along with black and white photographs of the local Inuit and early prospectors.

"Wow."

She heard Brad and Ross chuckle.

"That's the common reaction," Brad said. "The guest rooms are upstairs, all eight of them. We deal with a pretty exclusive clientele; at least they like to think of themselves in that way." Lacey smiled and Brad sighed. "They're a little arrogant for my taste, but as long as they keep the place running, I won't complain."

"Why don't you go sit by the fire, Lace," Ross suggested. "Brad and I will check the packs."

Lacey took off her jacket and turned to them. "Don't you need me to do anything?"

Ross shook his head. "I always pre-pack the gear before I leave, that way it's ready for the next trip. I'll double check everything, and then we just have to wait for our friends to roll out of bed."

"If you want a cup of coffee, there's a pot right over there," Brad said, pointing to a long narrow table set up against one wall. On it rested two pots of coffee, one labeled regular, the other decaf, alongside a tray of fresh, sliced fruit and a basket of muffins, croissants, Danishes and other breakfast breads. "Help yourself to anything. We won't be gone long."

Lacey's stomach growled and she nodded. "Okay. I'll be right here."

Ross followed Brad to a small room down a narrow hallway where his packs were kept. As Brad unlocked the door, Ross noticed the smile twitching about his friend's mouth, and he frowned. "What?"

"Friend, huh?" Brad said with a mischievous twinkle in his eye. "You sure do have hot friends."

Ross rolled his eyes. "She just moved here. I'm helping her get to know the place."

Brad nodded, trying to look serious. "Of course, you're a regular welcome wagon, Ross ol' buddy."

"Lay off, Brad. She's a friend, an employee, for Pete's sake, nothing more."

Brad gave him a sidelong glance. "Is that your choice, or hers?" Ross snorted and started to inspect the packs, ignoring Brad's amused chuckle. "Okay, Ross. I'll be up front, entertaining your *friend.*"

Lacey sat in a plush chair near the roaring fire, a cup of coffee in her hands when Brad reappeared. She looked for Ross then turned her eyes to Brad in silent question.

"He's almost done." He sat on the couch across from her, rested his elbows on his knees and smiled. "He says you just moved here."

Lacey nodded. "From California."

He gave her a quizzical look. "May I ask why?"

She sipped her coffee and watched him thoughtfully. "I needed a change of pace." She shrugged. "And I was curious. A friend of mine took a cruise and raved about how beautiful it was here. So, I decided to take the plunge."

Brad shook his head. "That is quite a plunge. Not many people think of *moving* to Alaska when they want a change of pace. Visiting, maybe, but moving? No."

Lacey smiled and sipped her coffee. *That's exactly why I chose it.*

"It's too early for this!"

She looked up in surprise as the voice carried down the gigantic staircase.

"Stop whining, Dennis. This was your idea in the first place, so suck it up."

"Yeah. You were the brain child behind this little excursion, so if anybody's *not* allowed to bitch it's *you.*"

Three men, dressed in jeans and flannel shirts, looking red-eyed and mussed, appeared at the top of the stairs.

"Oh, thank God. Coffee," the one in the middle said as he hurried down the stairs and made a beeline for the pot.

Lacey glanced at Brad in amusement as the three of them hovered around the table, downing coffee as if there were no tomorrow. When they'd each consumed two cups in as many minutes, they turned, their eyes widening when they saw Brad and Lacey.

Brad immediately got to his feet. "Good morning, gentlemen. I'd better make some more coffee." Lacey nodded at the men then turned her eyes to the fire.

"Well, hello there," said the tallest of the three. She looked up at him as he walked over and took the seat Brad had vacated. He was handsome in a bookish sort of way, with blonde hair, blue eyes and sharp features. Slightly built, he was the thinnest of the three. "I'm Dennis Lechter, as in Hannibal." He saw her expression and chuckled. "Just kidding. This is Mark Young and Steven Parkes, my partners in crime, so to speak."

The other men looked like brothers, with brown hair, brown eyes and athletic builds. Dennis held out his hand and she shook it briefly. His grip was neither firm nor limp and she recoiled inwardly. Something about the way he looked at her made her uncomfortable, as if he recognized her. Her mind flew back through the dinners, cocktail parties and social events Lucas had taken her to, but she couldn't recall anyone named Dennis Lechter. As much as his touch repulsed her, she knew she would remember him if they'd met before. He smiled at her, but the warmth never reached his eyes.

"Lacey?" Ross called. "Oh, good morning, gentlemen."

Relief swept over her when she saw him, and she nearly spilled her coffee as she leapt to her feet. The three men rose and turned, Lechter's eyes narrowing slightly as Ross strode forward, hand extended.

"Hello, I'm Ross Devlin. I'll be your guide."

Dennis Lechter shook his hand, and Lacey thought she saw a flash of annoyance in the man's eyes.

"Lechter, Dennis Lechter. Call me Dennis. As I was telling this lovely lady, this is Steven Parkes and Mark Young, my associates."

Lacey could barely hide her surprise when Ross put an arm around her shoulder and pulled her against him. "This is Lacey," he said.

Dennis smiled a cold smile as his eyes swept over her. "May I call you Lacey?" he asked politely. She hesitated then nodded, unable to think of a good reason to deny his request. He inclined his head. "Such a pretty name; it suits you."

She gave him a tight smile, relieved when Ross held her close to his side.

Dennis looked at her a moment longer, then turned his gaze to Ross. "How long have you and your...*wife* been doing wilderness tours?"

Something inside of Lacey recoiled at the man's tone, but Ross only chuckled and gave her shoulders a squeeze. "Well, I've been doing them for most of my adult life, but this is the first time I've been able to talk Lacey into coming along." He looked at her with affection and she played along. "If you gentlemen will excuse us, Lacey and I have to double-check the supplies. We'll be ready to leave in about fifteen minutes, so fill up on coffee now if you've a mind to."

He took her hand and led her down the same narrow hallway and out a door to the rear of the lodge. When the door closed Lacey pulled away and crossed her arms over her chest.

Ross held up his hands. "Now, before you say anything, I didn't tell them we were married. What's-his-name is *assuming* we are."

She stared at him for a moment, insides churning. "I would say thank you, but your little lie of omission has brought up a range of other questions that will need to be answered."

Ross looked surprised. "You're not angry?"

Tipping her head to the side she studied him then shook her head. "I should be, but I'm guessing Mr. Lechter would entertain the idea of sneaking into my tent had you not intervened." He blinked and Lacey continued. "Which brings us to one of the *other* questions."

His brows drew together and he frowned. "What?"

"Who *is* going to share my tent, dear hubby?" Ross's mouth dropped open as realization hit him and he put his hands on his hips. Lacey nodded. "Exactly."

He snapped his jaw shut. "Oops." They stared at each other for a moment then Ross sighed and shrugged. "Well, I don't bite, and it *is* only for one night." He caught and held her gaze. "I can handle it if you can."

Lacey licked her lips, self-conscious, and focused on the tree line. She'd become good at making quick decisions, and this one was a no-brainer. Ross or Lechter. Setting her chin, she looked at him directly. "I don't think one night will kill me. As long as you don't snore."

He took a step toward her and grinned. "I've never had any complaints before."

Heat surged into her cheeks, but she returned his gaze without flinching. "If I have any, I'll keep them to myself." Her chin tilted up a little. "I wouldn't want to damage your fragile male ego. Now, come on, let's get this over with." When she turned he grabbed her arm lightly. She jerked away and nearly fell backwards down a set of stairs.

"Whoa, Lacey," he said softly, holding her arms to keep her upright. "Relax."

She blinked several times, expecting to feel fingers dig into her arms. When nothing happened, she looked up and realized it was Ross holding her.

"Lacey, what's wrong?"

She tried to smile, and Ross released her when she started to twist away from him. "N - nothing," she replied, her lungs fighting for air. "You startled me, that's all." He brushed a curl from her cheek and she flinched. Her face went hot and she swallowed hard when she saw his frown. She tried to make light of it. "I guess all this excitement has me on sensory overload. Sorry."

His eyes were shadowed and he gazed at her speculatively. "It's okay." Pausing, he studied her face. "Let's get our clients before they decide to cancel this outing and spend the rest of their trip at the bar."

***

"What is the meaning of this?" Lucas demanded, tossing aside the newspaper he'd been reading. His frown darkened when he saw Frank Milligan, his former attorney, flanked by two muscular men, standing on the other side of his desk. Milligan smirked and opened his briefcase, then tossed a sheaf of papers at him.

"I'm sorry, Mr. Davenport," said Kelly, his secretary, her eyes wide with fear. "I tried to stop them."

Lucas silenced her with a wave of his hand and decided he would teach her a lesson later that night after their dinner date. When he was done with her, she'd know the true meaning of the word obedience. "It's all right, Kelly. Close the door on your way out."

"Yes, sir."

Lucas waited until the door clicked shut, then picked up the papers and looked at them casually. "Are you going to give me the Cliff Notes version, or do I actually have to read these?"

Milligan's smirk deepened. "Those are your divorce papers. It's final, Mr. Davenport. You are legally a free man."

Excuse me? Lucas glanced at the papers and was barely able to hide his shock when he saw Milligan was quite serious. "What is...I didn't sign any...what kind of joke is this?"

Milligan sat down in a nearby leather chair and crossed his legs, grinning like a madman. "It's no joke. Your wife, or should I say, *ex-*wife, retained me for the divorce." He brushed an imaginary speck of lint from his suit. "That *is* your signature, isn't it?"

Lucas flipped through the pages and his eyes widened. "Yes, but..."

"Am I to assume from your surprise you didn't bother to read the documents your wife asked you to sign?"

Lucas searched for the date and his mind flew back. Closing his eyes, he ran a hand over his face. *Oh, Lindsay, you are going to pay for this.* "Of course I didn't read them. I signed so many papers while the construction was underway. My wife said they were..."

"So, you signed these documents without bothering to read them?"

A hot burst of anger ripped through him and he shot Milligan a harried look. "You worked for me. You know I never read things like this. That's for my advisors to do. I sign where they tell me..." His voice died off and he sat down, realizing what he'd done and said.

"So, that *is* your signature, and you didn't sign under any type of duress?"

Lucas shot to his feet. "Of course I wasn't under duress, you ass! I thought I was signing an electrical contract!"

Milligan stood and glanced at his companions. The look they exchanged was significant, but Lucas knew they wouldn't let him in on their secret. "But you didn't even look at the documents to verify that, did you, Mr. Davenport?"

"No!"

Part of him realized he was playing into Milligan's hands by reacting, but rage was searing through his veins like molten venom. Visions of what he would do to Lindsay when he eventually found her danced in his brain and his vision edged in red. He tried to pull himself in.

"Then our work here is done," Milligan said. "Thank you, Lucas." The man reached into his breast pocket, touched something, and Lucas heard a click. A recorder. With a satisfied smile Milligan turned and walked toward the doors.

A sense of impending doom wound coldly around his esophagus. "You can't do this to me!" Lucas shouted.

Milligan turned back to him, looking immensely pleased with himself. "I didn't do anything to you, Mr. Davenport. You did it to yourself." A look of loathing crossed Milligan's face and he screwed up his mouth as if in distaste. "Be thankful your wife is not greedy, arrogant, and self-centered like you. If I'd had my way, you'd have signed over every bit of this company to her, but she wanted nothing of yours. I tried to talk her into it, but she refused, and left with only the clothes on her back."

For a second he was surprised, but then his fury boiled back up. *Of course she didn't. She wouldn't dare.*

Milligan's smile reappeared. "It appears you should start doing your own reading, if you want to avoid a similar incident in the future, that is. Good day, Mr. Davenport."

***

Lacey sat down near the campfire and stretched her hands towards the flames. Ross fished down the river a ways while Steven and Mark stood close by, watching him intently. She looked across the fire, met Dennis Lechter's eyes, and repressed a shudder.

"So, how long have you been married?" he asked.

Lacey rested her elbows on her knees. "How long have you?"

When he looked surprised she pointed to his hand where a wedding band glimmered. A sheepish smile crossed his face and he twisted the ring on his finger.

"I'm divorced, actually." He paused. "I guess I wear it to remind me of what went wrong, so I can avoid it in the future."

"Avoid what, exactly?"

"Marriage."

"Ah. So one bad marriage has soured you on the institution altogether, has it?"

A flicker of something, regret maybe, crossed his face. "No, *two* bad marriages." He stared at the ring. "My first wife left me. Just packed up and left, no note, no explanation, no reasons." Lacey felt extremely uncomfortable, and got slowly to her feet, but he didn't notice. "I divorced my second wife because she didn't understand the meaning of fidelity."

"I'm sorry. It's none of my business." She gave him a small smile and pointed to Ross. "I'm going to see if he needs any help."

She felt his eyes boring holes in her back as she walked away. Steven and Mark had taken the spare rods Ross had brought and were trying their hand at fishing downstream. She walked up behind Ross and hesitated, then slipped her arms around his waist in what she hoped looked like a natural motion. To his credit, Ross didn't even flinch.

"What are you doing?" he asked in a low voice.

Lacey stood on tiptoe and rested her chin on his shoulder. "Looking wife-like, I hope."

He laughed softly. "Mr. Lechter getting too chatty for you?" She nodded in reply as she closed her eyes and inhaled his scent. He chuckled again. "Well, don't take this the wrong way, but I don't mind at all."

She looked at him out of the corner of her eye. "As long as you don't start to *enjoy* it, we'll be okay."

He grinned wickedly and kissed her temple. "Enjoy it? Me? Now what man do you know that wouldn't enjoy camping in the woods with a beautiful woman wrapped around him?" She scowled and poked him in the ribs, and he laughed when he nearly dropped his pole. "Hey, watch it. You almost lost us our dinner."

Lacey leaned close to his ear. "You watch it, or you'll lose more than dinner." He turned to look at her, a grin on his face, his cheek nearly touching hers. She went absolutely still, his nearness sending her heart into overdrive. They stared at each other for a moment.

"Of course you know Lechter is watching us," he whispered. Lacey nodded imperceptibly and Ross's smile faded. "You realize he probably expects us to kiss right now, don't you?" Lacey's breath caught and she gave him another slight nod. His expression softened. "Relax, Lacey. I already told you, I don't bite."

Anxiety raced along every nerve. "I'm saving your butt by going along with this," she said under her breath.

His brows rose and he smiled. "Funny, I thought I was saving yours."

Indignation replaced the apprehension with a hot flash. She glared at him. "I don't need saving." His mouth was so close she felt his breath on her cheek, and strange shivers fanned across her skin. A devilish glint entered his eyes, their piercing depths holding hers captive.

"Prove it," he said softly.

She didn't move, but after several seconds he did. Lacey froze, her heart pounding out a brisk tempo against her breastbone. What she expected to feel, and what she actually felt, were so different it stole her breath as his mouth slowly covered hers. His hand cupped her head gently and she closed her eyes. His lips were warm and firm and a flush crept over her skin as he kissed her. She returned his kiss. She couldn't remember the last time she'd been kissed and enjoyed it, the taste and texture of his mouth sending heated, pleasurable ripples through her. Finally, to her secret chagrin, he pulled away and pressed his lips against her brow.

"Well, you certainly convinced me," he said in a low voice. "Let's hope Lechter believes what he saw." He looked at her and gave her a wink. "Why don't you go back to camp? I have enough fish for dinner."

She averted her gaze, not wanting him to see the effect he had on her. "D-do you need any help?"

He chucked her playfully under the chin and shook his head. "No. Just stoke the fire and see if we have enough wood."

"I'll go get some more." She turned to leave and he ran a finger over her cheek, stopping her cold.

"Stay close to camp, okay?"

She forced herself to look at him, and was taken aback by the expression in his eyes. Apparently, she wasn't the only one affected. With a nod, she stepped carefully over the rocks and set off into the woods.

She made sure to keep the campfire in sight as she gathered what pieces of wood she could find. With her arms full she walked back to camp, and relief crossed Ross's face when she stepped out of the trees. She gave him a jaunty smile and carefully put her burden aside. Several large trout were spitted over the fire and a pot of ranch-style beans bubbled on the coals.

"Smells delicious, hon."

His eyes widened slightly at the use of the endearment. Then he smiled.

"It certainly does," Dennis said, glancing between them. "Now, when I go to Tavern on The Green, I can tell them I've had trout so fresh it was swimming only minutes before I ate it." He laughed, and Steven and Mark did likewise, as if on cue.

"This was a good idea, Dennis," Mark announced while he poured himself a cup of coffee. "And here I thought you were all work and no play."

"A regular stick in the mud," Steven added.

Lacey saw the tightening about Dennis's mouth but said nothing, and moved to help Ross as Steven continued.

"But no more. I'll bet you haven't thought of the merger or Davenport Pharmaceuticals all day, have you?"

Lacey felt the blood drain from her face, and she was very thankful her back was to the others. Ross must have felt her stiffen because he looked at her.

"You okay?" he asked in a whisper.

Lacey forced a smile, hoping her knees would hold out, and nodded.

Chapter Six

Ross watched Lacey carefully as the evening wore on. While she didn't say or do anything out of the ordinary, he saw a shadow in her eyes and a tightness about her mouth that hadn't been there earlier. His gut told him something was wrong, and he'd always listened to his gut.

Dinner was over, the cooking utensils washed and stowed for the night. Lacey sat on the ground next to him, as the five of them roasted marshmallows over the fire. She stared into the flames, her marshmallow on fire and dripping, but she didn't notice.

"Lacey?" Steven said as he watched the melting confection. "Lacey, you're not going to eat that, are you?"

She blinked and looked at him blankly.

"The marshmallow," Ross whispered in her ear.

When she saw the charred candy she grimaced and tossed the stick into the flames with a chuckle. "Sorry. Guess I wasn't paying attention."

"Guess not," Dennis agreed. "May we inquire as to where your mind was?"

Ross tossed Dennis a glare, but the man was focused on Lacey. As she returned Lechter's gaze Ross rubbed her shoulders. He felt the tension there and wondered at it.

"You may ask," she replied at last, her voice neutral, "but I'm not going to answer." She tossed Ross a glance then turned back to Dennis with a sinful smile. "I don't think you'd be particularly interested in what I was thinking about."

Ross knew she was lying, but she achieved the desired effect. Dennis looked away uncomfortably as Steven and Mark exchanged wry looks. Ross only grinned, took his perfectly browned marshmallow, and popped it into his mouth.

"Well, I'm ready to call it a night," Dennis said as he got to his feet. He nodded at Ross. "See you in the morning."

Ross inclined his head, put another marshmallow on his stick and propped it over the fire. Steven and Mark mumbled good night as the three men retreated to their separate tents.

"So," Ross asked after several minutes of silence, "do you want to tell me what has you so spooked, or are you going to keep it to yourself?" He kept his voice low, even though they were far enough away so his clients wouldn't be able to hear them. "I heard one of them mention a merger with some pharmaceutical company, and you froze."

"I – I used to work for the company they were talking about. Small world, huh?"

Again, Ross knew she was lying, but he wasn't about to press her. "Very." He watched her covertly, her eyes turned translucent by the firelight. "I'm going to gather the trash and food and stow it away from camp." He got to his feet and held out his hand. "Wanna come with?" She looked up at him uncertainly for a moment then placed her fingers in his. He pulled her to her feet.

She helped him gather the debris and the remaining food, and followed behind as he trekked toward the river and then moved upstream. The night was cold. Snow crunched underneath their boots, and a half moon lit the icy patches with an eerie glow. She waited on the riverbank as he opened one of several bear-proof canisters and stuffed the bag inside. He then replaced the lid and put it on the ground near the trunk of a large tree. He stored the food and other bear-attracting items in another canister and placed it next to the first one.

"Have you ever wanted to leave here, Ross?" she asked quietly.

He turned toward her. She stood on a large rock, bundled in her coat with her back to him. From the angle of her head he could tell she was looking at the stars, and he was careful not to startle her as he moved to stand behind her.

"Sure, when I was younger. I *did* leave, in fact," he replied. "Went to NYU, and once I graduated I spent two years working on Wall Street before I decided it was time to hightail it home." He tucked a stray curl behind her ear and was thankful she didn't flinch this time. "Alaska gets under your skin. You don't realize it until you leave, and then every other place you go feels too small."

She closed her eyes and breathed deeply. "*I* feel small here," she said, her voice barely above a whisper. "I feel like I could disappear."

"Is that why you came here? To disappear?" To his surprise, she didn't even falter.

"Yes."

He didn't know what to say to that and stared at her. The only sound was the soft gurgling of the river and the lonely hoot of an owl. She turned her face toward him and he studied her profile, wondering what she was thinking and why she was smiling. When she lifted her eyes he was struck by how pretty she was, and he ran his finger across her cheek before he realized what he was doing. Her expression didn't change but he felt suddenly awkward and his hand dropped.

"It's cold out here. Let's get back to camp," he said in a stiff voice.

"That's it?" she asked, eyes wide. "You're not going to ask me anything else?"

He turned and started walking. "I'm sorry, Lacey. It's none of my business."

"Ross."

He stopped and looked at her, questions swirling in his brain. He clenched his jaw and waited for her to speak.

She hopped down from the rock and stood in front of him. "Thank you."

His brows drew together. "For what?"

She smiled and looked at her boots. "For being you." He was surprised when she glanced up, a twinkle in her eye. "Come on, hubby. Let's go back to *our* tent."

His eyes narrowed and he stared at her for a moment then burst out laughing as he draped an arm around her shoulders. "Okay, wife. And maybe I'll let you rub my feet before we go to bed." Her horrified expression made him laugh again, and the sound echoed through the mountains. She poked him in the ribs and stifled a giggle.

Quarters were close in the small tent, with barely enough room for them to turn around. A small lantern emitted enough light for them to see what they were doing, and Ross watched her from beneath hooded eyes. She took off her boots and sat them at the foot of her sleeping bag, then took her jacket and rolled it up as a pillow. He smiled as she crawled into her sleeping bag fully dressed.

"Um, don't take this the wrong way," he began, "but you'll be warmer if you take most of your clothes off." Her head snapped up and she stared at him. Clearing his throat, he started to undress. "Just leave your long-johns on. All the layers of clothing prevent your body heat from reaching the sleeping bag, so you end up sleeping in a cold bed all night."

"You're serious."

He glanced at her and smiled when he saw her eyes were focused on the door of the tent, as if she was contemplating escape. "Very," he replied. He turned off the lantern. "Honestly, Lacey. I have no desire to be up all night listening to your teeth chatter." He undressed and slipped into his sleeping bag. "I promise I won't look."

She didn't reply, but by the rustling noises he knew she was following his advice. Gradually his eyes adjusted to the darkness, but he could only see a faint outline of her body. Something inside him tightened as she slid her jeans over her hips and he looked away, not wanting to feel the tightening in his gut, the pull of attraction. He turned onto his side with his back to her and closed his eyes.

Ross didn't know how much time had passed before he heard her breathing even out and deepen, telling him she was asleep. He rolled over, propped his head in one hand and looked at her. Wispy tendrils of blonde hair escaped the neat braid, curling around her face, and he absently wound one gossamer strand around his finger. Asleep, she looked like a little girl; lips parted slightly and one hand tucked beneath her cheek. He frowned and released her hair, lay on his back, and settled his hands behind his head.

What was it about her? She was attractive, sure, but she wasn't the only attractive woman in town. He liked her spirit, yes, but most Alaskan women had that independent, pioneer sort of grit. Delicate flower types didn't usually fare well in the vast expanse of America's last frontier.

With a soft snort, he shook it off. He was obviously plagued by the same ailment every other man in town was. She was new, attractive, mysterious, and that was interesting. He closed his eyes, thankful that once he got to know her better this attraction would fade. It always did. After all, he was a confirmed bachelor, and proud of it. He had his apartment, he had his bar, he had his friends, and the afternoon ice hockey games. Until six months ago, there had been two single women he saw when he felt the need for female companionship, and he'd told them up front he wasn't the type for commitment. They'd have dinner, see a movie, and then go back to his place, but they'd never stay the night. Or, if they went to her place, he'd stay long enough not to be rude, then go home. It was his unwritten rule. They would talk, laugh, have sex, and then go their separate ways. That was the way he worked, and played. For him, it had always been what he wanted, and it had always been enough. He'd seen the harsh reality of Alaska ruin too many relationships to want to risk it himself. Now the appearance of one pretty, unpretentious female had him questioning things he'd never before given a second thought.

He turned to look at her again. Her eyes moved rapidly beneath tightly closed eyelids. A frown creased her brow and she mumbled something unintelligible, then, moving restlessly, turned her back to him. After watching her for a moment longer, he closed his eyes and started counting backwards from 100. After the third time his eyelids started to droop, and before he could finish counting he was asleep.

***

The twitter of birds teased Lacey from sleep, but she fought it. She was warm and comfortable and didn't want to wake up yet. She desperately wanted to go back to the dream where she and Russell Crowe in his Gladiator splendor, were strolling hand in hand through a field of wheat, and he had eyes only for her. Unfortunately, the birds weren't following her telepathic commands to be silent.

Something shifted behind her and it was then she realized something was draped over her waist, something that felt like an arm. Her eyes snapped open and she bolted upright. She couldn't remember the last time Lucas had touched her, and her stomach twisted at the thought. She threw the arm off and scuttled back against the side of the tent, her heart pounding like a jackhammer.

"Wh - what is it?" Ross mumbled, rubbing a hand over his face as he sat up.

Lacey stared at him, her mind still fuzzy with sleep even as a surge of adrenaline sent her pulse skyrocketing. He frowned and reached out to her. His eyes widened when she slapped his hand. It was an automatic reaction for her and it took a moment to register. When she realized what she'd done, she blinked several times and slowly sat down.

"I - I'm sorry," she whispered, swallowing hard. "I forgot where I was for a minute." She chanced a quick glance at him but his expression was neutral, giving nothing away. Averting her eyes, she ran a hand over her hair self-consciously. "I'm not accustomed t-to waking up...w-with someone." She licked her lips. "I'm sor – I'm sorry." She felt him watching her and closed her eyes, mortified.

"It's okay," he said, his voice low. "I probably would've done the same thing had I been you." He chuckled. "It's okay, Lacey. Really."

Lacey sat as still as stone while he dressed and her heartbeat gradually returned to normal. As he laced up his boots she dared a quick look at him, surprised to find him watching her with a small smile.

"Get dressed. I'll get breakfast started." Whistling softly, he opened the tent flap enough to squeeze out and left her alone. Lacey listened to him for a minute as her heartbeat returned to normal, hearing the clink of the pans and the crackle of the fire as he added more wood. After taking a shaky breath, she pulled her clothes on, then undid her braid, brushed her hair out quickly and re-braided it. After that was done, she rolled up her sleeping bag and packed the meager belongings she'd brought, and rolled up Ross's bag as well. Just as she finished, Ross stuck his head in the tent flap.

"I'm coming," she said. "Just wanted to get the stuff ready." The sound of male voices reached her and she looked at Ross in silent question.

He smiled. "They're already up." His eyes narrowed on her face. "Are you sure you're all right? You're kind of pale."

She looked away. "I'll be fine. My heartbeat's finally back to normal."

"Lacey, I'm sorry—"

"Don't be." Smiling, she shook her head. "Don't be sorry, you didn't do anything. In fact, you were a perfect gentleman." As if to prove her words true he extended his hand to her, and she put her fingers in his. He helped her up and out of the tent, and his eyes widened slightly when she planted a kiss on his cheek. Heat crawled lazily up her neck. "Don't want our guests getting suspicious, now do we?"

A grin twitched about his mouth. "Certainly not. That would *never* do."

"Ah, the lovebirds."

Lacey glanced at Dennis, and the man looked as grouchy as he sounded.

"It does my heart good to see that love is still alive, somewhere," he said. He returned her gaze, eyes narrowed a bit. "Now, where is the coffee?"

After breakfast, Lacey and Ross left the men to gather their belongings as they cleaned and stowed the cooking utensils. Since this was a regular camping spot for Ross, he kept a supply of pots, pans and miscellaneous supplies in a locked, metal, bear-proof box just outside the perimeter of the camp. After Lacey put the wire cooking grill inside, he closed the lid and snapped the lock shut.

"This is handy," she said as she dusted her hands off.

"Yeah. I used to pack all this stuff out here, but Brad suggested the box when I started using this spot on a regular basis." He smiled and put the key back in his pocket. "It's a helluva of a lot easier than hauling everything out and back."

"I'll bet," she agreed. An enraged shout came from the direction of camp and Lacey rolled her eyes. "Speaking of hauling out and back..." Ross laughed and she couldn't help but smile. "Why don't you tend to your clients, and I'll get the canisters." He nodded and set out for camp.

Lacey took her time as she walked up the bank of the river. Sun glimmered off patches of snow. Pines rose like white-crusted soldiers, their boughs heavy with the icy stuff. The air was cold and crisp, and she inhaled deeply, a profound peace enveloping her as snow crunched underfoot. When she reached the spot where Ross had stowed the food and trash, she picked up the canisters and held one in each arm. Turning, she came face to face with Dennis.

"I know you from somewhere," he said. "I can't remember from where, and it's driving me crazy."

Her stomach twisted at his sudden appearance but Lacey forced herself to remain calm. "What are you doing here? Shouldn't you be back at camp?"

"I wanted to talk to you, alone."

She stepped around him and started walking. "Why?"

"I'm trying to figure out how I know you."

She stopped and faced him. "You don't. I get that all the time. I have one of those faces everyone seems to recognize." A smile tugged at the corners of his mouth and Lacey wished she could slap the smug expression off his face. He reminded her so much of Lucas it scared her.

"Then why are you so upset?" he asked.

Her eyes narrowed and she frowned. "This isn't upset. This is annoyed." Turning her back, she started walking again.

"That's okay. I'll remember eventually."

"Good," she said over her shoulder. "And when you do, call me so we'll both know." His laugh sent a shiver up her spine and she forced herself to keep her pace sedate when everything inside of her said to run.

The hike back to the lodge seemed to take forever, and Dennis's eyes bored holes into her back the entire way. Ross looked at her questioningly several times but she only shook her head, her lips pressed into a thin line. They crested the last ridge just before noon and Lacey almost cried in relief.

"Looks like your ride home is here," Ross commented, gesturing toward the second pontoon plane now secured to the dock.

"Nah," Steven replied. "We don't leave for two more days. That's probably the rep from Davenport Pharmaceuticals."

Mark laughed. "Yeah. Dennis is wining and dining one of the company's top executives. Thought a trip to the Alaskan wilderness would impress the man, since the only state bigger than Texas is Alaska."

Lacey thought she was going to be sick and tripped over a rock as her vision wavered. She would've fallen had Ross not caught her arm.

"Something wrong, Lacey?" Dennis asked. Ross frowned and glanced at the man.

"Nothing that wouldn't be fixed by paying more attention," she answered immediately, her survival instinct kicking in. The last thing she needed was for this man to connect her with Davenport Pharmaceuticals.

"You okay, hon?" Ross asked.

Lacey gave him a smile and nodded. "Of course. I was just daydreaming. I should know better, especially after all the time you and I have spent hiking." Turning, she looked at Dennis. "Thank you for your concern, Mr. Lechter." He inclined his head slightly and Lacey looped her arm through Ross's.

As they neared the lodge, the three men quickened their pace and passed them, dropping their packs at the bottom of the stairs that led to the huge front deck. Lacey slowed even more and Ross didn't question. When they reached the stairs, Lacey stopped.

"Why don't you tell me where those packs go and I'll put them away," she suggested. She looked up at him. From the look on his face, she knew he wanted to question her, but he didn't.

"The back door, first room on your right." He pulled a key out of his pocket and pressed it into her palm. "I'll settle up with our buddies then give you a hand."

She nodded, gathered up the three packs, and made her way around the back of the lodge, following Ross's directions. Once inside the room, she closed the door, put the packs down, and collapsed on a metal chair, her head in her hands. The fluorescent light flickered and buzzed.

She wondered who the men were meeting with. Lacey knew it

wouldn't be Lucas. He never did his own dirty work, preferring lackeys to do it for him. Nevertheless, she knew all the top executives at Davenport and they knew her. If she was seen, she was dead.

Tears filled her eyes as frustration rose up in her. She didn't have the resources to keep running, but most of all she didn't have the heart. It had taken her more than four months to get here, endless days of meandering through the U.S. and Canada to shake off any possible pursuers. She was tired of running. Sniffing, she wiped her eyes and started to unload the packs.

"Need some help?" Ross asked from behind her.

She chuckled, her eyes filling again. "Yeah. I have no idea what I'm doing." He moved to her side and she averted her face, not wanting him to see her tears.

"You're doing all right so far. Now, take the sleeping bags and put them in that bin over there." He pointed to a laundry cart in the corner of the room. "Brad will have them cleaned, and we'll re-pack with these." He pulled several already rolled up sleeping bags from a shelf. In no time at all, they had the packs finished and ready for the next trip. Lacey imitated Ross and propped the rig up next to the supply shelf. He smiled at her. "Not bad. You're hired."

Lacey rolled her eyes. "I already work for you, remember?"

"So you do. Which reminds me." He paused and fished in his pocket for something. "Mr. Lechter gave me this for you." A one-hundred-dollar bill appeared and he held it out to her. "It's a tip."

Lacey stared at the money and wished she could take it and throw it in the man's face.

Ross pressed it into her palm. "It won't bite, Lacey. Take it."

After a moment's hesitation she pocketed the bill. "So, when do we leave?"

"Right now, if you want," he replied.

"I do."

He studied her for a moment then nodded. "That's a good idea actually. We'll have enough time to get home and take a nap before work tonight."

She gave him a tight smile. "That was my plan."

"Let's go then. We'll say goodbye to Brad and be on our way."

He grabbed her hand but she held back.

"Where are Mr. Lechter and his friends?" she asked, her voice small.

"I'd rather not run into them."

Ross faced her, his expression serious. "Did he say or do something to you?" His eyes narrowed. "I saw him follow you up the river this morning. Tell me what he—"

"He didn't do anything," she assured him, and she realized with a start he still held her hand. She was surprised she didn't mind the contact. Her cheeks flushed and she looked at her boots. "I – I don't like the man, that's all." She felt him watching her, but was even more aware of his thumb rubbing her fingers.

"He and his friends are with the man from that drug company, in a meeting room on the second floor." He squeezed her hand. "I doubt we'll see them again."

Lacey closed her eyes briefly, praying that was true. "Okay. Let's say goodbye to Brad and get out of here."

Ross locked up the room then draped his arm over her shoulders as they walked down the narrow hall toward the front desk. Brad was just hanging up the telephone when Ross leaned his elbows on the counter.

"Hey, you two about ready to head home?" Brad asked with a smile.

"Yep. I've got to get Lacey out of here before Mr. Lechter appears again." He glanced at her then grinned at Brad. "By the way, if he asks, Lacey and I have been married for...gee, how long have we been married, hon?" Brad's jaw dropped as Ross gazed at Lacey expectantly.

Pursing her lips, she gave him a baleful look. "Three years," she replied.

Brad gaped at them and Ross laughed. "Mr. Lechter was getting a little too friendly, so when he asked how long my *wife* and I had been doing wilderness tours, I didn't bother to correct him." He chuckled, put a finger under Brad's chin and closed his mouth. "Oh, come on, Brad. You knew it was bound to happen someday, marriage I mean."

Lacey propped her chin in her hand and rolled her eyes. "Oh, please. As if."

At that Brad smirked and looked from one to the other, his eyes alight with amusement. "You two better be careful what you start pretending," he warned them with a laugh. "Keep it up and you might forget it's an act."

Lacey yawned.

Ross grinned. "Come on *wife*, let's get going." He rapped his knuckles on the counter. "See you next time, Brad. Take care."

"You too; have a safe trip home."

Lacey shook his hand then gave him a smile and a wave as they walked out the huge front doors and across the deck. Stopping at the top of the staircase leading to the dock, she closed her eyes and breathed deeply. Now that she was leaving Dennis Lechter and his link with Davenport Pharmaceuticals behind, she felt as if the world had been lifted from her shoulders. As they walked toward the Piper Cub her steps were almost jaunty.

She got in and Ross untied the plane, giving it a shove before hopping onto the pontoon and into the cockpit. After checking all his instruments, he started the engine and went through his pre-flight checklist. Lacey glanced back toward the lodge over her shoulder. Her heart stopped and her eyes widened. Standing on the deck was Dennis Lechter, his hands resting on the railing as he watched them leave.

Chapter Seven

"So, I hear you went camping with Ross."

Lacey put Jack's beer on the table and gave him a bored look. It had been four days since her trip with Ross, and she was surprised Jack was bringing it up now. Then again, he'd drunk nearly a six pack since coming in, and his gaze had been like a weight on her all evening.

"Yes, I did." There was no use denying it since it was all over town. "Do you have a problem with that?"

Jack looked up at her and took a long drink of his beer. "You can't go to a movie with me, but you'll spend the night in the wilderness with Ross Devlin."

Lacey didn't like his tone and her hackles prickled. "That'll be $4.00."

"He's not your type, you know; doesn't believe in commitment. There were a couple of women in town he used to sleep with on a rotating basis, but he never let them stay longer than a few hours. He'd have his fun then kick 'em out."

She frowned. "Ross Devlin's sex life is none of my business, and frankly, I'm not particularly interested." She put her free hand on her hip and glared at him. It was on the tip of her tongue to tell him the trip had been completely innocent, but her indignation rose. She didn't have to explain anything to anyone. Let them think what they wanted. "Are you going to pay for your beer, or not?"

He stared hard at her, his eyes narrowing. "I want an explanation."

A hot burst of anger blazed beneath her sternum. "I don't give a damn what you want, and it's really none of your business. Now, are you going to pay for your beer, or not?" She waited another moment and her brows drew together. "Forget it. The beer's on me." She started to walk away and he grabbed her arm. She reacted instinctively and jerked away from him. Her tray clattered to the ground as she swung her other hand around and brought it across his cheek with a sharp *crack*.

Jack had come halfway out of his chair to grab her, and his rear-end thudded back onto the wooden seat as he stared at her in shock. Lacey returned his stare with one of her own, her mouth open. She backed up several steps, her throat tight with anxiety, her heart somersaulting.

"I - I'm sorry," she whispered. She turned on her heel and walked away. She went past Ross and out the back door into the cold night air.

Less than a minute later she heard the door open and glanced up, her cheeks flaming. Eyes brimming, she ran a hand over her face and sighed heavily.

"I'm sorry, Ross. It was..."

"A reaction. I know; I saw what happened. You okay?" She nodded, her hair hiding her face. Ross sighed. "Lacey, he deserved it."

"Did he?"

Ross shrugged. "He shouldn't have grabbed you like that." He tucked her hair behind her ear and chuckled softly. "Hell, if it'd been Hilda, she would've bench pressed him a couple of times and then tossed him into the snow. All in all, I'd say he got off pretty easy."

She fought a smile and glanced at him. "So, I'm not fired?"

He rolled his eyes and snorted. "Hell, no. Good waitresses are too hard to find." There was a clatter from inside and Ross looked at the door. "I'd better get back in there. Why don't you take a break?"

Lacey heaved a sigh and got to her feet. "No. I'm all right."

He watched her for a moment. "Okay, but give me a couple of minutes to get rid of Jack, if he's still here." She nodded, and Ross gave her a smile as he disappeared inside.

Lacey leaned against the railing and something cold brushed her arm. Her eyes widened when she realized it was snowing, and a smile blossomed on her mouth as she turned her face skyward. A low laugh escaped her, the delicate flakes falling softly on her forehead and cheeks, melting almost as soon as they contacted her skin. She walked down the short staircase to the back parking lot, stretched her arms out and opened her mouth as she spun slowly in a circle.

"It's three times, isn't it?" Ross asked from the doorway. He smiled and looked around. "I don't see a map."

"It's snowing," she said, closing her eyes and feeling the snow on her lids. It was a ridiculous statement, and she laughed.

"Yes, it is," Ross replied. "Believe me you'll get tired of it after a while."

"I think it's wonderful." She stopped spinning and looked at him. "And yes, it's three times. But, I've spun around at least six or seven, so even if I had a map it wouldn't work."

He chuckled softly, the smile softening his usually harsh features. "Jack's gone. Left on his own."

Reluctantly, Lacey climbed the stairs, taking one last look at the falling snowflakes before she opened the door and stepped inside. After the cold, the heat was almost stifling. The crowd quieted as she walked back into the bar area, but the silence was short-lived. As she looked around she realized no one seemed upset by her actions, and relief flooded her. She picked up her tray, which had been collected and placed on the end of the bar along with, to her great surprise, all of her cash. Ross put a hand on her shoulder and gave her a grin, and the noise resumed almost immediately. It was as if he'd flipped a switch, and Lacey gave him a strange look as she resumed her duties.

The remainder of the night went on without incident, except for the usual drunken brawl, which was broken up in short order by Ross and Burke. As the patrons filed out, there was no mention of the incident with Jack. Apparently, they considered her reaction justified and that was that. After the last customer had gone and the door was closed and locked, Lacey sat on a barstool and sighed.

Ross watched her from behind the bar as he pulled the cash drawer out. He paused, sat the money aside and took a couple of beers out of the cooler. He opened them, sat one in front of her, and smiled when she looked at him in surprise.

"What's this for?" she asked.

"It's your one week anniversary," he replied. He picked up his bottle and held it up as if to toast her. "Congratulations, Lacey. You made it."

She smiled. Pursing her lips, she picked up the beer and tapped his bottle with hers, then took a small sip. Her brows drew together and she looked at the label. "Hey, that's pretty good. It's been a long time since I've had a beer."

Ross grinned. "You seem like a white wine sort of girl to me."

Lacey took another drink and looked at the bottle wistfully. Lucas had never allowed her to drink except for an occasional glass of wine on social occasions. He'd never allowed her to do anything. It still overwhelmed her sometimes when she realized how much freedom she now had, and all because she'd finally grown a spine and walked away.

Shaking her head, she took a long swallow and savored the tangy brew. The bubbly liquid tickled her tonsils as she swallowed and she gave Ross a smile.

"I don't think I've decided what I am," she said. "I'm still experimenting." His expression shifted slightly but she ignored it. She knew he wouldn't question her.

He said nothing and, once they finished their beers, they went back to work. After the tables were cleared and cleaned, Lacey hummed softly as she swept the floor, pausing when she noticed Ross's annoyed expression. He cursed under his breath, the adding machine clicking and whirring as he punched in the numbers.

"Dammit."

She walked toward him, leaned the broom on the bar and looked over his shoulder. "Something wrong?" she asked.

He glanced at her, dark brows drawn together in a fierce scowl. He tossed aside his pencil, moved to the other side of the bar and got another beer. "Yeah; me with an adding machine. Y'know, this is the part of owning my own business I like the least. And, I think that adding machine is cursed."

Lacey glanced at the papers and slid onto the seat Ross had vacated. She chuckled softly, and her eyes narrowed as she looked over the numbers. After she went over the figures, her fingers moved automatically to the calculator.

Ross said nothing as she started tapping on the machine, his eyes intent on her face. Her brow was furrowed in concentration as her fingers flew over the keys. The tip of her tongue stuck out from a corner of her mouth, and as he looked at her lips his mind went back to the kiss they had shared. He remembered how it had felt to have her lips against his, and how it had felt to wake up next to her. He had enjoyed both experiences, and he shouldn't have. That wasn't how he worked *or* played, and he was too set in his ways to change now. *That kiss, though.* When his heartbeat jumped he put the beer to his lips and drank deeply. The tightness in his chest; the nearly magnetic pull toward her stirred his lust and his anger; anger at himself. *Get over it, Ross. She's new, that's all it is.* When she smiled and looked up his pulse took another unwelcome leap, which only fueled his temper. He clenched his jaw and tried to keep his expression cool, but when her smile faded he knew he'd failed. A shadow of apprehension darkened her eyes and she bit her lip.

"I gave you a job as a waitress." He spoke in a neutral voice and saw her convulsive swallow. He hated himself for feeding her anxiety but his mouth kept going. "If I'd wanted an accountant, I'd have hired one."

"I - I'm sorry," she said as she dropped her gaze and slid off the barstool. She flushed crimson, grabbed the broom, and resumed sweeping on the far side of the room.

He watched her for a moment longer, and narrowed his eyes when her spine straightened and she turned to him. She walked to where his papers were, picked up the pencil and circled something.

"There's the problem," she said. "If you add it up now it should equal out."

He wanted to smile as she put the pencil down, but he forced himself to retain the aloof expression. Ross had a feeling it had taken every ounce of courage she could muster to face him again, but damned if she hadn't done it anyway. Like it or not, he had to respect that kind of backbone. She stared at him, but he only nodded and remained where he was until she'd gone back to sweeping.

He plopped down on the barstool and looked at the numbers, not at all surprised when he proved her right. He added up the column again and shook his head, then spun around to look at her. Her hair hid her face as she scooped a pile of debris into a dustpan and he knew she was avoiding looking at him.

"So, you're a CPA, too?"

Without saying a word, she walked into the kitchen to dump the contents of the dustpan in the trash then came back out to get the rest. "Almost," she replied as she swept up the last of the debris. "I was one semester away from my degree, but I had to leave school."

Ross felt like a heel. "Why?"

She paused, glanced at him, and averted her eyes. "Family problems." With her head held high she walked into the kitchen to empty the dustpan and put it away. Ross heard the water in the deep sink and knew she was preparing a bucket so she could mop. Sighing, he watched as she rolled the pail out.

"I'm sorry," he said.

"That's okay," she replied. "I shouldn't have stepped in without asking. You're right; after all, you hired me to be a waitress. The finances are none of my business."

He wished she would look at him, but she concentrated on mopping, her eyes glued to the floor. Finally, he got to his feet and took the mop from her.

"No, it's not okay. You were only trying to help, and I shouldn't have snapped at you like that." He chuckled and put the mop back in the water. "I guess my ego was a little annoyed that you figured out in three minutes what I couldn't in fifteen."

Lacey looked at her boots and scuffed her toe against the well-worn floor. "You would've figured it out eventually. You simply needed a fresh pair of eyes to look at it." A rueful smile curved her mouth and Ross found his gaze drawn there as she continued. "When I used to get stuck I'd leave for a while, go for a swim or a ride, and when I came back it would all work."

He chuckled and she glanced at him. "Next time I'll do that," he said. "Or, I could let you take care of the books from here on out." Her eyes widened and she opened her mouth as if to speak, but nothing came out. He continued. "Of course, you'd get a raise and you'd have to give up sweeping and mopping, which I know you'd *hate*, but life is full of compromises."

She watched for several seconds, uncertainty clear in her caramel colored eyes. "Yes, it is." She chewed her lip. "Let me think about it?"

After a moment he nodded. "Don't take too long. There are people beating down my door for this job, as you can see."

She chuckled and glanced toward the door. Boomer stood there with a grin on his face. Lacey went to the door, opened it, and let Boomer in.

"Hey there, folks," he greeted them, shaking the snow off before removing his parka. "Saw you two chatting and decided to stop in and say hello."

Ross gave him a wry look. "Spill it, Boomer. You don't stop by at this hour unless there's something on your mind."

Boomer looked at Lacey with an annoyed scowl. "How do you work with this guy? Thinks everyone has an ulterior motive."

Lacey laughed and Ross crossed his arms over his chest as he waited for the sheriff to answer him. Boomer returned his expectant stare mutinously, then sighed and dropped his chin.

"Oh, all right. Fanny said if I had a chance, to stop by and invite the both of you to dinner again on Sunday." He glanced at Ross. "Looks like Monday nights have been moved, bud."

Ross threw his head back and laughed. Lacey shook her head as she walked away and resumed her mopping. He called after her.

"What do you say, Lacey? Should we let Fanny be Cupid, or do we dash her hopes now?"

Rolling her eyes, she ignored them, finished the floor, and disappeared into the kitchen.

"Aw, come on, you two," Boomer said. "The four of us had a good time last Sunday, admit it."

Lacey reappeared and sat on a barstool. Ross looked at her and when their eyes met, the memory of their kiss came to his mind. As he replayed the scene in his head, Boomer's voice was strangely muted.

"Fanny even went out and bought some games for us to play. She got Boggle and Guesstures and...Yahtzee I think. Or was it Uno? Oh, I don't know." He looked at them, imploring with his eyes. "It'll break her heart if you don't come."

Ross stared hard at Lacey and she seemed unable to look away, even though he could tell she wanted to. Her eyelids fluttered several times and she swallowed hard, making him wonder if she was thinking the same thing he was.

"Well, Lacey?" His voice was low and she blinked slowly.

"I – I don't see the harm in a little dinner," Lacey replied. "We did have fun last time, and I'm pretty good at Boggle."

"So, you think we should let Fanny down slowly?" Ross asked. Lacey nodded, their eyes still locked. Boomer watched this interaction with amused interest and Ross frowned at him. "Okay, Mr. Lawman. Wipe that smirk off your face and tell your wife we'll both be there."

Boomer grinned and clapped Ross on the shoulder. "Now that's more like it. I would've hated to be you if I'd told Fanny you'd said no." Ross turned to look back at Lacey but she was gone, the back door clicked as it shut. He glanced at Boomer and scowled. The sheriff was unaffected. "Oh, get off it, Ross. Stop being so damned bacheloric."

Ross gaped at him. "*Bacheloric?*"

Boomer shot him a glare. "Well, maybe it's not a word, but it should be." He grabbed his parka. "It's no crime to like a woman, and for more than a roll in the hay, or...*snow*, as location would have it." Ross looked at him expectantly, arms crossed over his chest, and Boomer frowned. "You know, Ross, you're going to end up a lonely old man one day. I should know. I was headed in the same direction until Fanny knocked some sense into me."

Ross chuckled. "I don't need any sense knocked into me. I'm happy the way I am."

Boomer smiled knowingly and pulled his wool cap down over his ears. "One day, Ross ol' buddy, you're going to eat those words." With a short wave, the sheriff stepped into the night and was gone. Ross stared after him, dumbfounded.

He gazed out the window at thick clouds of swirling snow for a bit then closed the blinds. After flipping the light switches he turned, and froze when he saw Lacey at the end of the bar.

"Everything's done," she said as she shrugged into her heavy coat. "See you tomorrow." She turned to go and, for some reason, Ross found he didn't want her to leave.

"Lacey, wait." She stopped and looked at him as she zipped the jacket. He floundered for something intelligent to say. "You've never driven in the snow at night before, have you?" It sounded lame, he knew, but she only stared at him and shook her head. He was hit with an inspired thought and grabbed his coat. "I'm going to follow you home. Or better yet, you follow me. Driving in the snow, especially at night can be a little scary until you get used to it."

"Ross, that's sweet, but I don't think—"

"I'm not expecting an invitation in," he interrupted as he moved to stand in front of her. She pursed her lips and crossed her arms over her chest. Ross took a breath and plunged on. "This is the first time it's snowed since you came here, and I want to make sure you get home in one piece. It's really coming down."

She contemplated him silently, and her gaze traveled to his mouth, albeit briefly. He couldn't help but smile and her cheeks turned pink as she looked away.

"I don't know, Ross. That's an awful long way for you to drive. Why don't I call you when I get home?"

"And if you miss the turn off? You won't be able to call anyone if you get lost out there, and there's no cell reception past the river bridge." He put a finger under her chin and turned her face to his, and that familiar shadow flashed in her eyes. "I won't be able to sleep unless you get home safely, and everyone knows how much I need my beauty sleep. I can't maintain this handsome facade without it." He saw the uncertainty in her expression, but he had the feeling he was winning his case.

"All right," she said, "but you're *not* coming in."

He held up his hands as if in surrender. "I didn't expect to, I already told you that."

Her gaze turned steely. "I know, I just want to make it extra clear."

Laughing softly, he put his hands on her shoulders, turned her around, and gave her a small push toward the back door. "Oh, it's clear, Miss Jamison. It's crystal."

***

Lucas sat on the edge of his desk and Roger stood nearby like a good guard dog. A smug smile graced his handsome face as Lucas looked meaningfully at the much larger Roger.

"What do you mean I can't go back to school?" Lindsay asked in disbelief. "I'm only one semester away from my degree."

"You know, that's one thing I've always liked about her, Rog. She is determined to finish what she starts." Lucas took a step toward her and Lindsay shrank in the chair as her fingers dug into the padded arms. Lucas smiled. "Unfortunately, dear wife, this is one thing you can't finish. I've been indulgent so far, letting you pursue this little fantasy, but enough is enough. You're neglecting your duties here."

Her jaw dropped. "My *duties*? We have half a dozen housekeepers, three cooks, four gardeners and six grooms. What *duties* do I have? Am I supposed to sit at home all day doing nothing, only to get up and greet you when you come home from work? If you decide to come home at all."

Lucas placed his hands over hers and his fingers dug into her wrists. "I married you because I knew you'd be a good, dutiful wife. You fulfilled all the requirements my father demanded in a *good, dutiful* wife."

Lindsay blinked. "What does your father have to do with this?" Lucas squeezed her wrists a bit harder and she bit her lip to keep from crying out.

"Oh, that's right. I never bothered to tell you." His lips curled in a sneer and he pushed away, as if he couldn't stand to touch her. "See, I didn't really want a wife, but my father said without one I'd never see a penny of the Davenport fortune. Out of all the women I brought home for his approval, you were the only one he liked. You're pretty, but not too pretty, you're smart enough to be entertaining without being intimidating and, despite the fact you're from a small, backwoods town, you're an elegant and gracious hostess. Yes, you fit the bill."

Lindsay wanted to kick herself. She'd realized shortly after their honeymoon that Lucas didn't care for her, but he'd never actually come out and said it before. This revelation wasn't really a surprise, but hearing it hurt nonetheless. As the tears gathered she took a deep breath, hating the pitying look she saw in Roger's eyes.

"Why don't you just divorce me?" she asked. "Your father is dead, you have control of Davenport. What do you need me for?"

Lucas snickered. "Why, I need a dutiful wife. Hadn't you guessed that? A public servant is nothing without his loving, supportive wife at his side, and I don't plan to spend the rest of my life as simply the CEO of Davenport Pharmaceuticals. No, darling, I have much bigger plans." Lindsay turned her face away as he stroked her cheek. "So you can take comfort in the fact that even if I don't *love* you, I do *need* you. However, I *do* not need another accountant."

"And if *I* leave *you?*" She hated the quiver in her voice, but could do nothing to stop it. Her heart hammered wildly, her breathing rapid and shallow.

"You won't." His fingers slid into her hair, his touch deceptively gentle, and Lindsay braced herself for what she knew was coming. Even so, she couldn't keep back the cry of pain when he fisted his hand and jerked her head back. His eyes bored into hers, his face scant inches away. "I *own* you. If you try to leave me, your life as you know it, and the life of your family, will end, like *that.*" He snapped his fingers in her face to emphasize his point.

Lacey's eyes snapped open and she sat up quickly, disoriented. The logs in the fireplace crackled again, and glowing embers flew against the screen as red sparks floated up the chimney. When she realized where she was, she heaved a sigh of relief. She was in the cabin, alone, neatly stacked bills on the TV tray in front of her. After counting her tips, she had closed her eyes for a moment as the warmth of the fire had enveloped her.

She shook off the memory and stood. After double-checking the locks, she took the money into the bedroom and stowed it in the strongbox before climbing into bed. She stared through the sheer curtains and watched the snow fall. The memory of Lucas's laughter echoed in her mind before she fell into a fitful sleep.

***

Snow continued to fall well into the next day. Lacey sat on the porch with her pad and pencils, snuggling deeper into her parka. It was cold, colder than she'd ever felt before, her breath freezing in front of her.

She'd learned that sketching with gloves on was a little harder than she'd anticipated, so for now she was content to watch the flakes float to earth.

The sound of an engine approaching broke through the quiet; the diesel hum echoing off the trees. Setting her things aside, she got to her feet and groaned inwardly when Jack Calhoun's truck came up the road. Despite the nervous flutter in the pit of her stomach she stood her ground. She leaned against the support post and crossed her arms over her chest.

She kept her expression neutral as he turned off the truck and got out. He looked at her sheepishly before he shuffled toward her.

"That's far enough," she said as he reached the bottom step. "What do you want?"

He took off his cap and twisted it in his hands. "I – I want to apologize." She said nothing and his eyes pleaded with her. "C'mon, Lacey. I'm sorry. I was drunk and jealous—"

"There's nothing for you to be jealous of," she interrupted, her tone brusque. "Neither you nor Ross Devlin, has any claim on me. I may be *fresh meat*, but I don't appreciate being treated like a piece of it."

"Now, Lacey, I didn't mean to—"

"I don't care what you meant." She descended the steps, her anger rising. The memory she'd relived last night was too fresh in her mind; the feeling of helplessness like a bad taste in her mouth. When she reached the next to the bottom step she poked a finger in his chest. "*No* man; not you, not Ross Devlin, not anyone, will *ever* put their hands on me again unless I want them to. You got that?"

He moved back. "Yeah, yeah, Lacey, I've got it." He studied her face for a moment. "I'm sorry. It's just...I like you. You're different, and I'd like to get to know you."

Her eyes narrowed and she shook her head. "I'm not different, I'm *new*. That's the only thing that interests you. And you don't know me well enough to like me." She ran a hand over her face, turned around and walked back up the stairs. "Just go, Jack. I accept your apology, and you're forgiven, but I don't want anything else from you."

"Lacey..."

She stopped with her hand on the doorknob and gave him a harried look. "Just go." They locked eyes for a moment and Lacey saw the pain of rejection in his gaze. She felt strange, like she wanted to laugh and cry at the same time, because she knew exactly how he felt. To want someone who didn't want you back really sucked. She softened her expression and that seemed to help a little, a small, pained smile curved his mouth.

"I'm sorry, Lacey. See you around?"

Giving him a short nod she went into the cabin and closed the door behind her. It was several minutes before she heard his engine start and the truck head down the road. Maybe she wasn't so different from her ex, being nice when it suited her and being cold when it didn't. The very thought started a cascade of dark, depressing emotions. She sat down in front of the fire, and laid her head in her hands as sorrowful tears streamed down her face.

Chapter Eight

Ross had just finished his breakfast when the bell on the café door rang, signaling another customer. He glanced up as Jack Calhoun approached him and took a seat two spots down. Annie looked from one to the other as she poured Jack a cup of coffee. Ross gave her a tight smile as she wisely retreated into the kitchen.

"Well, it looks like the way is clear for you now," Jack said, his voice low. He poured some cream and sugar into his cup.

"What way would that be?" Ross asked, not sure he wanted to hear the answer.

Jack stirred his coffee, a small smile on his face. "I went to apologize to Lacey yesterday afternoon." He chuckled and shook his head. "She told me she accepted my apology then ran me off. Said she didn't want anything else from me."

Ross fought a smile and rubbed his chin. "And this affects me...how?"

"The competition has been eliminated. She's all yours now."

Ross laughed and gazed heavenward. "You are *un*believable." Turning on his stool he looked at Jack, incredulous. "That's your whole problem, Calhoun. You viewed Lacey as some sort of medal you were competing for. Did you think she didn't know that?"

"I didn't—"

"Yes, you did." Ross got to his feet and tossed some bills on the counter. "You don't think of women as people, you think of them as trophies."

Jack frowned. "And what about you? You fool around, you have your fun, but you never make any commitments. What makes you so different?"

"The women I spend time with know *exactly* what they're getting, up front, and you don't see me chasing every skirt in town. With you, sex is like a spectator sport, the more people who know about it the better."

Jack laughed shortly. "As if your flings are any secret."

Ross ground his teeth together and resisted the urge to punch the younger man. "There *are* no secrets in a town like this. You of all people should know that. The difference between us is *I* don't advertise my sex life. The women I spend time with know they won't be the topic of the locker room, or have their names bandied about the bar along with colorful descriptions of their talent, or lack thereof."

"I'd never do that to Lacey. She's...different."

Ross choked back a laugh. "You're right about that, Jack. And, in case you hadn't noticed, Lacey keeps to herself and tries to avoid attention. What you did the other night made her the center of attention."

"Yeah, and she paid me back for that."

"What did you *expect* when you grabbed her in front of the entire town?"

Jack got to his feet, lines of anger harsh about his mouth. "Well, what do you think she's going to do when the whole town finds out about the two of you? She ain't even been in town two weeks and already you've put another notch in your belt."

Ross scowled. "What are you talking about?"

"I saw the two of you leave town together that night," Jack replied with a smirk. "I know what's going on, and it's only a matter of time before everyone knows. How do you think she's going to like you then?"

Ross stared at him for a moment, then threw his head back and laughed. Annie appeared in the kitchen door with the cook right behind her. "I know you're young and immature but I didn't realize you were *stupid.* I guess you weren't conscious to see me drive *back* into town half an hour after I left. She's never driven in snow at night before, you idiot."

Jack scowled and threw a punch, but Ross dodged it easily. The younger man's momentum carried him forward and he fell onto the worn linoleum. Before he could get up Ross planted a booted foot between his shoulder blades and held him down.

"Don't, Jack. There's no reason for this."

He waited until Jack nodded before removing his foot. He took a step backwards while he kept a close eye on the younger man. Slowly, Jack got to his feet and straightened his jacket.

"Just watch yourself, Ross," Jack warned him. "When you get tired of Lacey, like I know you will, I'll be there waiting to pick up the pieces.

So, have your fun while you can."

Ross didn't reply, content to watch as Jack strode slowly out of the café. When the door closed behind him, Annie walked over, shaking her head in disbelief.

"He always has been a sore loser," she commented. "I've never seen him so agitated before. You'd think they were engaged or something." She turned to Ross and looked at him with wide eyes. "I think I'm going to have to come over to Lights one night and see what all this fuss is about. I mean, she's pretty, but what is it? Does she serve topless or something?"

Ross pulled on his coat. "It's a whole lot of nothing, Annie. A whole lot of nothing."

"There has to be something, Ross. Two of Cooper's Ridge's most popular bachelors, fighting over some woman who hasn't been in town long enough to knock the snow off her boots." She nodded. "Yep, there has to be something."

***

"Fangs!" Ross yelled as the last card dropped into the slot. Lacey shouted triumphantly and Ross jumped to his feet. Fanny and Boomer laughed as she ran over and hugged him. Ross swept her up in his arms and spun her around.

"We win," Lacey announced.

Ross laughed, put her back on her feet, and turned to their hosts. His arm was around her shoulders and she was relaxed against him, but when Fanny and Boomer exchanged a knowing glance he felt her tense up. He grinned and let his arm drop to his side. To his relief, Lacey returned his smile.

"That's three out of four," Fanny griped, looking sideways at her husband. "Maybe if I had a better partner..."

"All right you two," Ross interrupted. "None of that."

Boomer leaned over and started to reset the game. "One more round," he suggested. "This time Fanny and I will smoke you guys."

Lacey shook her head and glanced at Ross. "I really have to go."

Ross checked his watch. "It's nearly eleven," he said, amazed.

Fanny and Boomer looked at each other, then at the clock over the bar, and both of their jaws dropped. Lacey leaned over and gave Fanny a kiss on the cheek.

"Thanks again for dinner." Fanny and Boomer got to their feet, following as she walked up the stairs. Ross was close behind them.

"Same time next week?" Fanny asked.

Lacey tossed her a smile over her shoulder. "Wouldn't miss it."

Boomer helped her into her coat. "And next time, we're playing something else, or changing partners," Boomer said with a glance at his wife. Fanny sniffed and put her nose in the air.

"Hear, hear," Fanny said. She gave Lacey a hug. "Drive safely, dear."

Lacey laughed and returned Fanny's hug. "I will."

Ross stood on the front stoop and looked up at the softly falling snow. "I'll make sure she makes it." When he saw Lacey's expression he grinned. "Do we have to go over this again?"

She arched one brow. "Let me guess. Beauty sleep?"

Ross looked at Boomer in mock surprise. "Boy, she catches on quick."

Boomer laughed and put an arm around Fanny's shoulders. Lacey waved to them as she made her way to the Jeep, Ross in step beside her. Boomer and Fanny waved back, then went inside and closed the door.

Ross watched as she crossed her arms over her chest and turned to him. He stuffed his hands in his pockets and gave her what he hoped was a charming smile. She didn't appear impressed.

"Are you going to guide me home every time it snows?" she asked.

"Yes. At least until I'm more comfortable with the idea of you driving in this weather." Her brows rose. Ross cleared his throat and glanced toward the house. "Alaska can be tricky. You never know when a gentle snowfall is going to turn into a raging blizzard."

Her posture didn't change. "And you have no ulterior motives?"

Ross looked at her innocently and shook his head. "Perhaps..." Lacey laughed as he continued. "You see, I have this theory." She waited for his explanation, an expectant look on her face. It took a moment to find the words, and even then he had trouble getting them out. "See...I find myself incredibly attracted to you, but I know it's because you're..."

"Fresh meat," she finished for him.

He winced. "I would have put it a little more delicately, but I suppose that's accurate enough." She continued to watch him carefully and he had the sudden urge to kiss her. He dropped his eyes and shuffled his feet in the snow.

"So, what is this theory of yours?" she asked.

Ross shrugged. His urge was to kiss her, but he forced himself to remain businesslike and as scientific as he possibly could. He cleared his throat softly. "Well, I figure if I spend more time with you, the newness will wear off and this attraction will fade. Then I won't have to worry about whether or not you find me attractive, because...it won't matter." He glanced at her but her expression gave no clue to her thoughts.

"I do find you attractive."

"We'll be friends and..." When what she'd said finally registered, he paused. "What did you say?" He thought she blushed but in the darkness he couldn't be sure.

She looked down at the ground and a small smile curved her mouth. "I said, I *do* find you attractive." When she finally raised her eyes to him, they were twinkling. "But I, too, have a theory."

"Go on."

"I think I feel this attraction because you seem to be a genuinely nice man. I'm sure once I get to know you better, I'll realize I'm wrong and it will wear off."

And there's that saucy side again. I like it. He grinned. "So, I'll lead?"

She got into the Jeep and rolled down the window. "Only if you promise to come in for a cup of hot chocolate."

He studied her then brushed the snow from her hair. For a second he debated dragging his fingers down her cheek that was close and looked so soft, but he decided to play it cool for now. "Do you have marshmallows?"

"Big ones or little ones?"

"You have both?" She nodded and he rubbed his hands together. "Hot damn. A woman after my own heart."

Grinning, Lacey started the Jeep and waited for Ross to get into his truck. Truth be told, she was relieved for the escort. He hadn't been kidding when he said driving at night in snow was frightening, and she knew if it hadn't been for him, she wouldn't have made it home these past couple of nights. The snow effectively hid the turn off for her driveway, at least from her eyes, but it didn't seem to affect Ross a bit.

When they pulled up to the cabin, Ross parked to the side so she could park in front, then he got out and waited for her. Butterflies bounced off her insides as she walked past him and up the front steps. After opening the door, she stepped across the threshold. She pulled in a breath and let it out slowly. *This is it, Lacey. This is the first time since you left Lucas that you're going to be alone with a man, really alone. With a hot man, a man who makes you feel more than Lucas ever did.* When the door closed behind him her train of thought derailed and she jumped.

Lacey started when she felt his hands at her neck, and she felt like an idiot when she realized he was helping her with her coat. Forcing herself to relax, she shrugged out of the parka and gave him a brief smile then walked over to the refrigerator. He hung his jacket up and moved to the hearth.

"Have a seat," she said, hating the slight tremor she heard in her voice.

He smiled and crouched before the fireplace, placing several more logs on the banked coals. As he stoked the fire, she took the milk out, got a pan from a rack over the stove and set it on the burner, then poured milk into it. He walked toward her, and Lacey was uncomfortably aware of his gaze.

"Need any help?" he asked in a low, buttery voice.

Lacey shook her head and forced a smile. "No. Hot chocolate I can do." His presence at her side was palpable, as if he was pressed against her and not standing a foot away. Awareness spiraled out from her core. His sexuality was a force of nature, like a brooding electrical storm she could feel but couldn't quite see yet. Goose bumps broke out on her arms.

"Why don't you put on some music?" she suggested. "The player's over there." She pointed to the far wall, hoping a little distance between them would settle her nerves. He tipped his head and smiled, then made his way over to the CD player. Lacey watched him as he went, admiring the width of his shoulders and the nicely rounded backside. As if feeling her stare, he turned, grinning when she blushed and dropped her gaze. She reached blindly for the tin of marshmallows and almost burned herself on the pan of heating milk.

He turned at her indrawn breath. "You okay?" he asked.

"Fine," she said as she retrieved the chocolate syrup from the refrigerator. However, before she could pour it, Ross took the bottle from her hand, set it aside, and pulled her into his arms. The sultry sounds of Barry White drifted from the stereo, and Lacey looked up in surprise as he smiled and twirled her into the living room.

"Dance with me?"

Unable to reply, she swallowed hard and focused on the buttons of his shirt. His body swayed gently to the music and, while he made no moves on her, it was still several minutes before she could relax. As if sensing her tension had eased, he pulled her closer, his arm around her waist and his cheek pressed against her hair. Lacey closed her eyes, trying to remember if she'd ever felt like this with Lucas. It startled her to realize she enjoyed Ross Devlin's embrace, his arms like a fortress around her. The warmth of his body sent shivers over her skin and, when she thought of their kiss, desire sparked inside of her. She gulped and pulled away.

"I - I've got to stir the milk or it'll scald," she said in a low voice. She averted her face and walked to the stove. Thankfully, Ross didn't follow, but his gaze remained fastened on her as she poured chocolate syrup into the pan. After ladling the cocoa into a pair of large ceramic mugs, she turned to him, and her heart skipped a beat at the warmth she saw in his eyes. Several seconds passed before she could speak. "Um, big ones or little ones?" His brows rose and a smile danced about his mouth as she flushed. "Marshmallows," she clarified.

"Little ones," he replied.

She returned his smile, dropped some marshmallows in his drink, and picked up the mugs. She handed his cup to him as she sat down on the couch, and he sat next to her.

"Is it so different, being alone with me?" he asked in a low voice.

She blinked at him. *Boy howdy, and I can't even begin to explain how much.* They'd been alone before, at the bar before opening and after closing, inside the tent, but this took it to a different level. Here, in her little cabin in the woods, there was the distinct possibility they would be intimate, and the thought both excited her and scared her to death. She wasn't sure how to answer him. Her mouth went dry. The clock on the mantle ticked as seconds stretched out.

"Wh-why would you ask that?" she asked at last, her voice little more than a whisper.

He sipped his cocoa and gazed at the fire. "You've been wound tighter than a spring ever since I stepped through the door."

Lacey stared at her cup. "I *am* a little nervous," she admitted. "It's a lot easier with Fanny and Boomer around."

He chuckled. "Yes, they tend to put everyone at ease." Pausing, he took another drink. "They really like you, you know."

She could feel his eyes on her, but couldn't look at him. "And I like them."

He shifted on the couch, put his cup aside and moved closer. "I like you, too, Lacey."

His voice was so close she jumped. When she turned her eyes

widened, his face was scant inches away. He took her mug and put it on the end table behind her, a small smile lighting his face. He put a hand behind her neck and leaned forward, and her eyes closed as his mouth covered hers.

His lips were warm and supple, and without even thinking she returned his kiss. Something inside of her responded to him, and that spark of desire began to glow a little hotter. It had been so long since she'd felt attraction, or experienced any form of passion, but even this small taste was enough to start not only fierce need but also cold fear curling inside her. When he touched his tongue to hers it was too much, and a low cry escaped her as she twisted away from him.

Lacey got to her feet and stood in front of the fire as she tried to get control of herself. Her hands shook and she rested them on the mantle, her breath coming in short, ragged gasps.

"It was just a kiss, Lacey. We've kissed before, remember? I had no expectations beyond that."

She chuckled, but it sounded hollow even to her ears. "I – I'm sorry. It's been...a long time since I've been...alone with a man."

"You spent the night with me," he reminded her. "We were alone then."

"Not completely. Your clients were only a few feet away."

"We were closer then than we are now."

A smile tugged at the corners of her mouth even as tears welled. "But we weren't *completely* alone." She glanced at him, distinctly uncomfortable beneath his knowing gaze.

He sighed heavily and she closed her eyes when he stood behind her. It was several moments before he spoke again. "And if you would've cried out, someone would've come to save you." Before she could stop herself she nodded. Her eyes stung and when he touched her cheek she pulled away, tears squeezing from beneath her lids. "My God, Lacey. What did he do to you?"

"Who?" she asked in a whisper.

"The man you're running from."

Her head snapped around and she found herself caught by those piercing blue eyes. His brows were drawn together, his expression filled with concern and tenderness. Shaking her head, she took a step away from him. "I...I don't know what you're talking about."

He said nothing, and she knew he saw right through her. After several moments she looked away, unable to hold his gaze. His footsteps took him away from her and she heard him slip into his coat. For some reason, she had the feeling that if he walked out that door she'd never see him again, and that frightened her.

"Ross, wait." Summoning all her courage she turned, but the words stuck in her throat. She forced herself to look at him, her lungs frozen as her heart thudded painfully. Slowly, he approached her and pressed a hand to her cheek, his thumb stroking over the trail of her tears.

"I'm not like him, Lacey," he said softly. "You don't need to be saved from me."

Tears brimmed, but she smiled as she closed her eyes and covered his hand with hers. "I know."

His lips brushed her cheek, then her mouth. "Thanks for the cocoa. I'll see you at work." She stood like a statue until the door closed behind him and she heard his truck roar to life. It was then her bravado crumbled. She ran to the door and threw it open, watching his taillights disappear around the curve in the road.

***

Ross stared at the phone for the longest time before picking it up and dialing. He felt the frown as he waited for an answer.

"Gateway Lodge, this is Brad. How can I help you?"

"Brad, it's Ross."

"Hey, Ross, what's up? You looking for work, because I have some celebrities coming in next week who said they might be interested—"

"No, that's not why I called. Remember those guys I took out last week?"

"Yeah, the charming trio who drank my liquor cabinet dry. What about them?"

"The man who met them the day I brought them back, can you tell me what company he's with?" He could almost hear Brad frown through the phone.

"What's going on, Ross?"

Ross rubbed a hand over his eyes and sighed. "I can't talk about it right now. Can you give me his company name or not?" He heard the shuffling of paper and took a relieved breath.

"Lechter picked up his tab," Brad said, "but according to his reg card he works for...Davenport Pharmaceuticals out of Texas. Does that help?"

Ross was silent for a moment as he wrote the name down. "Yeah, thanks buddy. I'll get back with you soon, okay?"

"Sure, and tell the 'wife' I said hi."

Ross smiled. "I'll do that. Later."

He hung up the phone and stared at the name, then started thinking over the conversations he'd had with Lacey. He remembered when he'd called her a society dame and she'd nearly passed out. Narrowing his eyes, he wrote that phrase down, underlined it several times and tore the page out of the notebook. After stuffing it in his pocket, he grabbed his jacket and headed out the door, his stride purposeful.

He walked into the library and waved to Pauline, the librarian. The woman returned his wave with a smile. Even though Cooper's Ridge was a small town, their library had state of the art computers. While he wasn't completely computer literate, he could maneuver around the world wide web well enough to accomplish whatever task he'd set his mind on. After sitting down at one of the monitors, he logged in and started clicking away.

He did a search for Davenport Pharmaceuticals, pen and paper handy. Several links came up as he scanned the screen and he clicked on the top one. He found that, based in Dallas, Texas, Davenport was one of the oldest and largest privately owned pharmaceutical companies in the U.S., and was set to merge with Parker-Raines sometime next year. He scrolled down and stopped when a picture of a familiar face appeared on the screen. Dennis Lechter. In the picture he stood next to a younger man, and Ross read the caption to find out the other man's identity. Lucas Davenport.

Ross wrote Lucas Davenport and Dallas, Texas, below his other notes. Then he did a search of the Dallas newspapers, scanning the society pages. He went back one year, then two, but found nothing.

Two hours later Ross rubbed his eyes, sighing heavily as he scrolled through what he decided would be the last society section of the day. Suddenly, he sat straight up and his eyes widened. Glancing around to make sure no one else was watching, he turned back to the screen and stared at the picture of Lacey, in a wedding dress, standing next to Lucas Davenport. The caption read "Real Life Cinderella Story: Lucas Davenport, CEO of Davenport Pharmaceuticals and a rising star shooting straight for the State Senate, weds small-town girl, Lindsay Price." He looked at the date. The picture was nearly eight years old. In the photo she stared at Davenport adoringly, but the man looked bored, almost as if he wished he wasn't there. There was no warmth in his eyes, no hint of the happiness reflected on Lacey's face, nothing but indifference.

Ross felt his lungs burn and realized he'd been holding his breath. After writing down her real name on the scrap of paper he folded it and put it back in his pocket. He cleared the website history to erase the evidence of his activity and logged off. He felt like the wind had been knocked out of him, and it was nearly a minute before he stood and headed toward the doors.

"Hey, Ross, you're going to play today, aren't you?" It was a moment before Pauline's voice registered.

"Yeah. See you there?"

Pauline smiled and nodded as she returned to her chair behind the desk.

Ross walked slowly back to his place, his breath freezing in front of him. The air was cold but it had stopped snowing, the sun finally breaking through the ominous cloud cover. He'd just unlocked his door when he saw Annie wave to him from the café. He paused, then re-locked the door and made his way across the street.

Annie held the door open. "Hey Ross, I was just waving. No need to come over."

He smiled and sat down at the counter. "I know, but I could use a cup of coffee. That instant stuff doesn't cut it."

Annie chuckled and poured him a cup. After placing the pot back on the burner she leaned against the counter. "All right, honey, out with it." His brows shot up and Annie gave him a knowing look. "You didn't come over here for a cup of coffee."

Ross stared at his cup. "You said Lacey was running from something, or someone, probably a man." He glanced at her. "How do you know that?"

Annie snorted and started wiping down the counter. "Well, I *don't* know for sure, it's a hunch. But I've seen that look before...in the mirror." She paused and studied him. "Let me guess. She's skittish around men, she overreacts or reacts violently when touched by a man, she avoids being alone with men." She waited until he nodded in affirmation. With a shake of her head she resumed her work. "Classic symptoms of a battered woman."

"You sound like you're speaking from experience."

"I am." With a sigh she tossed the dishcloth beneath the counter and walked toward him. "A long time ago, in another lifetime, I was married to a man who liked to vent his anger on me. I couldn't find the nerve to leave until he nearly killed me, and even then it took more guts than I knew I had." Her gaze turned speculative. "What's wrong, Ross? Did you discover something about Miss Jamison that has you upset?"

Ross thought of the paper in his pocket. "No. I was just wondering."

"Well, honey, if she *is* running from an abusive man, she's got quite a bit of steel beneath that sweet exterior. It takes a lot for a woman to leave everything she's got."

Knowing Lacey had been married to a billionaire, Ross couldn't even imagine what she had left behind. He finished his coffee, and when he searched his pockets for some change Annie put a hand on his arm.

"It's on the house, Ross. See you at the hockey game later."

He got up and kissed her cheek. "Thanks, Annie. You're a doll."

"Yeah, well, if I'm right about Lacey, keep it in mind she's wounded." Annie gave him a wry look. "If you're sweet on her, you have to remember that."

Ross grinned and chucked her under the chin. "Why, Annie, you know the only girl I'm sweet on is you."

She rolled her eyes and groaned, then turned her back on him and disappeared inside the kitchen. Ross laughed and left the café.

***

Lacey was curled up by the fireplace, a book in her hand. Her eyes were focused on the flames, and Ross's image swam in and out of focus as she cursed herself. What had come over her? He was nothing like Lucas, but when he got too close she couldn't keep the fear away. The two men seemed to become one and the same. She'd never felt with Lucas what she did with Ross, and she knew instinctively he'd never hurt her, but after so many years of keeping her guard up she didn't know how to let it down. She was fine at the bar, or with Fanny and Boomer, and she'd thought last night would be a step in the right direction. Unfortunately, things hadn't worked out as she'd expected.

The phone rang and Lacey started violently, the book falling to the floor. The phone rang again before she moved, and she practically tripped over the rug getting to the receiver.

"Hello?"

"Hi, it's Ross."

Lacey closed her eyes and swallowed hard, the deep timbre of his voice making her heart thud. "Hi." Her voice came out in a hoarse whisper and she ran a hand through her hair. Clearing her throat, she repeated herself. "Hi."

"I'm not disturbing you, am I?"

She smiled and sat down in a chair. "Well, I've read the same page of my book about a hundred times, and I still don't know what it says, so yes, you are. But, I don't mind."

He chuckled. "Maybe you should try a different book."

"Yeah, maybe."

There was a brief pause.

"Are you busy later this afternoon?"

Lacey straightened up in her chair. "Um, I'd have to check my social calendar, but I don't think I'm *completely* booked. Why?"

"How'd you like to come to the hockey game? Boomer and I are playing. Fanny will be there, and I'm sure she'd love to have your help cheering us on."

Her cheeks burned as she remembered the fiasco of last night. How could he want to see her after what had happened?

"Lacey, you there?"

"Yeah, I was just, uh, checking my calendar." The residents of Cooper's Ridge attended the Monday afternoon hockey games more religiously than church, weather permitting, though Lacey hadn't had the nerve to go yet.

"I'd like you to come, too," he added.

That swung it. Playing with the phone cord, she smiled. "I – I didn't think you'd ever speak to me again after last night," she said in a hushed voice.

"That's what you get for thinking," he replied. "So, you going to come or not? I figure, after the game, the four of us could go to Joe's and get pizza, or something. What do you say?"

"The game starts when?"

"Three o'clock."

It took her less than a moment to decide. "I'll be there," she said, "with bells on."

Chapter Nine

Dennis Lechter looked at his watch and frowned. His appointment had been for 3 p.m., and it was now ten after. Drumming his fingers on the arms of the chair he reminded himself this slight was nothing new. If he wanted this merger to go smoothly, he had to make allowances for Davenport's juvenile behavior. He stood, went to the window and looked out across Dallas; the traffic and pedestrians below looking like hundreds of children's toys scattered on the ground. When he turned around his gaze fell on a framed picture on the desk, and his eyes widened.

Moving to the other side of the desk he picked the photograph up and stared at the image. He *knew* he'd seen her somewhere before. His head snapped around and he looked toward the bookcase where he'd seen another 8 X 10, and it all clicked. He put the picture back on the desk and walked to the bookcase.

"I'll be damned," he said under his breath. He ran his finger over the cool glass that covered the photo, a smile dancing about his mouth. "Well, well. I knew I'd seen you before Lacey, and now I know where."

***

The hockey rink was in the center of town, and Lacey had to park several blocks away. It seemed as if the entire town had turned out for today's game. The air crackled with excitement and anticipation as a low drone rose from the stands. She pulled a wool cap over her head and tightened her scarf, then put on her gloves and started walking toward the outdoor arena. People ran by her, obviously headed to the game. She couldn't help but smile.

As she walked up to the edge of the rink, she saw both teams were warming up. She turned, looked into the packed stands, and grinned when she saw Fanny stand up and wave, a large bundle of banners and flags clutched to her chest with the other arm.

"Lacey! Over here!"

She made her way to Fanny, and was surprised at the number of people who smiled and said hello. Fanny had great seats in the center section about six rows up, and soon as Lacey sat down, the woman pressed a flag into her hand.

"I was so tickled when Ross said you were coming," Fanny said, waving a banner as a line of men skated by. "Our men are the Hawks in black; the other team is the Bears."

Lacey recognized Boomer as he lifted his stick and grinned at his wife. Ross was right behind the sheriff, and when he met her eyes he smiled. He looked even larger in all his hockey gear, and when he waved she waved back, her heartbeat speeding up.

As the opposing team came around the ice, Lacey was surprised to see Jack Calhoun. He looked directly at her and smiled, but the warmth never reached his eyes.

"This ought to be a good game," said a woman to Lacey's left. Lacey recognized her as the waitress from the coffee shop. The woman smiled and extended her hand. "Hi, I'm Annie. I've waited on you at the café, but we've never been formally introduced." Her manner was warm and sincere, and Lacey shook her hand firmly.

"It's a pleasure," Lacey replied. "I'm Lacey."

Annie grinned. "That you are." She studied Lacey's face for a minute. "You're even prettier than I remember. It's no wonder Ross and Jack are both so taken with you." Lacey blinked and Annie laughed. "Oh, don't worry, honey, you're safe. Ross will never push himself on you, and Jack will stay away because he's afraid of Ross, though I imagine the hostility between the two will add flavor to today's game."

"Hostility?" She gaped at the redhead. "Because of *me*?"

Annie laughed and patted Lacey's hand. "Not really. Those two have never cared for each other. Ross has always been liked and respected, and Jack has always *wanted* to be liked and respected. Too bad his ego and his big mouth get in the way. Jack's not such a bad guy, if you can get past his attitude."

"I guess. He's a little pushy for my taste."

Annie gave her a knowing look. "Oh, honey, you have *no* idea."

At that moment a voice came over the loudspeaker, asking for the crowd to rise and sing the national anthem. A young man of about fifteen skated to the center of the ice, and the players lined up in a row behind him. Lacey stood up and laid her hand over her heart, closing her eyes as the youth's voice came through the speakers. Tears came to her eyes as he sang; each note perfect. When he was finished, the fans burst into applause, then took their seats as he bowed and skated off the ice.

The announcer, who was also the town mayor Fanny told her, stepped back to the microphone and smiled as the crowd cheered for him.

"Thank you, thank you." He cleared his throat and continued. "Now, I know you all heard about Ted Foster, and how he was killed last week in that accident at the mill, leaving behind his wife, Stephanie and two young boys." He paused for effect and a murmur went through the crowd. "Well, the town council was trying to figure out a way to help Mrs. Foster, when Sheriff Madison suggested we take a collection today. Mrs. Foster has decided to move back to Seattle to be closer to her and Ted's family, so we want to raise enough money to pay for movers, airline tickets for her and the boys, with maybe enough left over for a little nest egg. So, come on, everybody. Get out your wallets and be generous, and if you can't give now you can head down to the Sheriff's Department any time before Tuesday of next week. Let's show Stephanie and the boys how much we care."

Lacey turned to Fanny. "Oh, that's awful."

Fanny sighed and opened her purse. "Yes. Ted was only 45, and the boys are 10 and 8." She shook her head. "Poor Stephanie."

"She loved Ted so much," Annie said with a sigh. She dabbed at her eyes with her sleeve. "They were high school sweethearts, you know. Never spent a night apart, those two."

Lacey's eyes stung. "How tragic," she said. "To lose someone you truly love..."

Fanny sniffed. "I don't know what I'd do if I were her," the woman said. She glanced lovingly at Boomer who was skating in circles around Ross, and a determined gleam entered her eyes. "C'mon, girls. Let's ante up. It won't make up for her loss, but every little bit helps."

Since leaving Texas Lacey had made a point of carrying cash on her, so when the hockey helmet came around she didn't even think about it. She had close to $200, and it took her four tries to transfer all the bills from the pocket of her jeans into the helmet. Fanny watched her with wide eyes.

"Forgot to take my tips out of my pocket," Lacey said as she dropped the last handful in. She pressed down on the money to make sure it didn't fall out, then handed the helmet to Fanny. Fanny continued to stare and Lacey shrugged. "What? I can always make more."

Fanny gaped at her, then shook her head, dropped her money in, and passed the helmet along without a word.

Lacey had never been to a hockey game before, so she relied on Fanny and Annie to tell her what was happening. After the first period, however, she started to get into it and cheered just as enthusiastically as the rest of the spectators. She sat on the edge of her seat as Boomer passed the puck to Ross, then jumped to her feet and shouted as Ross rifled it into the goal. Fanny was also on her feet and the two women embraced, cheering until they were hoarse.

As the third period drew to a close the game was tied, but the Hawks had the puck. Boomer and Ross set up as before, and Lacey held her breath as they raced down the ice. As Boomer passed the puck to Ross, Jack Calhoun came up behind him and, using his stick like a baseball bat, brought it across Ross's shoulders. Ross went flying and crashed into the side of the rink. The crowd let out a collective gasp and jumped to their feet.

Lacey covered her mouth with her hands as Boomer shoved Jack violently out of the way and skated to Ross's side. Her heart stopped as she waited for him to move. "Come on, Ross," she whispered, "come on, get up."

Fanny and Annie each grabbed one of her hands as they watched in horrified silence. Boomer knelt on the ice next to him. When Ross rolled over and sat up Lacey nearly collapsed with relief. Closing her eyes, she sent a prayer of thanks heavenward.

People around them started shouting and Lacey looked back at Ross. As Boomer helped him to his feet, the entire team descended on Jack and he was lost in a sea of black uniforms. Then the Bears joined in and there was a full-fledged riot on the ice. Boomer, Ross and the referees stood to the side. It was several minutes before things calmed down and the players retreated to their respective boxes. Lacey felt an immense burst of satisfaction when she saw Jack's teammates help him to the bench because he couldn't skate there on his own.

"Jack got off easy, if you ask me," Fanny grumbled.

The angry sparkle in Fanny's eyes told of her loyalty to her husband and Ross. She was petite and usually dignified, but it was obvious she could be a firecracker when provoked.

The game resumed, and Ross seemed no worse for wear. Lacey

looked at the scoreboard and fidgeted, chewing on her lower lip while the seconds ticked away. Once again the three women linked hands as Ross and Boomer took the puck down the ice. Boomer passed to Ross who headed for the goal, but at the last minute he peeled off, and the puck rocketed toward Boomer. With a slash of his stick, Boomer shot the puck. The goalie was taken off-guard by Ross's last minute change of direction. The crowd roared as the puck went in, and time ran out.

***

Lacey wiped her mouth and laughed as Boomer described what the game had looked like from the players' vantage point. The extra large pizza was nearly gone. Ross finished the last piece and threw her a wry look as Boomer gestured wildly. Joe's Pizzeria overflowed with people, players and spectators alike, and it seemed as if similar conversations went on at almost every table. Lacey had come to realize the weekly hockey game was a much loved tradition in Cooper's Ridge, and it wasn't hard to see why.

"Well, I thought it was exciting," she said once Boomer had finished his narrative. "I've never been to a hockey game before."

Ross and Boomer looked at her in surprise. "Never?" they asked in unison.

Lacey shrugged. "Never had a reason. I'm from California, remember?"

Ross raised one brow. "Ever heard of the Los Angeles Kings? San Jose Sharks? *The Mighty Ducks?*"

Lacey chuckled and sipped her Coke. "All right, all right. So I've lived in a cave all my life. But now I've seen the light. It's official, I'm a fan."

At that moment a waitress appeared with a pitcher of beer in one hand and four glasses in the other.

Boomer frowned. "What's this, Amy? We didn't order any beer." The girl smiled and inclined her head to the left. Jack Calhoun and some of his buddies sat in a booth on the far wall, and Jack raised his beer in salute, a dark glint of challenge in his eyes.

"Jack sent it over," the girl said. She turned admiring eyes to Ross. "Great game, by the way."

"Thanks, Amy."

Amy put the beer and glasses down, giving Ross one last adoring look before she left their table.

"So," Boomer started, staring at the pitcher, "do we keep it? Or should we have Lacey perform her famous beer dump?"

Ross scowled, and Lacey was glad his back was to Jack. Between the scuffle at the hockey game and the look on Jack's face that seemed to say, "Give me a reason," the tension was already high. If Jack saw Ross's expression, Jack's alcohol-fueled bravado would no doubt take affront and then the brawl on the ice might very well reignite inside the restaurant.

"It's probably the only apology you're going to get, Ross," Fanny said.

Ross snorted. "It's not an apology. It's a taunt. He wants to see what I'm going to do, *and* he's itching for a fight."

"So, why don't you send him a pot of coffee?" Lacey asked. "It looks like he could use some."

Ross looked at her in surprise. After a moment he put an arm around her shoulders and pressed his forehead to hers. "That, my dear Lacey, is an excellent idea."

It wasn't hard for Ross to catch Amy's eye. The girl hurried over as soon as he waved. She looked puzzled when he told her what he wanted, but when he smiled she didn't hesitate.

Lacey chuckled. "I bet she'd do anything you asked her to, as long as you smiled at her."

Ross wiggled his eyebrows. "If only all women were so accommodating." Lacey gasped and poked him in the ribs. "Ouch!"

"Hey, cool it," Fanny said. "The coffee is being delivered."

The foursome watched as Amy sat the coffeepot and mugs on the table. The girl shrugged her shoulders when Jack asked her about it. After a moment he turned and looked their way, and Ross lifted his beer in salute. Jack frowned, turned his back to them, and Fanny laughed softly.

"Well done," she said, "well done indeed."

A moment later Ross's cell phone went off, and a scowl darkened his features. Without even looking at it, he excused himself from the table and stepped outside. In less than a minute he was back, but Lacey noticed it was several more minutes before the cloud seemed to lift.

It was nearly 9 p.m. when they left the restaurant. Boomer and Fanny headed down the street toward the sheriff's station, a tipsy Boomer leaning heavily on his wife. Lacey watched them go, a smile on her face.

"So, where you parked?" Ross asked from beside her.

"Close to the mercantile," Lacey replied as she pulled her scarf a little tighter.

"I'll walk you."

Lacey was about to protest, but when she looked up at him she decided it wouldn't be such a bad thing. Smiling, she inclined her head and started walking.

"How long have you been playing hockey?" she asked.

Ross stuffed his hands in his pockets and chuckled. "As long as I can remember. I could skate before I could walk, practically. But, I'm getting a little old for this. It's time for the young bloods to take over, and let us old timers have a rest."

Lacey shot him a reproachful glance. "From what I saw, you can out-skate most of the guys on either team. You and Boomer both."

He looked at her out of the corner of his eye and smiled ruefully. "Maybe, but it costs us a lot more." He grimaced, shrugged his shoulders, and then rubbed his neck. "That shot Jack gave me...I'll feel it until the next game, if not longer. A few years ago, it wouldn't have bothered me."

"Are you hurt? Should you see a doctor?"

"No, I'll be okay. I'm just sore."

"Rub some menthol cream on your shoulders and then apply ice. That'll bring down the swelling and help with the pain."

He chuckled. "Well, the ice I can handle but the cream is another matter. My arms don't bend that direction, Lace."

Before she could stop herself, the words fell out of her mouth. "I'd be happy to..." Her voice died and she looked up at him. He studied her intently and she averted her gaze, feeling like a fool. "Maybe not."

"If you're volunteering, I'd be much obliged," Ross said. "And I promise, no kissing."

She glanced up at him and gulped when she saw his smile, heat flooding her cheeks as she tried to gather her wits. The thought of seeing him half-naked sent strange shivers through her. She closed her eyes briefly, and imagined herself massaging those muscular shoulders. Unable to speak, she nodded and started walking.

Once they reached the Cherokee, she drove to the bar and parked in back. Ross got out, somewhat gingerly, and opened the back door. He waited for her, and Lacey straightened her spine as she walked past him into the bar's dimly lit interior. She was relieved to see the blinds were drawn, and made her way to the kitchen.

"What do you want me to do, Miss Nightingale?" he teased.

Lacey pretended not to hear him. She grabbed a box of gallon zip-top bags and then reached for the ice maker. "Go get the cream and two hand towels."

"Those are big bags. You planning on helping me, or putting me on ice?"

She faced him and put her hands on her hips. "The latter, if you don't behave yourself."

His grin was disarming, and with a mock bow, he went up the stairs with considerably less energy than usual. While he rustled around his apartment, she retrieved a bottle of ibuprofen from beneath the counter, a glass of water, and put them on the bar. Within minutes he reappeared, a jar of pain relief gel in one hand and towels in the other, naked to the waist.

Lacey took the towel from him and tried not to stare. His stomach was hard and flat, and gave new meaning to the term washboard abs. There was very little hair on his chest, and again the image of her hands on his skin entered her mind.

"Sit down," she said, her voice barely above a whisper as she gestured to a chair. He did so, spinning the chair around so he could straddle it and rest his arms on the back. She put the towels on the bar and stood behind him, and her breath caught at the gentle ripple of his muscles. "The cream?"

He held up the jar. "Am I going to make it doc?" he asked, his tone light.

After scooping out a dollop of the blue gel, she smiled and rubbed it between her hands. "I give you a fifty-fifty chance," she replied. "The next twenty-four hours are critical. Oh, before I get started, take four of those." She nodded toward the capsules on the counter and he tossed her a look over his shoulder before popping the pills into his mouth and washing them down. Lacey was impressed. "Good. My, my, you're quite docile when wounded."

He laughed. "Only for you, Lacey. Only for you."

Her heart jumped as she spread the gel across the width of his shoulders. "Now, this may hurt a little, but I promise you'll feel better afterwards. We used to do something like this with the horses..." She stopped and bit her lip, but Ross didn't seem to notice her sudden discomfort.

"So, I'm a horse now." He gave her a grin and wiggled his eyebrows. "I hope I'm a stallion and not a gelding."

Lacey rolled her eyes. "I wouldn't know."

He chuckled wryly. "A man can dream, can't he?"

"There's no law against it."

He only shook his head, grinning all the while. With one last look over the muscled expanse of his back, Lacey took a deep, steadying breath and started massaging his shoulders.

At first she applied only gentle pressure, until she felt him relax. She closed her eyes, ran her hands down his biceps and back up, and then over his back, kneading the taut muscles. His masculinity was almost overwhelming, and she fought to retain her focus. She couldn't remember the last time she'd actually touched a man, or had cause to touch a man in a way that wasn't defensive. Her heart pounded, and she wondered if Ross could hear it.

When she rubbed his shoulders where Jack had hit him he grunted once, but was otherwise silent. She kept the pressure of her fingertips relatively light, applying more of the gel as she worked. After several minutes she returned to massaging the rest of his back.

"That feels *amazing*," he said softly, his chin on his chest. "You've done this before."

"Once or twice," she replied.

"You can do that all night if you want. Would you like a raise? Just name a figure..."

Her lips curved in a smile and she ran her hands down his back one last time, enjoying the feel of him beneath her fingertips. The scent of menthol made her eyes water, and she walked quickly into the kitchen. After washing her hands, she filled two of the Ziploc bags with ice and took them back to the bar. She put one towel over his shoulders and then laid the ice-packs over the swelling area.

Air hissed from between Ross's teeth. "Yikes."

"Sorry," she said. "Guess I should've warned you."

Ross chuckled and used his foot to pull a chair out. "No worries. Have a seat, doc." She smiled and sat down, avoiding his gaze. He was silent for a moment, and she glanced up as he started to speak. "Tell me about yourself. I want to know where you got your medical training."

Lacey looked at her hands. "The school of life," she replied. She quickly thought over the bio Peebo had created for her, wondering what she could say without compromising her cover. "My dad trained thoroughbreds and quarter horses. He used to let me help sometimes."

She chuckled. "I wanted to be a large animal vet, but after he passed things didn't work out." Glancing up, she found herself trapped by that piercing azure gaze. Suddenly, she wanted to tell him everything. She bit her tongue and gave him a tight smile. "That's life."

He nodded. "Yes, it is."

They chatted comfortably, and Lacey sensed he was sticking to more benign topics so as not to make her uncomfortable. She sent him a silent thank you. After 20 minutes or so, she got to her feet and took the ice-packs from his shoulders. "Don't move, I'll be right back." In less than a minute she reappeared with fresh ice. She gave him a pointed look. "Brace yourself." The muscles in his arms tensed as he gripped the back of the chair tightly, but he didn't make a sound when she settled the bags back in place and covered them again. She started to walk back to her chair, surprised when Ross grabbed her hand gently. Lacey froze and looked at him.

He studied her fingers, as if by doing so he could decipher all the unanswered questions in the universe. Turning her hand over, he ran his thumb over her palm, then kissed the same spot. Lacey sucked in a breath, her eyes widening. A wistful smile tipped the corners of his mouth and he released her, his gaze slowly traveling up to meet hers. When their eyes met Lacey's heart began to thud. There was something different in his expression, a *knowing* that sent nervous chills racing up her spine. She felt cornered. Turning abruptly, she grabbed her coat from the bar.

"I – I've got to go," she said in a breathless rush. "Give yourself about ten more minutes with the ice. It's going to be tender and you'll probably have a nice bruise, but you should be okay." Ross remained motionless as she yanked on her coat and headed for the back door. As she pushed it open, she stopped and faced him. "Thanks for inviting me to the game. I really had fun."

Ross watched her go with a mixed sense of frustration and disappointment. He didn't move until he heard the Jeep's engine turn over and the crunch of snow as she drove away. After putting the ice packs and towels aside, he reached into his pocket, pulled out the rumpled piece of paper with his notes from the library, and smoothed it between his hands. *Lindsay Davenport.* He frowned as he read the name again, and a sense of foreboding put his nerves on edge. Carefully, he folded the slip of paper and stuffed it back into his pocket.

"How long until you run again Lacey?" he asked the empty room. "And what will happen to you when you can't run anymore?"

***

The phone jerked Ross from sleep; the harsh ringing echoing off the cavernous walls of his apartment. Rolling over, he groaned when the device clattered to the floor. He reached blindly for the cell phone, finally found it, and put it to his ear.

"This better be good."

"Sorry, Ross, but I didn't think this should wait." It was Brad.

Ross came fully awake and sat up. "What's wrong, Brad?"

His friend hesitated. "Well, I got a package, from that Lechter fellow, the guy you and Lacey took out."

"Yeah, and?"

"It's for Lacey, sent care of you by way of the Lodge." Ross frowned as Brad continued. "And that's not all. I should've told you last time we talked, but you sounded upset, so I didn't."

"Told me what?"

Brad sighed. "Lechter was asking all sorts of questions about Lacey, about you; about where you were from. He wanted to know how to get in touch with you, personally, and when I asked why, he said he was thinking about hiring you to do a week-long tour through the Klondike."

"What did you tell him?"

"Nothing. I said you and Lacey had been married about three years, like you said, but I couldn't tell him anything else. I offered to have *you* call *him*, but he wanted no part of that."

Ross snorted and ran a hand over his eyes. "Big surprise."

"Ross, what's going on?"

Ross sighed. "I don't know, Brad. I honestly don't know."

"What should I do with this package?"

"Hold onto it and I'll ask Lacey what she wants to do."

"Okay."

"And, Brad, thanks for covering. I'm sorry to put you in that position."

Brad chuckled. "No problem. I enjoyed pissing Mr. Lechter off. Take it easy, Ross."

"You, too. Thanks again."

After hanging up the phone, Ross looked around and wondered what to do now. What was Lechter's game? It couldn't be good, given his fascination with Lacey and his connection to Davenport Pharmaceuticals. Ross decided he had to speak with Lacey. She needed to know something was up. He only hoped she would let him help her. For some reason he couldn't fathom, the thought of her leaving didn't sit well, especially since he was just getting to know her. He was surprised to realize he liked her, and despite his theory that the attraction would fade with time, the more he got to know her, the more he liked her. Looking at his reflection, he frowned.

"Way to go Ross. You really know how to pick 'em, don't you?"

Chapter Ten

Lacey sat on the porch swing, teacup in hand, her charcoals and sketch pad next to her. A half-finished sketch of Ross topped of the pile of drawings. She smiled as she looked at it and sipped her tea. It really was a good likeness, especially around the eyes. When she was finished, she'd give it to him as a gift. She only hoped he wouldn't hang it in the bar.

The sound of a vehicle approaching made her look up, and her heart skipped a beat when she saw Ross's truck. She slid the portrait quickly inside the portfolio and stood. Smiling, she moved to the porch steps, her fingers wrapped around the warm mug. When he got out and she saw the look on his face her smile vanished.

He walked slowly toward her and with each step her unease multiplied.

"Ross, what's wrong?"

He stared at her for a minute. "We need to talk."

"Okay. What about?"

He took a deep breath and looked away from her, scanning the trees that surrounded the cabin. His actions made Lacey distinctly uneasy and a chill fanned over her skin.

"Can we go inside?" he asked.

Her eyes widened slightly, but she nodded and opened the cabin door. He walked past her, stood in front of the fireplace, and stretched his fingers toward the blaze. Laccy watched him for a moment before closing the door and putting her tea aside.

"What's this about, Ross?"

"How do you know Dennis Lechter?" he asked at last, his voice low.

She frowned. "I don't, at least, not any better than you do."

Ross faced her. "Brad called me this morning. There's a package at the Lodge for you, from Mr. Lechter."

Her stomach flip-flopped. "I can't imagine why. I've never met the man before." She sat down on the couch and stared into the flames. "He said he thought he knew me from somewhere, but," she paused and looked up, "I *don't* know him."

Ross crouched in front of her and took her hands. Her fingers were ice cold, and he massaged them absently. "What is your tie to Davenport Pharmaceuticals? Why did you freeze up when you heard that name?"

"I – I told you..." She stared at him. "I used to work for them." His gaze cut straight to her soul.

"We both know it's more than that."

A chill of uneasiness danced through her chest. "What's going on, Ross? Why the interrogation?"

He sighed and lifted her hands to his lips briefly. "I can't help you if you won't trust me, Lacey. Or...should I call you Lindsay?"

Her heart stopped. "Wh-what did you say?"

"That's your name, isn't it? Lindsay Davenport?"

For a moment Lacey couldn't move or even breathe. The floor dropped from beneath her feet. Her mouth worked soundlessly and tears welled in her eyes. Without a word, she removed her hands from his, stood and headed for the bedroom, in full survival mode. She ticked off a mental inventory as she went. *Clothes, cash; the rest of it I can leave. If I go now, I'll be halfway to Vancouver before...* Halfway there she stopped and faced him.

"How did...?" Her voice died, words strangling in her throat, and it was nearly a minute before she could speak again. If Ross had figured out who she was, it was possible Lechter had as well. And if Lechter told Lucas, it would *not* be good for her husband to find her with Ross. She gulped. "I want you to leave. Right now." Turning on her heel, she disappeared into the bedroom and strode into the closet.

Ross followed her. "Lacey, wait."

Lacey ignored him and pulled one of the canvas bags from a shelf, her pulse thrumming against her windpipe. She opened the duffel, jerked handfuls of clothes from their hangers, and shoved them into the tote. When she grabbed a stack of blue jeans Ross grabbed her arm.

She wrenched away from him and her chin trembled. "*Don't* touch me!" She backed up against the wall, holding the armful of denim tightly against her chest. She couldn't look at him as the panic expanded through her. Her heart spun wildly in her chest and her stomach clamped into a knot. "I've – I've got to go. Please, I have to leave, right now." Her voice broke and she stifled a sob. "If I leave right now, maybe...maybe I can get away again. Maybe he won't find me..."

Ross cupped her chin and forced her to look at him. "Lacey, let me help you."

Tears fell and she shook her head. "You can't...you can't help me. Nobody can help me."

He held her chin more firmly, freezing her with his gaze. "He doesn't know where you are, or he'd already be here, wouldn't he?" She paused and Ross continued. "Lechter doesn't know where to find you, or he wouldn't have sent the package to the Lodge, right?"

The steel in his voice and the calm, even expression on his face cut through her fear, and Lacey realized he was right. The adrenaline kicked off, her knees buckled, and she slid down the wall to the floor.

Ross took the clothes, tossed them on the bed, and knelt beside her. Her breathing was sharp and shallow as the tears continued to fall. When Ross ran a finger over her cheek, she closed her eyes and swallowed hard.

"How did you...?"

"I did some research on Davenport Pharmaceuticals, and Lucas Davenport. Imagine my surprise when I came across your wedding photo in the society section of the Dallas paper."

"Why?"

He sat down next to her. "I'm not sure. I guess I wanted to know what it was you were running from."

A sharp, humorless laugh escaped her. "And now you know."

Ross shook his head. "No, I don't. I don't really know anything, other than Lechter finds you more than a little interesting, he's working with Davenport Pharmaceuticals, and you're married to Lucas Davenport." He studied her. "The rest, I can guess at."

Lacey swiped at her eyes and covered her face with her hands, despair swirling in her belly and pulling on her lungs like a whirlpool. "You don't want to get in the middle of this, Ross," she said. "Believe me, you really don't."

"I'm already in the middle of this. I'm your husband, remember?"

Her gaze flew to his face. *Oh, if only. It would be so nice to love someone instead of fearing them.* A smile twitched about his mouth and she continued to stare. After a few moments he wiggled his eyebrows, and when he did she started to laugh softly. Then she began to sob.

Ross pulled her close, his arms tightening around her. It felt so good, so safe in his embrace; as if nothing bad could touch her as long as she stayed close to him. Lacey clung to him, her fingers clutching his shirt, her face pressed against his chest.

Ross buried his face in her hair, his hands stroking her back. When her weeping finally subsided, she still held him tightly, and he seemed content to let her. He neither moved nor spoke, and it was several more minutes before she left his embrace. Sniffling, she wiped her eyes.

"I – I'm sorry."

He pressed a hand to her cheek and turned her face to his. "Don't be."

She pulled away from him, stood, and plopped down on the edge of the bed, her stomach still pitching in her belly. "You don't understand. If Lechter's figured out who I am and he's told Lucas, it won't be long before Lucas comes here." She took a deep breath and studied her hands. "Lucas is a spoiled, ruthless child with tens of millions of dollars at his disposal." Tears filled her eyes again as she looked at him. "He wouldn't hesitate to get rid of anything, or anyone, that stood in his way. And with his money and connections, he can get away with it."

Ross scowled. "I'm not afraid of him."

"You should be. *I* am." She laughed and looked at the ceiling, fighting the hopelessness that threatened to consume her. "He would wipe out this entire town if it meant getting me back."

"Don't take this the wrong way, but why? Do you really mean that much to him? If your wedding photo was any indication, it looked as if he didn't care about you at all."

She shrugged, took a deep breath, and rubbed her eyes. "You're right, I mean nothing to him. But his pride and his image mean *everything* to him, and I damaged both by leaving. This isn't about undying love or obsession; this is about getting back something he thinks belongs to him. This is about regaining control over his meek, dutiful wife who had the brazen audacity to disobey him. In all actuality, this has very little to do with *me*."

He sat down next to her. "Maybe we should fly up to the Lodge and see what's in that package."

Lacey dried her eyes and looked at him. His expression was resolute, and her throat tightened at the silent pledge of loyalty she read in his eyes. "What about work?"

He shrugged. "I can either close the bar tonight, or see if Burke can handle things."

She was so tired, and she longed to have someone to lean on; someone who would help her, but she was loathe to get *anyone* she cared about involved. "Why? Why would you do that for me?"

He smiled and chucked her playfully under the chin. "Isn't that what friends are for?" She said nothing, and his expression sobered. "Hey, if your husband is going to come and wipe out Cooper's Ridge, I'm kind of obliged to try and stop him."

Anger sparked in her chest. "*Ex*-husband."

He nodded slowly. "Okay. *Ex*-husband." He watched her silently for a moment, and she looked away from him. "Should I call Brad and let him know we're coming?"

Did she dare accept Ross's help? After she and Lucas had married, her husband had cut her off from anyone and everyone in her life. The few times she had rebelled against the stranglehold he had on her, he had used her friends and family to strong-arm her into behaving. She didn't want *anything* to happen to Ross or Fanny or anyone else in Cooper's Ridge. Her throat tightened with uncertainty.

He seemed to recognize her hesitance. She jumped when he pressed a hand to her cheek and turned her face to his.

"Let me help you, Lace," he said softly, his fingers tracing the line of her cheekbone. "You don't have to do this alone."

She stared into those deep blue eyes and felt the sting of tears. His expression never wavered. Finally, Lacey nodded, got to her feet, and picked up the armload of clothes. She walked into the closet to put her things away. After several moments, she heard Ross leave the room; his footsteps fading as he walked down the hall to the living area.

She put the last hanger on the rod then reached up and pulled the string to turn off the one bare bulb that shone overhead. Her mind spun a million different directions at once. While she was relieved to have Ross's support, she was also terrified to let him help her. A shudder ran the length of her spine as she thought of what Lucas would do if he thought she'd been unfaithful, and, given Ross's harsh good looks, it wouldn't matter if she denied sleeping with him. Lucas would think the worst and act accordingly.

She shuffled out to the living room and collapsed on the couch. Ross's voice drifted to her from the porch. She wanted to scream, cry, rage to the heavens about the unfairness of life, but it would do no good. The only thing she could do, other than run, was find out what Lechter knew and what he wanted.

"Lacey?" She looked up as he sat next to her. "You okay?"

She smiled briefly but shook her head. "No." She pulled her knees to her chest and wrapped her arms around them. "I should've known better than to get comfortable here. It had to end sometime."

He touched her cheek, a frown creasing his brow. "You're wrong." He shook his head slowly. "The running has to stop, Lace. You can't live moving from place to place, never setting down any roots; never making any friends. Nobody can live like that."

Tears filled her eyes and she laughed softly. "Oh, Ross. You have no idea."

"So tell me. Give me an idea. Help me understand."

She swiped at her eyes. "It's a long story."

Ross took her hand and pulled her up with him. "Good. You can tell me on the way to the Lodge." His gaze turned pensive and he pressed his hand to her cheek. "Go pack an overnight bag. Brad said if we're going all the way up there, the least we can do is stay the night, on him."

Lacey closed her eyes and nodded, loving the feel of his skin against hers. His fingertips were slightly rough and they slid into her hair, cupping her head as he pulled her gently toward him. She pressed her face to his chest, her arms around his waist, and it was several minutes before she moved away.

After she packed, he took her bag and went outside, waiting in the truck as she locked up. When she climbed into the cab next to him, her gaze lingered on the cabin, sadness swirling like a cold, dark vortex inside her.

"What is it, Lacey?"

She sighed. "I have the feeling I'm not going to see it again."

Ross narrowed his eyes on the quaint cabin, but he said nothing as he put the truck in gear and drove away.

***

Lucas walked into the security room with his arms crossed over his chest, and looked at Roger in annoyance. The brawny man studied a video monitor intently, fast-forwarding and rewinding, and was apparently unaware of Lucas's presence. Lucas cleared his throat and Roger looked up.

"Oh, you're here," Roger said.

Lucas tapped his foot on the floor. "Yes, I'm here. Now what was so urgent that you interrupted my meeting?"

Roger turned to him with a sly smile. "I was going over the surveillance tape of the meeting with Lechter the other day and found something I thought you'd find very interesting." Roger gestured toward a chair. "Have a seat and I'll start the show." Lucas huffed in irritation but sat and looked at the monitor with disinterest. Roger grinned and pushed the play button.

The tape showed Lechter wandering around the office before Lucas's arrival, obviously upset at being kept waiting. He moved to the window, then turned and picked up the photo on Lucas's desk. He stared at it for a moment then put it back carefully. Then, he walked to the bookcase and picked up another photo of Lindsay. Roger hit the pause button.

After a moment Lucas glared at him. "This is what you brought me down here for?" He snorted and got up. "So, he finds my wife attractive. That's not a *huge* surprise. I'd never marry an ugly woman, Roger."

"Maybe not, but listen to this." He hit the play button again and Lechter spoke.

"I'll be damned." There was a brief pause as Lechter studied the picture. "Well, well. I knew I'd seen you somewhere before, Lacey, and now I know where."

Lucas was paying attention now. He grabbed the remote control and rewound the tape to listen to it again. A menacing smile spread across his face.

"Call Dillon. Tell him our friend, Mr. Lechter, may have some valuable information regarding my wayward wife." Roger nodded and Lucas left the security room, whistling.

***

Lacey stared out the window of the plane, trying to lose herself in the broad, blue expanse of sky. If only it was that easy. She felt his gaze on her and glanced at him.

"So, how did you end up with Lucas Davenport?" Ross asked as he maneuvered the plane with practiced ease.

Lacey rolled her eyes. "What? You didn't research *that?*" He had the decency to color slightly, and she chuckled. "It's simple really. Lucas needed a wife to gain control of the family fortune, so he wined, dined, and romanced me. I was a small town girl; he was rich, handsome, and sophisticated. I fell...hard." She paused and her heart thumped hard against the inside of her chest. Taking a deep breath, she gave herself a mental shake and continued. "After we were married, I guess he assumed I'd be forever indebted to him for bringing me into a life of wealth and privilege. I thought he loved me." She snorted softly. "It wasn't until our first anniversary that I realized what a fool I'd been."

"What happened?"

Her mind spun as the enormousness of that simple question almost short-circuited her brain. "You *can't* really want to hear this." He nodded and she groaned. "Fine. Well, since Lucas was heir to a rather... *large* fortune, his father insisted on a pre-nuptial agreement. Now, I was convinced Lucas and I would live happily ever after, so I signed it without hesitating. After all, I came into the marriage with nothing, and if things didn't work out, I'd leave the same way. No big deal. Once that was done, Harlan Davenport, Lucas's father, signed over control of the company to Lucas. Our first year together was relatively benign, though I began to see a side of him I'd never seen before; a cruel, selfish side." Her voice caught as she recalled the first time Lucas had hit her. She gulped and forced herself to continue.

"For whatever reason Harlan liked me, so, on our first anniversary he threw a huge party for us at his mansion outside of Dallas. Unfortunately, he wasn't in the best of health. He had heart problems and was in a wheelchair, but that didn't stop him from enjoying the festivities. After dinner Lucas stood up as if to toast his father, but instead of a toast, Lucas pulled out the pre-nuptial agreement. He sneered, ripped it into little pieces, threw it in Harlan's face and announced that his father couldn't control him any longer. Lucas then took out a copy of what he said was his new will, naming me as sole beneficiary for the estate. I thought it was a joke, then I looked at Harlan. I've never seen anyone so furious in all my life. He was absolutely livid. I was worried he'd have a stroke right then and there." Lacey ran a hand over her eyes. "Two days later Harlan had a massive heart attack and died."

Ross's eyes widened. "Whoa."

"Yeah," she said, "and Lucas...*celebrated.*" Her throat tightened as the memory of the funeral vaulted into her mind's eye. Tears stung. Her father-in-law had his faults, but he'd been kind to her and she had been very fond of him. She blinked rapidly and ran a hand over her brow. "That should give you a clue as to what kind of man Lucas is."

Ross snorted. "I think the word *man* is too good a description for him." He studied her profile. "How did you get away from him?"

"I planned and I plotted for almost six years. Lucas's one mistake was to think I didn't have the brains to pull it off; but that was mistake enough. I saved every penny I could; hoarded it away and waited until I saw the opening then ran without looking back. I spent four months just...driving around, tracking through almost every state in the Union and most of Canada before I came here. I thought this was the last place Lucas would ever think to look for me."

Ross shook his head. "And then fate sends Dennis Lechter across your path."

She had always known life wasn't fair, but with this twist of fate it was hard to keep the bitterness at bay. Choking it down, Lacey sighed heavily. "Yes. I don't remember meeting him before, but I suppose it *is* possible. Lucas prides himself on throwing the biggest, the best, and the most frequent parties."

"And I suppose you were obliged to play hostess."

She chuckled. "Of course. That's where I learned how to fend off drunken men and still maintain a smile, be polite to people I really didn't care for and serve them as if they were my own family." Ross looked at her in surprise and she smiled. "I remember the way you grilled me that first day."

His expression turned sheepish. "I'm sorry about that."

"Don't be. You forced me to stand up for myself." Lacey turned her eyes out the window. "When you've been under someone's thumb for years you forget how to do that."

"You recovered your memory quickly," he commented with a chuckle. "You may not be big, but you're definitely feisty."

Her cheeks warmed, and she smiled. Ross said nothing more, and Lacey was happy for the comfortable silence.

Her watch read half past three when they flew over the last ridge. Again her breath was taken away by the sheer presence of the building, and the snow of the last few days only added to the Lodge's appeal. Ross made a pass over the resort, then banked and began his approach.

Lacey saw Brad jogging down the long staircase, and he waved to them as Ross landed and then taxied toward the dock. Brad tied the plane and opened Lacey's door.

"Hi, Lacey," he said amiably. He took her hand and helped her onto the dock. "Good to see you again."

Lacey smiled and turned to catch her bag as Ross tossed it to her. "You, too. Ross says you have a package for me?"

Brad nodded. "It's up at the desk." He took Ross's bag and waited for him to join them.

"Let's take a look," Ross said. He put a hand in the small of Lacey's back and followed her as she trailed behind Brad.

"That Lechter guy sure took a liking to you, Lace." Then he smiled. "But then again, what's not to like?"

Lacey rolled her eyes. "Not you too." She shook her head. "You guys really should move back to the contiguous United States where there are more *women*."

Brad's brows rose and he spread his arms wide as he breathed deeply of the crisp air. "What? And miss all this? Not on your life."

Once inside, Ross and Lacey walked to the desk as Brad went through a side door to the back office. Lacey put her bag on the floor and shrugged out of her coat, and a minute later Brad appeared. He had a brown paper wrapped package in his hands, about the size of a large cereal box. Lacey blinked slowly, then took the parcel from him and ran a hand over the front.

She couldn't find the courage to open it and her hands were shaking. She glanced at Ross, then Brad, then put the package back on the counter. I can't."

Brad smiled and reached into a drawer. He pulled out a key and tossed it to Ross. "Here. I gave you guys one of the two bedroom suites, so you should be more than comfortable." He tossed Ross a meaningful look that was lost on Lacey. "Why don't you go on up and get settled in, relax for a while. Dinner is at seven."

Ross reached out and shook Brad's hand. "Thanks, Brad."

"Don't mention it. At least now I have someone to dine with. I hate eating alone."

Ross cupped her elbow and Lacey looked up as she took the package and held it to her chest. She was silent as they made their way up the broad staircase, his arm around her shoulders. Lacey leaned into him and closed her eyes with a soft sigh.

When they reached the suite, Ross opened the door. Lacey stepped inside and gasped at the opulence. She'd hardly expected such grandeur at a lodge in Alaska, but the room rivaled the finest suite at any hotel she'd ever stayed at. Thick, cream-colored carpet covered the floor; the walls were painted in a pale gold with gold-leaf accents. The furniture was big and richly appointed, the couch and wing-backed chairs plushly cushioned; the rich, wine-colored fabrics accented with throw pillows of cream and gold. Directly across from the entrance were two sets of ornately carved double doors that no doubt opened to the bedrooms. Ross looked at her and smiled.

"Which one do you want?" he asked.

Lacey shrugged. "As if it matters."

"Turn in a circle three times and point," Ross suggested, a twinkle in his eye.

"That only works if you have a *map*," she said with a grin.

"There are only two ways to go here. You don't need a map."

She put the parcel on the desk. "Fine. I'll take the one on the right."

Ross frowned. "But I wanted that one." She gaped at him, and he laughed. "Go on. I'm kidding."

She rolled her eyes and walked across the plush carpeting, and her eyes widened when she opened the door. The bedroom was even more lavish than the living room. A huge four-poster bed dominated the space, and, for a moment Lacey felt as if she'd been transported back in time. Thick velvet curtains of a deep claret color hung at every post, tied back with gold rope, and a matching down comforter covered the king-sized mattress. She blinked, deposited her bag on a chair, then threw herself onto the center of the bed.

She sank down into the feather mattress and closed her eyes. A sigh of pleasure escaped her as the bed enfolded her like a lover's arms. Ross's image flashed in her mind and her eyes snapped open, her heart thudding as she shook her head. This was going to have to stop.

"You look comfy," Ross said from the doorway. "Luxury suits you." She watched him as he walked over and sat down on the edge of the mattress, his fingers moving over the rich velvet-covered spread. "I always knew you were more fitted to satin and lace than flannel."

"And how did you know that?"

"You're too elegant for a place like Cooper's Ridge. Kind of like a..." He searched for the words. "Like...a figure skater in the middle of a hockey game."

"I'm a small town girl, Ross," she said. "I never had satin or lace before Lucas."

Ross narrowed his eyes on her. "Some women are born regal. Not all classy dames come from the city."

His expression shifted slightly and the thought of making love to him on this huge bed popped into her mind. Heat crept up her neck and she looked away, her pulse quickening. He pressed his hand to her cheek and she jumped, turning startled eyes to him.

"Not all ladies are born into nobility," he whispered. He stared at her a moment longer and she saw reflected in his eyes the very emotions that swirled inside of her. When he spoke again, his voice was low and husky, sending a shiver up her spine. "I'm having a problem, Lace."

She gulped, but was unable to look away. "What's that?"

"My theory isn't holding up under research." He inched a little closer. "The newness isn't wearing off. The attraction isn't fading."

Her mouth formed a silent "O" and her lashes fluttered down to conceal her eyes. "Maybe you haven't given it enough time," she said, her voice barely above a whisper. "Research takes time, lots of...time."

"Does it?" His voice sounded so close. Her heart jumped as she looked up and saw him on all fours over her. How had he done that without her realizing? Fear raced through her and he seemed to sense it. A tender smile curved his mouth. "I'm not Lucas, Lacey. I'll never hurt you, not ever."

She licked her lips and her gaze fastened briefly on his mouth. The flame inside her grew hotter. Again the image of the two of them, naked in the middle of this gigantic feather bed filled her mind, and she closed her eyes.

His lips feathered over her cheek and she gasped softly. As gentle as a summer breeze on her skin, he kissed her jaw, eyebrows, temples, even the tip of her nose, his fingers following behind. He grazed his thumb over her lower lip, and with each gossamer touch she lost a little more of her tightly held control as desire pulsed through her like a drug. Her breath came in short, shallow gasps and there were other parts of her that longed for his caress, but his hands never strayed below her neck. It was as if he were a blind man, memorizing her face with the tips of his fingers. Lacey had never imagined something so simple could be so intimate and arousing. She'd never felt like this, ever.

"May I kiss you?" Ross asked in a ragged whisper.

Lacey couldn't speak, her vocal chords paralyzed, but she could nod. Just before his lips found hers, she regained her voice. "Yes..."

His kiss was like sunlight on her lips, and warmth fanned to every part of her body. There wasn't an inch of her that wasn't abuzz with sensation as his mouth moved with delicate slowness over hers. Her fingers worked into his hair, relishing the soft thickness and crisp curls. He leaned down on his elbows and his body covered the length of hers, their lips never separating. She welcomed the weight, her breasts aching as they were crushed against his chest, her hips moving forward to meet his.

Part of her was terrified, but another part yearned for this contact. It had been so long since she'd experienced anything remotely resembling this; and it felt like she'd been lonely forever. While his movements were lazy and unhurried, Lacey felt the tension in him, in her, and she wanted to give in to it. She wanted to let go of her fears with him.

The thought of losing control sent a bolt of pure terror through her and, again, he seemed to know it. Before she could pull away, his arms enfolded her and he rolled onto his back, taking her with him. She straddled his waist and reared up, hands planted on his chest.

He smiled. "Now *you're* in control, Lacey. *You* have the power. Don't be afraid to use it."

Ross threaded fingers into her hair and slowly drew her to him. He saw the pulse racing in her throat, and his own did a nice job of keeping pace. He'd never tread so carefully with a woman before, but it had never been Lacey in his arms before. Even her name was delicate, and he wanted with everything inside of him to protect her, to keep her safe, to kiss her until they were both lightheaded and breathless. He saw the alarm in her caramel-brown eyes as he continued to pull her down, and released her. More than anything else, he wanted her to come to him on her own, with no fear, no pressure.

Lacey froze when his hand fell to his side, scant inches separating them. She looked at his mouth and touched it gently with her index finger, and a gasp escaped her when he nipped playfully at the digit. He lifted his head, looked into her eyes, and then kissed her again. He ran his hands up her thighs, around her waist and up her back. He would have preferred skin beneath his fingertips, but for now, the softness of her sweater would have to be enough. He deepened the kiss, but held himself in check. If she wanted to pull away, now would be the time, but she didn't.

His tongue slid into her mouth and Lacey moaned softly. She met his tongue with her own and he tensed, his fingers thrusting into her hair as his lips slanted over hers with increasing ardor. He was hard and she moved her hips to better fit against him. Ross growled low in his throat as fire shot along every nerve, and Lacey pulled away, her breathing ragged.

Ross looked at her, blonde spirals of hair wild about her shoulders, eyes glazed with passion, her lips swollen from his kisses. His breath caught when she pulled off her sweater, her breasts thrust forward as she reached to unhook her bra. She tipped her head to the side and watched him carefully as she slid the straps off her shoulders, her tentative movements more arousing to him than the most erotic striptease. She was self-conscious, he knew, but he couldn't hide his reaction when the bra fell away.

"Wow."

He saw the uncertainty in her eyes and the pulse fluttering in her throat. Her eyelids fluttered and she tried to cover herself with her hands, but he grasped her wrists gently and stopped her.

"My God, you are beautiful," he breathed. He released her wrists and cupped her breasts, thumbs stroking lightly over the taut nipples. She bit her lip, closed her eyes and her head dropped back. Ross slid a hand up and over her chest, his fingers curling around her neck. When she looked at him he pulled her down, his mouth claiming hers with ruthless intent.

Suddenly, the phone shrilled. Lacey jumped and jerked away from him, and it was as if they'd been pulled out of a dream and thrust rudely back into reality. Ross closed his eyes, sighed, and handed the sweater to her as he got to his feet.

He grabbed the handset. "Yeah, what?"

"Ross, I've got Dennis Lechter on the phone."

Ross looked at her, but she avoided his gaze as she fumbled with her bra and then slipped the sweater over her head. "What does he want?"

"I don't know. As soon as he identified himself, I put him on hold and called you."

Ross paused. "Okay. We'll be right down." He hung up the phone and turned to her, hands on hips. She studied her toes and he saw the flush in her cheeks, surprised that even her contrite expression could make him want her.

"That was Brad. Lechter's on the phone."

Her head snapped up, eyes wide. "Wh-what does he want?"

He walked over to her, extended his hand and smiled. "That's what we're going to find out." She slipped her fingers into his and he jerked her up and against his chest. Her eyes widened in alarm, and she blinked when he pressed a hand to her cheek. "Don't worry, Lacey. I'm here, and I won't let anyone hurt you." She opened her mouth to speak, but nothing came out. He kissed her quickly. "Come on. Let's go see what this asshole wants."

Chapter Eleven

Brad looked decidedly nervous and was pacing behind the counter when Lacey and Ross walked up to the front desk. When he saw them he sighed in relief.

"Good, you're here." He was silent for a moment and then he frowned. "What should I say to him?"

She had been thinking about that since she and Ross had left their room. "Ask him how you can help him," Lacey said, her voice low, "and put him on speaker." She tried to appear cool and calm, but a flush crept into her cheeks when she saw Ross's expression. Lacey glanced at Brad and leaned her elbows on the counter. "Go on, before he gets suspicious."

Ross's face was set in stone. Brad nodded, glanced at Ross, and pushed the button to activate the speaker-phone.

"Sorry to keep you waiting, Mr. Lechter, problem with a guest. How can I help you?"

"Um, yes. Brad, what was the name of that tour guide you set me up with?"

Brad and Ross exchanged a glance. "Devlin, Ross Devlin."

"Yes, yes, that's it. Well, I sent a package to you for his wife...Lacey, I believe her name was. I didn't know where else to mail it, and I was wondering if you'd received it yet. I want to make sure she gets it."

She leaned forward and motioned for Brad to keep him talking.

"A package?" Brad asked.

Lechter laughed, but it sounded forced. "Yes. It's a thank you gift. Nothing fancy, just a small token of my, I mean, *our* appreciation."

Brad frowned. "I don't remember seeing anything for Lacey, but if you'll hold again I'll check in the back."

"Of course, I'll wait."

Brad pushed the hold button and Lacey let out the breath she'd been holding. Ross leaned against the counter, relaxed, but he watched her carefully, as did Brad. She chewed absently on her bottom lip as her brain kicked into overdrive.

"Well, Lacey?" Brad asked. "What now?"

Nervous flutters pinged off the inside of her stomach. "I can't get you involved in this, Brad."

Brad looked at Ross, and then back at her. "Yes, you can." She shook her head and Brad reached across the counter to cover her hand with his. "Lacey, if this guy is bothering you I'm more than happy to help." He waited, and when Lacey finally pressed her lips into a thin line and nodded he grinned. "So, what now?"

Lacey shrugged. "I don't know."

"Did anyone have to sign for the package?" Ross asked.

Brad frowned as he thought about it and then shook his head. "No. They might have signed for it at the mailbox place, but it was sent regular mail and delivered today with the rest of the stuff."

Ross rubbed his chin, his expression thoughtful. "Tell him you don't have it."

Brad followed Ross's line of thinking and nodded. "Right-o." He pressed the button. "Mr. Lechter. It must not have gotten here yet. There's no package for Lacey, or anyone else for that matter."

"Hmm. I mailed it several days ago, but I suppose the mail could be a little slow. It is going to *Alaska* after all." He was talking to himself more than Brad, and there was a pause. "Well, could you give me a call when it gets there? I'd really appreciate it."

Brad looked at Lacey and she nodded.

"Sure, Mr. Lechter," he said. "I have your number. Is there anything else?"

"No. Thanks, Brad."

"Anytime, Mr. Lechter. Good-bye."

After he hung up, Brad gazed at her and Lacey didn't know what to say. Her insides were tight with anxiety, fear, and gratitude. Thank you seemed so inadequate. She swallowed the frog in her throat and found her voice.

"Thanks, Brad. I know I owe you an explanation, but..."

He interrupted her with a wave of his hand. "Don't worry, Lacey. You don't have to explain anything to me."

Lacey closed her eyes and took a deep, slow breath.

"Maybe a couple years from now," Brad continued, "after you and Ross are married for real, we'll all go camping and you can tell the story around the campfire. Until then, it'll keep."

Lacey glanced at Ross who watched her with hooded eyes, a small smile on his mouth. She then turned to Brad, her eyes stinging. "Thank you," she whispered. The stinging intensified and she blinked rapidly. "I think I'm going to get some air. If you two will excuse me?"

"Want some company?" Ross asked.

Lacey thought about it for a moment, but shook her head. Unable to meet his gaze, she walked past him and out into the dusk.

Ross looked after her for a bit then turned to Brad. "Thanks, bud."

"Don't mention it," Brad replied. "Hey, is this guy stalking her or something?"

Ross gazed in the direction Lacey had gone. "Something like that, though it's a whole lot more complicated." He chuckled. "It's probably best you don't know anything."

Brad rested his elbows on the counter. "She's not in some kind of legal trouble, is she?"

Ross smiled. "I thought you took down your shingle."

Brad glanced toward the front doors and shrugged. "I'm still a member of the Bar."

Ross smiled at his friend, then clapped him on the shoulder. "I'll let you know."

"Good. Now why don't you go after her? She looks like she could use a shoulder and you've got plenty to spare."

"Thanks again, Brad."

Brad waved him off. "Forget about it. Now get out of here. I do have other guests to take care of."

Ross laughed and went in search of Lacey. After leaving the lodge he scanned the deck for her, and spotted her at the far end of the dock, leaning against a large piling. The log was bigger than she was, and her blonde hair contrasted starkly with the dark, treated wood. He stuffed his hands in his pockets and glanced at the crystal clear sky, then started down the long staircase.

Lacey stared out over the tranquil waters of the lake, imagining the chaos that had created this beautiful scene. At one time this land had been molten and heaving, earthquakes and explosions arranging and rearranging the land until it left this in its wake. She wondered if she'd look any different when the turmoil in her life finally came to an end, if it ever did.

The sky was a pale purple, deepening with the encroaching night, and it seemed as if there were already a million stars overhead. Her breath froze on the air and she wrapped her arms around herself, wishing she'd had the foresight to wear her jacket. The air was frigid and growing even colder, and the wind cut right through her sweater.

"You must be freezing," Ross said from behind her.

Had she not already sensed him near she would have been startled, but as it was she merely turned and looked at him. Heat surged into her cheeks as she remembered what had transpired between them only minutes ago, and try as she might she couldn't hold his gaze. He was too handsome, too rugged, and being near him sent her pulse racing.

"I'm all right," she replied.

He chuckled, stood behind her, and pulled her against his chest. After wrapping his jacket around her he zipped it, effectively clothing both of them inside the oversized garment. Lacey didn't protest and closed her eyes as the heat of his body warmed her.

"Liar," he said. "You're shivering." She leaned her head back against his shoulder and he pressed his cheek to her ear. "I know you said you didn't want any company, but you didn't set a time limit." Lacey smiled and tears slid down her cheeks. Ross frowned. "What's wrong, Lacey? Talk to me."

She stared up at the ever-darkening sky and shook her head. "I...I don't know how to deal with all this," she said at last, her voice barely above a whisper.

Ross's reply was immediate and hushed. "Running isn't the answer."

"No, I don't mean that."

He pressed his lips to her temple. "Is it about what's happening between us?"

She didn't answer for a moment. His breath was warm on her skin and she felt his strength, his heart beating in steady rhythm against her back. She enjoyed his closeness for a minute longer, then gathered her courage and spoke. "Jack told me about your...girlfriends."

Ross didn't even flinch. "Did he now? What exactly did he say?"

Swallowing hard, Lacey dropped her chin, resting the bridge of her nose against the zipper of his jacket. When she spoke, her voice was muffled by the thick down. "Nothing much. He said there were two women you...saw, on a regular basis."

Ross laughed and shook his head. "Knowing Jack Calhoun, I doubt he put it so politely." He paused, and a sigh escaped him. "But he's right. There were a couple of women I used to spend time with, until they moved, but they're friends, nothing more."

"I'm sorry. It's none of my business."

They were silent for a moment, but when Ross spoke his voice was low and firm. "Lacey, I'm not looking to make you another...*girlfriend*, if that's what you're thinking."

Lacey groaned inwardly. She was so very bad at this, communicating with men, and it frustrated her to no end. With a curt laugh she unzipped the jacket and stepped away from him. The temperature change was dramatic, and a shiver ran through her.

"That's not what I'm thinking. Hell, I don't know *what* I'm thinking." Sniffing, she wiped her cheeks and faced him. "My whole life, what little there is, is up in the air. My feelings are so jumbled I'd have better luck figuring out a Rubik's cube right now."

Ross's expression was resolute. "Talk to me, Lacey. Maybe I can help."

Lacey stared at him for the longest time, searching for the words and coming up dry. Unable to maintain his gaze she looked down at her shoes. "It's cold. I'm going back to the room."

"Lacey, wait."

She paid him no heed, and quickened her steps until she was running.

Ross watched her go, his feelings a mixture of sadness and frustration. He couldn't begin to imagine what she was going through, and while his head understood her reluctance to trust him, her retreat stung. He stared at the Lodge until the last vestige of sunlight vanished, then walked slowly back.

Brad was nowhere to be seen when he entered the grand lobby, but he wasn't looking for Brad. Ross mounted the stairs, taking them two at a time, but his pace slowed as he got closer to the room he shared with Lacey. After stepping into the suite, he closed the door softly and looked for her, but the area was empty.

His eyes fastened on a ball of wadded up wrapping paper on the desk, and he moved to look at the framed photograph next to it. His jaw clenched as he picked up the picture, which had a 3x5 yellow sticky note attached to the glass. Lucas Davenport looked at him from that black and white copy, his bride at his side, and Ross felt his anger boil when he read the message.

Lacey, I know who you are. Call me or I'll have to tell your husband where he can find you, and I don't think either of us really wants that. I'll be expecting to hear from you soon. Dennis.

With a growl Ross tossed the photo back on the desk, his eyes sweeping the room as he removed his jacket. He stopped when he saw the open bottle of scotch on the bar, half empty, and it was then he heard splashing. The bathroom door was slightly ajar, and he walked slowly toward it. After pushing it open he leaned against the jamb.

A large ball and claw tub sat near the window, and right now it nearly overflowed with bubbles. Lacey, her hair knotted atop her head, was neck deep in the foam, her eyes closed and a large glass of scotch in one hand. Steam filled the room, her skin glistening with moisture, damp curls clinging to her cheeks and neck. A bolt of lust went through him at the same time she opened her eyes and looked at him. Without even blinking, she put the glass to her lips and took a long, slow drink. Ross was mesmerized.

"I suppose you saw it," she said.

Ross nodded. She sat up, the bubbles barely covering her breasts, and his breath caught. He remembered all too clearly the feel of her in his hands, the satin smoothness of her skin, the warm roundness and weight against his palms.

Lacey pulled her knees to her chest and wrapped an arm around them. "What do you think I should do?"

"What do you *want* to do?" The tone of his voice made her look up. Their eyes locked, and Ross smiled when he saw the color rise in her cheeks. Obviously, they were thinking along the same lines. The moment soon passed as Lacey turned her face away and sank in the water.

"Well, as you said, running isn't the answer, and I guess murdering Lechter isn't an option either."

He grinned at that, and saw the frown that creased her brow. He wished he could smooth that frown away, he wished he could make her safe and happy, he wished a lot of things.

"Oh, Ross," Lacey said, "I'm sorry for dragging you into this, Brad too."

"I'm not," was his automatic reply. "And neither is Brad." She wouldn't look at him, her eyes focused on the bubbles as he continued. "You didn't drag me anywhere, Lacey. I went looking, remember?"

"That'll teach you," she said.

Indeed, Ross thought. *Indeed*.

She took another drink, and her next question nearly floored him. "Care to join me?"

He gaped at her as she looked absently at the nearly empty glass. Before he could stop them, the words tumbled from his mouth. "In a drink...or in the tub?" Her head swiveled around and he wanted to slap himself. She stared at him, her cheeks bright with color.

The ideas going through her head mortified her *and* turned her on. She'd known this man for hardly more than two weeks, and here she was, fantasizing about making love with him in the tub, on the plush, burgundy bedspread; in all sorts of places and in all sorts of ways. A shiver of desire ran the length of her body and settled between her thighs as a pulsing ache that threatened to drive her mad. She closed her eyes, shot the last of the scotch, and leaned against the back of the tub as she put the glass aside.

Ross sighed heavily. "Lacey...I'm sorry." He paused, then said again, "I'm sorry."

When she looked up he was gone, and for one insane moment she almost called out for him to come back. She wanted him, more than he knew. With a sigh of resignation, she got out of the tub, dried off, and wrapped herself in a thick velour robe, courtesy of the Gateway Lodge. After tying the sash, she picked up the now empty glass and walked into the living room.

He sat on the couch, a tumbler in his hand and the scotch bottle on the coffee table in front of him. When she walked out he looked up, and a flicker of regret shone briefly in his eyes before he turned his gaze back to his drink.

She chuckled. "We're quite a pair, aren't we?" she asked as she sat next to him and held out her glass.

He looked at her out of the corner of his eye, poured her a drink, and poured himself another. "That we are." He downed the scotch and put the glass on the table. "I am sorry, Lacey. Here you are, fighting for your life, and I'm making passes. It's not well done of me."

She smiled. "It's okay, Ross. It's not as if I discouraged you."

He shook his head and splashed another dose of scotch into his tumbler. "You're frightened, vulnerable, and I took advantage of that."

Lacey took a sip of the amber liquid. "No you didn't. I...I wanted you." He turned to look at her. She averted her eyes as her cheeks went hot. Keenly aware of his scrutiny, she stood and walked around the back of the couch as she moved toward her bedroom door, butterflies dive-bombing her belly. She paused, one hand on the knob. "I...still...want you." She went into her room, closed the door, and leaned against it.

Ross stared at the door, his jaw hanging slack. Her admission shocked him, and he was amazed she'd be willing to make herself even more vulnerable than she already was. Blinking slowly several times, he turned back around and emptied his glass.

"You may be scared, Lacey," he said under his breath, "but you're definitely not a coward." He stood, put the glass in the sink on the bar, and put the bottle away. After another long look at her door he went to his room to change.

Half an hour later Lacey sat on the edge of her bed, staring into space, her mind spinning. A knock brought her back to earth. She glanced at her reflection then turned toward the door. "Come in."

Ross opened the door and stuck his head inside, hand over his eyes, peeking between his fingers. He smiled when he saw her fully dressed. "We're supposed to have dinner with Brad. Unless, of course, you'd rather not."

Lacey smiled and shook her head. "No, let's go. I owe him at least that much."

A frown creased Ross's brow and he stepped into the room. "Lacey, you don't owe him, or me, anything."

She stared at him for a moment then got to her feet and walked over to him. Standing on tiptoe, she kissed his cheek. "Yes, I do. Now, let's agree not to talk about this for the rest of the evening, and enjoy ourselves, all right?" She looked up and saw something in his eyes, and for a moment she thought he was going to kiss her. Surprisingly enough, she wanted him to kiss her, and when he didn't she could barely conceal her disappointment.

"Okay, boss," he agreed. "Let's go."

The dining area was located off the main lobby, with six four-person tables and four larger tables that could have seated twelve or more. Fine linen covered the polished wood and antique oil lamps flickered in rustic centerpieces made of pine branches and polished stones from the lake bed. A huge, antique chandelier hung in the center of the room, the candles of old replaced with tiny white bulbs that glinted off the polished brass and copper. Another enormous hearth dominated the far wall, a fire crackling merrily. It was gorgeous.

Two of the four-person tables were occupied. She thought she recognized one of the couples as a recent Hollywood joining, but she didn't want to stare. The couples glanced briefly at them and then returned to their conversations. She'd almost expected to see Dennis Lechter, and the mere thought turned her stomach. Pushing the image aside, before she lost her appetite, she glanced at Ross who seemed completely at ease in the grand room.

"There you are," Brad said from behind them. "Sorry I'm late. I was on the phone with a client in Anchorage." He moved to Lacey's side and offered her his arm, giving Ross a wink before he turned his best smile on her. "Mademoiselle, may I escort you to your table?"

Lacey laughed at his attempt at a French accent, and replied in kind. "But of course, monsieur. Lead ze way."

Brad led them to a table near the hearth, and as they were seated a uniformed waiter appeared with menus. Ross held out her chair for her, receiving a grateful smile and a murmured thank you for his effort. He grinned and sat beside her as Brad sat across from them.

"I don't know about you guys," Brad started, glancing over the menu, "but I'm starved."

After they ordered they sipped wine and chatted, and Lacey enjoyed the easy conversation and comedic banter between Ross and Brad. The two were obviously good friends, and Lacey wondered briefly if Lucas had any close friends, other than Roger. And *he* didn't really count, since Lucas *paid* him to hang around. She shook her head, and turned her thoughts from her ex-husband to the debate Brad and Ross were having about the logging trade.

Before she knew it dinner was over, the dishes had been cleared, and they had started their second bottle of wine. Leaning back in her chair, Lacey sipped the merlot, surprised to find she was totally and completely relaxed. When Ross had shown up that morning knowing her real name, she'd thought her entire world was coming to a swift close. And now here she was, sitting with two very handsome men, eating fine food, drinking fine wine, and quite unable to recreate the fear that had nearly consumed her earlier. It was most odd.

The warmth of the fire seeped into her bones and before she could stop herself she yawned. Both men looked at her in surprise.

"Oh, don't mind me," she said. "I'm relaxed, and a bit tipsy I think."

Ross and Brad exchanged a glance and Ross took her glass. "I think we'd better get you to bed, Lacey. I don't want you hungover tomorrow. Hangovers and Piper Cubs don't mix."

"What? Don't you have those little air sickness bags?" Brad teased.

She threw him a withering look. "For your information, I have never been drunk, or *hungover* in my life."

Ross laughed softly. "You have to be drunk before you can be hungover, Lace. Now come on, it's getting late anyway."

She frowned. "Hey, I thought you said I was the boss."

He got up and hauled her to her feet, his arm going around her shoulders when she swayed unsteadily. "Given your present state of intoxication, I'm relieving you of your post," he said with a grin. "You can either walk, or be carried, back to the room."

Her jaw dropped and she gaped at him. Both men fell into gales of laughter. She narrowed her eyes on Ross but she didn't leave his side, her legs quite rubbery and out of sorts. She looked at Brad and smiled, then leaned forward to kiss his cheek. "Thanks for dinner, Brad. The food, and the company, was magnificent."

She giggled when he blushed and looked away in embarrassment. Ross seemed as surprised by Brad's reaction as Brad seemed to be, and Ross couldn't help but laugh. Brad glared at him then turned his most charming smile on her.

"Anytime, Lacey. I've got some things to do, so if you'll excuse me?"

She nodded, and Brad grinned as he exited the room.

Ross watched him for a moment then chuckled. "I've known him since high school, and I don't think I've ever seen him blush before." He looked at Lacey with what looked like respect. "Well done, Lacey. Very well done."

They strolled back to their suite, and Lacey leaned heavily on him. She glanced up and saw his smile as he toyed with a lock of her hair. After letting them into the suite he closed the door with one foot then escorted her to her room. At the edge of the bed, he released her and she collapsed face first onto the mattress. The memory of what had happened last time she'd been on this bed vaulted into her mind's eye and a shiver of delicious heat settled low in her belly. *I wonder if he remembers?* She decided to find out, flipped onto her back, and stretched like a cat. Ross watched her, his expression guarded.

"Would you like to tuck me in?" she asked with a come-hither smile.

Ross scowled and smiled at the same time. "Are you flirting with me, or is that the liquor talking?"

Lacey knew herself well enough to know it was a little of both. Without liquid courage she would *never* have been so forward with him, even if she wanted to. Pouting, she got to her knees and draped her arms over his shoulders, the wine bolstering her. "Don't you find me attractive?"

The smile vanished leaving the scowl behind. He gently disentangled himself and gave her a light push, sending her sprawling on the bed. "I think you know the answer to that."

She lifted her arms over her head and stretched again, giving him a slanted look. She saw the convulsive swallow as his eyes focused on her breasts straining against the soft material of her sweater. The female in her clearly recognized the desire in him and the heat in her core expanded outward. His frown deepened and he lifted his gaze back to her face.

His scowl didn't deter her. "Show me," she said in blatant invitation.

Lacey hadn't really expected him to take her up on her proposal, but he did, and with lightning speed. In the blink of an eye he covered her body with his, his mouth descending on hers with brutal swiftness. She was already tipsy, and as he deepened the kiss her head spun, sending that urgent warmth spreading through her. His lips were a contradiction, at once soft and hard, and she knew she could easily get addicted to the feel and taste of him. When their tongues met desire burst inside her, and she wondered briefly how she'd survived without this. She felt like she was floating. The sensations he roused in her were heady, intoxicating, and she wanted more.

To her dismay, he jerked away and got to his feet, standing over her with hands on hips as his eyes bored into hers. Lacey wanted to reach for him, to pull him back, but her arms refused to cooperate.

"Satisfied?" he asked, his voice barely above a whisper. Without waiting for an answer, he left the room and closed the door behind him with a little more force than was necessary.

Lacey stared after him, her lips swollen and tingling. She sighed, looked at the ceiling, and willed the room to stop its interminable spinning. With another glance toward the door she ran a hand over her eyes. She thought about following him for a moment, but decided against it. "Satisfied?" She shook her head. "Not even close."

***

It was half past eight when Lacey woke up, and as soon as her eyelids opened embarrassment burned into her cheeks. When she thought of facing Ross the flush intensified until she thought her hair would burst into flame. Now she wished she'd drunk more, because, unfortunately, she clearly remembered everything she'd said and done last night. She wanted to disappear into the mattress, but there was little point in putting off the inevitable. A frustrated sigh escaped her and she forced herself out of bed.

After taking a quick shower and dressing she took a deep breath and left her room. She had expected Ross to be waiting on the couch for her, but the living area was empty. The door to his bedroom was wide open, but he wasn't there either. The apology she'd been poised to give died in her throat, and she frowned. She left the suite and made her way to the lobby.

Pausing on the second floor landing, she saw Ross and Brad seated near the hearth, drinking coffee and talking amiably. As if sensing her presence, Ross turned and looked at her, and a smile curved his mouth.

"Good morning," he called. "Care to join us?"

Lacey descended the stairs and poured herself a cup of coffee before approaching them. When they moved to get up she waved a hand at them, and plopped down in a large, overstuffed chair at Ross's elbow. Their eyes met and heat surged into her cheeks. She dropped her gaze and sipped the hot coffee carefully. Ross seemed unaffected, and for some reason that irritated her.

"Sleep well?" he asked.

"Very," she replied. She glanced at him then looked at Brad, who watched her with a knowing smile. She dropped her gaze. "And you?"

Ross grinned. "I slept quite well, thank you."

"So what's on the agenda today?" Brad asked.

She glanced at Ross, brows raised in silent question.

"We're going back to Cooper's Ridge," Ross replied.

Brad looked surprised. "What about Mr. Lechter?"

Ross took a sip of his coffee, his expression level. "What about him?"

"Do you think he'll give up that easily?"

"No," she said. She studied her coffee, and looked up when she felt both men staring at her. "But now I have a little time to figure out what to do."

Ross leaned forward in his seat and rested his elbows on his knees.

"You're not in this alone, Lacey. I'm in."

"Me, too," Brad piped up. "And in case Ross forgot to mention it, I *am* a lawyer. I was lead prosecutor for the Anchorage District Attorney before giving it up for all this, so if you have a need for my services..." His voice trailed off and he looked at her with all sincerity.

Her eyes stung and she blinked rapidly. "Would you two stop being so chivalrous?" she said after a brief silence. "I don't know how to deal with it."

"Accept it," Ross said. "Stop questioning it and accept it."

They stared at each other for a moment. He was smiling, but his eyes spoke volumes more and Lacey finally had to look away. She took another sip of her coffee and jumped when Ross slapped his hands against his thighs and stood up.

"Well, darlin'," he said, "get your bags. We'd better be heading out."

"Already?" Brad asked as he stood. "I figured you'd stick around for lunch."

"I've got a business to run, old buddy," Ross replied. "I can leave Burke in charge for one night, but two? Burke's a good guy, but graceful he's not. I already know I'll have to replace at least a dozen glasses, and probably a few tables and chairs."

Lacey smiled, knowing all too well the large, burly man who seemed all thumbs. "I'll get my stuff," she said. She stood, smiled at Brad, then walked over and gave him a hug. It was a moment before he responded, his arms enfolding her slowly, and when she pulled away his face was crimson. She chuckled and kissed his cheek. "Thanks for everything, Brad."

He stuffed his hands in his pockets and shook his head. "Don't mention it. A guy likes a little excitement now and then."

Lacey turned, glanced at Ross, and gave him a quick smile before heading up the stairs to their room. She'd almost finished tossing her things into the duffel bag when the outer door opened. A moment later, Ross stuck his head in her room.

"Almost ready?" he asked. She zipped the bag shut and nodded, tongue tied and eyes averted. Ross grinned and picked up her bag, his own already in hand. "Good. Let's go home."

Chapter Twelve

Lacey stared out the window of the plane, her mind spinning. Bouncing around inside her head were thoughts of Lucas and what would happen if he found her, Dennis Lechter and what he wanted from her, and Ross. She didn't know what *Ross* wanted from her, other than the obvious, and she was unable to figure out what it was she wanted from him, other than the obvious. But, it wasn't only sex she was interested in, of that much she was sure. She'd never been able to separate emotional attachment and intimacy from pure, physical sex. She'd never *had* pure, physical sex. Then again, maybe that *was* all she wanted. With a groan of frustration, she ran a hand over her face and looked heavenward.

"Wrestling with the weight of the world?" Ross asked, his voice low.

Lacey glanced at him but he wasn't looking at her. "Wrestling with something."

"Maybe I can help."

"I seriously doubt it," she replied. He looked at her then, and the intensity of his gaze was as tangible as if he'd touched her. She remembered how it felt to have his hands on her and averted her eyes as heat rose in her cheeks.

"If it's about what's going on between us..."

"It's more than that."

"Tell me."

Focusing on a distant fluffy cloud she tried to relax her taut vocal chords enough to reply. She cleared her throat softly and forced herself to look at him. "If Lucas finds me it won't *matter* if there's anything between us or not," she finally managed to whisper. He didn't respond. Her heart twisted and she closed her eyes. "Please don't take this the wrong way, but for the time being can we put whatever *this* is aside? I need to deal with my ex and Lechter first."

"Agreed."

He sounded almost relieved and for a moment Lacey was insulted. Was she *that* easy to dismiss? As quickly as the thought had come she pushed it aside, irritated at her own reaction. Getting angry because he agreed to do what she wanted was beyond ridiculous. Silence prevailed for several moments, but when he spoke again she heard the humor in his voice and snuck a glance at him.

"However, Lacey, when this is all over, we *are* going to have to deal with the failure of my theory."

Her throat tightened and she turned her gaze to her lap. "By that time, your theory may very well have proved true." The very thought was depressing.

He chuckled. "I seriously doubt it."

A shiver went through her and she knew her voice would fail so she didn't respond. The drone of the plane's engine dulled the quiet. Lacey chewed her thumbnail as the thought of Dennis Lechter and his 'gift' weighed heavily on her mind. "What does he want?" She didn't realize she'd spoken out loud until she heard Ross's voice.

"Lechter? It's anybody's guess. Maybe it has something to do with the merger."

Lacey frowned. "Maybe. I'll never know unless I contact him, and I don't plan to do *that* if I don't have to." Ross was studying her, she could tell, and she kept her gaze forward.

"What will you do until then?" he asked.

As far as she was concerned her options were limited. The sight of an eagle caught her eye. "Prepare. If I have to run, I will. Hopefully, if I can learn enough about Mr. Lechter, I won't have to."

"Amen to that." When she looked at him Ross grinned. "Hey, I like having you around. Makes my job much easier, and much more profitable."

"Yeah, right," she said dryly, "and it also makes your life much more complicated."

He thought about that for a second and shrugged. "I don't think of it as complicated, I think of it as...interesting."

Lacey didn't argue. She knew it would do no good. If she'd learned anything about Ross, it was that he was stubborn as a mule. There weren't many who trifled with him, and those who did learned the hard way he didn't take crap from anyone.

"Maybe for you it's interesting," she said, "but from where I sit, it's anything but." She looked at him and he returned her gaze, his expression somber. With a short nod he turned his eyes back to the sky.

***

Ross's eyes followed Lacey while she flitted about the bar, tray balanced overhead as she made her way to a table. Her cheeks were flushed, a smile on her lips as one of the men said something amusing. She threw the logger a look filled with mock reproach and put a beer in front of him. The man laughed and she returned to her duties after patting his cheek fondly.

"You look like someone shot your dog," Boomer said casually as he nursed his cup of coffee. He followed the direction of Ross's gaze and smiled. "What did you expect, ol' buddy? She was bound to make some friends, and given the ratio of men to women in Cooper's Ridge, a few of them were destined to be of the male persuasion."

Annoyance flared in his chest. "I'm glad she's making friends," Ross growled. "I wish she wouldn't be so...*flirty*. She's going to start a fight."

Boomer watched Lacey for a moment then shrugged. "She doesn't seem any more sociable than normal. Besides, I seem to recall Hilda being more than a little flirtatious with some of the customers. Remember the night she gave Bob McTavish a lap dance?"

Ross glared at him and stalked to the other end of the bar to serve a customer. Boomer was right, of course. Lacey didn't act any differently than any of his other waitresses had, but he'd never been interested in any of his waitresses before. It had been nearly ten days since their trip to the lodge, and it irked him how easily she'd reverted to being simply an employee and friend. It was as if their kiss, the kiss that still burned inside him, had never happened.

"Well, Ross Devlin," a sexy female voice said. "Don't you look like an absolute grizzly bear?" Ross turned toward the sound, but he already knew who it was. Slanted green eyes gazed at him with open admiration, and hair the color of pitch brushed slender shoulders. "I know *just* what you need to put a smile back on that handsome face."

Ross walked around the end of the bar. "Renee. It's been a while."

Full lips tipped up in a feline smile as the petite woman ran her hands up his chest and laced her fingers behind his neck. "Yes...it has..." When she pulled his head down he didn't resist.

Her kiss was familiar and his body responded, memories of the many nights they'd spent together sending heat through his veins. He pulled away and her gaze turned questioning.

"Ross?"

After gently disentangling her arms from around his neck, he pressed a hand to her smooth cheek and smiled. "I'm working, Renee. You know I don't mix business and pleasure."

Renee smiled wickedly and hopped up onto the nearest barstool, giving him a look that spoke volumes. "I can wait," she said, her voice husky. "After all, it's almost closing time. Once business is done, we can begin the...pleasure."

His body leapt in response as she licked her lips provocatively, and he remembered vividly how talented those lips were. "We'll talk after I close up."

Renee leaned forward and her breasts nearly popped out of the low-cut sweater. "Oh, Ross. I didn't come all the way from Juneau to *talk*." Her implications were clear, and all Ross could do was nod. He gave her a tight smile and went back to his place behind the bar.

He realized with a start that Lacey was at the waitress stand, waiting and watching him, her expression guarded. At once his ardor cooled. After wiping his hands on a towel and tossing it aside, he approached her.

"What do you need?" he asked. His tone was brusque, and he saw the surprise in her eyes before she looked down at her pad.

"Um, martini, extra dry, two beers and a scotch, neat."

"Coming right up," he answered, in what he hoped was a lighter tone. As he prepared the drinks he noticed she looked anywhere but at him. For a moment he felt guilty, because he knew Lacey must have seen him kissing Renee. At that thought he frowned. What did he have to feel guilty about? It wasn't as if Lacey had some kind of claim on him. He glared at her, angry at her for making him feel like this, angry at her for making him confused when things should be simple. He was a free man, free to see and spend time with whomever he chose. So why did he feel guilty, as if he had cheated on her somehow?

He shook the martini vigorously and noticed Lacey staring at him. "What?" he demanded.

She blinked and took a step back, and several people at the bar turned to look at him.

"N-nothing," she replied softly. "It's just...I'm sure it's mixed by now."

"So now you're going to tell me how to tend bar?"

She looked at him as if he'd slapped her, eyes wide and disbelieving, and he felt the stares of the people sitting within earshot. He hated himself for acting like such a jerk, but it was as if he couldn't act any other way. Now he knew how Jekyll and Hyde felt. He was angry at her, at himself, even at Renee. It was absurd.

"I'm...sorry," she said. After placing the drinks on her tray, she paid for them and didn't even wait for the change. Ross hung his head and rested his hands on the edge of the bar.

"Way to go," Boomer said, his expression speculative.

Ross was not in the mood. "Can it, would you? I feel bad enough."

Boomer drained his coffee cup and got off the barstool as he tossed some bills on the counter. "Yeah. I could tell." After giving him a nod, Boomer pulled on his parka and headed out into the icy, cloudless night.

The remainder of the evening went quickly, despite the obvious chill between him and Lacey. When she ordered her drinks her tone was clipped and concise, and his responses were either nonexistent or limited to single syllables. There was no more easy banter between them, no joking about the customers' drinking habits, no friendly play. When she approached him her smile vanished, only to reappear once she returned to serving the customers. It was beyond strange, but Ross envied them, even though he knew he had no one to blame but himself. He was an idiot.

"Ross, honey," Renee called.

After giving the guy at the counter his beer, Ross walked slowly down to the end of the bar, and she smiled at him. At least he hadn't alienated *her*. "Yes, Renee?"

Renee slid off the barstool and stood in front of him, hooking her thumbs in the belt loops on his jeans. She tipped her face to his and gave him a look that would melt the polar ice caps. "I think I'll wait in your office until you're all done out here, okay?"

Ross nodded, the sensual fragrance of her perfume reaching his nostrils. Maybe spending the night with Renee would finally prove his theory true. Perhaps his attraction to Lacey *was* simple, old-fashioned horniness. There was only one way to find out.

"Fine," he said, "but it'll be about half an hour."

Standing up on her tiptoes, Renee pressed her body against his and kissed him, giving the term global warming a whole new meaning. Thankfully, she pulled away before she embarrassed both of them. "You're worth the wait, honey."

He watched her as she sidled down the hall to his office, and she blew him a kiss before she went inside and shut the door. Another spurt of guilt twinged his conscience, but he quashed it and let his inner caveman take over as he moved behind the bar and gave last call.

Lacey said good night to the last customer, closed the door, and shut the blinds with a sigh of relief. Ross watched her as she turned and caught his eye, and her steps faltered a bit. She looked away; obviously uncomfortable. He didn't know what to say; the silence heavy between them until she finally spoke, her voice hushed.

"Do you want me to run the totals tonight, or should I come in early tomorrow and do them before my shift starts?"

Ross's brows shot skyward. She'd taken over the books when they returned from the Lodge, and seemed to relish the work. After the bar closed her fingers would fly over the adding machine while he swept and mopped and cleaned up, and she never left until the figures were perfect. Now, if her expression was any indication, running the receipts was the last thing she wanted to do. Then it hit him. She knew Renee was waiting, and she probably knew why.

"That's fine," he replied.

Nodding once she strode past him, giving him a wide berth. She took her jacket from the hook in the kitchen, put it on, and grabbed her purse. Never once did she look at him as she went out the back door. Ross ran a hand over his face, sighed heavily, and dropped his chin to his chest. He hadn't thought he could feel worse but he did, and he doubted even Renee, as skilled as she was, could improve his mood.

The tears froze on her cheeks as the screen door slammed shut behind her. Lacey stood on the back stoop for a moment, her breath puffing in the frigid air, her throat constricted painfully as the icy wind cut through her clothing. Her head throbbed and her feelings were so jumbled that for a moment she thought she was going to vomit. Clutching the snow-covered rail, she walked down the short staircase and practically ran to her Jeep.

Once inside the vehicle, her hands shook so badly it was close to half a minute before she could get the key in the ignition. Without turning the engine over she grabbed the steering wheel then pounded it with her fists. What on earth was wrong with her?

She'd seen the petite brunette and she'd seen her kiss Ross. But that really wasn't what was bothering her. It was more his tone of voice when he'd spoken to her, and the glare he'd given her. His scowl felt like a slap in the face, and the look in his eyes had hurt her more than words ever could. What had she done?

It was true they'd put some distance between them since returning from the Lodge, but she was under the impression they'd agreed to do that. Was *that* what was bothering him? Lacey couldn't fathom why he would suddenly turn from friendly to malicious in the blink of an eye. But then, Lucas had done that. Maybe Ross wasn't really so different after all. The idea made her ache.

Lacey huffed in annoyance and swiped at her tears. She reached down and turned the key but nothing happened. Again she turned the key, and still, nothing. Groaning, she rested her forehead against the steering wheel. After several moments, she pumped the gas then tried to start the Jeep once again. Silence. Complete, utter silence.

"Great." She leaned back in her seat and looked toward the rear of the bar. Why did things like this always happen to her? The last thing she wanted was to go back inside, especially with Ross and his lady friend in there. More than the thought of interrupting something, the thought of those piercing eyes and his angry glare made her loathe to face him. However, she had little choice. At two-thirty in the morning there wasn't a soul awake in Cooper's Ridge, except for Ross, his 'girlfriend', and her. Lacey grimaced at the thought.

The sound of her own teeth chattering made her realize she had to do something. The longer she waited, the more likely it was she'd freeze, or she'd *really* interrupt something. She got out of the Jeep and walked up to the back door.

When she stepped into the darkened hall she was surprised to hear the jukebox, the volume turned up. Light spilled from the open door of Ross's office onto the floor, and she paused outside the entrance.

"Ross?" she said. She peered around the door jamb into the office and was relieved to see it empty. With a sigh, she walked past the office and toward the main room.

As she turned the corner, Lacey halted in her tracks, heat searing her cheeks. There, on one of the larger tables sat the brunette, her sweater pulled down to reveal her cleavage and lacy black bra. They weren't having sex, *yet*, but they were obviously headed there, her legs wrapped around Ross's waist and his hands in her hair as he kissed her. He trailed his lips down her neck and a moan of desire escaped her, her head dropping back. As if sensing another presence in the room the woman opened her eyes and turned her head. Her eyes widened when she saw Lacey.

"Ross!"

Ross paused and followed the direction of the woman's gaze. His jaw dropped when he saw her standing there.

"I – I'm sorry," Lacey whispered as she backed away. She blinked, and without another word she turned, ran down the hall and into the sub-zero air. Hearing Ross behind her, she quickened her pace, sprinting around the side of the building and down the street.

"Lacey! Wait!"

But she didn't wait, moving as quickly as her legs would carry her, and she didn't stop until she was certain Ross wasn't following anymore. When she turned a corner, she saw the hockey rink and skidded to a halt, her lungs protesting vigorously against the frozen air she inhaled. After a brief pause, she walked slowly toward the rink, snow crunching underneath her boots, the ice giving off an eerie glow beneath the light of the fingernail moon. She leaned against the bleachers, sank to the ground, and cried.

It was after 3 a.m. when she walked into the sheriff's station. Boomer was at his desk, feet kicked up and newspaper open. A little bell connected to the door tinkled, announcing her presence, and Boomer practically jumped to his feet when he saw her standing there, shivering and teeth chattering. She knew it was obvious she'd been crying, but she put up a brave face and smiled. Boomer came around the counter to stand in front of her, eyes filled with concern.

"Lacey, what are you doing here?" He glanced at the clock, frowned, and looked at her. He took her arm and stood her in front of a glowing space heater. "What happened?"

Lacey took a deep breath and stretched her hands toward the heat. "M-my car w-wouldn't start," she said at last, thankful her voice didn't crack. "I th-think the b-battery's d-dead."

Boomer's expression was thoughtful, and he rubbed his chin. When he spoke his voice was gentle. "Why didn't you get Ross? He has a set of jumper cables in his truck."

Lacey gulped and looked down at the floor. She blinked against the tears that wanted to come and shrugged, unable to meet the sheriff's gaze. "I – I would've, but he was...he was...b-busy."

She glanced at him. Understanding dawned and Boomer's mouth formed a silent "o" then he clapped a hand on her shoulder and smiled. "I get it. Once you're warmed up some, we'll get that old jalopy started so you can get home."

Lacey nodded and gave him a grateful smile. "Okay."

***

Ross recognized the sound of Boomer's Suburban as it pulled up behind the building. Renee was in the bathroom, and he glanced toward the closed door before getting off the bar stool and moving to the window set in the back door. He gazed through the half-closed blinds and watched as Lacey got out of the truck and into the Jeep. Boomer popped the hoods of both vehicles. He had a pair of jumper cables over one arm, and Ross was half tempted to see if they needed any help, even though he already knew the answer. Starting a dead battery was not rocket science, and Boomer was more than capable.

Ross jumped when smooth fingertips grazed his cheek, and Renee laughed softly when he turned startled eyes to her. The sound of the Jeep roaring to life drew their attention back out the window and Renee pressed herself up against his side. As they watched, Lacey got out of the Jeep, exchanged a few words with Boomer, and then the two embraced. Ross didn't realize he was frowning until Renee ran a finger over his lips, a knowing smile on her full mouth.

"So, *that's* why you're so far away," Renee said. She walked behind the bar and poured herself a cup of coffee.

He frowned. "I don't know what you're talking about."

Renee stopped what she was doing and gave him an indulgent look. "Oh, don't get so defensive," she said, adding creamer to her mug. She stirred the hot brew, the spoon clinking against the ceramic. "I'm not taking it personally, Ross. I had a feeling from the moment I kissed you it wasn't going to happen."

He stared hard at her. "I *did* kiss you back."

One dark brow arched. "I didn't come all the way from Juneau for a *kiss*."

"I'm sorry," he replied, his voice laden with sarcasm, "but I didn't realize I was required to perform on demand for you. Next time perhaps you should give me some notice." His gaze drifted back out the window, his chest tight with irritation and regret. He ground his teeth together. "It's been a really long day and I'm not in the mood."

She laughed and put the mug on the counter. "Since when has Ross Devlin ever *not* been in the mood?" When he glared at her she lifted her hands as if in surrender. "Relax. I wanted more than a make-out session, but I'll survive. I'm just disappointed it wasn't *me* you were kissing."

He leaned against his closed office door and stared at the opposite wall. He was frustrated, confused, and tiring of this conversation, quickly. "Well, I don't see any other woman around here, so it must've been you."

Renee walked up to him and her fingers stroked lightly over his shirt. "It's okay, Ross. We're friends, friends with...benefits. At least we *were*." He felt her watching him and kept his expression impassive, but when she spoke again he heard the pensive note in her voice. "But that's all changed, hasn't it?"

It was more a statement than a question, and Ross looked at her. "Why would it?"

"Because of that pretty waitress. I saw the way you watched her, and I saw the jealous spark in your eyes every time she smiled at someone who wasn't you." She studied him closely, and her eyes widened a bit when he didn't argue. "I'm right, aren't I?"

Ross huffed in annoyance and stepped away from her. "You're being ridiculous." He went to the window, hoping for one more glimpse of Lacey, but the Jeep was long gone. Behind him, he heard Renee sigh.

"I suppose it was bound to happen eventually," she said. "I never thought I'd see the day when Ross Devlin would fall in love."

He clenched his jaw and glared at his reflection in the window. "I'm *not* in love."

Another delicate, feminine laugh. "Oh, yes, you are. You may not know it yet, in fact you're probably fighting it every step of the way, but you've got it, bad."

He clenched his fists at his sides and resisted the urge to yell at her. "I'm. Not. In. Love."

She sauntered to his side and wound an arm around his waist. He kept his expression neutral and a sad smile blossomed on her lips. She kissed him on the cheek and placed a hand over his heart. "Don't worry, Ross, I'm happy for you. And I don't even mind that you said her name while I was trying to...get you in the mood." She paused, her palm flat against his chest. "Lacey. It's a pretty name."

Ross gaped at her as she gathered her jacket and purse, exited the bar, and closed the back door softly behind her. It felt like he'd been sucker-punched. He didn't remember saying Lacey's name, but he couldn't deny he'd been thinking of Lacey during his brief and unfruitful interlude with Renee. And there was no other way Renee could know Lacey's name. Renee had moved to Juneau more than six months ago, and he hadn't seen or spoken to her until tonight. He walked back to the bar, planted his elbows on the counter, and dropped his head into his hands.

He remembered vividly the expression on Lacey's face when she'd discovered them, the hurt and disbelief so clear in her caramel-colored eyes. Self-reproach rose like bile. He'd been an ass, a complete ass, and he had no idea what he was going to do now. At the Lodge he'd told her he wasn't trying to make her another 'girlfriend' yet he'd made a pass at her anyway. And now this.

Renee had been right, but then, Renee was always right. That was why they'd gotten along so well and managed to maintain their friendship even with the sex. She was a realist, as was he. When he'd seen Lacey smile at other men he *had* been jealous, and that was totally out of character for him. It was a new sensation, and not an entirely pleasant one. It coiled and undulated like a serpent before striking the inside of his chest cavity. Then Renee had arrived, and his behavior had gone from bad to worse.

He'd thought to banish Lacey from his mind and his heart by having a night of wild sex with Renee, but things hadn't gone as planned. After Lacey's interruption and subsequent flight from the bar, Renee had used every feminine tool in her vast repertoire to regain his interest. She had failed. Instead of feeling the burn of lust and desire he felt restless, guilty, and bewildered. Then she'd decided a practical conversation was in order, and that also proved fruitless. He wasn't a man who *talked it out.*

Not one to be discouraged, Renee had reverted to seduction, a skill she'd mastered ages ago. At first his body had responded as if on autopilot. However, as soon as he'd cupped her breast he'd realized it wasn't Renee's curves he wanted his hands on. It wasn't Renee's mouth he wanted to claim. It wasn't Renee's gasps of pleasure he wanted to elicit. Not only did he not want Lacey less, he wanted her *more.*

Frustrated to the boiling point, Ross strode to the back door, jerked it open, and stepped onto the landing. He turned his face to the sky, his breath turning into frothy puffs in the freezing air, and yelled at the top of his lungs. His feral howl echoed off the buildings and traveled through the dark, cold streets like the mournful cry of a wounded wolf. When the sound finally faded in the distance he went back inside, closed and locked the door, and went to the bar to retrieve a bottle of single malt scotch and a glass. Then he stomped up the stairs to his apartment. It wasn't until the first blush of dawn colored the sky that he finally found sleep. The empty scotch bottle sat on the nightstand like a silent sentinel as the tumbler slipped from his fingers and fell to the carpet.

Chapter Thirteen

Lacey pulled up behind the building and stared at the back door for several moments before she shut the engine off and got out. She didn't want to be here but she had a job to do. As she walked up the stairs she saw an envelope sticking out of the screen door. She frowned, took it, and slid her finger beneath the flap. Inside was a note from Ross that said to see Annie at the café.

"Annie?" she said. "Why?" After reading the note one more time she shrugged. She stuffed the paper into a pocket then made her way around the building and across the street. A bell rang as she pushed open the café door, and Annie appeared almost immediately. A smile broke out on her face when she spotted Lacey. After wiping her hands on her apron, she approached.

"Afternoon, Lacey. How's it going?"

Lacey slid onto a seat at the counter and returned the woman's smile. "All right I guess."

"Want a cup of coffee?"

"No, but a cup of tea would be nice."

Annie grinned and nodded, red curls dancing. "You got it."

Lacey watched as Annie bustled around, gathering one of those little silver teapots, a cup and saucer, and a tea bag. Glancing around the café, Lacey nodded and smiled at several people, then turned her attention back to the vivacious redhead as she put her tea on the counter. "Thanks, Annie."

Annie shook her head and leaned against the counter. "No problem. Now what brings you here? You don't usually come into town this time of day."

Lacey stopped in mid-drink. "Ross left me a note telling me to come see you. I have some book work to do, and I thought he would be in the bar, but he's not."

"Oh." Annie's eyes widened and she searched her pockets. Finally, she pulled out a key and handed it to Lacey. "I forgot. It's a key to the bar. Ross had to run some errands, and he said to give this to you when you came by."

Lacey looked at the key for a moment then slipped it into her pocket. "Thanks, Annie." Part of her was relieved that the inevitable face-to-face with Ross had been postponed, while another part of her just wanted it over with.

The cook tossed a plate underneath the warmer lights and barked something unintelligible in their direction. Annie glanced at him in annoyance then turned back to her. "Don't mention it. Hey, are you okay? You look...tired." The cook growled again and Annie frowned. "Don't go anywhere. I'll be right back."

As the vivacious woman bustled off with the plate of food, Lacey thought about ducking out but decided against it. The last thing she wanted to do was alienate any of the friends she had in Cooper's Ridge. She'd already done a bang up job with Ross, so she stayed put.

After Annie deposited the plate, she checked on the other customers in the café then made her way back to where Lacey sat. Instead of standing behind the counter she came around and sat down next to her, her eyes filled with concern.

"So, tell me what's wrong."

Lacey looked down at her tea. "Nothing's wrong. You're right, I'm a little tired." She felt Annie studying her, and was unable to meet the woman's eyes.

"Hey, Lacey," she began, "whatever you're going through...you're not alone. If you ever need to talk..."

"I'm fine," Lacey said, forcing a smile.

After a few moments, Annie sighed in resignation. "All right, if you say so. Hey, you want a sandwich or something? I can make it to go."

"No, thank you," Lacey replied with a grateful smile. "Maybe later."

Annie patted her hand and gave her a quirky grin. "All right. And, Lacey, like I said...if you ever need someone to talk to..."

This was *not* a conversation Lacey wanted to have. She nodded, finished her tea, and stood. "Fanny told me that, next to her, there's no better therapist in training than you." She said her goodbyes then walked back to the bar.

With the lights out and the jukebox quiet, there was an eerie feel to the place, and a shiver ran up her spine as she closed and locked the door behind her. She flipped a switch, and the lights over the bar nearly blinded her as they came on. She hung up her jacket and purse and gathered the paperwork. Her gaze swept the bar, falling on the table Ross and his lady friend had used for their lip-lock. She stutter-stepped and her throat tightened. *It's a table. Get over it.* She gave herself an inward shake and straightened her spine. After getting herself a soda, she sat on a barstool and went to work.

Her fingers tapped rhythmically on the keys of the adding machine, a pencil between her teeth. Since last night had been a relatively easy night, it didn't take her long to finish the totals, and before she knew it, she was done. After folding up the tapes and sliding all the papers into a manila folder, she decided to work on the inventory. She pulled the receipts out of a file in Ross's office, then sat back down and got to work.

Half an hour later she was stuck, and frowned at the totals in confusion. Either her math was way off, or she was missing a receipt. Deciding it was probably the latter, she hopped off the stool and started her search. After going through the bar area and Ross's office, she still came up empty. Ross had told her this happened occasionally, and he'd joked that if the receipt wasn't in the office or the register, it was probably upstairs in his pants pocket. He'd also told her to feel free to look. She blew a curl out of her eyes, plopped down on a barstool, and looked at the staircase in annoyance. The *last* thing she wanted was to venture into Ross's space, a space where he and his *friend* had no doubt ended their evening. The thought sent her heart plummeting.

"Perfect." She moved to the bottom landing and stared at the door. Her stomach knotted. "I wonder what it would take to talk him into computerizing everything. Then I wouldn't have to worry about missing receipts *or* invading his privacy."

After much internal debate she squared her shoulders and mounted the stairs. He had given her a raise to do a specific job, a job she couldn't do properly without all the necessary paperwork. He'd also given her permission to enter his private domain if needed. Swallowing hard, she stopped on the upper landing and grasped the doorknob. She knocked soundly with her free hand. Nothing. Even knowing his apartment was empty, it was several moments before she gathered the courage to open the door.

She stepped into Ross's apartment, her nerves on edge. *Okay, if I was a receipt, where would I be?* The first thing she saw as she perused the space was the bed. It sat under a large window along the north wall, and to her surprise it was neatly made, with hospital corners even, a thick down comforter folded at the foot of the mattress. An image of Ross and the dark-haired woman entwined on that mattress blossomed in her mind's eye, but she shoved it back. *Concentrate, damn it.*

There were no blinds on the windows, only thin, sheer curtains, and the floor was covered with thick beige carpet. The apartment was more like a studio; one giant room with a sitting area in the southwest corner made up of large, comfy looking chairs that circled a pellet stove. A wheeled, portable clothes rack and milk crates turned on their sides served as the closet area in the opposite corner. A large desk took up the wall near the bed, the surface so organized it looked more like a display in an office furniture store than a work space. With a shake of her head, she opened the only other door and glanced into the small bathroom, where a large ball-and-claw tub with a shower attachment dominated the space.

She felt like an intruder here, as if she were spying on him. Annoyed at herself, she started looking for the missing receipt, and was amazed at how neat everything was. The place was almost sterile. The walls were bare except for a grouping of photos on the wall near the fireplace. Tempering her curiosity, she walked over to the clothes rack and started going through the pockets of his jeans. When that yielded nothing she went to the kitchen area, feeling immensely guilty as she pulled out the drawers. Even those were neat. Lucas would've been impressed.

After nearly ten minutes she'd found nothing, and stood in the middle of the room with her hands on her hips. She turned in a full circle, trying to see if there was anywhere she'd forgotten to look. Rolling her eyes, she slapped herself in the forehead. The desk.

A search of the drawers yielded nothing. Granted, there was plenty of paperwork and files, but she didn't look at anything unless it resembled a receipt for supplies for the bar. She was about to give up when she saw a piece of paper on the floor behind the desk. She got down on her hands and knees and crawled underneath the piece of furniture, her fingers searching blindly.

"If you're trying to find my little black book, I can assure you, I don't have one."

Lacey started violently and yelped in surprise when she cracked her head against the underside of the center drawer.

"Ouch!" Holding a hand to the back of her head, she scooted out from beneath the desk and plopped down on her rear.

Ross was at her side in an instant. "Are you okay?" When he reached for her she jerked away from him and frowned as she got to her feet. Her eyes widened when she pulled her hand away and saw bright red blood on her fingers. There wasn't a lot, but there was enough that his reaction was immediate.

"Sit down," he commanded.

Lacey was too shocked to protest as he steered her to the bed, and forced her down on the edge of the mattress. Without another word he went to the kitchen, got a wet towel and a first aid kit. He returned and pulled her forward until her forehead rested against his stomach. He brushed her hair aside, pressed the wet towel against the throbbing area and held it there for what felt like minutes. His legs straddled one of hers, and Lacey realized with a start that her face was practically rubbing against his crotch. She jerked and he cursed under his breath.

"Hold *still*." His voice had an edge that froze her, and she complied. He lifted the towel and inspected her head. "It's a small cut, and the bleeding has pretty much stopped. I'll disinfect it, but I don't think it's life threatening."

Her face was hot with embarrassment, and the humor she heard in his voice made her cheeks burn even hotter. When he finally moved away it was all she could do not to run from the room.

Ross handed her the towel so she could wipe off her fingers, then he pulled a gauze pad from the first aid kit and liberally soaked it with alcohol. To her mortification, he positioned himself as before, and Lacey thought she'd die from the humiliation. What made it even worse were the lurid thoughts running through her mind.

"Get on with it," she said from between clenched teeth.

Ross chuckled softly then leaned forward. "Okay. Brace yourself."

Air hissed from between her teeth when he pressed the alcohol-soaked pad to the cut, and Lacey was surprised at the amount of pain for such a small wound. After a few moments she pushed him away and put her hand over the gauze. "I think I can take it from here."

Ross held up his hands and stepped back, then grabbed a chair and spun it around so he could straddle it. When the burning finally faded Lacey pulled the gauze off and looked at it. There was a small spot of blood, but that was all. He was watching her, she could tell, so she forced herself to speak.

"I suppose I should thank you." She glanced up then averted her gaze. "Thank you."

"Don't mention it," he said. "After all, it was my fault, sort of. If I hadn't scared you, you wouldn't have hit your head."

Lacey pressed her lips into a thin line and nodded, unable to meet those piercing eyes. At least he wasn't growling at her, which was good. Nevertheless, she jumped when he spoke again.

"Now, do you want to tell me what you were doing?"

Lacey dropped her chin and pinched the bridge of her nose. Finally, she looked up, surprised to find him smiling. That gave her pause, and for a moment she forgot what she was going to say.

"I...I was looking for a receipt," she said at last, her cheeks flaming. It sounded like a lame excuse, even though it was true. Ross lifted one brow and she looked down at the ground. "You told me if one came up missing, and it wasn't in the office or the register..."

"Then it would probably be in one of my pants pockets," he finished. "Did you find it?"

When she looked up, the picture of him with that woman popped into her mind and she jumped to her feet. "Um, no. So...I'll go back downstairs and look again." Without waiting for a reply she walked quickly out the door and took the stairs two at a time.

Ross watched her go and fought the urge to call out to her. When he'd walked into his apartment and seen that nicely rounded backside as she wiggled around under his desk, his initial reaction had been anger at her for invading his privacy. Then, as she wiggled some more, his anger had turned into lust. The temptation to run his hands over that enticing derriere had been so strong it had taken every ounce of willpower not to. He was amazed at the effect she had on him, and wondered briefly if she felt even a tiny bit the same. Judging by her reaction when he'd tended the cut on her head she couldn't stand to be near him. Given the drama of the previous evening he understood her wariness, but given the power of his attraction to her it was still disconcerting. It was time to put an end to this. He huffed in annoyance and stuffed his hands into his pockets. Paper crinkled and he pulled out a rumpled receipt, no doubt the one she was looking for.

Lacey heard his footsteps on the stairs and braced herself. She hated feeling like this, on edge, as if she was on a tightrope suspended hundreds of feet in the air where one tiny misstep spelled disaster. It reminded her too much of Lucas. She'd always been on eggshells when her husband was around, treading carefully and quietly so as not to raise his ire. She didn't want to be like that with Ross, or with anyone for that matter.

She pretended to look over the numbers again and waited for him to say something. He sat on the barstool next to her and slid a piece of paper toward her.

"I believe you were looking for this."

His voice was soft, low, but as much as she loved looking at him she couldn't at this particular moment. She picked up the receipt and smoothed the rumpled paper. "Thank you."

"Lacey, about last night—"

She immediately slid off the barstool and held up her hands. "That's okay, Ross," she said in a rush, "you...you don't have to explain anything to me."

He gave her a beseeching look. "*Yes*, I *do*."

She returned his gaze, took a deep breath, and squared her shoulders. "No. You don't. It's none of my business and, frankly...I don't want to know."

He got to his feet and stood in front of her, making her feel very small as she craned her neck to look up at him. A half-smile danced about his mouth, and Lacey wondered what he found funny. "At least you're looking at me again," he observed, his voice like velvet. "Lacey, I'm sorry I hurt you."

She flushed to the roots of her hair and lowered her eyes, hating the jump in her pulse. "You didn't."

"The way you ran out of here..." His voice trailed off and he nudged her chin up with his knuckles.

Lacey swallowed hard and looked briefly at his mouth. Even though those lips had been kissing the raven-haired woman mere hours ago, the thought of kissing him now sent a stab of heat through her. She squeezed her eyes shut and jerked away from him, mortified by her body's reaction to a simple mental image. "I was...*shocked*," she said, "and embarrassed. Should I have pulled up a chair and waited for you to finish?" She felt him studying her, and wished he'd look elsewhere as her flush burned hotter.

"So...you don't mind that I kissed Renee?"

Kissed? Oh, sure, all you did was kiss. *Riiiight.* She walked to the front doors and opened the blinds, needing to put some space between them. "Why should I mind? After all, we're just friends, right?" She gathered her courage then turned and looked at him.

His eyes narrowed slightly and he tipped his head to the side. "Really? The way you've been acting lately, I'd hardly say we're friends. Ever since we got back from the Lodge, I keep expecting you to start calling me *Mr. Devlin* again."

Anger blossomed in her chest and her jaw dropped. "The way *I've* been acting?" She stared at him and the amused glint in his eyes only fanned her temper. She moved to stand toe to toe with him and poked a finger in his chest. "*I* wasn't the one biting *your* head off last night!"

Ross chuckled softly. "That's better. At least now you're fighting instead of scurrying around like a frightened mouse."

Lacey realized she'd been baited and narrowed her eyes. "I've spent the past seven years being a mouse," she said under her breath. "If it's a fight you want, I'll be happy to oblige you."

He smiled wistfully as he wrapped a long, golden curl around his index finger. "It's not a fight I want," he said, studying the shining ringlet. "I've been fighting myself long enough. What I want...is you."

Lacey felt like she'd been punched in the gut. She slapped his hand away and pulled back. When her lungs finally started to function again, she took a deep breath and turned her back to him as she rested her hands on the bar. "You've got a funny way of showing it," she whispered. Her head started to throb and she closed her eyes for several moments.

"I didn't think I *should* show it. We agreed to put this attraction between us aside for now, and while my head understood that, the rest of me wasn't listening." He paused and his expression shifted from earnest to concerned. "Lacey? Are you okay?"

"I'm fine," she bit out. "Wonderful." A glance at her reflection said otherwise. Her face was pale and dark circles shadowed her eyes. Even her voice sounded strained. "You want me, so you decide the best way to handle it was to have sex with someone else on a table in the middle of the bar." She pressed her fingers to her temples and sat down. "Makes *perfect* sense."

"Lacey," he began, resting a hand on her shoulder, "I didn't–"

"Stop," she interrupted in a growl, pushing his hand away. "Just stop."

At that moment she decided she'd had enough. Her head was killing her, and her emotions were in such turmoil she couldn't think. She jumped to her feet and went behind the bar to get the bottle of pain reliever, popped four of the pills into her mouth and downed them with a tall glass of water. Once she'd done that she returned to her paperwork, added the receipt to her stack of bills and ran the figures again. When the totals came out, she stuffed everything in a folder and handed it to Ross, none too gently.

"There. The books are done, inventory is up to date, and everything totals out fine. Now, if you don't mind, I'm going to go take a nap."

Ross stared at her as she got her coat from the hall. "And, exactly *where* are you going to do that?"

Lacey paused, her hand on the knob, and looked at him, feeling weary. "In the back of my Jeep. I keep a sleeping bag in there for just such emergencies."

Ross frowned, put the folder aside, and walked up to her. "You'll do no such thing. There's a very warm, very comfortable bed upstairs."

Lacey gaped at him and her hand fell to her side. "The same bed where you and your friend got...*reacquainted* last night? I don't think so."

He huffed. "Renee and I didn't *get* reacquainted last night, so use it, or you're fired."

Her jaw dropped. "You wouldn't."

His expression darkened and he leaned toward her. "Try me."

Instinctively, she shrank from him but she couldn't look away. They battled visually, and as much as she wanted to defy him she really didn't have the energy. Plus, the back of the Cherokee wasn't exactly comfortable. Finally, she nodded and he stepped back. His features softened and a ghost of a smile warmed his mouth as she walked past him and up the stairs. She wondered at the smile, but she didn't stop to ask, her heart fluttering. When she heard his footsteps following behind the quivering in her chest grew stronger. Without looking back, she opened the door and walked into his private domain.

Lacey had to admit that by the time she sat down on the edge of the bed, she was exhausted. She'd hardly slept the night before, and with all the emotional turmoil she'd been in, she was completely drained. She lay back, her feet still planted firmly on the floor, and closed her eyes with a sigh.

Her head snapped up when Ross took her foot in his hand, his fingers nimbly untying the laces on her boots. He knelt in front of her, and when she rose onto on her elbows he looked up.

"Relax. I'm just helping you with your shoes." His voice was like a caress, and for the first time she realized how long his eyelashes were. As he stroked her ankle, his fingers slid inside her shoe to slip it off her foot, and strange shivers of warmth ran up her leg. His eyes never left hers, and everything in the background faded in comparison to their brilliant blue. She gulped when he did the same with her other foot, moving as if in slow motion.

The thought of those fingers straying higher, caressing and stroking, made her suck in a breath. She couldn't believe that despite what she'd walked in on the previous night she was still wildly attracted to him. Would he always affect her this way? She lay back down, stared at the ceiling, and tried to regulate her breathing.

"There," he said at last, "all done. Now, why don't you stretch out and get comfortable."

Lacey swung her legs onto the bed and laid her head gingerly on the pillow. With one flick, Ross opened up the comforter and settled it over her, then moved to her side. The bed dipped as he sat down on the edge of the mattress and pulled the coverlet over her shoulders. His expression was almost...tender, and her heart skipped a beat when he smiled.

"All snug?" he asked.

"As a bug in a rug," she replied. He opened his mouth and she waited for him to speak. Instead, he snapped his jaw shut and got to his feet.

"I'll wake you when it's time for your shift," he said at last.

She nodded. He stood there for a while, looking down at her, and for a second that guarded expression slipped a little. She thought she saw remorse in his gaze, but the shield went back up so quickly she couldn't be sure.

"Get some rest," he said, and then he turned on his heel and left the apartment.

Ross walked softly down the stairs, his insides wound tighter than a spring. He wanted to tell her what had really happened, defend himself, but he knew now was not the right time. She wouldn't believe him anyway. He puffed out a slow breath and walked to the bar.

The manila folder lay on the polished wood and he glanced briefly at her figures, not surprised when everything totaled out perfectly. It was the best thing he'd ever done, letting Lacey handle the books. She could do in an hour what would normally have taken him two or more. He smiled at the same time a cool spurt of sadness chilled his heart. He took the papers, tossed them on his desk, and then set about getting ready for the Friday night crowd. It was the fifteenth, payday. Tonight they'd be busy.

At six o'clock Ross went back upstairs to wake Lacey. He walked over to the bed, looked down at her and felt the smile despite the melancholy that tightened its grip on him. In sleep she had no worries. A small smile curved her mouth; her hair lay tousled and riotous about her face. She looked peaceful, and he hated to wake her. Carefully, he sat down on the edge of the bed and tipped his head as he brushed an errant curl from her cheek.

It felt good seeing her in his bed, though he couldn't explain why. He remembered what it was like to wake up next to her, and his thoughts automatically shifted to what it would be like to make love to her, to fall asleep with her in his arms. He was tired of fighting these feelings, of being careful not to step over the 'friendship' boundary. It wasn't friendship he wanted from her.

Was he willing to take on the all baggage that came with an exclusive relationship? He knew Lacey had a lot of baggage, potentially dangerous baggage. But the thought of not having her in his life, never again seeing the smile that lit up a room, never again smelling the scent of her hair or hearing the warmth of her laugh...*that* frightened him more than anything in her past. No, he could deal with her baggage. It was not having her he didn't think he could deal with.

She murmured in her sleep, her smile deepened, and he had the sudden urge to kiss her. Before he realized what he was doing he did just that, his lips feathering over hers once, then again. Something inside him tightened when she smiled against his mouth and her arms wound about his neck.

Lacey didn't think she'd ever been so warm, or felt so safe. It was a wonderful dream, having Ross kiss her. His touch was so light it made her ache for more, and when his lips gently demanded entrance to her mouth she gave in with a small sigh. Her fingers sifted through his hair, and she was amazed at how real it all felt. She hoped she'd never wake up, never have to see Ross scowl at her again, or hear the growl in his voice when he snapped at her. Here was where she wanted to stay, snug, protected, and thoroughly kissed by a strong, beautiful man who made her tingle all over. It was wonderful.

Ross knew he needed to stop, but she was so warm and soft and responsive. He kissed her deeply, leisurely, as if he had all the time in the world to simply savor her. Finally, he pulled away, knowing if he didn't stop he wouldn't be able to. Her eyes fluttered open and she smiled up at him, a sleepy, beautiful smile that made him want her all the more. He ran a finger over her cheek and returned her smile.

"Wake up sleepy head. It's after six."

At that her eyes widened and she bolted upright. She pressed her fingers to her lips then looked at him in silent accusation. Before she could protest, he put a hand gently over her mouth.

"No, don't yell at me. I've decided I don't want to put aside the way I feel any longer, and you're going to have to deal with that." She blinked at him, and he chuckled. "I thought sleeping with Renee would make me want you less, get you out of my head." He kissed her on the cheek and rose. "But, it didn't happen and rest assured, she won't be back. She wasn't very happy that I called her by your name while we were making out."

Lacey frowned. "I don't...understand."

"I didn't sleep with her," he explained. "I *couldn't*, because I don't want *her*." His fingertips grazed her jaw. "There's more than friendship here Lacey, and I think you know that." He delved the golden depths of her eyes as his thumb rubbed her lower lip. "I think we need to explore that a little bit, if you're willing to forgive me." Again, sorrow pulled on him. "Please, say you forgive me."

"I...I..." Her voice died and she averted her gaze.

Chuckling, he sat down and cupped her chin. "I know you're scared, especially after last night." He leaned his head to the side so he could see her eyes. "Talk to me, Lace."

She shook her head. "Ross, I can't be one of your...*girlfriends*." Pausing, she closed her eyes and took a deep breath. "I'm not made that way."

He slid his fingers into her hair and she went still, as if waiting for the kiss. When his lips brushed hers he heard her sharp intake of breath before she melted against him. Then he claimed his prize. Her hands fisted in the front of his shirt as he explored her mouth. When he pulled away he pressed his forehead against hers, her breath warm on his cheek.

"There won't be any other girlfriends. I don't want anyone else." Just then a knock sounded on the front door. Ross kissed her again, as passionately as he could in three seconds, and got to his feet. "We need to finish this conversation, but right now I have to get the door." Lacey opened her eyes and simply stared at him, a look of complete bewilderment on her face. He laughed at her expression then bounded down the stairs. Whistling, he opened the front doors, surprised to see a UPS guy standing there.

"Ross Devlin?" the man asked. Ross nodded and the guy immediately handed him the package. "Package for you. Please sign here." He held out the electronic board and Ross signed, looking at the box in puzzlement as he shut the door. It was a 10"X13" box about two inches thick. There was no return address, so he looked for any indication of the sender. Seeing the city of origin, his eyes widened.

"What is it?" Lacey said from behind him. She must've seen his face in the mirror, her expression turning curious as she moved to his side and looked at the package. He pointed to the postmark and when she read it she turned wide eyes to him. New York.

Ross sighed heavily. "Time's up, Lacey. What do we do now?" He looked at her, and his gut wrenched when he saw the fear in her eyes. He put an arm around her shoulder, pulled her close and hugged her tightly. "Don't worry, Lacey. I won't let him hurt you. I won't let anyone hurt you."

Chapter Fourteen

The bar was packed that night and Lacey was thankful. She was so busy she didn't have time to think about Dennis Lechter or the package or what was inside it. Even now it lay untouched on Ross's desk. They'd agreed not to open it until after work.

"Hey, waitress!" a male voice called loudly from behind her. Lacey smiled at the man she was serving, handed him his beer, and turned toward the voice. She rolled her eyes and groaned inwardly. Jack Calhoun and his friends watched her and, judging from their bleary eyes, they'd started to drink long before they ventured in here. She forced a smile to her lips and approached the table.

"Hi, Jack, fellas. What can I get you?"

Jack leered at her. "I heard Renee was in town yesterday, and I hear she spent the night with Ross."

Lacey gave him a tolerant smile. "Well, I don't know her name but he did entertain a beautiful little brunette after closing," she replied smoothly. "In fact, I walked in on them making out on this very table." She gave him a wry grin. "Don't worry, I disinfected it...twice. Now can I get you something to drink?"

His friends snickered and looked at Jack out of the corners of their eyes, gauging his reaction to Lacey's apparent indifference. Jack's expression turned sour. "You know, Lacey, you're no fun. No fun at all."

She leaned over, got in his face, and smiled seductively. "Oh, Jack," she whispered, giving him an inviting look, "you have no idea how much fun I am." She kissed the tip of his nose, then straightened up and sauntered back to the bar. Behind her she heard the raucous laughter and fought to keep the grin off her face. Ross narrowed his eyes and looked past her to Jack's table where Jack's friends continued to rib him unmercifully.

"What was all that about?" he asked. Before she could answer the sound of a table being toppled made her jump and she whirled around to see Jack push one of his friends out of his chair. Jack then grabbed the man's shirt, but before he could do anything Ross grabbed him from behind and wrestled him off. "Jack! Cool it, bud. You don't want to do this."

People scattered and the man on the floor looked at Jack in disbelief. Jack struggled briefly, but he was no match for the taller, stronger Ross, and finally he stopped struggling.

Ross turned toward the door, released him, and gave him a light shove. "Go home, Jack. I think you've had enough to drink tonight." Without a word or a backwards glance, Jack left, slamming the door behind him. Lacey helped the man to his feet, and Ross came over and set the table to rights. Almost immediately the normal chatter and noise resumed.

The rest of the night was relatively uneventful, with only three other brawls which were easily broken up. As Ross gave last call, Lacey slipped behind the bar and took some more painkillers. She picked up her tray and returned to the floor before he could question her. She tossed him a smile when he frowned and thankfully, he returned it. He watched her, she knew, but at least he wasn't scowling.

After the doors shut for the night, the calm Lacey had felt before started to waver. She turned slowly to look at Ross and hesitated, and he nodded. Without a word she sat down at the bar, surprised when he poured each of them a glass of his best cognac. After picking up his glass, he gestured for her to do the same.

"No better time for liquid courage than the present," he said, his voice low.

Lacey took a small sip, savoring the amber liquor as it warmed her throat. After taking a long drink, Ross put his glass aside and got the package from his office. He watched her carefully as he pushed it across the bar toward her.

"It's addressed to you," she pointed out, hands clasped in her lap. "Maybe it has nothing to do with me. You went to school and worked in New York. Perhaps it's from someone you knew there."

His expression never changed. "All right. I'll open it."

Lacey held her breath as he stripped away the wrapping, and her heart dropped when the gilt picture frame was revealed. Ross laid it flat on the counter and Lacey saw there was an envelope taped to the glass. Frowning, Ross peeled away the envelope, revealing her and Lucas's "official" wedding photo. She took a shaky breath, unable to tear her eyes from the picture. She heard the rustle of paper as Ross opened the envelope.

"Read it, please," she said as she picked up the picture and stared at it.

"Dear Mr. Devlin, this is the second time I've mailed this particular photo. Apparently the first is lost somewhere inside the US Postal Service. We both know the woman in the photo is the same woman you claim is your wife, and we both know she isn't your wife. If you care for her at all, as I suspect you do, I urge you to have her contact me. If her husband were to discover her whereabouts, I can assure you his reaction wouldn't be pleasant." He paused, took a breath, and held up a business card. "It's signed simply, Dennis Lechter."

Lacey took another sip of her cognac, amazed that she hadn't dissolved into tears or hysterics or rushed home to get her "go" bag and hit the road. Then again, she'd had nearly two weeks to prepare for this, and having someone with her was a whole different scene than if she'd been alone. She looked at the photograph from her wedding. Now she saw how contrived it looked, and wondered why she'd never noticed before. She ran her finger slowly over the glass then put the picture aside.

"Lacey?"

Ross's voice was low, and she looked up when he placed his hand over hers. Suddenly, she knew what she was going to do, but there was something else she had to do first.

"So we're clear," she began softly, "you *didn't* sleep with Renee."

He wound his fingers through hers. His gaze was direct and unwavering. "No, I didn't."

"Why not?"

His expression didn't change, not even a little bit. "Because I realized as soon as I touched her that it wasn't Renee I wanted to touch. It was *you* I wanted my hands on, not *her*."

She slipped off the barstool and walked around to where Ross stood, her heart fluttering in a crazy rhythm. She laid her hands on his chest, smoothing the fabric of his shirt with absent strokes, her gaze focused on the buttons. Slowly, she slid her hands up and over his shoulders, and wound her fingers around his neck. His skin was smooth and warm and she closed her eyes as she imagined what the rest of him would feel like. She dragged her hands back down over his shoulders and her breathing quickened.

He stiffened when she began to unbutton his shirt and gently grasped her wrists. "Lacey, you don't have to—"

"Shh," she whispered. When he didn't release her she pressed her lips to his fingers, then turned her face to his. He was stiff, unyielding, but she continued on, standing on tiptoe. She found and kissed his mouth. At first there was no response, but when she ran her tongue over his lower lip he sucked in a breath. He released her wrists and cupped her face. She looked at him then, and the depth of emotion she saw reflected in his eyes made her insides coil. Her pulse pattered against her windpipe and she stroked his beard. "I...still...want you..."

It was obvious he remembered the phrase. She gripped his waist as he thrust his fingers into her hair, his mouth descending on hers with breathtaking intensity. The feel and the scent and the taste of him made her dizzy, and heat coiled low in her belly. She finished unbuttoning his shirt and warm pulses shot through her when she contacted his skin. As she stroked his chest Ross growled low in his throat, an animal sound that sent shivers of anticipation through her. He deepened the kiss, and she was helpless to resist him.

A startled cry escaped her when his arms locked beneath her derriere and lifted her up. She gripped his muscular shoulders, her legs encircling his waist as she looked down, her hair falling like a curtain around them. His breathing was ragged, as was hers, his gaze hot on her face.

"If you don't want this," he began in a rough whisper, "stop me now." For an answer she lowered her head, nipping softly at his bottom lip as she settled herself more intimately against him. He closed his eyes and groaned, his hands moving over her backside. "Lacey–"

She slid her tongue past his lips and that was all it took. He strode from behind the bar, across the room and up the stairs with her still wrapped around him, as if she weighed nothing. She had no idea how he got the door to his apartment open, but once inside he kicked it shut. He marched across the room and fell onto the bed, leaning on his elbows to avoid crushing her. He plundered her mouth ruthlessly, as if he demanded her very soul. Lacey let go of her fears and surrendered to him.

Ross felt her yielding and pulled back, searching her face for any sign of uncertainty or apprehension. Her gaze was warm and completely trusting, a small smile on her mouth. He brushed the hair from her brow and simply stared at her. He trailed a finger over her cheek then traced the outline of her lips.

"I don't want this to be a one-time thing," he whispered.

Her lashes fluttered down and she kissed the fingertip that lingered near her mouth. "Neither do I," she replied, her voice husky. "Now quit talking and kiss me..."

It was all the urging he needed. Their tongues met and fire shot through him as her hips moved to accommodate him more fully. He felt the heat of her, and the need to feel her skin against his nearly overwhelmed him. He moved carefully and deliberately until he was on all fours over her, their lips never separating. Then he put a hand behind her back and sat back on his heels, pulling her to a sitting position. A murmur of protest escaped her when his lips left hers, until she realized what he was doing.

He hooked his fingers in the bottom of her t-shirt, pulled it up and over her head in one smooth motion, and tossed it aside. She moved to unfasten her bra but he stayed her hand and shook his head. When she opened her mouth to object he silenced her with a kiss, all the while pushing her slowly onto her back. Once he felt her yield again, his mouth trailed leisurely down the slender column of her throat as his hands cupped her breasts. He felt the hardening of her nipples through the fabric of her bra as his thumbs rubbed rhythmically. Her fingers twined in his hair and a gasp of pleasure escaped her as he kissed each rounded swell.

She was panting when he stood up, her eyes hooded as she watched him move to the end of the bed. After kicking off his shoes and shrugging out of his shirt, he removed her boots and socks. He massaged first one instep, then the other. Then he slid his hands up her calves and thighs, and her stomach muscles contracted involuntarily when he unfastened her jeans. He straddled her legs and pressed his mouth to her belly as he worked the pants down over her hips, his lips following as each new inch of skin was exposed. When he looked up, he saw her eyes were closed, teeth worrying her lower lip and hands fisted in the thick down comforter. Her jeans fell to the floor and he stood up, his eyes roving over the sleek legs, the rounded hips, the narrow waist and ample bosom. His hands itched to stroke every inch of her skin, to hear her moan with pleasure as he taught her how it was supposed to feel when two people made love. There would be no fear here, no domination, just pleasure.

"Turn over," he said. She gazed at him for a moment, her tongue darting out to wet her lips, but she did as she was told. She rested her cheek on her hands, and waited.

Ross straddled her again, then brushed the mass of curls aside to expose her neck and back. He leaned over and placed hot, wet kisses along her shoulder and the curve of her neck, stopping to nibble her earlobe as he nimbly unfastened her bra. Her skin was so soft. His fingers moved across her shoulder blades and downward, his lips following, leisurely and unhurried. By the time he reached her lower back she was trembling, and he paused.

"Cold?" He smiled when she shook her head. He chuckled and continued his exploration. "Good. Because if you are, it means I'm not doing something right."

"I'll let you know if you do something wrong." Her voice was hushed and he laughed softly.

He ran his hands over her backside, the fabric of the white bikini panties shimmering in the dimly lit room. When he slipped his fingers inside the waistband she tensed and inhaled sharply as he slowly retreated from her, removing them and letting them fall to the floor. For a moment he stared at her, and the sight of that firm, rounded bottom did strange things to his heartbeat. She looked even better naked than she did in her jeans, and *that* was saying something.

When he came back to his senses, he smiled and rubbed his hands together. As far as he was concerned, this was where things really got started. He slipped out of his jeans and briefs, fully aware that she was watching him. He hardened and throbbed. Her eyes widened slightly and then she closed them, her teeth sinking into her lower lip when he slid one hand over each calf. The bed dipped as he straddled her legs again, and a tremor went through her when he placed a kiss behind one knee, then the other, his tongue leaving a hot trail up the back of her thigh and over her derriere. She jumped when he nipped gently at one rounded buttock, then she settled back with a sigh as he pressed his lips into the small of her back. His tongue darted out as he gradually worked his way up her spine, and her body trembled beneath him.

Lacey was certain she would die from this sweet torment. Never in her life had she felt anything like this, her body so alive it was hyper-sensitive to each touch, each kiss; each caress. When he nuzzled her ear again she turned her head, seeking his lips. She found his mouth and rolled slowly onto her back, her arms lacing around his shoulders. It felt like she was on fire everywhere he touched, yet she didn't want him to stop. She massaged the muscles of his back and tried to press him closer.

Unable to move him, she dropped her arms to the side. His kiss stole her breath and her strength. She was so lost in him she didn't realize he'd removed her bra until his hand touched her bare breast. Her back arched and a low moan escaped her. His fingers plucked softly at the taut peak, sending urgent, spiraling sensations humming along every nerve. He pressed his lips to the pulse that raced in her throat, and then ran his tongue down to her cleavage as he cupped her breasts, pressing them inward and upward.

"Ooh...Ross," she said, her voice breaking as he nuzzled her, "how long are you going to...torture me...like this?"

He lifted his head and smiled. He rolled the dusky nipples between thumb and forefinger and chuckled when she gasped softly. "As long as it takes," he replied in a throaty whisper. "Trust me, Lacey. I'm just getting started."

Lacey burned as maddening, mind-numbing pleasure pulled her insides tight. When she thought she could stand no more, he dipped his head and his tongue swirled lazily around one nipple, then the other. His mouth traveled back and forth, slowly, deliberately. A soft cry was wrenched from her lips and she felt him smile. It was infuriating. He wasn't in any hurry, even though she could feel him, hot and hard, against her leg. Without thinking, she bent one knee and her thigh rubbed against him. He froze, but only for a moment.

He nibbled her breast, his whiskers tickling and sending shivers over her skin. When his hand slid over her belly she jerked, and his fingers came to rest at the juncture of her thighs. The ache that had settled there at his first kiss sharpened intensely, and she moved against his hand. She didn't just want him...she *needed* him.

Ross waited, knowing she was going crazy and that he was half crazy himself. But he loved her breasts, loved the weight and warmth of them, the way her nipples hardened against his tongue. Even so, he longed to be inside her, to have her tight around him, to feel her muscles contracting as she climaxed. He was a patient man. There was only one first time with a woman, and he was determined that his first time with Lacey would be as special as he could possibly make it. Tonight, he would set the standard.

Despite his determination, maintaining his composure became increasingly difficult. Her breathless cries and moans of pleasure steadily chipped away at his resolve. As he gently suckled her, he ran his fingers through the crisp hair at the juncture of her thighs but went no further, and smiled when she growled, clearly frustrated. Her hands clutched the comforter, her hair in wild disarray. He looked up and saw her watching him with passion-glazed eyes, her lips parted slightly and her breathing ragged. His gaze fastened on her mouth and he lifted his head.

When his tongue met hers he slipped one finger between her legs, and lust surged through him. Her flesh was hot and wet and he buried his face in her neck with a groan. Gritting his teeth, he probed gently, rewarded when he grazed that tiny nub of flesh and her hips jerked. With feather light strokes he massaged the swollen button, and her legs quivered in response. Frantic whimpers rose in her throat and her fingers dug into his shoulders.

"Please . . ." she gasped. "Ross...I need you..."

He moved slowly, deliberately. His fingers continued to stroke her as he knelt between her thighs and sat back on his heels. Picking up a small, silver packet from beside him, he opened it and took the condom out. Lacey's eyes widened slightly as she watched him put it on. His actions seemed to inflame her even more, and a wicked smile curved her mouth.

"Next time, I get to do the honors," she said in a sultry voice.

He only nodded as his fingers resumed their intimate caress. Air hissed out from between her teeth as her hips moved to meet his hand.

"Oh, Ross...that feels so good..."

He smiled as she closed her eyes and gave over to the pleasure. He slid one hand beneath her bottom and pulled her toward him until her backside rested against his upper thighs. Slowly, he moved forward and lifted her hips to meet him.

Lacey felt him pressed against her, nearly beside herself as the torturous pleasure threatened to snap her in half. She planted her feet on the mattress on either side of him and pushed her hips up. He surged forward and came into her powerfully. Lacey cried out as he shuddered and groaned deep in his throat. He clenched his jaws and remained absolutely still. Then, after a few delicious seconds, he started to move. Slowly, rhythmically, he pulled back until he nearly left her body, and then gradually pushed forward. It was agonizing, it was wonderful, and it was driving her crazy.

Ross had never imagined making love could be like this. She was so tight around him, and everything inside of him wanted to speed things up, but he forced himself to hold back. It was the sweetest agony, this intense, tender mating. It was unbearable and it was heaven, and he never wanted to stop feeling this.

"Ross! Please...!"

He picked up the pace, just a bit, and her hips matched his rhythm. Her cries grew more fevered and frantic, fueling his desire. With a mighty thrust he forced her onto her back, seating himself to the hilt as her legs wrapped around him. He found her lips and matched the thrusting of his body into hers with the thrusting of his tongue into her mouth as her fingers fisted in his hair.

He pressed his face into her neck, his hands cupping her bottom as he lifted her slightly. He felt the entrance to her womb and sucked in a breath as she shuddered beneath him. For a moment he thought he was going to lose control. He went absolutely still and took a deep, steadying breath.

"Oh...please...don't stop...!"

Her impassioned plea nearly snapped his resolve, and his hips jerked involuntarily. He clenched his jaw and left her body, unable to contain his own groan of frustration as he did so. Leaning on his elbows, he laid his brow against her chest as he got hold of himself.

Without a word he stretched out beside her, his hand stroking leisurely over her breast. She stared at him, her eyes wide and uncomprehending.

"Well?" he asked. "What are you waiting for?" She blinked and he smiled. He put a hand behind her neck, pulled her close and kissed her deeply. Backing away a fraction, he gazed into her eyes. "You're in control now, Lacey. You have the power. Don't be afraid to use it."

She stared at him for a moment, and then something in her expression shifted. After getting to her knees she straddled him, but didn't mount him. She planted her hands on his chest and a wicked smile curved her mouth as she began to rub against him. He saw the flush of pleasure in her cheeks, her eyes closing as he lifted his head to suckle her breast. Her teasing drove him crazy, and finally he could stand no more.

When she moved forward he arched his back and thrust up. Lacey gasped and froze as he entered her, her mouth open, hair wild about her shoulders, eyes locked with his. She bit her lip and began to move. She proceeded slowly, cautiously, and Ross was unprepared for the amazing sensations that washed over him. Needing to touch her, he slipped one hand between their bodies, his thumb rubbing her clitoris, while the other hand stroked the round firmness of her breasts.

Her tempo increased and she leaned forward on her hands. Her breasts were so close, and she sucked in a breath when he took the sensitive tip into his mouth, suckling her. Her moans reached a fever pitch and he moved more quickly, his body in complete control now. He felt her shudder and she reared up. Her muscles contracted around him and she threw her head back.

Lacey couldn't have stopped had she wanted to, the tension in her building to a frenzied pitch. It wound low in her belly, expanding, contracting, and expanding again, tingles traveling along every nerve ending until her entire body hummed. The feel of his fingers on her, of his body joined with hers was too much. His movements were hard and fast, their bodies moving together in a breathtaking rhythm.

"Oh, Lacey...that's it...come on, baby..." Hearing the urgency in his voice, the coil between her legs broke, spiraled outward, and just when she thought she'd reached the limits of sensation, she exploded. She shuddered violently and cried out as intense, throbbing pleasure traveled through her like lightning. Then she felt Ross stiffen, and he gripped her hips as he climaxed. Groaning, he thrust up, lifting both of them off the mattress and sending her reeling. Lacey moaned softly as the shockwaves finally softened and she collapsed against him.

She rested her head on his shoulder, her limbs like rubber. They were both breathing heavily, heartbeats drumming in tandem. They lay like this for several moments, then, in one swift motion, Ross flipped them over. Their bodies were still joined as he leaned on his elbows and looked at her.

His expression was so serious that Lacey felt a flutter of nervousness in her stomach, and she looked at him in silent question. His eyes narrowed as he lightly trailed one finger over her skin.

"You are so beautiful," he said at last, his gaze fastened on her mouth, "and so very dangerous."

Lacey blinked. "What do you mean?"

He rubbed his thumb over her bottom lip and studied her, a frown creasing his brow. "You make me feel and think things that scare me."

"Such as?"

"Such as...what would it be like to make love to you every night, and wake up with you every morning?" Lacey gulped and he stared at her mouth again, his eyes narrowing ever so slightly. "Such as...why is it when I'm with another woman only my body is involved, but when I'm with you...my body, my heart, my mind, *everything's* involved?"

Lacey squeezed her eyes shut. "It's the novelty," she ventured in a whisper.

"I don't think so." His voice was hard and she looked up, surprised by the vehemence of his tone. He framed her face with his hands. His expression softened and he searched her eyes, as if he would find an answer to his questions there. "I've always been a confirmed bachelor, Lacey. I never wanted anything more, until I kissed you."

She held her breath as his mouth covered hers, teasing, tasting, and then he pulled away. After brushing his knuckles over her cheek he got up and went to the bathroom, closing the door softly behind him.

While he'd been near she'd been warm, but now a chill went through her and it went deeper than an absence of his body heat. The sensation spurred her off the bed and into an anxious search for her clothes. She found her panties and bra, and then her t-shirt. After putting them on she looked for her jeans and frowned. She got down on all fours and peered under the bed.

"Why is it every time I walk into this room, I'm greeted by the sight of your cute butt up in the air?"

Lacey jumped and tossed him a reproachful look as she pulled her jeans from beneath the bed. He stood in the door of the bathroom, still naked, and the sight of him made her breathing hitch. She sat on the edge of the mattress and put one foot in the leg of her jeans.

"Why are you getting dressed?" he asked.

She went absolutely still when she saw his scowl. "I – I was cold."

A smile twitched about his mouth as he walked slowly toward her, and it was all she could do to keep her eyes on his face. When he stood in front of her, he leaned over and yanked on her jeans, then tossed them on a nearby chair. He extended his hand to her, his eyes twinkling as she looked at him, uncertain. Finally, she put her fingers in his and he pulled her to her feet. She gulped and averted her gaze, focusing on his chest, hoping he wanted her to stay but unwilling to ask.

"That's why I have a down comforter, Lace. It's really warm when you're *underneath* it."

She glanced at him, and heat crept up her neck at his meaningful smile. His expression said much but she needed to hear him say it. "I...I wasn't sure you'd want me to stay."

He put a finger under her chin and tipped her face to his. His lips feathered over her cheeks, her brow, her lips. His hands slid under the hem of her shirt and she lifted her arms as he peeled it off. Next came her bra, and when he slid her panties down and pressed a kiss to her belly she sucked in a breath, amazed that she could want him so much, so soon after they'd just made love. He stood and his arms wound around her waist as he pulled her close, the friction of their skin sending desire radiating through her again.

"Didn't you hear anything I said?" he asked, nuzzling her ear. "I want you to stay." His lips found hers, and her arms snaked around his neck as he kissed her. When he pulled away she whimpered in protest and he laughed softly. "Get back in bed, Lacey. I'm not finished with you yet."

Chapter Fifteen

It was near dawn when Lacey slipped out of bed as Ross slumbered peacefully. Quite accustomed to moving about a room silently, she dressed and then went to the desk. She pulled out a sheet of paper, wrote him a note and folded it carefully, before laying it on the night stand. He murmured in his sleep and rolled toward her. Lacey looked at him and stroked his hair. For a moment she considered abandoning her plans, but only for a moment. She brushed her lips over his brow, picked up her jacket and purse, and left the apartment.

***

Sunlight streamed through the windows when Ross finally pulled himself from the deepest sleep he'd had in months. Yawning, he stretched and then reached for Lacey. His eyes snapped open when all he found were cold sheets. He sat up, looked around the apartment, but there was no sign of her. He swung his legs over the edge of the bed and reached for his pants, stopping when he saw the note on his night stand. He stared at it for a couple seconds then picked it up. His heart began a hard, steady drumming inside his chest.

Ross, please don't be angry with me. I need to put my past to rest before I can move on, and I want to move on. Thank you for being there for me, for making me stand up for myself, for helping me realize I don't have to run. I'll be back soon, and you can scowl at me then. Lacey.

"Oh, no," he said as he reread the flowing script. "No, Lacey, no." He jumped to his feet and went to the window. Sure enough, the Jeep was gone. "Shit."

He picked up the phone and dialed her number, then slammed the receiver down when no one picked up after nearly twenty rings. *Damn it, why won't you get a cell?* He frowned, picked up the phone, and dialed another number. His foot tapped the floor, and finally a man picked up on the other end.

"Cooper's Ridge Airport."

"Mike, this is Ross. You haven't seen Lacey by any chance, have you?"

"As a matter of fact, I did. She chartered Dave to take her to Anchorage, and they left about two hours ago. Is something wrong, Ross?"

Ross cursed under his breath and ran a hand through his hair. "No. Thanks, Mike." He hung up the phone and stared out the window, cold barbs of fear spearing through him. "What are you doing, Lacey? What the hell are you doing?"

***

Lacey leaned back in her seat, the drone of the plane's engines lulling her nearly to sleep. She shook herself, stood up, and walked toward the lavatory; a flight attendant gave her a smile as she passed. She took her credit card and slid it into the slot for the phone. After taking the handset out of its cradle she slipped into one of the empty rest rooms. She locked the door and lowered the toilet lid, dialing Frank Milligan's cell phone as she took a seat. She knew he might not answer because he wouldn't recognize the number, and said a quick prayer he wouldn't look at the display first. She fidgeted as she waited for Frank to pick up the line, and when he finally did so relief swept over her.

"Hello?"

She pulled in a breath. "Frank, it's me."

"Lindsay? My God, I'm glad you called. You said you'd contact me when you got settled, and that was nearly six months ago. I've been worried sick about you."

The concern was clear in his voice, and she smiled. "I'm sorry, Frank. I was going to call, but things haven't quite worked out as I'd hoped. I thought I was settled, but it turns out I might not be."

His reply was immediate. "What can I do? Do you need money, new documents, what?"

"Not yet and hopefully not at all. What I *do* need is a favor."

"Anything."

Lacey paused and steeled herself against the guilt simmering inside her. She didn't want to do this, but she had little choice unless she wanted to run again. "I need you to find out everything you can about a Dennis Lechter. He's a suit for Parker-Raines."

"I know who he is," Frank replied, his voice conveying obvious distaste. "He's handling the merger for PR. How do *you* know him?"

Because life sucks and Fate has a twisted sense of humor. "I ran into him and he recognized me. *How* I don't know. Now he wants me to contact him or he says he'll tell Lucas where I am."

Frank was silent for a moment. "What does he want?"

Lacey sighed and rubbed a hand over her eyes. "I have no idea." Again the line was silent, and she could tell Frank's mind was working furiously.

"Where are you now, Lindsay?" he finally asked.

Lacey chuckled. "About thirty thousand feet. I'm on my way to New York."

"What? Why?"

She sighed. "I'd rather confront him in his territory, than have him come into mine and unwittingly lead someone to me. I'm planning to meet with him and I'm hoping you'll find something for me to bargain with."

"Does he know you're coming?" Frank asked.

"No. I'll be landing at JFK in about two hours."

He didn't reply for several seconds, his tongue clicking against his teeth. "Hmm, I think I can help you. An ass like Lechter is bound to have a past." He paused. "Y'know, I wanted to mail your divorce papers to you, but I didn't know where to send them. Why don't I send them along with whatever I dig up?"

Lacey sucked in a breath. "It's over?"

"Yep."

"He didn't contest it?"

Frank laughed, a sinister laugh, and she held her breath. "He did, but when I met with him and his lawyer, he had a change of heart. I guess he wasn't keen about his abuse becoming public knowledge. The pictures were especially convincing." Frank clicked his tongue again several times. "I knew things weren't *good* between you two, but I wish you would've told me how bad it really was, Lindsay. I could've helped you."

Tears stung and she blinked them back. "No, you couldn't have," she replied. "I had to help myself first."

He seemed to ponder that for a moment then sighed. "One day you have to tell me how you got copies of the medical and police reports; reports that supposedly no one else could find. That was a stroke of genius."

Her past rushed by in a blur of fragmented memories that chilled her. "Money opens a lot of doors," she whispered.

"That it does," Frank replied in a low, serious voice. "But let's get back to the matter at hand. I'll have my researcher get on it right away. Where do you want me to send the information when I get it?"

Hope blossomed. If anyone could help her it was Frank. "How long will it take?"

"I can have it by the end of the day, barring any major power outages or computer crashes. There's a reason I pay my head geek almost as much as a partner. I can have it to you by tomorrow morning. I'll fly it in by private courier if I have to."

Tears welled, and this time she didn't bother to blink them back. "Thank you, Frank. I owe you my life, again."

"No, you don't. You have no idea how much I enjoyed trumping that little bastard, and not just once, but twice. Now, where should I send it?"

"I'm staying at the Waldorf."

"Under what name?"

"Elle Jamison." She heard him scribbling and smiled. "You wouldn't be able to hand deliver that, would you? It'd sure be nice to see a familiar face."

"I wish I could. It'd be nice to see you, too. Dallas isn't nearly as pleasant a place without you in it."

She let out a disappointed sound. "Well, if your schedule opens up I'll treat you to dinner. If not, some other time."

He laughed softly. "Deal. Now, you'd better get off the line before you max out your card. Those airline phones are expensive."

"You're right. Thanks again, Frank."

"Anytime, sweetheart. It's been a pleasure doing business with you."

"Bye."

Lacey was smiling when she got back to her seat. With a happy sigh borne of relief she closed her eyes and fell into a peaceful sleep.

* * *

According to her watch, it was seven twenty-three p.m. when she walked into the lobby of the Waldorf Astoria Hotel. Lacey smiled as the doorman tipped his hat to her. After checking in and dropping her bags in her room, she left the hotel to do some shopping. She'd decided when she met with Dennis Lechter, she didn't want to look like a small-town girl. She wanted to look like a woman in control of her own life, a woman who didn't intimidate easily. At that thought she laughed softly. Boy, appearances could be deceiving.

As she strolled down the street her thoughts turned to Ross, and her cheeks warmed. What a night they'd spent! Just the memory of their lovemaking made her heart race. Now she understood why Renee kept coming back. Granted, including Ross, she'd only had three lovers in all her life, but she could honestly say she'd never felt anything like what she had with Ross.

She'd hated to leave like she had, but if she'd told Ross of her plans she knew he would have insisted on helping. He was already more involved than she wanted, and she couldn't risk his getting hurt. This was her mess, and she was determined to clean it up.

When she returned to the hotel room her arms were laden with packages. She dumped them on the bed, collapsed in a chair and kicked her feet up. A clock on the night stand read 9:30 p.m., and she glanced at the phone. She took a deep breath and sat on the bed, her hand hesitating over the receiver. Nearly a minute passed before she found the courage to pick it up and dial the bar. Ross answered on the second ring.

"Lights."

Her voice failed her and she gulped, and Ross immediately responded. "Lacey? Lacey is that you?"

Oh, how she loved his voice. "Hi." It was all she could manage; her throat was tight and growing tighter.

"Wait. Let me change phones." She heard the jukebox, then a click as he picked up the phone in his office. "Lacey, where the hell are you? I've been going out of my mind here." He sounded hurt, worried, and a little angry.

She bit her lip then cleared her throat softly. "Ross...I'm sorry."

"Where are you?" he asked, his voice low.

She sighed. "I can't tell you that."

"You're either in Dallas or New York. Now which is it?"

Her pulse began to notch up. "Why? Are you going to come here? Look, I don't want you any more involved in this than you already are." He was silent for a few moments, and for a second Lacey thought he'd hung up on her. Uncertainty flared in her chest. "Ross, are you there?"

When he spoke, his voice was tightly controlled and she winced. "Lacey, I'm *already* involved, up to my eyeballs." He took a deep breath. "Didn't last night mean *anything* to you?"

She gasped softly. "You know it did."

"Then why did you leave? Damn it, Lacey, you don't have to do this alone."

His anger stung, and so did her eyes. "Yes, I *do*. I have to close this chapter of my life, for good, before I can start writing any new ones."

"So what was I? Research?"

Lacey blinked and the tears rolled slowly down her cheeks. She felt as if the wind had been knocked out of her and her lungs started to burn. The line was silent, but she knew he was still there. She finally took a soft breath and sniffled. "I'm sorry, Ross. I wanted you to know I was okay. I'll talk to you later."

"Lacey, wait..."

She dropped the receiver back onto the cradle and dissolved into tears. Rolling onto her side, she pounded the mattress with her fists then pulled a pillow to her chest, and sobbed.

***

The Monday morning news droned in the background as Lacey looked at her reflection. The deep chocolate color of the pantsuit looked great against her skin. She put her hair up in a loose chignon, several curls springing loose at her ears. As she slipped into the black leather trench coat she felt ridiculous, like she was the star of a bad James Bond parody. Black leather gloves and large, dark sunglasses completed the ensemble. At any other time this getup would seem absurd, but she wasn't taking any chances. Besides, no one in the City would even notice.

Frank's package had arrived as promised Sunday morning by private courier. Lacey was shocked at what he'd found. After reading a little of what he'd dug up she'd had to stop, her stomach rolling uncertainly. She hated this. It wasn't in her nature to be mean or vicious, and right now she was acting like her ex-husband. The very thought nauseated her. She shoved the papers back into their envelope, tucked them into her purse, and left the room.

She stopped in the lobby long enough to ask the front desk clerk to make several copies of the documents for her, and to have the extras delivered to her room. She doubted she'd need them, but in case she did...

The doorman hailed her a cab and her thoughts centered on Ross as the cabbie headed for Central Park. So far, it was not a good morning. She was nauseated by what she was about to do to Dennis Lechter, but she was also heartsick about what she'd already done to Ross. She felt guilty; not only because she'd left without a word, but because she'd left without a word after spending one of the most amazing nights of her life with him. She'd left him without a waitress; though that was really the least of her worries. He'd been angry when she'd called, and rightly so. She only hoped she'd be able to make it up to him. She hoped he'd let her.

"Here we are, ma'am. Ma'am?"

Lacey shook her head and gave the cabbie a sheepish smile as she handed him the fare. After getting out of the cab, she paused and took a deep breath. She double-checked her pocket for Lechter's business card, then squared her shoulders and started walking.

The paved path was smooth and wide; joggers and people with fat babies bundled in their strollers passed her. Even in winter the park was beautiful, and Lacey smiled at an elderly woman feeding one of the many flocks of pigeons that lived in the city. Squealing children played on a nearby playground as the adults watched, and a snowball whizzed by her followed by several young boys. She paused and grinned as they ran by in a tornado of arms and legs, then she started walking again. In a small square near the center of the park Lacey stopped, found a payphone and dialed Lechter's office.

"Good morning, Parker-Raines. How may I help you?"

"Dennis Lechter, please."

"One moment."

Lacey took another deep breath. If she was this nervous about speaking to him over the phone, she hated to imagine what she'd be like face to face. *Get it together, Lacey.*

"Mr. Lechter's office."

Lacey throat went taut, and it was a moment before she could speak. "Dennis Lechter, please."

"Mr. Lechter is in a meeting," the secretary replied in that monotone usually reserved for telemarketers. "May I take a message and have him return your call?"

"No."

The woman seemed startled. "Excuse me?"

"Tell him it's Lacey. I'm sure he'll take the call."

"But..."

Lacey made an exasperated sound. "Just tell him." There was a pause.

"One moment."

While she waited, Lacey popped another couple of quarters into the phone to avoid being interrupted. As the last coin slid into the slot there was a click and her nerves went taut.

"Lacey," he said, drawing out her name as if it had several a's in it, "so good to hear from you. I take it you finally got my package?"

His flippant tone kicked her from apprehensive to irritated. Sarcasm usually wasn't her style, but it seemed appropriate at this particular moment. "No, this is a *social* call. I wanted to ask you if you had any plans for lunch." He chuckled, and her irritation began to morph. Now she was angry. This was her life she was trying to protect, and he was laughing.

"I see you haven't lost your sense of humor," he said.

"No, but I have lost patience."

"Then I'll cut right to the chase..."

"No," she interrupted. "I want to speak face to face, not over the phone."

He was silent for a moment. "I can't get away right now. I'm right in the middle of an important meeting. And a trip to Alaska is out of the question for at least a week."

"Good, because I'd rather not have you back in my territory anyway."

"Then how—"

"I'm in New York," she said as she glanced at her watch. It was nearly 11:30 a.m. "I'll be in the square in the middle of the park for another hour. If you're not here by then, I'll assume we have nothing to discuss." Before he could reply she hung up, but it was several moments before she released the handset. Finally, she let go and found a park bench at the edge of the square.

Once her nerves were calm, she searched out one of the many street vendors and bought a cup of coffee. She returned to the bench, sat down, and took out the papers Frank had sent. Forcing herself to remain emotionally detached, she perused them again, committing certain particulars to memory. When she was certain she had them down, the papers went back in her bag and she sipped her coffee.

By the time he showed up she'd relaxed almost completely, enjoying the beautiful snow-covered landscape. As soon as she spotted him her heart vaulted into her throat and she rose. For a moment, she thought about bolting and her body tensed for flight. In the end, her brain won out and she stayed put. She put on what she hoped was an expressionless mask and watched him as he approached. When he gave her a smile she did not return it.

He stopped when he was directly in front of her. His eyes traveled the length of her, widened slightly, and she returned his gaze, unblinking.

"Well, well," he drawled. "This is a far cry from the freshly-scrubbed, dressed-down woman I met in Alaska. I'd thought then that flannel and blue jeans suited you fine, but this...you are gorgeous. Yes, now you look like the wife of a billionaire. I'm impressed."

"Don't be." She was surprised at the calmness of her voice. "What do you want?"

He seemed taken aback for a moment, and switched to charm mode. Giving her a wide smile he gestured toward the bench. "What? No pleasant 'hello, how are you?' Why don't we sit down and chat a bit?" She sat and crossed her legs, giving him a bored look as he sat beside her. "You're not in the best of moods today, are you, Lacey?"

"What. Do you. Want?"

He turned toward her and draped one arm across the back of the bench. "All right. If that's the way you want to play, fine." She remained silent as he studied her, and it was several moments before he spoke. "You know, your husband is not a pleasant man to deal with, Lacey. Or should I call you Lindsay?"

"Lindsay Davenport no longer exists, and if my *ex*-husband was a pleasant man, I wouldn't have moved to Alaska and changed my name, would I? Now, what do you want?"

He nodded, a small smile twitching about his mouth, and she wanted to hit him.

"Well," he began slowly, "your husband is making some rather outrageous demands. Parker-Raines is so desperate to have this merger go through, they're telling me to give him whatever he wants, regardless of the cost. I don't want to do that."

She made lazy circles in the air with one hand. "So you come to me because...?"

"I'm going to meet with him in a few weeks to finalize the details. I want you to give me something I can use to get him to...ease up a little, lighten his demands."

Lacey stared at him, disbelieving. "*You're* going to blackmail *Lucas*?" She blinked.

Lechter appeared offended. "Blackmail, that's such a crass way to describe it."

"But accurate."

He ignored her interruption. "I prefer to think of it as...*creative persuasion.*"

"No," she said flatly.

Lechter's smile vanished. "No?"

"No."

"Just like that?"

She pressed her mouth into a thin line, unable to believe Lechter's stupidity and arrogance. "Just like that."

He smiled indulgently and covered her hand with his. "Lacey, I'm only trying to protect my company's interests."

She jerked away from him, her eyes narrowing. "And I'm trying to protect my *life*. Forgive me if I don't think the two are comparable." She stared at him for a moment, her breathing fast and shallow. "Do you want to know what Lucas gave me for my 30th birthday, Mr. Lechter?" He looked puzzled, but inclined his head. "A brand new Z8 Coupe, fully loaded."

"That's very generous."

She felt tears sting as fear and anger churned inside of her. "Indeed. He drove it when he picked me up from the hospital. Of course, I couldn't drive it because of my broken arm, the broken arm he'd given me the night before." Lechter's mouth opened in surprise and Lacey laughed. "That's right. And that wasn't the first time he put me in the hospital, nor the last. You have *no* idea who you're dealing with."

For a moment he stared at her, apparently at a loss, and then his expression hardened. "I'm sorry for what you went through, but that has little to do with me and the present situation."

"The hell it doesn't," she said, anger warming her chest. "I have good reason to fear my husband, and if you had *any* sense...you would, too." She paused. "I came here to ask you, as a decent human being, to forget you ever saw me. Please...don't tell my husband where I am."

Lechter watched her carefully, and Lacey thought he'd give in. She prayed silently, hoping beyond hope he'd cooperate. Using his past against him was the last thing she wanted to do, but she was prepared to do just that if she had to. Her heart sank when he shook his head.

"I'm sorry, Lacey. As much as I dislike wife-beaters, I can't let emotions get in the way of business. Give me something I can use to soften Lucas up, or I'll tell him where you are."

She let out the breath she'd been holding and her chin dropped. Tears welled but she forced them down, blinking rapidly as she pulled the papers from her bag. "No, you won't." She handed the sheaf to Lechter and got to her feet. He stared, uncomprehending, then looked at her questioningly.

"What are these?"

She'd seen Lucas do this before, swoop in for the kill when he had the person right where he wanted them. It had always made her wince, the gloating way in which he felled an opponent. Now, however, what she'd seen would serve her well. Taking a deep breath, she steeled herself.

"You were quite a handful when you were a teenager, weren't you, Mr. Lechter?" She heard the papers rustle and his sharp intake of breath as he realized what they were. "Lewd acts with a minor, and at the tender age of thirteen. But that *is* what you were charged with. Of course, the original charge was forcible sodomy, on a ten year old boy, if I remember correctly." She glanced over her shoulder and wished she could exult in the sickly pallor of his face, but his shock brought her no joy. Regardless, her voice took on a hard edge. "It's lucky you were born when you were. Had you been arrested for something like that today, you'd be facing some far more serious consequences than a slap on the wrist."

He stared up at her, eyes wide and dilated. "Wh-where did you get these?" he asked in a whisper. "Th-these records are s-supposed to b-be s-sealed."

"It doesn't matter where I got them. What matters is I *have* them, copied and ready to be delivered to every executive officer at Parker-Raines, Davenport, and let's not forget the local media." She felt a twinge at the lie, but continued. "Tell me, what would your life be like if your criminal history became public knowledge?"

"You can't do this," he said, staring at the papers in horror. "It would ruin me."

"And I won't, *if* you agree to my terms." She paused, but there was no reaction from the stunned man. "I propose this; you forget you ever saw me, and these records go away. You don't know me, we've never spoken, and I was never in New York. Do we understand each other?" Lechter's hands shook and Lacey actually pitied him. It was terrible to live with a past. She knew; she was there.

Finally, after a long silence, he looked up at her. "I would never have guessed from looking at you that you could be as ruthless as your husband. But then, you had more than seven years to study him, didn't you?"

Lacey looked at the toes of her designer boots. "Even a mouse will fight back when cornered, Mr. Lechter." She closed her eyes, her stomach pitching and heaving. "Please believe me when I say I'm sorry I had to do this, but...you left me little choice."

He stood and laughed, a sharp, ugly sound that made her wince. "Don't apologize. I've always admired a worthy opponent. I underestimated you, Lacey, badly."

He still sounded shaken, but there was a note of respect in his voice and she looked up.

"That was my husband's mistake," she said. "He never thought I'd have the backbone to leave him, but I finally made it happen." She gazed up at the overcast sky and a pigeon flew overhead. "I guess when that survival instinct kicks in, all bets are off."

Lechter stood up, folded the papers and stuffed them in the pocket of his overcoat. "Well, I don't suppose there's anything left for us to talk about," he said at last. "Your secret is safe with me. I don't know you, we've never spoken, and you were never in New York." She merely nodded, and he sighed heavily. "You have no idea what you've done, Lacey. No idea at all."

Lacey's brows rose. "Yes, I do," she replied. "I saved your life. If you'd tried to blackmail Lucas, at the very *least* you'd have lost your job. At the other end of the spectrum, I'd really hate to watch the news and see them pull your body out of the East River."

Lechter laughed, but when her expression didn't change his humor faded. "You're not kidding, are you?"

Lacey finished her coffee and tossed the empty cup in a nearby trash can. When she turned back her expression was deadly serious, and Lechter's eyes widened a bit.

"Let me give you a little advice, Dennis. If you like your limbs the way they are, find another way to convince Lucas to ease up, a *legitimate* way. To understand Lucas a little better, you need to know your place in his world. I was a possession, I was *his*. The only person I *wasn't* protected from was *him*. If anybody else so much as looked at me sideways, they faced his wrath. You, on the other hand, are merely an irritant he has to deal with until the merger is final, kind of like an ant at a picnic. If the ants really bother him, he just steps on them, or he has someone step on them for him." She sighed. "Think about it. He broke my nose and knocked two of my teeth out for spilling champagne on his new Armani suit, and I was his *wife*. I was no threat to him or his livelihood. What do you think he'd do if you tried to mess with his *billion-dollar business*?" Lechter gaped at her, and she gave him a ghost of a smile. "So, you'll forget all about me?" He gulped and gave a short nod. Her smile widened a bit. "Good."

Lacey turned and walked away, but she felt Lechter's eyes on her. When she'd gone about twenty steps she stopped and faced him again, searching for words to verbalize the remorse and regret that pooled coldly inside her. Slowly, she walked back up to him.

"Thank you," she said at last. "And could you do me one more favor?"

Lechter's expression was wary. "Do I have a choice?"

She looked at the ground for a moment. When she turned her gaze back to his she didn't hide her regret. "Don't make the same mistake with Lucas you made with me. And...be careful." Lechter seemed thoroughly confused by her apparent duality. She stared at him for a moment then she turned away, leaving him staring after her open mouthed.

Chapter Sixteen

The flight home was uneventful, if she discounted the businessman in the next seat who kept flirting with her. At least he made her laugh which, after the last couple of days, was a welcome change. He was handsome, but Lacey didn't feel the slightest bit of attraction despite his warped sense of humor. She kept wishing he was Ross.

She'd planned to return to Cooper's Ridge shortly after bidding Lecther goodbye, but she'd been so drained she'd changed her flight to early Tuesday afternoon. In the interim she had done nothing but relax, spending hours in the huge tub, getting a facial and a massage, and indulging in room service. On Tuesday, after a couple hours of shopping and an early brunch at Tavern on The Green, she'd boarded a plane. The flight had a brief layover in Seattle before continuing on to Anchorage, and home.

Home. To her own surprise, she'd come to think of Cooper's Ridge as home, even though she'd been there less than two months. She had the cabin, she had her friends, and a job she enjoyed. After seven years of virtual imprisonment one would think she'd be out to sow her wild oats, so to speak, but that wasn't her. She was a small-town girl at heart, and she liked simple, homey things. Plus, she had Ross. At least, she *hoped* she still had Ross.

The businessman got off in Seattle, much to his disappointment, and Lacey was actually sorry to see him go. For the leg to Anchorage she was stuck next to an elderly lady who was hard of hearing, and spent the better part of an hour telling Lacey in a very loud voice about the problems her son and his wife were having. Lacey didn't think she'd ever been so happy to get off an airplane.

After retrieving her bags, she left the terminal and caught a shuttle to the hangar housing the charter service; anxious to get going. She'd called from New York to reserve a ride back to Cooper's Ridge, and the man had promised to have a pilot waiting. As the mini-bus meandered toward the far reaches of the airport, her foot tapped the floor impatiently. The driver stopped the bus in front of the service, and Lacey gave him a grateful smile and a tip as she disembarked.

The charter service was in a small office inside the hangar, and the door squeaked loudly as Lacey opened it and walked in. Made of corrugated metal and frosted glass, it housed two desks that faced each other, two computers, three filing cabinets, numerous maps, charts and clipboards hanging from hooks on the walls, and one telephone. A second door directly across from the entrance had the company name inscribed on the door in large black letters, with a man's name, Ron Chambers, in smaller script beneath.

The door closed behind her, and a man behind one of the desks tossed aside the crossword he'd been doing as he hopped to his feet. He was short and stocky and he stared at her for a moment before coming around the desk.

"You lost or something, ma'am?" he asked. He pointed behind her. "The main terminal's back that way."

Obviously the man didn't recognize her, and she smiled. She'd forgotten she wasn't dressed in jeans and a sweater, as she had been the first time she'd met him. Wearing a suit of rich hunter green with a cream-colored cashmere sweater, she looked more like she belonged on Wall Street. She put her bags down and shrugged out of her coat.

"Mr. Stein, you don't remember me, do you?" When he shook his head she smiled. "We met Saturday. Dave Jenkins flew me in from Cooper's Ridge. I'm Lacey Jamison."

It took a minute for it to register, and then his eyes went wide. "Wow. You go to New York for a makeover or something? You look like you should be on a runway there, not a runway here."

Lacey blushed and dropped her eyes. "Thank you. Anyway, I called earlier about chartering a flight back to Cooper's Ridge?"

"Oh, right, right." He turned around, grabbed a clipboard and flipped through the papers. "Ah, yes. Here it is, and it looks like you're all set. Pilot's in with the boss, but I'll let him know you're here."

"Thank you."

Stein gave her another once over and shook his head. "You sure look different," he muttered as he turned and entered the office. Lacey heard a brief, muted conversation and a moment later he came back out. "Let me take your bags out to the plane, Ms. Jamison. Pilot'll be out in a minute."

"Thank you. It's those two there."

Stein gave her a smile and picked up her garment bag and overnight case, whistling as he left the office. Perched on the edge of the empty desk, Lacey untied the scarf from around her neck and absently fingered the colorful fabric.

When the owner's office door opened she stood up with a smile, ready to greet the pilot. Her eyes met familiar, piercing blue ones and Lacey's heart stopped. Ross looked surprised, his gaze traveling from the top of her head to the pointed toes of her high-heeled boots and back. She felt her eyes widen as she realized he'd shaved his beard, revealing a sharply squared jaw and chin that made him appear even harsher than he had previously. She gulped. Her hand fluttered self-consciously to her hair, which she'd put up in a French twist, and heat seared her cheeks as he continued his stunned perusal. The owner, obviously having been forewarned, retreated to his office and left the two of them alone.

Lacey's pulse ran a mile a minute, her breathing rapid and shallow. His expression gave no hint as to his feelings, other than shock at her appearance. She was torn. Part of her wanted to run into his arms, and the other part wanted to run away. Taking a deep breath, she averted her eyes.

"Hi," she said in a whisper.

"Hi, yourself."

She blinked several times, still unable to meet his gaze. "Wh-what are you doing here?"

"I was worried about you. I asked Ron to get a hold of me when you called in for a flight to Cooper's Ridge."

Her head snapped up. "And what if I hadn't used this particular service?"

He chuckled. "There are a limited number of services that fly into Cooper's Ridge, Lace. I have friends at all of them."

"Oh." She licked her lips self-consciously and dropped her chin, her mouth suddenly dry. "After our last conversation, I'm...I'm surprised you bothered." She jumped when his finger feathered over her jaw and he tipped her face up. He searched her eyes, took a step closer, and she gulped as his presence engulfed her.

"I bothered. Isn't that enough for now?"

Tears stung and she nodded. Her eyes closed when his hand slipped behind her neck and pulled her close, his arms tightening about her like a protective fortress. She laid her head on his chest and sighed as he buried his face against her hair.

"I was so worried about you, Lacey, and...I've missed you."

A smile blossomed. "I missed you, too." They embraced for several long moments then Ross pulled away. She pressed a hand to his face, his skin smooth beneath her fingers. "You...you shaved your beard." She touched his naked chin. "Why?"

"Spring is coming." She blinked at him and he chuckled. "I know it's a couple of months off, but I'm hot-blooded. I get an early start."

Running her fingers over his cheek again, she smiled. "I like it."

"Good." He grinned. "Now come on, beautiful. Let's go home." He held up her jacket so she could put it on. Lacey nodded and shrugged into the coat with a smile, then linked arms with him as they strolled out of the office and across the tarmac.

"So, how'd everything go?" he asked, his voice neutral. "Lechter grant you a pardon?"

She looked at him out of the corner of her eye. "You figured out I went to New York, eh?"

His expression was somber. "When you hung up on me I used my phone to search for the number on the caller ID and it was the Waldorf. That kind of answered my question."

She sighed. "I guess it would." She went silent, her eyes on the ground as they walked, her insides coiled into knots. He said nothing else and she was content to let it go. She knew it would be a short-lived reprieve.

When they reached the airplane, Ross stood with his hand on the door latch and watched her expectantly. "So...?"

She shrugged and swallowed her misgivings. "Oh, I can't say things went *well*, but yes, I've been granted a stay of execution, so to speak. Mr. Lechter will not be revealing my whereabouts."

Ross tipped his head, studying her with narrowed eyes. "And things didn't go well?"

Lacey gave him a weary look. "Can we talk about this later? It's a long story and I'd really like to go home."

He stared at her for a moment then nodded. "Sure, but first I have to tell you...you look amazing." She blushed and looked away, but he pressed a hand to her cheek and turned her face back. "And I have to do something."

He leaned toward her and her breath caught. "What?" she asked in a whisper.

He smiled as his lips met hers, his mouth warm, soft, and insistent. One hand moved to cup her head as he deepened the kiss, and Lacey flattened her hands against his chest. Heat fanned over her skin as his tongue teased hers. When he pulled away she was breathless and tingling. He opened the door for her, giving her a small bow and a grin.

"Hop in, Lacey. Let's get out of here."

With a short, dazed nod, she climbed into her seat and buckled up. Within minutes, they were off the ground and heading for home.

Lacey was silent as the plane winged through the crystal blue sky. She'd done a lot of thinking while in New York, especially after the telephone conversation she'd had with Ross. After taking a long, hard look at herself, she now wondered if he hadn't been right, at least to some extent. Over the years she'd seen Lucas use so many people. Had she watched it for so long she'd become like her ex-husband? The thought nauseated her.

"You're awfully quiet, Lacey. Lacey?"

Her head snapped around and she stopped chewing her thumbnail. "Huh? Oh, I'm sorry, Ross. I was just...thinking."

He gave her a sidelong glance and an amused smile twitched about his mouth. "Must be something serious, judging by the look on your face."

She turned her gaze back out the window. "Yeah, I guess."

Ross watched her for another moment as she stared into the distance, but he knew she wasn't really with him. Her expression was vague, introspective. He wanted to ask her what had happened in New York, but he decided to wait. If she wanted to talk, he would let her initiate the conversation.

His gaze wandered over her briefly, and again he was surprised at the change. She looked polished, professional, her clothes and makeup perfect for the cutting-edge style that was typical New York. But then, that was probably the look she'd been going for. It was quite a difference from the freshly-scrubbed, blue-jean wearing Lacey he'd gotten used to, which he preferred. This woman was different; beautiful in an almost cold sort of way, and self-assured to the point of near arrogance. If he hadn't known her, he would have admired her beauty from a distance but never approached. A Wall Street businesswoman wasn't his type. At that thought he chuckled, amused by his own hypocrisy.

"What's so funny?" she asked.

Ross laughed again and shook his head. "Just thinking funny thoughts."

She lifted one brow and pursed her lips. "So...want to share?"

He looked at her for a moment. "I was thinking that, looking as you do now, you're really not my type." She blinked at him and he chuckled again. "Just shows how shallow I am, because when you're wearing blue jeans and flannel you're exactly my type."

Lacey snorted softly and rolled her eyes. "Judging a book by its cover?" she teased. Ross didn't reply and she smiled. "That's okay. Looking as I do now, I'm not really my type either."

He laughed as she wrinkled her nose, yanked her scarf off, and pulled the pins from her hair. She shook her head and freed the long curls. Blonde corkscrews tumbled down around her shoulders and Ross's insides tightened. The pink that surged into her cheeks told him she'd seen his change of expression and understood it. She bit her lip and looked down at her hands. A flash of something, guilt, regret, he wasn't sure, darkened her eyes and his heart gave a sharp jerk.

"Lacey, what's changed?" His throat constricted when he saw the apprehension flit over her features.

"A lot has changed," she answered in a low voice.

"I mean, between us." He felt the frown. "Lacey?"

She looked at him, blinked several times then turned away. "Please," she whispered, "we need to talk, but not now. Not here."

He heard the quiver in her voice, and his heart twisted again when she glanced at him. The shadow in her caramel-colored eyes had darkened and she bit her lip. Steeling himself, he gave her a curt nod. "Okay. Name the time and place."

She said nothing and turned her gaze back out the window.

They landed in Cooper's Ridge without incident, but Lacey's continued silence ate away at him. He had the feeling she was going to say she didn't want to see him again, and, while his bachelor ego told him that was fine, another, more sensitive part of him, said that was anything but fine. He'd only known her a few weeks, but he wanted her in his life. He wanted her; period.

When they taxied to a stop, Dave Jenkins ran out of the hangar and stood nearby as Ross shut the engine down and went quickly through his post-flight checks. Once the prop stopped spinning, Dave chocked the wheels. Then he opened Lacey's door and helped her out. In his mid-fifties with salt-and-pepper hair, Dave was a friendly, fatherly sort, and his grin widened as his gaze swept over her. Ross exited the plane and walked around to the other side, trying to keep his concern on a low simmer and off his face.

"Wow. New York looks great on you." Without waiting for a reply he hauled her bags out, and his eyes widened in surprise when Ross took them abruptly from him. Dave started to say something, but Ross shot him a look that stopped him. He glanced uncertainly from one to the other.

"Thanks, Dave," Ross said, wincing inwardly at the curt note in his voice. He cleared his throat and forced a smile. "We'll take care of the post-flight inspection and refueling later." Dave blinked and nodded; his mouth halfway open. Without another word Ross turned and strode toward the Jeep.

Lacey stared after him, her insides pitching. The silence between them had been taut and heavy, and the closer they'd gotten to Cooper's Ridge, the worse it had become. Now, staring at his broad, stiff back she sighed, patted Dave's arm, and gave him an apologetic smile.

"Thanks, Dave," she said. "I think we can take it from here."

Dave glanced at Ross then back at her. "You sure?"

Although she wasn't, she nodded anyway. "Yeah. Thanks again." He touched the brim of his baseball cap with two fingers and headed toward the hangar. Lacey took a deep breath, squared her shoulders, and straightened her spine as she followed Ross.

He stood near the rear of the Jeep as she approached; his face like stone and his eyes unreadable. When she looked at him he stepped away so she could open the hatchback and her heart twisted. Obviously, he was not going to make this easy. She tried, unsuccessfully, to unlock the hatchback, her hands shaking. Finally, his fingers closed over hers and he helped her slide the key into the lock. The contact was brief but it was enough to rattle her nerves, and her resolve. She opened the hatch and moved back, gulping as he moved past her and loaded her bags. When he slammed the door shut she jumped.

"So, when do you want to have this talk?"

His voice was cold, emotionless, and Lacey glanced up at him in surprise. He wasn't looking at her; his eyes were focused on the horizon. She felt her courage evaporate.

"I...I don't know."

"How about tonight?" he asked flatly.

Lacey licked her lips and her heart thudded when he turned those eyes on her. Unable to hold his gaze, she looked down at the snow-covered ground. "What about work?"

"When Ron called me I decided to close the bar for the night." The wistful note in his voice made her head snap up. He sighed and scrubbed a hand over his face. "After your trip, I thought you'd want to spend some time together, alone."

Her mouth opened in dismay. "Oh, Ross...I..."

He interrupted her with a wave of his hand. "Look, Lacey, if you don't want to see me anymore, you can tell me now as well as later. Let's not prolong this."

She was taken aback. "Is that what you think?"

His brows shot skyward and he searched her face, clearly confused. "That's not what you want to talk about?" She blinked at him and shook her head slowly. Ross looked perplexed. "If not that, then what? Why so serious?"

At that her cheeks went hot and she dropped her eyes. The words whirled in her mind but stuck in her throat. Finally, she turned on her heel and opened the driver's door, then slid behind the wheel. She rolled down the window and looked up as he approached. "Come out to the cabin around eight. I'll even make dinner."

He stuffed his hands in his pockets and tilted his head. "Lacey–"

"Please, Ross. It's not that I don't want to see you anymore. It's just...well, after I say what I have to say, *you* may not want to see *me* anymore." The very thought made pain blossom in her chest. She started the engine and tears stung as she pulled away leaving him standing in the parking lot.

***

Lacey checked her appearance in the bathroom mirror one more time, staring at her reflection uncertainly. She looked more like herself, the self she was comfortable with; designer suits and shoes had been stowed in the closet. A bell rang and she jumped, a soft sigh escaping her when she realized it was the timer on the stove. She fluffed her hair one final time and hurried out to the kitchen.

A fire crackled cheerily on the hearth and she tossed another log on as she went by. The wood snapped and hissed as the flames embraced it. She glanced at the kitchen table again, but it was set. The only thing missing was candlelight, but she wasn't planning a romantic rendezvous. She pulled on her oven mitts and took the bubbling pan of lasagna from inside the appliance. The tangy scent of parmesan cheese, tomatoes, and spices drifted up to her. She put the dish aside to cool and slipped the tray of garlic bread into the oven, then tossed her mitts aside and set the timer. There. All she had to do now was wait.

The thought of Ross's impending arrival sent her heart into a painful, steady staccato against her ribs. She looked at the open bottle of wine, poured herself a glass and downed it quickly, the liquid settling warmly in her belly. *Relax, Lacey, you will survive this.* She pulled in a deep, cleansing breath, then filled both glasses and put them on the table. After tweaking the napkins, she walked over to the CD player. She'd just turned the music on when the sound of an engine coming up the road drew her attention, and she moved to the window. She held the curtain aside and watched as Ross parked his truck. When he got out, a she smiled as he strode confidently over to the porch, ruggedly handsome as always.

Before he could knock, she opened the door, and butterflies launched themselves against her insides. Their eyes met and the electricity was instantaneous. The teal colored sweater made his eyes appear even bluer than they were. She leaned against the door, tipped her head and gestured for him to come in. For a moment he didn't move as his gaze swept over her. Finally, he smiled.

"Now that's the Lacey I'm used to," he said. "There's nothing like a pair of great fitting blue jeans on a nice butt." He tipped his head back and sniffed the air, then turned to look at her. "Is that...lasagna?"

She closed the door after he stepped inside. "Yes," she replied with a smile, "and we're ready to eat. Why don't you sit down and have some wine while I take the bread out of the oven?" She walked past him toward the kitchen.

Ross lifted one dark brow, a half smile on his mouth. "Trying to get me drunk?"

Lacey ignored him, turned off the oven, and pulled out the tray of perfectly browned bread. She sliced it, put it in a basket, and handed it to Ross. He held the basket under his nose, inhaled deeply, and sat down at the small table.

"Mmm," he said, "this smells wonderful."

She took the lasagna to the table and put it down on a trivet next to the salad bowl before retrieving a spatula. She stood with the utensil hovering over the food and looked at him.

"How hungry are you?" she asked.

Ross grinned. "Why don't you get yourself some, and I'll eat the rest."

Lacey chuckled, scooped out a large piece of lasagna, and plopped it on Ross's plate. As she served herself, he piled a heap of salad next to the pasta, grabbed a piece of garlic bread, and then waited for her to pick up her fork. After she did he picked up his own and dove in.

They ate in relative silence, though Ross made occasional compliments regarding the meal. She only smiled or nodded in reply, not really hearing his praise, her mind whirling and her stomach in knots. She only hoped the evening turned out as well as the lasagna. As he ate, she continued to mull over what she wanted to say, and the words blended into a verbal goulash inside her head.

"Okay, Lacey," he said. "Lacey!" Her head snapped up. He gave her a tolerant smile, wiped his mouth, and put the napkin aside. "The food was fabulous, but that's not why you invited me here. So, why don't we cut to the chase and get on with it?"

She took another drink of her wine. Truth be told, she was as anxious to get this over with as he was. "Very well. Why don't you refill our glasses and go sit on the couch while I clear the table?" His eyes narrowed on her face and she had to look away as something hard and abrasive materialized in her throat.

"I can help with that," he said.

She gave him a curt shake of her head as she stood, picked up his plate, and placed it in the sink along with her own. "No. Oh, and add another log to the fire, would you please?" She knew he was studying her, but he finally retreated to the living area with their wine. All too soon the table was cleared, the food put away and the dishes in the sink waiting to be washed. She thought briefly about washing them but decided against it. With a silent prayer for strength, she walked over to the couch.

Ross stood in front of the fireplace with his hands on the mantle, the flames turning his skin golden and casting burnished highlights on his dark hair. Her breath caught as she studied him; admiring the strong profile and sheer masculinity. As if feeling her gaze, he turned his head and locked eyes with her. He looked different without his well-kept beard. She focused on his generous mouth and remembered the feel of those lips on hers. Heat surged into her cheeks and she looked away. She took a deep breath and sat down. To her relief he remained standing and turned to face her, his back to the fire.

"Okay, Lacey, this is your show. Talk."

She looked around for her glass of wine, picked it up, and took a long drink. *Liquid courage, that's what they call it, don't they?* Her fingers clutched the cool stem of the crystal goblet, her knuckles white. Finally, after sucking in a huge gulp of air, she stepped off the cliff.

"I did a lot of thinking while I was in New York, especially after you accused me of...of using you for research."

He took a step toward her. "I shouldn't have said that. I was angry, I was worried..."

She looked at him and held up a hand. "It's okay, Ross. Really." She paused and dropped her eyes. "You were right...sort of...I think."

"Lacey—"

"Please, let me finish." She waited until he nodded, his mouth set in a thin line and a frown darkening his brow. Now that she had his undivided attention however, she wasn't sure where to go from this point. Uncertainty gnawed on her gut and her stomach twisted. She got to her feet and started to pace, floorboards creaking softly beneath her feet as she continued. "From what you said the other night, what happened between us was more than...*casual.*" She looked to him for confirmation, and again he nodded.

"For me, it was," he replied. His voice was low and even, but there was an underlying tone that made Lacey wince.

"It was for me, too," she said. "But then, sex, what little I've experienced, has never been casual for me."

"Lacey—"

"Anyway," she rushed on, ignoring his interruption, "what you said made me think, and I'm not certain I liked what I was thinking." She stopped pacing and faced him, forcing herself to look him in the eye. "You're the first man I've been attracted to in more than six years. After Lucas, I wasn't sure I *could* be intimate with a man again, ever. What happened when we were together was amazing. I've never felt...*anything* like what I felt with you."

He frowned. "Is that wrong?"

She bit her lip and looked at the ground. "It is if I did it for the wrong reasons." She waited, but he remained silent, and after a few moments she started pacing again. "It was wrong if I *was* using you, like you said...for research, so to speak."

"Were you?" The tone of his voice made her look up quickly.

"I don't know," she said, stricken. "And *that's* what I really want to talk about." He looked puzzled but said nothing, so she plunged on. "I want to know if all these feelings I have inside me are real, and not some knee-jerk reaction to the chemistry we have or some...*rebound* thing." She stopped pacing and looked at the ceiling, unable to maintain his gaze. "I want to know that I truly care for you, and not because you make me feel safe and protected and beautiful..." Her voice died and her eyes stung. "I can't figure that out and be sexually involved with you at the same time, I can't." She turned her back on him and swiped angrily at her eyes. "I'm sorry."

There was a pregnant pause, and for a moment Lacey thought he'd somehow managed to leave the room without her hearing him. Even so, she couldn't find the courage to turn and see if she was right. Part of her wanted to be right because then she wouldn't have to hear him say they were done.

When he placed his hands gently on her shoulders she tensed, and he started to knead the taut muscles.

"So, you still want to *see* me, you don't want to *sleep* with me." To her surprise, he didn't sound angry. Instead, his voice was warm, rough velvet with a resonance that called to her. Unable to reply she nodded slowly and closed her eyes as he turned her to face him. "Okay. If that's what you want, you got it."

She blinked and looked at him in surprise. His lips curved into small smile and he picked up a lock of hair, slowly rubbing it between his thumb and forefinger. His gaze turned pensive and he pressed a hand to her cheek.

"Allow me to introduce myself," he said softly. "Ross Devlin's the name, and I was wondering...would you like to go out with me sometime? We could have dinner, catch a movie, go for a stroll along the nearly frozen river. You know, typical dating...stuff."

Lacey gaped at him, unable to believe what she was hearing, and he chuckled softly.

"Did you think this would send me running the other direction?" he asked. She nodded, and he grinned. "Well, Lacey, you were wrong. However, it's been a while since I courted a woman, so you'll have to forgive me if I'm a little rusty."

"I...don't...I don't understand."

He framed her face with his hands. "Hey, if nothing else, I want to be your friend. And don't take this the wrong way, but I've already made love to you." He searched her eyes, his expression wistful. "You're worth the wait."

Chapter Seventeen

At first there were whispers and raised eyebrows, but after nearly three months the sight of her and Ross together had become as common as the Monday afternoon hockey games. It was because it was spring, the people decided, and even Jack Calhoun seemed resigned to the fact she and Ross were now a 'couple'. And no two people could have been happier than they were, except maybe Fanny and Boomer.

"Here to cheer on your honey, are you? See? I knew you and Ross would get on well." Fanny beamed and handed her a flag as Lacey sat down.

Lacey rolled her eyes and scanned the ice for Ross. "So you keep telling me," she replied. "I will never again doubt your matchmaking powers, oh mighty Aphrodite."

Fanny laughed heartily and jumped to her feet when the men skated into the rink.

The game was well into the second period when Annie joined them. Fanny had a flag for her, too, and soon all three of them were waving and cheering loudly. The crowd seemed especially boisterous today, and Lacey guessed it was because they were playing the team from Glacier Hill, a small town down-river and their chief rival. Looking around at the people and the idyllic setting she sighed happily. She liked the landscape the chaos of her former life had carved.

"You're glowing," Annie whispered in her ear. "Love certainly agrees with you."

Lacey blushed and watched as Ross stole the puck. "I am *not* in love," she replied.

Annie laughed and nodded, red curls bouncing. "Oh, yes you are. You haven't told *him* yet." Lacey couldn't meet her gaze and Annie chuckled again. "Don't worry, honey. He's got it as bad as you do." Lacey's head snapped around and she looked at the older woman with wide eyes. Annie grinned. "Oh, he hasn't said anything, but when you're as old as I am you recognize the signs. Trust me. He's toast."

Lacey laughed and shook her head, then turned her attention back to the game.

Toward the end of the second period, the sound of a woman's voice shouting Ross's name drew Lacey's attention, and she scanned the bleachers. Her stomach dropped. She'd never been formally introduced to the woman, but she'd never forget her. It was Renee, the woman she'd caught Ross kissing in the bar. Her silence had apparently drawn Fanny's attention. Fanny squeezed her hand.

"Don't worry about her, Lacey," Fanny said, her eyes narrowing on the stylishly dressed brunette. "She's got nothing on you."

"Hear, hear," Annie agreed.

Lacey swallowed the lump in her throat and nodded, but confident she was not. She tried to watch the rest of the game, and found her gaze drawn time and again to the beautiful woman. As if sensing she was being watched, the woman turned, a feline smile curving her generous mouth when their eyes locked. Renee inclined her head slightly, and then turned her gaze back to the rink.

The team from Glacier Hill was victorious that day, but only by one goal. Regardless of the loss, the crowd was exuberant as they filed out of the bleachers. Fanny muttered that the winning team had cheated. The woman's loyalty warmed Lacey, but the feeling soon evaporated.

As they approached the edge of the rink she saw Renee standing near the wall, her eyes locked on Ross who was still on the ice, messing around with Boomer. He hooked his stick in Boomer's legs and sent the man sprawling, then raced toward the bleachers as Boomer hopped up and gave chase. Ross neared the wall and Renee stepped forward to open the gate for him, giving him a look filled with lusty intent. Ross gave her a tight smile and a "Hi, Renee," and Lacey's heart soared when he turned to look for her.

When their eyes met, Ross grinned and he walked toward her, his steps sure despite the fact he still had his skates on. He stopped in front of her, dropped his stick and shrugged out of his arm pads, then flicked his helmet off. Lacey cried out in surprise when he put his arms around her and lifted her up. Her hands automatically clutched his shoulders. His hair was slick with sweat but he smelled wonderful, like Christmas.

"Hey, beautiful," he said. "Sorry I couldn't win the game for you."

She smiled back, and her grin widened when she saw Renee's annoyed expression. The woman was watching them, hands on hips, her eyes narrowed and a frown marring her otherwise perfect brow. Lacey couldn't have been happier.

"Hey yourself," she replied. "And you know I don't care if you win or lose. You're still the MVP in my book."

He kissed her, and his lips tasted of salt and the peppermint gum he chewed during a game.

"Oh, yeah," she heard Fanny say from behind them. "He's got it *way* bad." Boomer and Annie laughed.

"Hey, Ross," Boomer called, "why don't you two get a room?"

Lacey smiled against his lips and he chuckled as he pulled back slightly, his eyes holding hers captive. "As soon as *she* gives the word, Boomer," he replied, then softer, so only she could hear, "as soon as she gives the word." Lacey's cheeks went hot and he chuckled before putting her back on her feet. He draped an arm around her shoulder and turned to face the others. "C'mon, Boomer. Let's get showered and changed. There's an extra-large pizza at Joe's with my name on it."

Boomer nodded and grinned. "Beat you back to the locker room," he challenged as he skated away. Ross shook his head and sprinted toward the ice, legs pumping furiously in an attempt to catch up with his friend. The women watched in amusement, and Fanny laughed heartily when Boomer tripped as he reached the door to the small cabin that served as their locker room. Ross stepped gingerly over the older man, raised his arms in exultation and disappeared inside the building.

"Well, you have him now, don't you?"

Lacey turned to Renee, and Fanny and Annie flanked her like protective older sisters. Renee gave them a tight smile, but there was no rancor in her gaze, only wistful disappointment.

"I wondered when the day would come," Renee said, "and now I know. Congratulations. Ross is quite a man." Without waiting for a reply she turned and walked away. Annie shook her head and Fanny stared after the woman in disbelief.

"Well," Fanny started, "*that* was interesting."

"I'll say," Annie agreed. "I'd never have thought she'd be such a gracious loser."

Fanny crossed her arms over her ample chest. "If she were Sue, she wouldn't be." She looked at Lacey out of the corner of her eye. "Be glad she's not Sue."

Lacey said nothing, watching Renee until the woman disappeared from view.

The three friends linked arms and strolled to Lacey's Cherokee, chatting amiably. Lacey opened the hatchback and sat down on the tailgate and Fanny followed suit.

"Well, it's been great fun, guys," Annie said. "But, I don't want to be a fifth wheel, so I think I'll head on home."

"Oh, no," Lacey said. "You have to come to pizza with us. And you're not a fifth wheel."

"Besides," Fanny ventured, "Dave Jenkins will probably be there." She gave Annie a sly glance and smiled. "He's awful sweet on you, and I'm sure we can convince him to join us."

Annie rolled her eyes and gave Lacey a dour look, a blush creeping into her cheeks. "You had to do it, didn't you?" Lacey's brows shot skyward, but she held her tongue and fought a smile as Annie continued. "Now that she thinks she got you and Ross together, none of the rest of us singles will be safe for a moment. Can't you tell her she had nothing to do with it, and clip her Cupid wings?"

"She's Aphrodite," Lacey corrected with a grin. "And she wouldn't believe me anyway. She's convinced the relationship between me and Ross is her doing."

"It was," Fanny interjected, studying her fingernails. "So both of you had better resign yourselves to that fact and allow me to work." She looked up and gave Annie an angelic smile. "Why don't you go on over to Joe's and get us a table while we wait for the boys. A table for *six*. We'll be right behind you."

Annie stared at her for a moment, then her expression softened and she smiled. "Right. A table for six it is." She turned and walked away, muttering under her breath, "I don't know why I let her do this to me. Get a table for six, Annie; let me work, Annie; he's sweet on you, Annie..."

Lacey giggled and looked sideways at Fanny when Annie was out of earshot. "How do you do that?" she asked.

Fanny's eyes twinkled and she smiled. "Talent, my dear. Pure, raw talent."

"All right, wife, what have you been up to?" Boomer asked, his gear slung over his shoulder and Ross right beside him. "I've seen that look, and it can only mean trouble."

Lacey spoke up. "She's trying to set up Annie and Dave Jenkins."

Ross and Boomer looked at each other then nodded in approval.

"That would be a great match," Ross commented, leaning against the side of the Cherokee. "I take it the *two* of them will be joining us for pizza?"

Fanny looked at him indignantly. "Of course," she replied, "*after* you and Boomer invite Dave to eat with us."

Ross and Boomer exchanged glances again, and then laughed.

"All right," Boomer conceded. "I'll do anything as long as I can get some food." He grinned and rubbed his not-so-flat stomach. "As you can see, I'm wasting away."

Fanny rolled her eyes. "Yeah," she agreed, her voice laden with sarcasm. "You're practically the poster boy for Feed the Children."

He grabbed her around the waist and hugged her. "We both are, my dear. We both are."

***

The yacht made its way through the harbor, a stiff breeze coming over the bow, moonlight dancing on the water. In the background the lights of New York sparkled, the city glimmering like a freshly minted coin enhanced by the cover of night. To him, it never looked so lovely in the day, when harsh sunlight accentuated the crowded streets; the noise and traffic, the unforgiving jungle of concrete, steel, and glass. Regardless, Dennis loved the city; its energy, the pulsating life that never seemed to abate even in the wee hours. He pushed away from the railing, turned and headed for the aft deck, wineglass in hand.

The party was going well, thank goodness. No matter how much he disliked Lucas Davenport, he had to admit the man knew how to throw a party. The merger had been finalized, and now all the key players from both Davenport and Parker-Raines were celebrating, courtesy of Lucas. Men in tuxedos and women in eye-popping cocktail dresses adorned the polished deck of the rented yacht as a string quartet played in the background. Uniformed waiters with shining silver trays flitted through the crowd like black and white butterflies. Yes, the man had taste.

The yacht had to be a hundred feet long if it was ten, and Dennis's legs wobbled unsteadily as he joined the celebrants. The wine and champagne flowed freely and he'd drunk more than his fair share. A waiter appeared from out of nowhere to exchange his empty glass for a full one. He smiled at the young man, catching Lucas's eye as he took a long drink. The ship lurched as he lifted his glass in salute to his host, and he nearly fell, bumping into a voluptuous brunette.

"Whoa there, big fella," she said with a laugh, dark eyes glittering as she helped to right him. He smiled at her, her lazy Southern drawl wrapping around him like a pair of warm arms. "Wouldn't want to go swimmin' this time of night. I'm Lisa, and you are...?"

He extended his hand and when she slipped her fingers into his he pressed a gentlemanly kiss to her soft, floral-scented knuckles. "Dennis Lechter," he answered with a charming smile. "And I think going swimming is a wonderful idea." His gaze roved boldly over her curvaceous figure and she returned his look in kind, one dark eyebrow lifted and her perfectly painted lips curved in a cat-like smile. He leaned closer. "Care to join me?"

"Dennis," Lucas said, approaching slowly. He gave the brunette a short nod and she immediately turned on her heel.

Dennis looked at Lucas, irritated. "Yes?"

"Before you do too much more...celebrating," Lucas began, "I wanted to go over your new contract. I've increased your yearly salary and added a few company perks I think you'll enjoy, so, if you wouldn't mind?" He gestured toward the hatch that led to the lower deck and the conference room. When Dennis hesitated, Lucas smiled widely and picked up two glasses of champagne as a waiter walked by. "All you have to do is look it over, sign it, and then we can truly begin the party. Yes?"

Dennis looked for the brunette, but she had disappeared. "Fine. Let's get on with it."

Lucas led the way, smiling and shaking hands with the tipsy guests as he went. Dennis followed behind. He resented having to trail the younger man like some obedient hound, but the sooner he signed his new contract, the sooner he could resume his search for...Lisa. Yes, Lisa was her name.

Dennis grasped the rail as he descended the ladder, and the music grew muted as the sound of the engine increased to a whispering hum. After sliding back the conference room door, Lucas indicated Dennis should precede him inside. Dennis spotted Roger almost immediately. The blonde bodyguard's considerable physique took up a lot of space in the small room. Unbidden, a chill went up Dennis's spine.

"Sit down," Lucas said as he slid the door shut and effectively cut off any outside noise.

Dennis didn't want to sit but he did as he was told and eased down on one of the plush leather chairs. Lucas reached past Dennis to hand the champagne glasses to Roger. Roger put the flutes on the table and then sat down, lacing his fingers over his rock-hard abdomen.

"All right," Dennis said. "Where's the contract? Let's get a look at this bad boy, and get back to the party." He looked at Lucas expectantly. The younger man smiled and sat down on the edge of the table, then turned Dennis's chair so they faced one another. Dennis felt vaguely uncomfortable with Roger behind him and another shiver ran up his back. "What's going on, Lucas? Where's the contract?"

Lucas tipped his head and glanced at Roger, his smile deepening a bit. "Well, that's the crux of it, isn't it?" he said cryptically. "Actually, there is no contract, Dennis. I needed to speak with you...alone." Dennis sat up in his chair, but Roger clamped a hand on his shoulder and a champagne flute appeared in his peripheral vision, Roger's thick fingers wrapped around the stem. Dennis glanced at the glass then back to Lucas, who nodded. "Go ahead, Dennis. Have a drink, and then we'll talk."

"I-I don't want a drink. I think I've had enough."

Lucas's smile vanished. "That wasn't a request." Slowly the corners of his mouth tipped up again as Roger stood, leaned over, and pressed the glass into Dennis's hand. "Drink. I have some questions to ask you."

Dennis felt the cold sweat on his brow and his mouth went dry. He lifted the champagne, but for some reason it looked different. It was fizzing, quite profusely, a tornado of bubbles spiraling up from the bottom of the glass.

"Questions about what?" he asked, his voice barely above a whisper as he stared at the golden liquid. The bubbles were thick on the sides of the fluted crystal, and foam gathered on the top. The sizzle seemed unnaturally loud, and that was when he noticed the manila envelope on the table. He looked at it through his champagne and lowered the glass as Lucas picked it up and opened it. Before Lucas even showed him the contents he knew what it was, and a hollow ache grew in his stomach. Lucas pulled a single sheet of paper out and flipped it over just as Dennis felt something cold and hard pressed gently against the base of his skull. The click made him jump, and he gulped, his gaze drawn to the photograph.

He remembered all too well how she had looked that day in Central

Park. Truth be told, he'd thought of her more than once since that meeting. Now, looking at the black and white image of him and Lacey sitting together on that bench, a flood of emotions coursed through him; regret, longing, fear, relief. Tearing his gaze from the picture he turned his eyes to Lucas. The younger man's expression was harsh; his eyes glinting with a cold fire that spoke of madness.

"Drink," Lucas ordered, his voice almost gentle. "And then you're going to tell me all about her."

***

Lacey stretched and yawned, then snuggled deeper into her comforter. A glance at the clock told her it was nearly eleven a.m. Sunlight sifted through the cracks in the mini-blinds and birds chirped outside the window. She watched the dust as it floated about the room, disappearing then reappearing as the light caught it. Getting up was an option, but since it was Sunday, she was content to stay where she was. The brief thought of hot coffee and fresh cinnamon rolls almost tempted her to get up, but she didn't have any cinnamon rolls. Yawning, she fluffed her pillow and rolled onto her side.

The sound of a truck coming up the road made her groan and she got to her feet. Thankfully, her slippers were where they were supposed to be and she scrunched her toes into the soft sheepskin, pulling on a robe as she lifted one slat of the blinds. It was Ross. She ran to the bathroom and pulled a brush through her hair, then brushed her teeth. Just as she hung the towel back up she heard his boots on the porch.

He knocked before she could reach the door. She opened it and looked at him, her lips pursed in mock annoyance. His eyes widened as they traveled the length of her.

"Did I wake you, sleeping beauty?" he asked.

She gestured for him to come in and pulled the thick velour tighter around her neck. "No, but you might as well have. I was thinking of staying in bed all day and then you decided to show up. So much for that idea."

He leaned over and brushed a kiss across her cheek as he walked past, and Lacey closed her eyes, inhaling his warm, male scent. He always smelled so good.

"Need some company?" he asked.

Lacey rolled her eyes, closed the door, and walked past him into the kitchen. "Coffee?"

Ross grinned and nodded as he shrugged out of his coat. He followed her into the kitchen and sat down at the two-man table, leaning back and watching as she measured the coffee. Lacey felt his gaze and one hand fluttered to her hair self-consciously.

"I know I have bed-head," she said. "You could've at least warned me you were coming." She glanced at him briefly, her cheeks going pink as he smiled.

"You look great. And I didn't want to warn you. I was trying to be...spontaneous."

After pouring the water into the coffee-maker, she took two large ceramic mugs from a cabinet and looked at him over her shoulder. "Spontaneous?" she asked. "How so?" She pulled out a chair and sat across from him.

"I figured we could go on a picnic," he said. "I've got a basket out in the truck that Annie did up for me. Oh, and I grabbed your mail from the box on the way in. When was the last time you checked it anyway?"

Lacey laughed. "All I ever get are bills, so what's the motivation there?"

"Well, you had more than bills this time," he said. "I'll run out to the truck and get it."

Lacey smiled as he got to his feet and left the cabin. With a glance at the pot she saw the coffee was still brewing, so she got up and went to her bedroom. As she dressed she heard the front door open.

"Lacey?"

"I'm getting dressed," she called, buttoning her jeans and pulling a light sweater over her head. "I'll be right out."

She put her hair up in a clip and then she went back out to the kitchen, smiling when she saw Ross had poured the coffee. He was reading a newspaper, a steaming mug held easily in one hand. Her brow furrowed when she saw the large, padded envelope on the table.

"What's this?" she asked.

Ross glanced up. "That's part of your mail. See, I told you there was more than bills."

She picked it up, glanced at the postmark, and a flicker of apprehension went through her. Dallas. The envelope was addressed to the P.O. box Peebo had set up, and forwarded to her here, but there was no return address. It was probably nothing but some junk mail. Shaking off the uneasiness, she dropped the envelope back on the table.

Ross looked at her strangely. "Aren't you going to open it?" he asked.

Lacey shook her head and sat down, then poured a small amount of cream into her coffee. "No. I'll open it when we get back from this picnic you're insisting I go on." He smiled at that and she smiled back.

An hour later they sat on the bank of a small lake, the sun shimmering off the deep blue water. A flock of ducks floated on the placid surface, their feathered behinds occasionally bobbing up into the air as they went under for food. Lacey smoothed the plaid blanket and inhaled deeply, smelling pine, water, and the thick patches of wildflowers that dotted the ground. The air was so crisp, nothing like Texas, and she savored it.

"Hungry?" Ross asked.

She nodded. "Starving. You did interrupt me just as I was going to have breakfast."

"Yeah, right. You were still in bed when I rolled up, so you said. How did I interrupt your breakfast?" He handed her a thick roast beef sandwich and Lacey's mouth watered.

"Well, you interrupted my *thoughts* of breakfast," she said. "That's close enough."

He laughed; a rich, rolling sound that warmed her. "I suppose you've got a point. I know there are times I've been thinking of you and had *those* thoughts interrupted. It's quite annoying, and it always happens when I'm getting to the good part." She felt her cheeks flame, and shot him a murderous look when he laughed again. "Relax, Lace. I'm only teasing."

Lacey said nothing and took a large bite of her sandwich. She felt him watching her and looked up as she swallowed her food. "What?"

Ross grinned. "You look great in pink."

Lacey glanced at her sweater, which was blue. "What are you talking about?"

"Actually, it was closer to crimson than pink." When he saw her expression, he smiled. "Your cheeks, Lace. Your cheeks."

Once again, heat surged into her face. She gave him a withering look, turned her back on him and continued eating. As she popped the last bite into her mouth, she felt lips at her ear. Instinctively, she flinched and pulled away. When she turned to him, she saw the brief flash of hurt in his eyes before it was masked. She reached for him but he backed up.

"Ross...I'm sorry."

His gaze was steady and unflinching, and Lacey found it impossible to maintain eye contact. She folded her hands in her lap and stared at her fingers.

"Lacey, don't you know by now I'd never hurt you?" he asked, his voice low.

A lump formed in her throat and all she could do was nod, tears stinging her eyes. "I'm sorry," she whispered. "It was..."

"I know," he interrupted. "It was a reaction."

She heard him sigh and closed her eyes. The blanket rustled as he got to his feet, and she felt him standing beside her. His hand dropped down on her head, gently stroking her hair, and she laid her cheek against his muscular thigh.

"I have something I need to talk to you about," Ross began, "but why don't we take a walk first? It's an easy hike around the lake. You brought your charcoals, didn't you?" She nodded silently and looked up. He gave her a tender smile and pulled her to her feet.

Lacey grabbed her charcoals and sketchbook. Ross took them from her and took her hand. They strolled leisurely, Ross pointing out different species of birds and other wildlife. It was enchanting, and Lacey felt as if she'd been dropped in the middle of a Thomas Kincaide print. On the far side of the lake they stopped and sat down on a log.

"Gimme," Lacey said with a smile as she took her pad and charcoals from him. As she opened the portfolio, several sketches fell to the ground, and Ross retrieved them before she could. He glanced through them, his eyes widening slightly when he saw the one of him. Lacey bit her lip and waited.

"Is this me?" he asked.

"Yes. Why?"

"Do I really...look like this?"

Lacey gazed at the sketch, and smiled. It was an excellent likeness, and she took the paper from him, holding it at arm's length. She picked up one of her charcoals and darkened the brows a bit, glancing at him every so often as she put the final touches on the image.

"There," she said, handing the sketch back. "Now it *really* looks like you, except you had a beard then." He stared at the picture, and Lacey couldn't tell if he liked it or not. "Bet you didn't realize you were so handsome, did ya'?"

He turned to her, touched her cheek and smiled. "You've got black stuff on your face." Lacey looked down at her fingers, which were quite sooty. Turning, she rubbed her hands over his face and smeared a goodly amount of charcoal on his skin before he managed to get away. Ross was laughing as he pulled a handkerchief from his pocket.

"What was that for?" he asked.

Lacey giggled and turned her pad to a fresh sheet of paper. "Now you've got black stuff on your face, too."

"We're quite a pair," he said, "aren't we?"

Lacey remembered the phrase, from the night at the lodge. Smiling, she started sketching the lake, and her eyes widened when a bear appeared out of the trees on the far side of the lake. Ross followed the direction of her gaze and his brows drew together.

"If you want your stuff, pack it slowly."

Lacey shook her head almost imperceptibly as she let the pad and charcoals slip slowly to the ground. "That's okay. We can always come back for them later. Right now, what do we do about that teddy bear over yonder?"

"Don't move," he said. He watched as the bear investigated the remains of their picnic, obviously finding some goodies as it tore apart the basket. While the animal was occupied, he grabbed her hand and pulled her into the trees.

"What do we do now?" she asked in a whisper.

Ross pressed her back against a large pine and covered her body with his as he peered around the tree. "We wait a bit. We're downwind so the bear shouldn't smell us."

"Shouldn't we run for the truck or something?"

Ross shook his head and pressed a kiss to her temple. "Rule number one, you can't outrun a grizzly. Rule number two, never forget rule number one." He gave her a reassuring smile. "Don't worry, Lace. Once the bear's eaten the rest of our lunch, it'll probably go back the way it came."

"Probably?" she squeaked.

While it was only about ten minutes, it seemed like forever before the bear ambled back into the woods. Lacey thought her heart would burst from her chest as the bear made its presence known to any and all within earshot. The beauty of the day seemed to fade, the trees taking on an almost menacing appearance, and she laid her head on Ross's chest. Her arms crept around him, and when he pulled her closer the forest returned to normal. She felt safe again.

Ross's heartbeat was strong beneath her cheek, and when the coast was clear, the tension seemed to drain out of him. She looked up and he gave her a weary smile, his forehead against hers. "Now," he said, "we run for the truck."

He gave her a brief kiss and took her hand, pulling her as they made their way quickly back to the truck. Lacey didn't have to be told. She jumped into the cab, slammed the door and buckled up. Ross started the engine, dust and gravel flying as he sped down the narrow road.

He didn't slow down, and neither of them said a word until he pulled up in front of the cabin an hour later. When the engine died they both sat there, and Lacey listened to the relative quiet surrounding her. Birds sang, crickets chirped, the breeze whispered through the treetops. She looked at Ross, who turned and looked at her. Her pulse ratcheted up.

As she gazed into those vivid blue eyes, the intensity of her feelings for this man finally broke through the wall; the wall of protection she'd erected around herself. She was acutely aware of his breathing, the slight rise and fall of his chest, the gentle flare of his nostrils. She thought of what might have happened with the bear, and knew he would've sacrificed himself to save her. She also knew she would've done the same for him.

The revelation hit her square between the eyes, and for a moment she was startled, and afraid. His brows drew together and he gently touched her cheek, as if he sensed her turmoil, and that small gesture was enough to dispel her fears. She wanted him, needed him. She loved him, and for the first time in a long time, the wall came down.

"What's wrong, Lace?" Ross asked in a low voice.

She shook her head. "Nothing. Nothing at all."

Chapter Eighteen

Lacey got out of the truck and came around to his side, her eyes never leaving his. She watched as he stepped out and closed the door behind him, and wondered if he could read the intent on her face. He stood completely still as she approached him, his expression guarded. When she stroked his cheek a hint of a smile appeared, and she ran a finger over his mouth. Her hands moved up his chest to sift through his hair, and she pulled his head down.

He came willingly enough, though Lacey sensed his hesitation. He let her lead, and the sense of power that gave her emboldened her. She kissed him, softly at first, but when his tongue met hers all bets were off. Passion spread like a wildfire through her and he seemed to sense it, his hands stroking her back and derriere with languid familiarity. Her skin itched to feel his touch, and she could wait no more. She grabbed his hand and practically ran for the cabin.

Once inside Lacey turned on him, and he met her hungry lips with his own. Clothing flew in every direction as they made their way to the bedroom, knocking a lamp off the credenza and a picture off the wall in the hallway. The bedroom door crashed open as they fell through it, laughter bubbling out. Ross's pants had gotten tangled about his ankles, and Lacey giggled as she yanked on the offending blue jeans.

She got to her feet and smiled wickedly as she stared down at him. Clad only in his briefs, he really was an amazing male specimen; a thin, dark line of hair traveling from his navel and disappearing beneath the waistband of his underwear. Below that, the evidence of his desire stood out vividly, and she licked her lips.

Her sweater, bra, shoes and socks were somewhere between the front door and the bedroom, and she watched his face as she slid her jeans over her hips. To her surprise, when she started to remove her panties, Ross's expression changed and he got to his feet.

"Lacey, wait."

Lacey froze, her heart doing double-time, and not for a good reason. "Wh-what?"

Ross's expression was serious as he pulled the pins from her hair and fluffed the golden corkscrews around her shoulders. "You are so beautiful," was all he said.

Lacey gaped at him. "But...?"

"You said something to me once about doing this for the wrong reasons," he said as he took a step toward her. "I don't want this to be something you'll regret." He paused, as if searching for the words. Lacey ran a finger over his abdomen in small, lazy circles, and he clenched his teeth. "Adrenaline can do strange things to a body."

Lacey smiled. "I know."

"It's like a drug. You get high off it, but then you come down."

She stepped forward and her breasts brushed his chest. "I know."

He seemed distracted by the contact of their bodies, and Lacey's smile deepened when he swallowed hard, then continued. "I'm trying to do the honorable thing here, Lace. You're not making it easy."

"I know." She ran her hand down his belly and over his groin, lust surging through her when he sucked in a breath.

He took her wrists in his hands and pushed her away, his expression resolute. "Stop it, Lacey. It's the adrenaline making you act like this. The bear..."

"The bear," she said, "has nothing to do with this. Except I need to find a big, fat salmon for him, or her, to say thank you."

He frowned. "What are you talking about?"

"The bear made me realize something," Lacey replied. "What would you have done if that grizzly had found us?"

His reply was automatic. "I'd have distracted it so you could get away. What do you think I'd have done?"

He sounded indignant, and Lacey smiled. "Just that; and I would've done the same," she replied. His expression told her he was confused, and she gently disentangled her wrists from his grip. As she framed his face with her hands, she wanted to say 'I love you', but the words stuck in her throat. Closing her eyes, she pressed her lips to his briefly, then pulled back and looked at him. "I would rather die than see you hurt, Ross. For the first time in a very *long* time, I wasn't worried about *my* survival. I knew I didn't have to, and that has *nothing* to do with the bear."

A glimmer of hope flickered in his eyes as he wound a stray curl around his finger. "I thought you didn't want to be with me because I made you feel safe."

"You make me feel safe, and every woman wants to be with a man who makes her feel safe." Her fingertips memorized his features. "But at the same time, you scare the hell out of me."

He searched her face, his expression dismayed. "Why?"

She lowered her eyes and splayed her fingers over his chest as her cheeks went hot. "You make me wonder what it would be like to make love to you every night, and wake up with you every morning." He put a finger under her chin and tipped her face up, his expression tender, and Lacey continued. "You make me wonder why, when I'm with you, not only is my body involved, but my heart, my mind, and *everything* else is involved, too."

"Lacey..."

"I want to be with you, Ross," she interrupted, "not because of the bear or the adrenaline, or because you make me feel safe. I..." Her voice died and she turned away, the 'love you' part once again frozen on her tongue.

Lucas had mocked her declarations of love, and the memory of his disdain had done its damage. Closing her eyes, she inhaled Ross's scent and squared her shoulders. If Ross didn't reciprocate her love, so be it. But it was high time she stopped letting what Lucas had done to her rule her every action. If she didn't, she'd never be free of him, ever. Tears gathered beneath her lids, and she cleared her throat.

"I...love you," she whispered. She heard his sharp intake of breath but kept her eyes closed, and her face averted. The tears slipped out silently, but she remained as still as a statue, even when he cupped her face gently. His thumbs stroked her wet skin, and slowly he lifted her face to his.

"Lacey, look at me."

She bit her lip and shook her head.

As gently as a butterfly's wings, his lips feathered over her face, planting soft, whispering kisses on her cheeks, her chin, her eyelids. Her heart broke even as her body swayed toward him, and when his mouth finally covered hers, she was lost. He picked her up and carried her to the bed, and she let herself go, never once opening her eyes.

***

Night had fallen nearly an hour ago, but his eyes had long since adjusted. Ross lay on his side, head propped in his hand. Lacey was next to him, and he wrapped a long blonde curl around his finger as he watched her sleep. Her confession had surprised him, but even now he smiled. The very fact she'd had the courage to say something so potentially damaging showed him the depths of her heart, and, to his surprise, his own responded in kind.

He'd felt it when they'd made love; that deep, spiritual connection that went far beyond the physical. It was more than her pretty face and voluptuous figure that drew him; it was everything about her. Despite what she'd been through, she still loved life, and, once she'd come out of her shell, her enthusiasm was contagious. He saw it in the way she dealt with people, in her generosity; the way she talked and smiled and laughed, and even in the way she drew. She saw the beauty around her and reveled in it, in spite of the ugliness she had experienced.

Lacey murmured in her sleep and rolled toward him, eyes still closed as she tucked her hands beneath her cheek. He wanted to touch her again and stroked her cheek lightly, marveling at the smooth texture of her skin. His fingers trailed down her slender neck, over her shoulder, and back up. Her mouth tipped up in a smile and he fought the urge to kiss her. He argued all the reasons he shouldn't, but his body didn't seem to hear him. He wanted her again.

"What the hell," he said softly. "Why fight it?"

Leaning over, he kissed her softly. At first there was no response, but when he ran his tongue over her lower lip she stirred and rolled onto her back, stretching like a cat. He tugged the sheet down, exposing her breasts, and her eyes flew open when he suckled her.

"Ross...!" she gasped. Before she could say anything else he lifted his head and kissed her deeply. She tensed at first, but he continued his relentless assault and gradually her uncertainty faded, her arms snaking around his neck. She sighed softly as he nibbled her earlobe, his hands brushing her breasts with deliberate intent. When she spoke, her voice was low and husky. "Ross, what are you doing?"

"What do you think I'm doing?" He rolled one nipple gently between his fingers and she sucked in a breath. "I want you, Lacey, all of you."

"Hmm..."

"Only this time," he said, lifting his head to look at her, "you're going to do something for me." She gazed at him through lazy-lidded eyes, and he saw the apprehension there.

"What?" she asked in a breathless whisper.

He covered her body with his, the friction of their skin making him harder than he already was. "This time, you're going to look at me while we make love. No more hiding, Lacey, not any more. Not with me." He waited until she nodded, and smiled at her. Leaning on his elbows, he gazed at her tenderly and pushed the curls from her face. "Don't worry, Lace. You're not in this alone."

Blonde brows drew together and she looked at him questioningly. "What do you mean?"

Ross's eyes narrowed on her face and he ran his thumb over her lower lip. He loved the shape of her mouth, and he traced the outline with his index finger, his expression somber. "I mean...I love you, too, Lace." He glanced up, reading the astonishment in her eyes. "I love you, Lacey, and we're in this together."

***

Lacey snuggled closer to Ross's side, his arm draped around her shoulders, his breathing deep and even. His heart thumped rhythmically against her cheek and she sighed softly. She didn't think she'd ever been so happy, or so at peace.

His face was softened in sleep and he looked so perfect, at least to her. He was handsome, strong, but it went further than good looks. Above all, Lacey loved him for his heart. She saw how he treated those close to him, with respect, loyalty, and love; and she trusted him with everything inside her.

She pressed a kiss to his cheek then disentangled herself gently from his embrace. He frowned as she moved away but did not wake, and she paused. After brushing a lock of dark hair from his forehead, she smiled and walked into the bathroom.

She took a hot shower, towel dried her hair, and shrugged into her robe and slippers. Her stomach grumbled loudly and she gave Ross one last look before leaving the bedroom. As she walked she picked up their clothing, laughing softly when she pulled one of his socks from a lampshade. She tossed the clothing in a heap on the couch, righted the picture and the lamp; her cheeks warming as she remembered how the light had ended up on the floor. After stirring the coals in the hearth, she tossed another log on and watched as the dry wood succumbed to the heat. Small flames licked upward and the log popped and hissed, smoke drifting lazily up the chimney. She stirred the coals again, then put the poker away and rose.

When she turned on the kitchen light, her eyes were drawn immediately to the envelope still sitting in the middle of the table. As earlier, a shiver of apprehension washed over her. For a second. she thought about opening it, and changed her mind as her stomach rumbled again. She frowned and shook her head.

"Food, Lacey," she said aloud. "You want *food*."

"Me, too."

Lacey started violently and whirled toward the voice, her hand pressed to her heart. Ross stood there in his briefs, leaning against the wall. Relief washed over her and she turned to rest her hands on the edge of the counter as she took a huge gulp of air.

Ross chuckled and walked up behind her. He wrapped his arms around her and rested his chin on her shoulder. "Sorry, Lace. I didn't mean to scare you."

"Well, Ross, y'did."

He chuckled and kissed her ear, and Lacey closed her eyes, loving the feel of him so close. She leaned back against him and he nibbled her neck, making her giggle.

"Stop it," she said.

Ross chuckled, turned her to face him, and kissed her mouth. "Don't wanna." He untied the sash of her robe and slipped his hands inside.

Lacey laughed as he tickled her. "Ross, stop." She pushed him away and knotted the sash, throwing him a withering look as she opened the refrigerator. "I'm hungry."

He grinned wickedly. "So am I."

"For food," she said. She leaned over to examine the contents of the icebox, and yelped when he smacked her backside. "Hey!" Straightening up, she faced him.

He immediately took her in his arms and lifted her onto the kitchen counter, positioning himself between her legs. Lacey's breath caught and this time, when he undid the sash of her robe, she said nothing. His eyes never left hers, even when he pushed the robe off her shoulders. It was as if he knew her body by memory, his hands brushing her breasts while they stared at each other. A soft gasp escaped her when his fingers moved lower, and she shuddered.

"Still hungry?" he asked, his voice low and rough.

Lacey couldn't keep from staring at his mouth as she remembered the wonderful things he had done to her with those lips. "What?"

He smiled. "I didn't think so." His voice trailed off, and Lacey closed her eyes as his mouth covered hers.

An hour or so later they lay on the couch, and Lacey felt his heart beating against her back. She stared into the fire as Ross played with her hair, his chin atop her head.

"You hungry?" he asked softly as he pulled the curls back to kiss her temple.

Lacey smiled and nodded. "I was hungry an hour ago. Now, I'm starving."

"For food?" Ross teased.

Looking at him out of the corner of her eye, Lacey tried to frown and failed. "Yes, for food."

"Darn," he said. Lacey laughed and moved to get up, but Ross put a hand on her shoulder and pressed her back against the cushions. "Don't move. I'll whip something up." He leaned down and kissed her, then climbed over her and jogged down the hall to the bedroom. Lacey looked after him, puzzled, until he reappeared in his jeans. As he passed by he gave her another lingering kiss, and then walked into the kitchen.

She stayed put until the smell of eggs and grilled ham reached her. The kettle whistled and, when she walked into the kitchen, Ross handed her a mug of peppermint tea.

"Thank you," she said, sitting down at the table.

"You're welcome." He smiled and flipped the omelet in the pan, wiggling his eyebrows at her. Lacey laughed and shook her head.

She found her eyes drawn to the envelope and, before she realized what she was doing, she had picked it up and opened it. Pausing, she took a deep breath and emptied the contents on the table. An unlabeled DVD and several newspaper clippings fell out, and Lacey shook the envelope to make sure nothing was left. A smaller envelope fell out then, and she pushed it aside.

"Whatcha got?" Ross asked as he put a plate in front of her.

She sifted through the clippings for a note of some sort, something to indicate who had sent them, but there wasn't one. "I don't know," she replied as she picked up the clippings. She slid off the paper clip that held them together, read the top headline and her eyes widened. Immediately, she went to the next one, then the next, and the next after that. Her stomach dropped and suddenly she wasn't hungry anymore.

She felt the blood drain from her face and closed her eyes against the sudden wave of nausea.

"Lace?" When she didn't answer he knelt at her side and took the clippings from her. He started to sort through them. "These are all about..." His voice trailed off and he looked at her. "These are all about Dennis Lechter."

"He's dead," she whispered. She pulled one of the articles from the pile and read it, her voice wooden. "Pharmaceutical executive's body discovered by local fisherman." Lacey's eyes swam and she took a deep, jerky breath. "Oh, God. He's dead, Ross. Dennis Lechter is dead."

Ross read through the remaining articles and his jaw dropped. "I don't believe this." He took all the clippings and put them back together. "There are six weeks' worth of articles, in chronological order, starting with his disappearance then the follow-up investigations. Here they called off the search, and here..." Ross took a deep breath. "Here, they find his body. This last one details the autopsy report and arrangements for his funeral."

"How...how did he die?" Lacey choked out.

Ross sat down across from her and laid each piece of newspaper carefully out on the table. Picking up the article regarding the autopsy, he scanned the print and his brows rose. "This says it was an accident. He drowned." He turned his eyes to a different story. "According to this, the last time anyone saw him alive was at a party hosted by...Lucas Davenport."

Lacey blinked and the tears spilled down her cheeks.

Ross paused briefly then continued. "They were celebrating the finalization of the merger. Witnesses report that Lechter was heavily intoxicated, and it wasn't until the yacht finally pulled into port that anyone noticed him missing. The seas were a little rough, and it was assumed he fell overboard. Autopsy results confirmed the police's suspicions."

"He didn't drown," Lacey said, more tears sliding down her face. "Lucas killed him."

"Lacey, you don't know that."

"*Yes*, I do."

"How?"

She picked up the smaller envelope and opened it, but somehow she already knew what was inside. When she unfolded the sheet and saw the picture of her and Lechter sitting in Central Park, she laughed curtly and handed the picture to Ross. "That's how." Lacey ran a fist over her eyes and heard Ross's slow exhale.

"He had Lechter followed," Ross said as he flattened the picture with his hands.

"Apparently," Lacey agreed. "What I don't understand is why? How could he have known Lechter and I even *met*? Dennis said he wouldn't say anything to Lucas, and I believed him."

Ross picked up the DVD and tapped it against the table. "Maybe this will tell us."

Lacey was numb as she followed Ross into the living room. The tears still fell, but she ignored them as she sat down on the couch and pulled a pillow to her chest. Ross popped the disc into the player and joined her. Wrapping an arm around her shoulders, he pulled her close and pressed a kiss to the top of her head.

When the DVD started playing, Lacey gasped at the first black and white images. An icy wave rolled over her. "That's Lucas's office in Dallas. I never knew he had cameras in there." They watched as Lechter moved about the office, and then picked up the picture on Lucas's desk. "That's my picture." Lechter then moved to the bookcase.

"Is that one you, too?" Ross asked.

Lacey only nodded, and coldness consumed her when she heard Lechter's softly spoken words. "So that's what tipped him off. I'll be damned." She covered her face with her hands and burst into tears. "It's not fair. It's just not fair."

Ross tried to pull her close, but she pushed him away and jumped to her feet. She picked up a nearby lamp, hurled it against the wall, and looked for something else. Oddly, the sound of shattering glass was comforting and she wanted more. Rage and despair burst inside her like fireworks; one hot, one cold, and the dueling sensations made her vision waver. "Why is it," she picked up her boot, "that just when I think things are going to work out," and threw it at the TV, "my ex-husband has to ruin my life all over again?" She missed her intended target and picked up her other boot, determined to destroy the television.

Before she could throw it, Ross grabbed her from behind and pinned her arms at her sides. She struggled briefly, screaming out her rage and frustration until her throat hurt, but Ross held her tight. He whispered softly but she continued to struggle, World War III detonating in the center of her chest. The battle raged and she could almost hear the shells and mortars exploding around her. When she finally stopped fighting, he let her go and she sank to her knees, her limbs refusing to support her. Ross knelt beside her and gathered her into his arms.

"Shhh, Lace," he whispered, "it'll be okay. Remember, we're in this together."

She shook her head vehemently, her body shaking with the depth of her anguish. It grew, like a cancer, eating through her with violent intent. "No, we're not. We can't be...or we'll die together."

***

The clock struck midnight, but Lacey hardly noticed. She lay on the couch, her head in Ross's lap, his fingers idly sifting through her hair. Her eyes were swollen, she was completely drained, and she doubted she could've gotten off the couch if she'd wanted to.

They'd watched the rest of the DVD, which had consisted of news stories regarding Lechter's disappearance and the subsequent investigation. The show had ended with the discovery of the body, and video of the funeral. Lacey hadn't been at all surprised to see her husband in attendance, and even less surprised when he'd looked into the camera and raised one perfectly shaped brow. It was a mannerism she was more than familiar with.

Ross sipped a cup of coffee as Lacey rolled onto her back to look up at him. He attempted a smile, but failed, and put his cup down with a sigh.

"I have to go, Ross," Lacey said quietly. "I have to leave before he gets here."

"You don't know he's coming." He continued to toy with her hair, and for the first time since she'd met him, he avoided her gaze. "Then again, he could already be here." When he finally looked at her, she saw the pain in his eyes and felt tears sting.

"He's not interested in you," she said, "but if you get in his way, he will be."

His brows drew together and he frowned at her. "So what are you going to do? Run? That will solve everything. He'll only follow you, and how long do you think you can avoid him? He's only a step behind you this time. You won't last a week on your own."

Lacey was too tired to fight. "Then what do you suggest? Should I send him a message saying I want a shootout at the OK Corral? Tell him to come alone, and we'll strap on our six-shooters and end this once and for all?" She sighed and shook her head. "This isn't the Old West, Ross. I can't stay here. It's too dangerous."

His expression darkened. "And it's too dangerous for you to leave. Come on, Lacey. He's not going to do anything where anyone can see him. I seriously doubt he's that stupid."

Lacey gaped at him and sat up. "He got rid of Dennis Lechter in front of 200 people."

"Yeah, and somebody could commit murder in Times Square at high noon, and no one would see a thing." He took her hands in his and faced her. "People in New York live differently. There, nobody knows anybody; you never make eye contact or look directly at someone. Everybody is a stranger. It's not like that here. Somebody new in town generates a lot of attention, and you, of all people, should know that."

Lacey couldn't argue with him there, because she knew he was right. She untangled her hands from his and rubbed her eyes. "So what do you want me to do, Ross?"

"Stay, and let us help you." He cupped her chin and Lacey looked at him, surprised to see him smiling. "I'm in pretty good with the local law enforcement, and this is the sort of thing Boomer lives for."

Hope sprang up in her chest, but she thought of Dennis Lechter and choked it down. "I don't know. If someone else got hurt, I'd never forgive myself."

"How do you think Fanny and Boomer would feel if you left, and they had to see news of *your* death on the six o'clock news?" He put a hand behind her neck and gave her a pleading look. "How do you think *I'd* feel?"

Her eyes brimmed and, when he pulled her to his chest, she went willingly. He was so warm and strong, and for a moment she could forget all about her exploding life.

"Lacey," he said, his voice low, "*someone* is going to get hurt in all this, that's pretty much a given. What we have to do is make sure it's your husband, and not one of us."

Lacey closed her eyes and the tears started again. She clung to him, his skin warm and smooth beneath her fingers. "I'm scared," she whispered.

His embrace tightened and he pressed his lips to her forehead, his hands roving slowly and rhythmically over her back. "Me too, Lace. Me too."

She hiccupped and buried her face in his neck. "Really? I was under the impression nothing scared you."

He snorted. "Whatever gave you that idea?"

"The fights at the bar, the hockey games, the bear." She sniffled and settled more comfortably against him. "And now this. You don't *seem* scared."

"Hey, I told you that *you* scare me. That alone should tell you it doesn't take much."

He was teasing, she knew, and she smiled through her tears. "Then why am I leaking like the Titanic but you're so Stoic?"

"Would you prefer it if I burst into tears?" he asked with a chuckle.

Lacey only shook her head, her eyelids growing increasingly heavy. Just like in the forest, being close to him made everything seem fine. She was warm, comfortable, and, for the time being, safe. It was a wonderful feeling, and she wished it would go on forever.

"Ross?"

"Hmm?"

"I love you."

She felt him smile and he kissed her forehead again.

"I love you, too, Lace. I love you, too."

Chapter Nineteen

The sound of gunfire jerked Ross from a sound sleep, and his heart nearly burst from his chest. At first he thought he'd imagined it, but when shots rang out again he jumped out of bed and jerked on his jeans. Suddenly, he realized Lacey wasn't beside him.

"Lacey?" He threw open the bathroom door. Empty. His anxiety rose and he ran down the short hallway into the living area. "Lacey?" Again, empty.

For a moment he froze, paralyzed with fear that rose like bile in his throat. Chills fanned over his skin. He started when two more shots split the air, but it was enough to spur him into action. Heedless of his bare feet, he ran out the back door and followed the sound of the gunfire. When three more pops shattered the quiet he honed in on their direction and set out at a dead run.

He jumped over fallen trees and low hanging branches slapped him in the face as his feet flew over the damp ground. Following a narrow trail that wound through the woods, he put on a burst of speed when several more shots rang out. The trail ended in a small clearing, and he skidded to a halt, his eyes wide.

Lacey wore a set of hearing protectors and shooting glasses, and, judging from her stance, Ross was pretty sure she'd done this before. Relief washed over him and his knees gave way. He sank down on a nearby stump and rested his head in his hands, trying to catch his breath and resisting the urge to strangle her. He jumped when she fired off six rounds in quick succession. His mouth fell open as she dropped the magazine and reloaded in the blink of an eye. Yes, she'd *definitely* done this before.

He looked toward the far end of the clearing where the ground rose and provided a perfect backstop for shooting practice. She had several targets set up; life-size silhouettes as well as the standard round targets. He held his breath as she sighted down the barrel and watched her carefully as she fired. She didn't even flinch. When that magazine was empty she reloaded, then slid the gun into the holster on the waistband of her jeans. She dusted her hands off and removed the earphones.

"Where'd you learn to shoot like that?" he asked. He expected her to be startled, but he didn't expect her to whirl on him, gun drawn. At least she didn't fire, but his arms went up as she continued to point the pistol at his chest.

Once she recognized him, she holstered her weapon, ran a hand over her face, and took a deep breath. "Don't *do* that! You scared the hell out of me."

He scowled. "I know how you feel," he said, slapping his hands against his thighs as he got to his feet. "I'm jerked out of a really great dream by the sound of gunfire, and when I look around, you're nowhere to be found." She had the decency to blush, and his anger evaporated.

She looked down at the ground and holstered her weapon, her voice small. "I'm sorry."

Her contrite expression undid him, and he put his hand behind her neck, pulling her roughly to his chest. He buried his face in her hair and inhaled deeply of the fresh, clean scent. "You can't begin to imagine what went through my head, Lacey," he said, remembering with vivid clarity how frightened he'd been. "I was afraid I'd find you all shot up, or...worse."

She held him tightly and pressed her face against his neck. "I'm sorry. You looked so peaceful I didn't want to wake you. I didn't stop to think the sound of the shots would do that."

He closed his eyes and rested his chin atop her head. "Well, they did. Now, you want to tell me what the hell you're doing out here?"

"Practicing."

He snorted and pulled away. "I can see that. Why?" She glanced at him only briefly, but he saw the wariness reflected in her eyes before she looked away.

"I figure if I'm going to stay," she said, "I'd better be prepared." He watched as her spine stiffened and she finally managed to look him in the eye. He remembered that same look from the day she'd applied for her job. Determination. "I don't want to be a helpless female always in need of saving."

His eyes narrowed and he smiled. "You left everything behind to escape what is, for many women, a hopeless situation. I've never thought of you as helpless. The very fact you left your husband, not to mention a life of luxury, proves you're anything but helpless." Her cheeks colored, and when she tried to look away, he took her chin and held her fast.

"I'm scared, Ross. Really scared," she said.

He chuckled. "Scared isn't synonymous for helpless, Lace. Now come on, I'm starving."

Lacey smiled and nodded. "Me, too. Let me get my stuff, and we're outta here."

As she ran to retrieve the targets, Ross picked up the empty magazines and tossed them in the small canvas bag with the rest of her ammo. Then, he sat down on the stump and waited.

She held up the targets for him to see and he had to admit, he was impressed. Her groupings were very precise, and on a person, they'd be deadly. The head and chest area of both silhouettes were completely blown away, along with the centers of the round targets.

"So, now you gonna tell me where you learned to shoot like that?"

She smiled and folded the mutilated targets. "A man named John Garrett taught me."

"And who is John Garrett?" Ross asked. He got to his feet and followed her as she started back to the cabin.

"He owns a motel I stayed at on my way here." She slipped the handles of the canvas bag over her shoulder and Ross fell into step beside her. "The Cherokee broke down in this little spot in Montana. Place didn't even rate a name. It was a freeway off-ramp with a motel, a truck-stop, and a mini-market."

"And...?"

"Well," she started, "the mechanic at the truck stop didn't have the parts to fix the Jeep, so he had to order them. Because, apparently, they order and deliver parts via carrier pigeon in that neck of the woods, I ended up staying in the motel for nearly two weeks. I was the only guest so Gunny, that's what they called John, made it his business to make sure I was okay. He'd eat with me, invite me to the office to play cards and watch TV. Said I reminded him of his granddaughter."

Ross looked at her out of the corner of his eye. "So, how'd you go from sitcoms to guns?"

Lacey chuckled and shook her head. "Fate, I guess. I bought the gun for protection before I left Texas, but I didn't really know how to use it. In fact, it kind of scared me. I was so afraid I wouldn't be quick enough that I kept it on the nightstand so I wouldn't have to open a drawer if I needed it. I think it was the third day I was there, I was taking a shower and Gunny must've come to make up the room."

"How do you know that?" Ross asked.

"Well, when I got out of the shower, the bed was made, and there was a stack of clean towels on the pillow next to the nightstand where the gun was sitting." She grinned. "That kind of gave it away."

"I guess it would." He paused, thinking again of the precise placement of her shots. "So, after that he taught you how to shoot?"

Lacey nodded. "Yep. Once I realized he'd been in the room and had seen the gun, I went to the office to try and explain. Before I could get a word out, he asked me if I knew how to shoot that thing. I said yes, and he said, 'no, I mean *really* shoot that thang.'" She sighed and continued.

"Next thing I know, we're out behind the motel at his makeshift shooting range. Nothing but a bunch of targets set up in front a whole lot of hay bales. And then he taught me how to shoot, but not just how to shoot, how to shoot to kill. Gunny was a Marine sniper. He didn't talk about it much, but he sure was an effective teacher."

Ross was thoughtful for a moment, and grabbed her arm when she tripped over a renegade tree root. "You seem to have been an apt pupil."

Lacey frowned at that, but nodded. "Gunny said I had a good eye, and good hands." She paused and pressed a hand to the pistol at her side. "He taught me so well I can disassemble this thing, clean it, and reassemble it blindfolded."

"Remind me never to make you mad," Ross teased.

She looked at him in surprise, her expression softening when she saw the grin on his face. "That's *not* funny."

"I wasn't trying to be funny. Who knows, one day I may say something inappropriate and end up mounted on your wall." He sighed and shrugged. "I'd rather be tied to your bed and mounted, but if I must be mounted to your wall, so be it. I like kinky."

Lacey gaped at him, her cheeks going crimson. "You're terrible, Ross Devlin."

He put an arm around her shoulders and nuzzled her neck. "That's not what you said last night."

"Oh, stop," she said with a chuckle as she pushed him away. "I'm armed, remember?"

Laughing, he kissed her temple. "I know. And for some strange reason I find that incredibly arousing."

"You'd find a cold shower arousing," she muttered.

"Only if you were in it, Lacey," he said. "Only if you were in it."

***

"You're glowing Lacey," Fanny said with a knowing smile. "So, is he as good in bed as they say?"

Lacey's jaw dropped and she stared at her friend in disbelief. The crowd in Joe's Pizzeria was boisterous and loud, and Lacey looked around quickly to see if anyone had heard Fanny's remark. Thankfully, Ross and Boomer were at the counter ordering their food, Annie and Dave were playing pinball, and no one else appeared to pay any attention to them. "Fanny!" Fanny laughed heartily and Lacey's cheeks flamed.

"Oh, come on, Lacey. Ross called us last night to say the two of you wouldn't be coming over for our Sunday night dinner, so I simply added two and two together. Or should I say," she paused and wiggled her eyebrows, "one and one. So, how was it?"

Lacey rolled her eyes. "I don't believe this."

"Come now." Fanny leaned closer. "Aphrodite must have details. It's for my memoirs."

"*Memoirs?*"

Fanny nodded. "Yep. All of my success stories will be chronicled and published, ensuring my fame." She paused and gave Lacey a long, assessing look before speaking again. "It's rumored he's very good in the sack; at least Renee and Sue always said so."

"Sue?" Lacey asked. She remembered Fanny mentioning a woman named Sue, but that brief conversation was the only time Fanny had spoken of her.

"Ross's other, um, for lack of a better word...girlfriend," Fanny said. "And I mean girlfriend in the *loosest* sense."

"Literally," Lacey said dryly.

Fanny laughed and slapped her lightly on the arm. "You are too funny. But now, I want details."

"Details about what, Fanny?" Ross asked. He placed the pitcher of soda on the table and handed out the glasses.

Boomer slid into the booth next to his wife and looked at her expectantly. "Yes, my dear. Details about what?"

Fanny turned pink and glanced at Lacey, who lifted her brows and returned Fanny's look with one of innocent anticipation. The woman gave a nervous chuckle. "Well, um, I was curious about...ahem. Why, I wondered how...I wanted to know...oh bother." She frowned and rested her chin in her hand. "It was nothing, really."

Ross smiled as he filled the glasses with soda. "It was spectacular, Fanny. Best sex I've ever had."

Lacey had just taken a drink and choked on her soda, her eyes going wide. As she coughed, she gaped at Ross, who tried not to laugh even as he pounded her back. When the spasms stopped, Lacey covered her face with her hands.

"Well, I knew it would be good for *you*," Fanny retorted with an indignant sniff. "I wanted to know if it was good for *Lacey*."

Lacey looked at the napkin dispenser in disbelief, and shook her head slowly. She glanced at Boomer, who sipped his soda as if nothing untoward had been said. Fanny grinned and so did Ross, and a thought suddenly popped into Lacey's head.

"Well," she started, drawing her words out slowly, "it was...okay. I've had better."

The table went silent and for a moment Lacey feared she'd crossed the line, but then Boomer burst out laughing. It wasn't long before Fanny was also chuckling, and she leaned close to whisper in Lacey's ear.

"Nicely done," Fanny said, a spark of pride in her eyes.

Lacey finally gathered the nerve to glance at Ross, and the look on his face sent her heart into her throat. She blinked several times, her mouth open in dismay, but then a slow smile blossomed on his lips.

"All right, all right," he said, nodding slowly. "But I still have a few tricks up my sleeve." He put an arm around her neck and pulled her close as his lips brushed her ear. "You're going to regret that flippant remark, because tonight, I'm going to prove you wrong."

He nibbled her earlobe and her breasts tightened, her body responding to his slightest touch. She pulled away just enough to look him in the eye. "If you're lucky."

He grinned and planted a lingering kiss on her mouth. "No," he said. "If *you're* lucky."

"All right, you two," Boomer interrupted. "Enough of that. You're going to get Fanny all riled up and then I won't get a minute's peace tonight."

Fanny gasped and smacked her husband's shoulder. "As if."

"Hi, Ross," a female voice said from the end of the table.

They looked up, and Lacey's eyes widened slightly as she found herself staring at a Nordic goddess. The woman's gaze flicked over her before returning to Ross, but Lacey recognized that look. Renee had looked at him the same way.

"Great game," she said with a feline smile.

"Thanks, Sue," Ross said. "When did you get back into town?"

The blonde flipped platinum hair over one shoulder and placed her hands on slender hips. "Yesterday. I went by Lights to see you, but you weren't there. And since you never answer your cell..."

Lacey looked at Fanny, who rolled her eyes as she took a sip of her drink. From her expression, Lacey guessed the goddess and Fanny didn't mix well, and that thought warmed her. At least she knew who her allies were.

"I was with my girlfriend," Ross replied, smiling when Lacey turned startled eyes to him. "Let me introduce you to Lacey Jamison. Lacey, this is Suzanne Montclare. She's an old friend."

The goddess's brilliant blue eyes swiveled her direction and a frown creased the smooth brow. Her perfect lips curved into a smile, but Lacey knew it was forced.

"It's a pleasure to meet you," Lacey said.

"Since when do you believe in girlfriends?" Suzanne asked, looking down her aquiline nose at Lacey while trying to appear nonchalant. She gave Ross a pointed look. "I never figured you for the type."

"People change," Ross replied with a shrug.

Suzanne twisted a long, shining curl around her finger. "So I see."

"But, enough about me," Ross said. He was obviously uneasy with this line of conversation. "What brings you back to Cooper's Ridge? I thought you'd be staying in Juneau permanently."

Suzanne tilted her head to the side and gave him a look filled with longing. When she ran a hand over Ross's cheek, Lacey felt him stiffen, but Suzanne seemed not to notice. "The job didn't pan out, so I'll be moving back. Besides, I missed you."

"So we see," Fanny said under her breath. Lacey hid a grin behind her hand and Boomer started coughing violently as he elbowed his wife in the ribs. "Ouch!"

"Excuse me?" Suzanne said. She lifted one perfectly plucked brow and looked at Fanny in annoyance. "Do you have a problem?"

"Yes, I *do* have a problem," Fanny replied.

"Fanny," Boomer said.

Fanny was indignant. "Well, I *do* have a problem." She turned back to Suzanne and her voice rose a notch. "You walk up here and start getting all touchy-feely, batting your eyelashes and such." Fanny planted her hands on the table and halfway came out of her seat, leaning toward Suzanne. "He's got a *girlfriend,* who is sitting right next to him."

Suzanne was taken aback. "I'm aware of that, and I don't see what you're getting all worked up about. I was just being friendly."

Fanny snorted. "Friendly, my ass! You've never been friendly with anyone you didn't plan on sleeping with later. Why don't you strip out of your clothes and see if Ross will do you right here on the table?"

Suzanne gasped, and a hush fell over the crowd as people turned in their seats to watch this little exchange. Boomer stared at Fanny as if he didn't know who she was, and Lacey looked at her in surprise. Ross rubbed his chin, a ghost of a smile hovering around his mouth. Suzanne's face went scarlet, and she glanced quickly around the room, her cheeks flushing deeper when she saw they had everybody's undivided attention. Fanny, on the other hand, didn't seem the least bit disturbed. In fact, she pushed Boomer out of the way and got to her feet, turning to address the room.

"For any of you who were unaware," she began, her voice carrying through the restaurant, "Ross and Lacey are a couple, an item, girlfriend and boyfriend, and involved with each other. They're happy, sappy, and hopelessly in love, and he is officially off the market. Any questions?" She gave Suzanne a pointed look, arms crossed over her chest. Suzanne's eyes blazed, but she said nothing.

The room was so still that when someone in the back finished their drink, the slurping of the straw made everyone turn and look. The guy seemed surprised, and slunk down in his seat. Attention returned to the two women who battled visually in the middle of the room.

"You've got a lot of nerve," Suzanne said from between clenched teeth.

Fanny looked bored. "No, Suze, *you* have a lot of nerve. Now, why don't you go flirt with someone who might lower themselves to take you home tonight? Ross is already booked."

Lacey was silent as Suzanne flounced away and exited the restaurant in a huff, and she looked at Ross uncertainly. Her eyes widened when he started clapping, and it wasn't long before the entire crowd followed suit. The applause rose and Fanny blushed, taking a small bow before sitting down.

"That'll show her," she said with an emphatic nod. "Hussy."

Boomer leaned over and kissed her soundly, then put his arm around her shoulders and pulled her close. "That's my girl."

"Thank you, Fanny," Ross said once the furor died down.

Fanny looked at him strangely. "For what?"

Ross looked at Lacey, and the warmth in his eyes made her heart skip a beat. "For saying what I should have said. Next time, rest assured, I shall act accordingly."

Fanny studied him for a moment. "Well, I must admit, Ross, sometimes you're too nice; to the women that is." She smiled broadly. "Fortunately, I don't have that problem." The four of them broke into laughter, and spent the rest of the evening in peace.

It was after nine when they left the restaurant, and Ross put an arm around Lacey's shoulders as they strolled in the direction of the bar. A half moon hung in the sky, casting a soft, silver glow over the streets. When they reached the back porch, Lacey stopped.

"I should probably...go home," she said as she fished in her pocket for the keys to the Jeep. When she pulled them out, Ross snatched them from her and held them behind his back, smiling as she tried in vain to retrieve them.

"You can't go home," he said. "I have some work to do."

Lacey's heart leapt and she stopped trying to get her keys. When she met his eyes the connection was made, and the mere memory of their passion heated her blood.

"You said you'd had better." His voice was a caress. "That doesn't bode well for my reputation." He ran a finger over her cheek and then her lips.

"I lied," she whispered.

His brows shot up and he smiled, his eyes twinkling with mischief. "You did?"

She nodded and her gaze traveled to his mouth, her cheeks burning when she recalled how much pleasure that mouth gave her. "You have nothing to prove, Ross. Not to me, anyway."

"I don't?"

Licking her lips, she continued to stare at his mouth and shook her head. "No. Your reputation as a magnificent lover is well-deserved and... quite intact."

"Are you sure?" he asked as he leaned closer.

Lacey swayed toward him, her lashes fluttering down. "Positive."

She sucked in a breath when he kissed her, one hand molded to her head as his lips teased hers. Wrapping her fingers around his powerful forearms, she marveled at how much she wanted him, and he only had to kiss her. The image of their bodies joined together flashed in her mind and she moaned softly as her knees wobbled. When he pulled away she almost cried.

"Let's go to your place," he said in a ragged breath, his lips feathering over her face. "The apartment's a mess." He pulled back and looked into her eyes. "Besides, I don't think we've broken in that rug in front of the fireplace yet, have we?"

Lacey shook her head even as she twined her fingers in his hair and pulled his mouth back down to hers. She needed him; she needed to feel him, to taste him. She couldn't get enough of him, and when their tongues met she wouldn't have cared if he'd thrown her on the ground and made love to her right there beneath that half moon.

"I don't know if I can wait that long," she whispered against his mouth. She ran a hand over his belly and he sucked in a breath when she rubbed against him. "I need you, Ross. Now."

He groaned and clenched his teeth, then pushed her away. Lacey looked at him in shock as he calmly unlocked the Cherokee. He held the passenger door open and gave her a small bow.

"Regardless of whether you meant it or not," he began, "a challenge was still issued." He smiled and walked up to her, his expression filled with promise. "I never back down from a challenge." He pushed her into the seat.

"But, Ross..."

He kissed her again, a hot, demanding kiss that made her dizzy. When he pulled back, his breath warmed her cheek. "Shut up, Lacey. I want to make love with you, not argue with you."

Dazed, she nodded slowly and sighed when he kissed her again, his arms wrapped tightly around her. The feel of his body pressed to hers brought even more vivid images to her mind, and that familiar ache swirled in her belly.

"Take me home now, Ross," she said against his lips, "or take me upstairs now. I don't care which."

He chuckled, reluctantly released her, and planted one more kiss on her lips before going around and sliding into the driver's seat. "Your wish is my command."

"It is?" she asked. He nodded and she gave him a wicked smile. She leaned across the seat, put a hand behind his neck and covered his mouth with hers, the fire burning hotter when their tongues met. She pulled away and looked at him through lazy-lidded eyes. "Then hurry."

***

Golden rays filtered through the curtains, teasing Lacey from the deepest sleep she'd ever had. Ross had definitely risen to the challenge last night, literally, and Lacey's cheeks flamed as she remembered their lovemaking. Never before had she experienced anything like what she shared with Ross. He brought out a side of her she hadn't known existed; a sensual, hedonistic side that had even surprised him with its intensity. Lacey groaned in embarrassment and buried her face in the pillow.

She rolled onto her side and dared a peek at Ross. Her eyes widened. She leaned up on her elbows and pushed the hair out of her face. On the pillow next to her lay a dozen daffodils, the flowers holding down a single sheet of note paper. She slid the note from underneath the green stems and read the sprawling script.

Lacey, I had to go into town and run a few errands before work tonight. Meet me at the café for a late breakfast around ten? See you there. Love, Ross

Lacey rolled onto her back and pulled the cluster of daffodils to her nose, inhaling the sweet fragrance. He'd remembered when she'd told him they were her favorite, and that simple fact made her love him even more. With the flowers in one hand, she got out of bed, went to the window and opened the blinds. Sunlight poured in, but the distant rumble of thunder told her it wouldn't last long.

"Oh, well," she said, pressing her nose to the golden flowers one more time. "Rain or shine, every day is a beautiful day with Ross in it."

Chapter Twenty

The sky was dark with thick rain-filled clouds as she parked behind the bar; a stiff wind bending the tops of the trees as it whistled through the branches. She glanced at her watch as she pulled on a jacket. 9:55 a.m. She was right on time.

She sprinted across the street to the café and darted inside; a gust of wind sending a pile of newspapers near the entrance flying. Lacey pulled the door shut, retrieved the papers and returned them to the wire rack.

"Here, let me help with that," Annie said as she placed a five pound bag of sugar on top of the renegade newsprint. "That'll teach 'em."

Lacey grinned and sat down at the end of the counter. "It sure will." Annie set a cup of hot chocolate in front of her and Lacey picked up the warm mug, cradling it between her chilled fingers. "Thank you."

"You're welcome," Annie replied. "After such a beautiful morning, it's sure turning nasty. A spring storm is headed this way."

"Good. I love rain."

Annie chuckled and shook her head. "So, Ross is meeting you for breakfast, isn't he?"

Lacey looked at the redhead, surprised. "Yeah, how did you know?"

Annie sighed and poked a pencil into the bun on the back of her head. "Honey, everybody knows everybody else's business in this town. But, he told me when he stopped in for coffee this morning." She glanced at the clock on the wall and frowned. "Hmm. It's not like him to be late. I wonder where he is?"

A strange shiver ran the length of Lacey's spine and she frowned. She shook it off and sipped her hot chocolate. "He said he had some errands to run before work. Maybe he's behind."

Annie didn't look convinced. "Maybe."

Again, that shiver shot up Lacey's back, only this time it wasn't so easily gotten rid of. "Did he say anything else about where he was going when you talked to him earlier?"

Annie's brows drew together and she tilted her head. "Come to think of it, he did say something kind of strange. Said he was going up to the lake to pick up some sketches, and what was left of my picnic basket, whatever that means."

The thought of the bear went through her head, but Lacey dismissed the thought. Ross knew how to handle himself, and she knew he'd never risk his safety to retrieve her sketchbook. "Oh, well," she said at last. "I guess I'll wait for him."

Patrons came and went, but Lacey hardly noticed; her eyes drawn to the clock every couple of minutes. Her stomach started to twist, as if curling in on itself in ultra-slow-motion. She finished her hot chocolate, which did nothing to dissipate the chill in her abdomen or the cramping in her belly. When 10:45 came, she met Annie's eyes and the woman walked over to her.

"Something's wrong," Lacey said.

Annie nodded and pulled a cell phone from her pocket. She dialed and shook her head after about a minute, her brow furrowed in concern. "You want me to call Boomer?"

Lacey shook her head and got to her feet. "No. I'm going to run over to the bar and see if he left a note or something."

"Okay, hon," Annie said. "Call me when you find something out."

Lacey nodded and headed back out into the wind. Soft fat raindrops pelted the ground; slowly at first, but gradually increasing in intensity until it was a regular downpour. Lacey ran to the back entrance and moved to slip her key into the lock, but stopped short when the door swung slowly inward. A stone of dread settled in her stomach and she felt the pulse in her neck as it thrummed against her windpipe. Fear slithered up her spine; cold, dark, and oily, and she stepped into the back hall.

An eerie stillness hovered over the place, and even the sounds of the storm were muted, as if a shroud that Mother Nature herself couldn't penetrate covered the building. She walked slowly, her shoes whispering over the wooden planks. Her eyes darted back and forth, alert for any movement, but there was nothing.

Something crunched underneath her foot. She went completely still and looked at the floor. Broken glass. That stone in her stomach got a little bigger, and she followed the trail of glittering shards. There were two more broken glasses on the floor by the end of the bar, and several large dark splotches. Lacey blinked rapidly, her lungs refusing to function as she knelt and touched one finger to the sticky substance. A terrified whimper escaped her when her fears were realized. Blood.

"Oh, God," she whispered. Her head swiveled to the right. A table and several chairs had been knocked over, and the railing on the stairs leading to Ross's apartment was broken; the balusters shattered and hanging haphazardly out over the main floor of the bar. Gulping, she straightened up and turned toward the stairs.

She walked carefully up the first flight, craning her neck to see up the second set to Ross's apartment. Alert for any sound or movement, she climbed the stairs and stopped in front of the door. A sliver of light spilled out into the darkened stairwell. Taking a deep breath, she pushed the door open.

At once her eyes were drawn to the foot of the bed where her portfolio lay. Large, rumpled sheets of art paper stuck out at odd angles. When she stepped into the room she saw her sketches had been ripped into little pieces and scattered around the room. Her eyes widened and welled with tears. It was the sketch on the bed that really caught her attention, however. Standing at the side of the mattress, she stared down at the shredded portrait of Ross, the pieces carefully arranged as if it had been a puzzle to start with.

"Oh, God, no," she said, tears spilling down her cheeks. "No."

The phone rang.

Lacey jumped and whirled, a scream caught in her throat. It rang again, and again, but she was unable to move, terror freezing her. Finally, after the tenth ring, she managed to unstick her feet from the floor and walk slowly over to the desk. Her fingers trembled visibly as she reached out and picked up the receiver.

"L-Lights," she choked out. The person on the other end of the line chuckled and her heart sank.

"May I speak with Ross Devlin? No, of course I can't, because he's not there."

Air whooshed out of her. "Lucas."

"Very good, Lindsay. After all this time you still recognize my voice. That is most encouraging."

"Where is Ross?" Her voice rose as panic set in. "What have you done with him?"

Another chuckle. "Oh, he's all right, for now. He and Roger had a…disagreement, so he's a little bruised and battered. But otherwise, he's fine."

A wave of nausea hit her and she ran for the bathroom, the cordless receiver still in her hand. She dropped it on the tiled floor as she knelt in front of the toilet, her insides cramping violently. When her stomach was empty and the spasms had passed, she leaned back against the wall and picked up the phone.

"Lindsay? What are you doing? Answer me!"

"I'm here," she said in a small voice. "What do you want?"

Lucas clicked his tongue at her. "You should know what I want. I want my wife back."

"Fine," she whispered, "you can have me. Just don't hurt him…please."

"As long as you follow my instructions to the letter your *friend* will be fine. Agreed?"

Lacey choked back a sob as tears slid down her cheeks, and that old, familiar feeling of helplessness enveloped her. "Of course."

Lucas sounded almost jovial. "Very good. I see you haven't forgotten your place, even during your absence. That's good to know. I'd hate to have to retrain you, and I doubt you'd like that either, would you?"

The last was more a statement than a question and the tears started in earnest now. "N-no, Lucas."

"I didn't think so. Now, I want you to go to that pathetic excuse for an airport and charter a one-way flight to the Gateway Lodge. Is that understood?"

Lacey sat upright, her stomach cramping again. The Lodge? "Y-yes."

"Tell the pilot you're meeting your boyfriend for a romantic getaway," Lucas said, his voice taking on a warning edge, "and make sure he believes you. Then, after he drops you off and his plane leaves, go up to the Lodge. Mr. Thornton will fill you in on the rest. And, I shouldn't have to tell you, but if you involve the police in this, your lover and Mr. Thornton will both meet a very painful end."

"You have Brad, too?" she squeaked. "Oh, God. Lucas, what have you done?"

The phone clicked and she realized he'd hung up on her. She stared at the receiver for a moment, then scrambled to her knees and vomited again.

Her legs were shaking when she stood up, her reflection revealing an ashen ghost of her former self. She turned on the tap, splashed her face with cold water and rinsed her mouth, then took a long drink. Her first instincts said to run back to the cabin, get her gun and money, and bolt, but she couldn't. She splashed her face again, rested her hands on the edge of the sink and looked at herself.

"Well," she said to her reflection, "this is it, Lacey. Someone's going to get hurt. Now, you've got to find a way to make sure it's Lucas, and not Ross."

The words sounded much braver than she felt; her insides quivering in fear. It was several moments before she found the strength to stand upright, and it took everything she had to get her feet to move. As she left the bathroom the phone rang again, sending her heart into her throat.

She picked up the receiver, pushed the button and pressed it to her ear. "Lights."

"Oh, Lacey, it's you. Thank goodness." It was Annie, and she sounded worried. "Have you heard from him?"

Lacey's mind was working furiously. "Um...yes, as a matter of fact I have. He called a minute ago and...um...I'm...I'm leaving...to meet him right now." Even to her own ears, her voice sounded wooden. She hoped Annie wouldn't notice.

"Oh, good." There was a pregnant pause. "Lacey, are you sure everything's okay? You don't sound so hot."

Damn, the woman was observant. Lacey tried to sound cheerful. "Of course. I'm in a hurry. I have to meet him at the airport."

Annie's voice changed. "Ah. He's taking you for a plane ride, eh? Quite the romantic, that Ross. You go, girl."

"Thanks, Annie," Lacey said, trying not to sound relieved. "I'll talk to you later."

After hanging up, Lacey walked over to the bed and sank down on the edge of the mattress as she covered her face with her hands. Her body shook as she sobbed; despair, fear, frustration and sorrow both scalding and chilling her. It wasn't fair.

When she had no more tears left to shed, she drew a hitching breath and got to her feet. She thought briefly of calling Boomer, but knew Lucas would kill both Brad and Ross if she did. And, even if he *was* charged with their murders they'd still be dead; he had enough money and attorneys to make the case go away. No, there was no getting around this. She had to handle it herself.

After locking up the bar, she got in the Jeep and drove back to the cabin. With a calm that was surreal, she took her gun, made sure it was loaded, grabbed three extra magazines and a box of ammunition. She tucked the gun into the waistband of her jeans and the extra ammo in the pockets of her jacket, then pulled the strongbox from under the bed and opened it. After stuffing a wad of bills in her pocket, she locked the box and hid it beneath a floorboard in a back corner of the closet. Her task completed, she locked the cabin and gave it a lingering look before driving back into town.

Dave Jenkins was only too happy to fly her up to the Lodge, and Lacey was glad for his friendly prattle. He chatted about Annie, about Fanny and her announcement at Joe's yesterday that the whole town was talking about, while doing his pre-flights, Lacey only half-listened to him, her mind a whirl as she tried to form some sort of plan.

"Lacey!"

Lacey's head snapped around. "Huh? What?"

Dave looked at her, smiled, and pointed to her seatbelt. "Buckle up."

"Oh," Lacey said with a nod as she fastened the belt.

"Are you okay?" Dave asked, studying her closely. "Have you been crying?"

His observation was endearing and frustrating at the same time, and Lacey resisted the urge to burst into tears and shout at him. "I'm fine, Dave. I think I'm coming down with a cold or something. It's nothing, really."

Dave's eyes narrowed slightly, but he gave her a smile and a nod. "All right. Minding my own business now."

Lacey sighed. "I'm sorry, Dave. I don't feel much like talking."

He chuckled and grinned at her. "Aw, that's okay. Annie says I talk too much anyway."

Lacey smiled and settled back in her seat, turning her gaze out the window. Part of her wanted to cry, and it took all of her will to keep the tears back. The thought of seeing Lucas again sent stark, chilling fear through the very core of her being, but the thought of not seeing Ross again scared her even more.

When they were airborne, a pair of eagles paced the plane, and a shaft of pain bored through her even as a smile blossomed. She wondered if they were the same pair they'd seen when Ross had first flown her to the Lodge. If they were, maybe it was an omen, a good omen. This time, she couldn't stop the tears, and averted her face so Dave wouldn't see them. After several minutes she wiped her cheeks unobtrusively and closed her eyes.

A million thoughts were springing to life in her head; so many that she imagined her synapses looked like a Los Angeles freeway at the height of rush hour. The inner noise was deafening, and she jumped when Dave rested a gentle hand on her shoulder.

"We're there, Lacey," he said.

Lacey looked around and her mouth fell open. How had she not noticed the landing? The plane was already pulling up at the dock. A second pontoon plane was tied up in another slip, and Lacey knew it was the one Lucas had used. An air of foreboding hung in the air, and Lacey wondered if Dave could feel it too. When they reached the dock, Lacey opened her door and hopped out.

"Thanks, Dave. I really appreciate the lift."

He smiled and gave her a two-finger salute. "No problem, Lacey. You sure you won't need a ride back?"

"If I do, I'll give you a buzz, okay?"

"All right. Now you and Ross enjoy yourselves, y'hear?"

With a smile and a nod, she closed the door, holding her hair out of her face as Dave reversed the engines and pulled away from the dock. She watched as he taxied over the placid lake and waved as the plane ascended into the air, streamers of water falling gracefully from the pontoons. She waited until he disappeared over the mountain, then turned and headed for the Lodge.

Once inside, Lacey looked around the great room, finding the air unnaturally still. A glance in the dining room told her it was empty, and even the kitchen was devoid of life. She walked toward the front desk and a muffled moan caught her attention. Leaning over the counter she saw Brad on the floor, bound and gagged. She ran to the side door but it was locked, so she boosted herself up onto the counter, swung her legs over and around, and dropped to her knees at his side.

"Oh, my God," she said as she took the gag off. Brad took a grateful gulp of air as her fingers worked to untie the ropes binding his hands. "What happened?"

"They've got Ross," he ground out. "And they told me you'd be coming." When his hands were free he flexed his fingers and grimaced as the circulation returned. Lacey freed his legs and helped him to his feet.

"Come on," she said. "Let's get you some water."

She helped him to the couch and sat him down, then ran to the kitchen. After a few moments of searching, she found some bottled water in one of the large coolers and sprinted back to his side. He was rubbing his wrists and gratefully took the bottle. She waited until he downed some of it and knelt at his feet.

"What happened, Brad? Where is Ross?"

"He's not here. They took him, grabbed some packs, and headed out. I don't even know where they were going because they wouldn't say."

"What *did* they say?" she asked.

Brad sighed heavily. "Well, after they cut the phone lines and smashed the radio and my cell, they tied me up. The smaller of the two said you'd be arriving soon, and then they took a set of walkies. They're going to call in and tell us what to do next."

Realization hit her and her belly cramped. Lucas was doing as he'd always done, divide and conquer. Now she and Brad were cut off, isolated; as her ex-husband had planned. "We need some help," Lacey said, desperation raking its razor-sharp claws against the inside of her abdomen. "Is there anybody else here?"

Brad shook his head and grimaced again. "There's no one else, Lacey. It's you and me. And there won't be anyone else showing up until Friday."

Those talons punched through her and the air left her lungs. "Wh-what do you mean? What about th-the maids, the waiters, Jason?"

He rubbed his eyes and leaned back against the cushions. "About a week ago, I got a call from a man who said he wanted to rent the entire lodge for several days, at triple the going rate. Only a fool would pass up that kind of money, so I agreed. Two days later I received an overnight package with my payment, in cash, and a note detailing what the man wanted. He wanted the entire place to himself, and only minimal staffing to ensure his privacy."

"Didn't you think that odd?" Lacey asked.

Brad took another drink. "Oh, that's not even close to the oddest request I've received. We get all kinds in here, Lacey; eccentric billionaires, politicians wanting a nice, private place to play hide the sausage with their secretaries, celebrities, you name it." He looked at the ceiling and a muscle in his jaw tensed. "It's not at all uncommon for someone with the means to rent the whole place for a week at a time, or longer, but they usually want *extra* staff on hand, not the opposite." He scrubbed a hand over his face. "The guy called to see if I'd gotten the payment, and to make sure I could meet his demands. I should've known something was up."

Lacey shook her head, her shoulders slumped in defeat.

"I had a feeling," Brad continued, his expression filled with self-recrimination. "It felt weird, but I dismissed it. I sent everyone home and waited for this person to show up. And when their plane landed and I saw them with Ross in tow, I realized something was wrong. I should've made a call then but I didn't. This is all *my* fault."

"No," Lacey said, her eyes brimming. "No, this is my fault." She sat down and lowered her head into her hands.

"Who is he, Lacey? The big blonde guy is muscle, that's obvious, so who is the other guy? Who's the guy with the diamond Rolex and the $1,000 hiking boots?"

Lacey took a shaky breath and swiped at her eyes. "My...my ex-husband. He's my ex-husband...his name is Lucas Davenport."

Brad sucked in a breath. "Davenport Pharmaceuticals." He waited for her to nod, and when she did he exhaled slowly. "Holy *shit*."

"I left him about a year ago, after seven years of marriage; seven years of hell," she said, tears falling unchecked. "I tricked him into signing divorce papers then I left him. Took nothing with me, except some cash I'd saved up and some clothes. I disguised myself until I was out of Texas, changed my name, and roamed North America for four months before settling here. And *still* he managed to find me."

"Lechter."

Lacey nodded, the weight of what was happening crushing down on her shoulders. "Yes. And now Dennis Lechter is dead."

She felt Brad start, and turned to him. His eyes were wide with shock, and he stared at her in disbelief. "You do realize if he's gone this far, he's planning to kill all of us," he said, his voice low.

"Yeah." Sniffling, she wiped her eyes on the sleeve of her jacket and nodded.

"So, what do we do?"

"Got any guns?" she asked, more serious than teasing.

"We keep a couple of rifles and tranq guns in case of bears, but muscle-head took the rifles and destroyed the others. They're in the fireplace as we speak. I've got a hunting knife, but bringing a knife to a gun fight is not my idea of smart."

"Then all we have is this," Lacey said. She pulled the Smith & Wesson out of her waistband and sat it on the cushion next to him, placing the extra magazines alongside.

Brad looked first at the pistol, then at her. "You know how to use that thing?"

Lacey nodded. "Oh, yeah."

A crackling broke the stillness and Lacey jumped. Brad leapt to his feet and hurdled over the counter, coming up with a two-way radio in his hand. Lacey got slowly to her feet as Brad came out from behind the front desk.

"Hello? Mr. Thornton, are you there? Oh, I forgot. You're bound and gagged, aren't you? Has my errant wife arrived yet? Lindsay, oh Lindsay! I saw the plane fly in, so you must be there."

Brad held out the radio to her and she took it with shaking hands, the sound of Lucas's voice was enough to send her into a near panic. Squeezing her eyes shut she took a deep breath then depressed the button Brad pointed to.

"I'm..." She paused and cleared her throat. "I'm here."

"Oh, good. And now the fun really starts."

"Where are you, Lucas? Is Ross all right? Can I speak to him?"

"You'll find out soon enough, yes, and no," Lucas replied. "I trust you've released Mr. Thornton?"

"Yes."

"Good. Now here's what I want you to do." There was a pause and some static, and Lacey sat down on the couch as her knees wobbled dangerously. "Lindsay, are you still there?"

She held the radio close to her mouth. "Yes, Lucas."

"I want you and Mr. Thornton to come to Half Moon Camp. He does know where that is, doesn't he?"

Lacey looked at Brad who nodded, his expression darkening. Swallowing hard, she pressed the button again. "Yes, he knows where it is."

"Wonderful. It's quite a hike, but that personal trainer I paid for helped you get in great shape. So, unless you've completely let yourself go since I last saw you, it shouldn't be too much of a problem."

"Then what?" Lacey asked, dreading the answer.

Lucas laughed. "Not so fast, my dear. You'll find out the rest as soon as you and Mr. Thornton arrive at our scenic little outpost. We'll expect you by nightfall."

"Lucas, wait!" But it was too late. She screamed in frustration and would've thrown the radio across the room, but Brad stopped her, grabbed her arm and took it from her. He gave her a pointed look and she sank to her knees, a vortex of rage, sorrow, and frustration pulling on her heart. She couldn't breathe and her throat burned; that weight on her shoulders crushing the air from her lungs.

"Take a breath, Lacey. C'mon, breathe."

The whirlpool stopped swirling just long enough for her to take a gasp of air and the tears started. Lacey ground her teeth together and fought them. Now was not the time.

"I'm okay," she lied, her voice low and shaking. "I'll be okay."

Brad stood, held out a hand, and helped her to her feet. Lacey watched as he walked over to the front desk and pulled a large sheathed hunting knife from beneath the counter. After he attached the sheath to his belt he pulled his shirt over it and turned to her. "Come on, Lacey, we've got to get going if we're going to make Half Moon by nightfall." He took her hand and laced his fingers through hers. "Ross is counting on us."

Chapter Twenty-One

They'd been hiking for nearly three hours and the sun hung low in the western sky. Stopping at a rushing stream, Brad handed her a canteen, then eased out of his pack and knelt by the water.

"How much longer?" she asked before taking a long drink.

Brad splashed his face and head liberally, then shook the water from his eyes. "Another hour and a half," he said. He reached for the pack, opened one of the many compartments and pulled a pair of binoculars out. He looked through them then handed them to her. "See that clump of trees on the side of the mountain?"

Lacey followed the direction of his pointed finger. "You mean that patch of green that looks totally out of place?"

"That's it. That's where we're headed." He rubbed a hand over his face. "It's called Half Moon because it's a half-moon-shaped divet carved out of the mountain. On the arc side you have sheer cliff going up, and on the other, a line of trees and a thousand foot drop. There's only one way in or out, by foot. You *can* land a helicopter in the clearing; they've had to airlift people out before, but you have to be a damned good pilot to do it."

She fought the dark, thick swirl of hopelessness that wound around her esophagus. *Isolated, alone, and only one way in or out. Just when I think it can't get worse...* Lacey sighed and handed the binoculars back. "What are we going to do, Brad?"

"I don't know, Lacey. I don't know your ex-husband."

"Lucas is smart," she said as she checked the pistol holstered in the waist of her jeans. "I doubt he's overlooked even the tiniest detail." Her eyes narrowed on the spot of green which seemed so far away. "Unless..."

Brad perked up. "Unless what?"

She turned to him. "Lucas never expected me to leave him, because if he had, I'd have been locked in the house under 24-hour guard. He didn't think I was smart enough. He didn't think I had it in me."

"Will he make that mistake a second time?" Brad asked.

She shrugged. "I don't know. But if there's one thing that *could* trip him up, it would be his ego. He thinks of himself as superior...to everyone."

Brad nodded and shrugged back into his pack. "Well then, let's see if we can make that work for us." He started across the stream.

Lacey followed behind, struggling against the sucking darkness that pooled beneath her heart. "At this point, I'll try anything."

***

Boomer knelt down and touched the dark stain. "It's blood."

Annie gasped as Boomer surveyed the rest of the damage then took the stairs to Ross's apartment two at a time. He walked over to the bed and stared down at the sketch of Ross. Annie moved to his side, her eyes widening.

"That's Lacey's," she said. "She showed it to me once, before it was finished." She clutched his arm. "What's going on, Boomer?"

He shook his head, unwilling to admit how worried he was. When Annie had first called him, he'd assumed Ross and Lacey had gone off somewhere together for some private time. He'd called Dave and discovered the older man had transported Lacey to the Lodge, but *only* Lacey. Ross's plane was still moored at the airport's dock. A deputy had been out to the cabin and reported it empty, and now this. Something was definitely wrong.

"I don't know, Annie, but I'm damn sure going to find out."

***

Lacey wiped an arm over her brow, her heart fluttering as the tiny golden arc that was the sun, sank below the horizon. "How much farther, Brad?"

"About a quarter mile," he replied, turning and extending his hand to her. This part of the trail had proved the most grueling; more vertical than horizontal, like a giant set of stairs. They would climb the rocks and reach a relatively level area, only to be confronted by another tumble of boulders. "You hanging in there?"

Lacey placed her fingers in his and he helped her up to the next plateau. She leaned against a rock. "I'm wishing I had an oxygen tank right about now."

Brad nodded and continued, easily finding foot and handholds. "It's the altitude. Try to breathe deeply and evenly, and if you get dizzy, let me know and we'll take a break. I don't want you hyperventilating or passing out on me."

"Right-o sir," Lacey replied, her muscles protesting as she continued the climb. Her fingers were sore and raw, and she ached in places she didn't know she had muscles. Her lungs cried out for more oxygen, but Lacey maintained her breathing pattern, refusing to give in to the urge to pant.

Brad reached the next plateau and turned to her, a grim smile curving his mouth as she stood at his side. "Good, you made it."

"Barely," Lacey replied, dropping cross-legged onto the ground.

"The hard part is over," he said. "There's the last leg of the trail, and it's an easy walk from here." He pointed north, and Lacey squinted against the rapidly encroaching darkness.

"Then let's go," she said, getting reluctantly to her feet.

Suddenly the walkie-talkie crackled.

"Lindsay? Mr. Thornton? It's nearly nightfall."

Brad unhooked the radio from his belt and scowled. "We're at the top of the rock falls. Be there in twenty minutes."

"Good. We'll be expecting you."

The radio crackled once more then went silent. Lacey closed her eyes and took a deep breath, then checked the gun which she'd holstered to her ankle. When she straightened up, she met Brad's eyes and nodded. "It's show time."

If it weren't for the knots in her stomach and her mind's furious spinning, Lacey would've been awed by the scenery. Ironically, a half moon rose in the east, the sky to the west was a deep shade of purple. Above her, a million stars blinked on, one by one. At one point on the trail, a waterfall cascaded down the rocks to her right, mist puffing up in incandescent clouds as the stream flowed across the trail and disappeared over the edge to her left. She saw it all, but her brain processed none of it.

Up ahead, a pinprick of light caught her eye and she put a hand on Brad's arm. "What's that?" she asked, nodding in the direction of the glow.

"Campfire, most likely," he answered. He saw her hesitation and rested a reassuring hand on her shoulder. "C'mon, Lacey. Let's get this over with."

The trail ended at the bottom of the half-moon shape where the arc met the straight edge, and a large bonfire burned in the center of the clearing. Lacey stepped through the trees and walked forward, Brad right behind her, but the area was empty. Her gaze swept first one way, then back; and that's when she saw him. She gasped and dropped her pack, then sprinted across the dry, hard-packed earth to Ross's side.

He lay sprawled at the base of a huge pine, his hands tied over his head and anchored to the trunk. Tears filled Lacey's eyes as she gently touched a large bump over his right eye, dried blood striped across his face. One eye was swollen shut, and his lip had been split, his shirt torn and stained with dark red splotches. His feet were splayed at an odd angle and she ran a hand over his shins. The bones were broken. She choked back a sob of despair. Roger had certainly earned his paycheck this time.

"So good of you to join us," Lucas said from behind her.

She spun around in time to see Roger materialize from the trees behind Brad. She jumped up, but before she could utter a word, Roger hit him upside the head with one granite fist. Brad dropped like a stone. The big blonde man cracked his knuckles and looked at her, a knowing smile on his face.

Slowly, Lacey turned her eyes to her husband, and she knew he smelled her fear. *She* smelled her fear. Her heart thundered like a base drum and she faced him. "Lucas."

He smiled at her whispered word, a surprisingly pleasant smile. He crooked a finger at her and his smile widened as she walked slowly toward him. When she got close, he touched her cheek and smiled when she flinched and pulled away.

"Hello, wife," he said, his voice deceptively soft. "It's good to see you again." He put a finger under her chin and turned her face to his, and Lacey gulped. Lucas grasped her upper arms, his touch deceptively light. "Don't you have a welcoming kiss for your husband? I think after all this time it's the least you can do."

Lacey steeled herself, her lips pressed into a thin, tight line as he covered her mouth with his. She stood as still as a statue, arms tight against her sides, eyes squeezed shut. She heard Roger chuckle and tried to twist away from Lucas's viselike grip. When he finally released her, she looked at him and ran the back of one hand over her mouth.

"I suppose you'd be more agreeable if it was *him* kissing you," Lucas said. He walked over to Ross and tapped the prone man's leg with the toe of his boot. Ross groaned but didn't open his eyes. Then Lucas looked at her, his expression unreadable. "He *has* kissed you, hasn't he?"

Lacey held her tongue. She knew it wouldn't matter what she said.

"Has he made love to you yet?" Lucas asked, his voice taking on a steely edge.

Again, Lacey remained silent. She forced herself to hold his gaze, knowing that if she looked away he would consider it confirmation of his accusation. He watched her closely, brows drawn together, and goose bumps prickled on her arms as she felt the weight of his stare. Lucas laced his fingers behind his back and walked around her in a wide, slow circle.

"Has he made love to you yet?" he shouted at her back.

Lacey jumped, her heart nearly leaping out of her chest. She wanted to shake her head, to deny it, but she froze. Tears rose in her eyes and ran silently down her cheeks as Lucas continued to circle her, like a predator surveying his next meal. Her blood rushed in her ears, her pulse at a full sprint. Her heart hammered between her ribs and lungs until she thought it would burst. A dull ache throbbed at the base of her skull. So this was what it felt like to face Death. Lacey prayed it would be over sooner rather than later.

Finally, Lucas stopped his pacing and looked at Roger. "Search her."

She didn't realize what he'd said until Roger touched her. Then her brain kicked into gear and sent her body into a flurry of activity. She tried to knee him in the groin but he had obviously expected that. He feinted to one side and sent his fist into her jaw. Stars exploded behind her eyes and the vibration shuddered through her entire face and skull. Heated pain blossomed in its wake. She felt herself fall. Air whooshed out of her as his ascending foot met her descending body. Pain mushroomed in her belly. The world spun as she flipped once, landed face-first on the ground and rolled several times. The taste of dirt and blood filled her mouth. Her diaphragm spasmed as her lungs fought for breath but, before she could inhale, fingers wound into her hair. It had to be Lucas, because she could still see Roger's boots in front of her.

She bit back a cry of pain as she was jerked first to her knees and then to her feet. Her legs wobbled as her ex-husband's arms hooked around hers; his hands lacing behind her neck and pushing on the back of her head, driving her chin to her chest. One of his legs thrust between and over one of hers, effectively immobilizing her.

"Feisty," Lucas whispered in her ear. "I think I like feisty, but if you do something like that again, lover-boy will be the one who pays for it." He pushed a little harder on her head and pain shot from her neck down her spine. "Do we understand each other?"

All she could manage was the slightest nod.

"Good." He laughed softly. "Roger, shall we try this again?"

Roger only cracked his knuckles in reply.

Lacey tried to catch her breath and looked up into Roger's hard, smiling face. He ran his hands over her shoulders and arms, then around her waist to her back. She closed her eyes, humiliation searing her cheeks when he explored her stomach and cupped her breasts, lingering there. He seemed to know exactly how long and thoroughly he could manhandle her without arousing Lucas's temper. His thumbs stroked once over her nipples. She cringed and he chuckled as he moved on. Her heart sank when he knelt in front of her, his fingers starting near her crotch and moving slowly down the length of her legs. He grunted when he found the pistol, one brow lifted as he looked first at her, then removed the weapon and showed it to Lucas. Lucas abruptly released her and shoved her to the ground.

Her body bounced once upon impact and her forehead snapped against the dirt. Fireworks crackled in her skull, blinding her. She felt the toe of a boot in her ribs and braced for the kick, but whoever it was merely pushed her until she rolled onto her back. Lacey tried to blink her stinging eyes and pull in a normal breath. Above her stars flickered on, their beauty in diametric opposition to what was happening on the ground. Then Lucas loomed over her, his face the only thing she could see in the encroaching night.

He looked at her, then looked at the gun as he turned the weapon over in his hand. Roger hooked his hands beneath her arms and hauled her to her feet, then retreated a few paces as Lucas walked up to her, his eyes boring into hers. Her legs were shaky, but she refused to look away. It was the only act of defiance she was capable of at this point. She flinched when she felt the barrel of the gun, warmed by her body, pressed against her cheek. He drew the muzzle across her jaw, trailing it down her neck and over her collarbone. Finally, he pressed the gun against her chest and looked at her, an expectant smile on his face.

"Bang!"

Lacey started violently. Lucas laughed at her reaction. When her brain finally processed the fact that the gun hadn't fired, she drew a ragged breath and closed her eyes. He leaned toward her.

"Relax, wife," Lucas soothed, his lips near her ear. "I'm not going to kill you...yet."

"Why wait?" she asked in a whisper. "Just get it over with."

He stood directly in front of her, his eyes wide, as if hearing her speak surprised him. "Why, Lindsay, that would ruin all my plans. There is so much we have to do first."

"Such as?"

Lucas smiled, an evil smile that made her blood run cold and her insides cramp.

"Why, we must take care of *them* first."

He nodded to Roger, who walked over to Brad and lifted him by the arms. Lacey watched as Roger dragged Brad's limp form toward the edge of the clearing. Alarm burgeoned and expanded in her chest with every step he took. When Roger released Brad and looked to Lucas, Lacey turned horrified eyes to her ex-husband.

"Lucas, no..."

Lucas inclined his head slightly, and she screamed as Roger gave Brad a kick, sending him over the edge of the cliff.

"*No!*" she cried again; disbelief, despair, and grief exploding upward from the deepest part of her soul. She tried to run to the cliff edge, but Lucas grabbed her from behind and held her fast. She struggled in vain, tears streaming down her face, broken sobs shaking her. When Lucas released her, she fell to her hands and knees. She pressed her forehead into the dirt, her fists pounding the ground as alternating waves of hot frustration and cold sorrow coursed through her. "No, no, *no*...!"

Suddenly, she sprang to her feet and flew at him, fists flying. "I hate you, you bastard! You worthless, cowardly son of a bitch!" Roger intercepted her, his arms encircling her like steel bands and effectively stilling her struggles. "You'll pay for this Lucas! I swear to you, you'll pay!"

Lucas walked up to her, his eyes alight with malice. "Perhaps, dear wife. However, you must remember one thing. *I* can afford it."

"You didn't have to kill him!" she sobbed, trying vainly to break free of Roger's unyielding grip. Despair flooded her in a chilling surge and her muscles went weak. She sagged against Roger's chest and continued to weep, her strength evaporating. When she spoke next, a hushed whisper was almost more than she could manage. "You didn't have to kill him."

Lucas smiled. "Oh, but I did, Lindsay. I couldn't very well dispose of you and leave witnesses. That would never do."

Her misery was all consuming. Guilt ravaged her, sending her into an emotional tailspin so steep and violent she felt the air whooshing by as she plummeted toward earth. Her lungs seemed to have collapsed, her heart beating double-time in a vain effort to restart her breathing. As the edges of her vision started to gray, a searing burst of rage detonated in the center of her chest. She started to fight again and almost broke free. Almost. "So kill me already!" she shouted as Roger tightened his hold on her.

Lucas seemed amused by her outburst, a half-smile lifting the corners of his mouth. "Not quite yet," he said. "You see, it's so easy, a brilliant plan, if I do say so myself."

Lacey's body went limp, her strength and fury vanishing like steam on the wind. "Then get on with it," she said flatly.

"Don't you want to hear about my plan first?" he asked in a petulant tone.

She stared at him and a cold numbness grew inside of her. She glanced at Ross. The numbness receded and her heart splintered into a million shards, tears spilling down her cheeks as the pain, sharp and cutting, threatened to rip her apart. "No. Just do it."

Lucas frowned. "No. You're going to hear me out first. See, I'm going to get away with all this, and I want you to know that before you die. I want you to know *three* murders will be committed here, and I won't even be charged with the crime."

Lacey shook her head and shrugged. "I don't care anymore, Lucas. I just don't care."

"You will," Lucas said. The edge in his voice drew her gaze. He smiled. "Because your lover is going to die before you do, and *you're* going to kill him."

Lacey blinked, and the ground dropped from beneath her feet. Her mouth opened in a silent 'o'; eyes widening as her lungs burned. She wanted to breathe, but for some reason she couldn't. Lucas's grin paralyzed her.

"It's really an inspired idea," Lucas said, sounding almost cheerful as he glanced at her gun. "You and Ross come up here for a romantic getaway, with Mr. Thornton as your guide. Unfortunately, Mr. Thornton has a crush on you and decides to make a pass, and Ross sees it. An argument ensues, a heated argument, and Ross pulls a gun." Lucas paused and lifted her .45, the metal glinting in the firelight. "Your gun. The two men struggle and they both go over the cliff, but not before the gun fires, hitting Ross. In your grief you decide you can't go on without him, and take your own life."

Lacey felt like she was drowning. Her vision tunneled and the pressure in her chest increased until even her heart was immobilized beneath the weight. Mentally, she gave in to it and resigned herself to what she knew was coming, welcoming the dizziness. In desperation, her body reacted and she gasped, taking in a huge gulp of air. Lucas's words came back to her and she stared at him. "You're insane," she whispered. "If you want me and Ross dead, you're going to have to do it yourself."

"Oh, no, dear wife," he purred. "You see, I have been planning this for *months*. I would've been here much sooner, but I had to wait for the investigation into Lechter's death to close, I had to finalize the merger, and I had to plan *this*."

Lucas gave her a slow smile and nodded to Roger, who released her. Lucas spun her and looped an arm around her neck. He backed up several paces then jerked her against him as Roger walked over to the tree where Ross was bound. Roger reached behind the trunk and picked up a canteen then stood over Ross and waited.

"What are you doing?" Lacey asked, fingers of dread curling through her abdominal cavity.

"Just watch, darling," Lucas purred in her ear. "Just watch."

Lacey felt Lucas nod and Roger emptied the contents of the canteen over Ross's head. Ross sputtered and jerked awake, his one good eye peering around in confusion. When he saw her, he tried to move, but his hands were still firmly anchored above his head. Lacey saw the realization dawn as he remembered where he was and a groan of pain escaped him.

She jumped when Lucas pressed the pistol into her hand. "Now," he said, "shoot him."

"No!" she cried. She tried to twist away from him but Lucas tightened his hold on her neck, his free hand covering hers in a death-grip.

"Listen to me, Lindsay," he began, his lips brushing her ear. "You can shoot him and end it quickly, or you can stand here and watch as Roger disposes of him." He paused and took a breath. "I don't know if I ever told you, but Roger was in Special Forces. He's an expert in interrogation and torture. Do you know, there are over 200 bones in the adult human skeleton?" He chuckled and Lacey squeezed her eyes shut, her stomach rolling. "Roger already had to break your lover's legs to keep him from fighting, but there are *so* many more."

Roger reached behind the tree and pulled a rifle from the shadows. His large, thick fingers flexed as he wrapped his hands around the barrel of the weapon and waited.

"Shoot him, Lindsay."

Lucas helped her aim the gun as she shook her head, tears streaming down her face, her body visibly shaking. "No!" she wailed. Then, a whisper started in the back of her brain. With her throbbing face, the adrenaline and the stark, unmitigated fear, it was difficult to understand, but it was there. She tried to ignore her ex-husband and focus on that soft voice.

"Shoot him, Lindsay," Lucas whispered fiercely. "Or I'll have Roger start on his ribs, which is extremely dangerous. One punctured lung, and he'll drown in his own blood. Do you want to watch him die like that?"

Her cry of protest was cut off as his forearm pressed down on her esophagus, his rage a palpable thing. The whisper in her head got stronger.

"Shoot him!" Lucas shouted. When she didn't pull the trigger she felt him nod.

Roger's arms pumped up, his massive shoulders moving with fluid strength.

"Wait!" she cried, her voice barely a rasp against the pressure on her windpipe. "Wait!"

Roger paused, the rifle poised unmoving over his head.

"I'll do it," she said, her voice breaking. "I'll do it." She blinked away the tears and sighted down the barrel. Ross looked at her in disbelief and her face crumpled. "I'm so sorry, Ross! Oh, God, I'm so sorry!"

She squeezed the trigger and the gun kicked back, the shot splitting the still night air like a cannon. Ross jerked, his eyes flying to her face in astonishment. Then, Roger stumbled backwards, blood quickly staining the front of his shirt.

"What the...?" Lucas said. In his surprise, he loosened his hold on her and she turned on him, but she wasn't fast enough. His hand came down on her outstretched arm, and the gun went flying as numbing pain shot up her arm and down through her fingertips. He backhanded her and sent her sprawling in the dirt.

She rolled over and scrambled to a sitting position, and froze when she found herself looking down the barrel of her own gun. Lucas stood over her, a maniacal grin twisting his features. He pressed the muzzle to her forehead.

"Now who's going to pay, Lindsay?" he asked, his breath coming in short, rasping gasps. "It's your turn, your turn to pay."

He straightened up and assumed the shooter's stance, the gun dropping to his side as he moved with exaggerated care. First, he brought to the pistol to his eyebrow in a mock salute, and then slowly extended his arm.

As he sighted down the barrel she thought she saw something behind him, the glint of firelight on metal, but it was gone so fast she was certain she had imagined it. Then, a split second later, she heard a wet hissing sound, the kind of noise made by cutting into a hard rind fruit like watermelon. Lacey stared as Lucas's eyes went wide and the gun fell from his hand. The look of surprise on his perfect features was almost comical and he reached behind himself, as if trying to scratch his own back. When a thin, dark line appeared at the corner of his mouth and ran down his chin she inhaled sharply. He coughed and fell to his knees, gurgling as more blood filled his mouth. Unable to look away, she watched as her ex-husband wavered. After several long, tense moments he fell forward with a large hunting knife embedded to the hilt in his back. She gasped and scrambled away from him, horrified.

Lacey looked up at Brad, sure she was hallucinating. He swayed unsteadily, blood oozing from the myriad of scratches and cuts, his left arm limp at his side, his right hand covered in Lucas's blood. He sank to the ground and stared at her, his gaze vague as he tried to focus.

"Sorry I'm late," he whispered. Then his eyes rolled back in his head and he collapsed, unconscious.

***

Lacey checked on Ross and Brad again, then added more wood to the fire. Flames shot skyward, red embers floating into the darkness and disappearing. She stared into the blaze for a moment, then stood up and walked over to where Roger lay. His blue eyes studied her, and she knelt at his side, pulling back the blanket and checking the wound once again. His fingers snaked around her wrist and she jumped, her gaze flying to his face. He was pale, and Lacey doubted he'd live much longer. He'd already lost a large amount of blood, and the wound continued to seep despite her best efforts.

"Why...are you...helping me?" he rasped. He coughed and blood trickled from the corner of his mouth.

She pulled the blanket up around his shoulders. "Because I'm not like him."

He nodded slowly, but continued to hold her fast. "Is he...?"

Lacey sighed heavily. "He's dead."

"He got...what he deserved." He took a hitching breath and the life left his eyes.

"Maybe," she said. "Did you?"

He exhaled slowly, for the last time. His fingers slipped from her wrist and his hand fell to the ground.

She moved back to the fire and checked the still unconscious Brad, then she collapsed cross-legged on the ground near Ross. He was sleeping, or unconscious, she couldn't tell, but at least he looked somewhat peaceful. Resting her head in her hands, she wept.

Something dropped on her leg and she jumped. It was Ross's hand. He reached for her and laced his fingers through hers. Tears blurred her vision as she gently stroked the raw marks on his wrist, droplets falling onto the back of his hand as she brushed her lips against the abraded knuckles. "I'm so sorry," she whispered. When she looked up he'd fallen back asleep and she smiled, taking a deep breath as she lay down beside him.

She wasn't sure how much time passed, but she heard the helicopter before she saw it. Bolting upright, she searched the sky, her view obscured by trees. A few moments later the aircraft cleared the trees and stopped over them, hovering. Its lights flashed against the inky darkness, a spotlight blinded her as it illuminated the area. Lacey jumped to her feet and shielded her eyes with one hand, her gaze turned upward. Gradually, the figure of a man being lowered by a wire became visible, and Lacey's heart leapt. It was Boomer.

***

Lacey leaned her head back against the wall and closed her eyes, exhaustion threatening to overwhelm her. Hearing her name, she looked up and smiled wanly as Fanny rushed over to her. The woman enveloped her in a hug and the tears started again. Fanny whispered soothing words as she let Lacey cry.

The noise of the hospital faded, and even the heady odor of antiseptic didn't bother her anymore. Fanny smelled warm and spicy, like fresh-baked apple pie, her hands stroking Lacey's hair as she rocked her gently.

"They won't let me see him," Lacey said as she took a hitching breath.

Fanny smiled and smoothed the curls back from her face. "I'll fix that," she said. "You wait here and I'll be right back."

A few moments later Fanny reappeared with Boomer, his arm draped over her shoulder. "C'mon, Lacey," he said, extending a hand to her. Let's go see Ross."

Lacey took his hand and followed him down the hall. "Is Brad going to be okay?"

Boomer nodded. "He had a dislocated shoulder, a broken arm, and a concussion, but aside from the expected cuts and bruises he's all right."

"Can I see him, too?"

He chuckled and gave her a sidelong glance. His arm slid around her shoulders and he pulled her close. "I'm the law, sweetheart. You can see whomever you want."

They stopped and checked in on Brad, who seemed in relatively good spirits despite what had happened. Lacey started to cry again and he took her hand, squeezing it.

"It's okay, Lacey. I'm fine, really."

She pressed his hand to her cheek. "I thought you were dead, Brad."

He laughed softly and shrugged. "I would've been, if not for the ledge that stopped my fall." His expression turned serious. "When I heard that gunshot, I thought you or Ross was dead." Then he smiled. "You really do know how to shoot that thing."

Lacey couldn't speak, choked with emotion. "I'm so sorry," she began, her voice breaking. "I'm so sorry you had to..."

"What? Kill that guy?" Brad shrugged his one good shoulder and gave her a lopsided grin. "He had it coming. As far as I'm concerned, that was just a little chlorine in the gene pool."

She smiled through her tears and Brad grinned back at her.

"Why don't you go cry on Ross's shoulder," he said softly. "I'm sure he's waiting for you."

Lacey kissed his cheek then Boomer cupped her elbow and led her down the hall to Ross's room. The doctor had just exited when they approached.

"How is he, Doc?" Boomer asked.

The doctor perused the chart. "Six broken ribs, both tibias and fibulas broken, several broken fingers, bruised kidneys, major concussion, lacerations, abrasions..." He paused and looked at them over the tops of his glasses. "Somebody worked him over pretty good, somebody who knew what they were doing."

"Will he be okay?" Lacey asked. The doctor must have seen the alarm in her eyes, because he gave her a small smile and nodded. Lacey closed her eyes and took a shaky breath. "Oh, thank God."

"He won't be leaving the hospital for a while, but there shouldn't be any permanent damage."

Lacey swiped at her leaking eyes. "Can I see him?"

The doctor pursed his lips, then smiled and opened the door. "Go ahead. He asked for you, but he's under sedation so I wouldn't expect him to be coherent."

Boomer let her go in alone and the door whispered shut behind her. Lacey covered her mouth at the sight before her. Now that the dirt and blood had been cleaned off, she couldn't decide if he looked better or worse. The bruises stood out starkly, the swelling gave his face an odd, misshapen look. Both legs had been placed in traction, and she grimaced as she imagined the sound of snapping bones. A shudder ran the length of her spine and she fell into a chair at his side.

He had IVs in both arms and a machine beeped softly in the background, the green dot dancing up and down on the display. Tears spilled down her cheeks but not a sound did she make. She reached out a tentative hand and laced her fingers through his, his skin warm and dry to the touch.

His good eye fluttered open, and he took a deep, hitching breath. Lacey waited as he perused his surroundings, blinking rapidly. He froze when their eyes met and she bit her lip.

"You...were going...you were going...to...shoot me," he said in a rasping whisper.

She blinked at him and her throat tightened. "Ross, no. I wouldn't have —"

"You...were going to...shoot..." His voice died off and his eye closed.

"No, Ross. *No*."

He didn't respond.

Her mind replayed his words and she gulped. *Oh, God. He thought I was going to kill him.* It didn't matter that he was wrong; she could only imagine what he thought of her at this moment. *Say something, Ross,* please *say something.* His eyes remained closed, his chest barely moving. Lacey stared at him in dismay and waited for the machine to sound an alarm, but it continued its soft, rhythmic beeping. He'd fallen back asleep. She jerked her hand away, as if it burned her to touch him, and scrambled to her feet. Her heart hammered against her ribs as she backed away from him, his accusation rolling over her and pulling a tidal wave of guilt along in its' wake. Spinning quickly, she yanked the door open and sprinted down the hall.

"Lacey?" Boomer called.

She ignored him, panic clawing at the inside of her chest. She had to get out of here. She had to get out of here *now.*

People gawked as she flew past them, but she saw nothing. Everything blurred; tears obscuring her vision, the halls passing in a haze of color and light. She didn't slow until the cool night air brushed her face. Skidding to a halt she surveyed her surroundings, and realized she was at the front of the hospital. A taxi waited under the portico, and a sob escaped her as she walked toward it.

Just as she reached for the door handle, fingers closed over her arm and she was spun around. The Nordic goddess towered over her, blue eyes glittering dangerously.

"Bitch," she seethed. "You almost got him killed."

Lacey took a step back, shaking her head. "No...I..."

"How could you?" Tears gathered in Suzanne's eyes. "How could you hurt him if you love him?"

"But I..."

Suzanne abruptly released her and stepped back. "This is your fault. He's in the hospital, and it's *all your fault.*"

Lacey stared at her, and shame made her knees weak. Suzanne sniffed in disdain and turned on her heel, her stride brisk as she walked into the hospital. Lacey leaned back against the cab and jumped when the horn tooted softly. She turned as the cabbie rolled down the window.

"Need a ride, lady?"

Without a word, Lacey got in the cab and never once looked back.

Chapter Twenty-Two

"Pumpkin, you all right?"

Lacey turned toward the sound of her stepfather's voice. Big John stood in the doorway behind her. They called him Big J and for good reason. He'd been a professional wrestler at one time, and a champion to boot. Standing 7'3", he had shoulders so wide he had to turn sideways to get through a door. Her mother had married him when Lacey was seven, two years after her father passed. He'd taken to being her dad as if she were his own. He intimidated everyone who didn't know him, but to her he was Pop, and to everyone else he was Big J, the biggest, nicest teddy bear around.

"I'm fine, Pop," she said as she propped her bare foot up on the porch railing. The porch swing creaked softly and crickets created a beautiful symphony in the warm air. The sky was a brilliant sea of orange and fuchsia as dusk fell with lazy intent. "It's good to be home."

Big J stepped onto the porch and leaned against one of the support beams. "Your mama's makin' fried chicken and mashed potatoes, your favorite."

He studied her and Lacey felt her guilt rise again. She hadn't seen her parents since her first anniversary. Shortly after the wedding, Big J had recognized Lucas for the type of man he was, and after their first anniversary party, he'd tried to convince her to leave him. Somehow, Lucas had found out about their conversation, and he'd forbidden her to have any further contact with them. The one time she'd defied him and visited them anyway, he'd put her in the hospital.

"It smells delicious," she said, forcing a smile.

"You sure you're not too tired from your trip?" he asked. "We'd both understand if'n you wanted to get some sleep."

Lacey blinked back tears, remembering all she'd left behind: Ross, Fanny, Boomer, and the simple homey life she'd built. She shook her head. "I'm fine. I want to spend some time with you and Mom." She dropped her gaze and bit her lip as the self-reproach wrapped around her like a heavy, wet blanket. If she hadn't already been sitting she knew she'd be unable to stand beneath its weight. "I - I'm sorry I've been away for so long, Pop."

Big J sat down beside her. The swing protested loudly and dipped beneath his considerable weight. He plopped a large arm around her shoulders, pulled her close and hugged her fiercely. "That's okay, Pumpkin. I know it weren't your fault. We tried to come see you, but that bulldog Roger wouldn't let us past the gate." He paused and took a deep breath. "Don't hate me when I say I'm glad he's dead."

Tears fell unchecked, and Lacey smiled through them. "I'd never hate you. And Pop?"

"Hmm?"

"I'm glad he's dead, too," she whispered, burying her face against his neck.

They sat in silence for a while, enjoying the encroaching night and the peace of the quiet country night. Frogs added their voices to the crickets, and Lacey closed her eyes. Immediately, a picture of Ross in his hospital bed flashed in her mind's eye and her heart twisted painfully.

"How long can you stay?"

Lacey sighed. "Not long. Once the media gets hold of this story, they'll descend like a million vultures on this town. I don't want to bring them down on you."

"I'm not worried about some sissy reporters," Big J scoffed.

"I know you're not, but I don't want them camping out in front of the house and the café." She rubbed a hand over her eyes.

The night was so still that the sound of a car coming down the gravel covered lane sounded like a tank descending on them. Headlights pierced the night and the crickets went still. Big J got to his feet as a black BMW sedan with tinted windows pulled in front of the gate and stopped, plumes of dust rising on the air.

Lacey held her breath as the door opened and she got up, moving to Big J's side. He put an arm around her shoulders, his expression darkening in a scowl. The person stood up and peered at them over the roof of the car.

"Frank?" Lacey called. "Frank, is that you?"

The lawyer's face broke into a smile and he came around the car. He opened the gate and stepped into the yard, then strode briskly up the walk. When he saw Big John, he stopped in his tracks.

"It's okay, Pop," Lacey said as she slipped out from under Big J's arm and walked down the steps. "This is Frank Milligan, my attorney. Frank, this is Big John Price, my dad."

Frank extended his hand. "Big John. I used to watch you wrestle. In fact, I won a bundle when you beat The Viper in that title match in... when was it?"

"1990," Big J replied. From his expression, Lacey knew he wasn't sure about the lawyer, but at least the two men shook hands and Big J didn't break Frank's fingers. "We're just fixin' to have supper. Care to join us?"

Frank looked at him in surprise then turned his gaze to her. Lacey smiled and shrugged.

"My Mom's fried chicken has won the blue ribbon at the county fair for the past ten years running," Lacey offered.

The lawyer looked impressed and smiled. "Thank you for the invitation. I'd be honored."

***

Ice clinked softly in the glass as Frank finished his sweet tea. Lacey looked at him silently as he put the glass down on the railing and turned to her.

"I'll bet you're wondering why I'm here," he said.

Lacey smiled. "Well, I know it wasn't for my Mom's fried chicken."

"No, though now that I've had it, it'd definitely be worth a trip back to have some more."

She laughed softly. "I'll be sure and tell her that."

Frank returned her smile. "You do that."

"So," she began, "why *are* you here, Frank?"

The lawyer sighed and leaned back on the swing as he loosened his belt a little. "I've just spent several days with Lucas's attorneys, and I was with the police up in Alaska before that."

Lacey dropped her eyes. "Then you know."

"Some of it." His expression grew solemn. "What happened up there, Lindsay?"

"Please...please don't call me that."

His brows rose, but he nodded slowly. "Very well, *Lacey*. What happened?"

"You said you spoke to the police," she said. "You must know."

"I want to hear it from you."

Tears stung her eyes and she despised the ache that filled her. "I'll make a deal with you, Frank. Next time we're at Javier's, I'll tell you what happened over a glass of wine and a stogie. Okay?"

He must've seen her tears because he smiled and patted her hand. "Very well. But there is something I need you to do for me."

"What?"

"I need you to come back to Dallas. We have to go over the details of Lucas's estate, and decide what you want to do."

Lacey laughed softly. "We're divorced, Frank. I have no part of Lucas's estate."

Frank put a finger under her chin and turned her face to his. "Yes, you do." She blinked and shook her head, but he nodded. "Lucas never changed the will."

Lacey's stomach dropped and she gaped at him. "What?" she asked in a whisper.

"Even after the divorce, he didn't change the will." A grim smile lit his face. "The will he used to humiliate his father with, the one naming you as sole heir to his entire estate, remember that?" Lacey nodded dumbly and he continued. "That was the last will he had drawn up, and his lawyers have confirmed that it *is* legal and binding, though they're not happy about it. Plus, there aren't any relatives or offspring to contest the will, so it's yours Lacey, all of it. The real estate, the company, the entire Davenport fortune is yours."

She felt like she was in a vacuum, her lungs refusing to draw air. It was several moments before she could speak, and when she did her voice was hushed. "I don't want it."

Frank nodded. "I gathered as much. That's why you have to come to Dallas. The Davenport estate is considerable, so you need to decide what you want to do with it." He smiled and patted her hand again. "Think, Lacey. You're a *very* wealthy woman now. You can buy your parents a new home, new car, donate to charity, but I suggest you don't give *everything* away. After all, you earned something for putting up with that bastard for seven years."

Lacey nodded as her mind spun. Frank got up and swung his suit jacket over his shoulder.

"I've got a room at the motel in town, but I'll be heading back to Dallas tomorrow around eleven." He paused and she looked at him. "You can ride back with me, if you like. Or, if not, give me a call when you're ready. We've got time."

"Sure, Frank," she replied. "Okay."

"Hey, thank your mom and dad again for me, will you? That was certainly the best fried chicken I've ever had."

Lacey nodded and watched him as he walked back to his car. She remained on the porch until his taillights had disappeared from sight, then got up and went to her room. After changing into shorts and a t-shirt, she sat on the edge of her bed and stared out the window, overwhelmed.

"Lins, honey? You all right?"

Lacey loved the sound of her mother's voice; soft, musical, and with a hint of Texas twang. She stood in the doorway, her dark, luxurious hair pulled up in a loose chignon, soft curls escaping to brush her ears and neck. Lacey smiled at her and patted the bed next to her. Her mother returned her smile and crossed the room gracefully, then eased down beside her.

"What is it, sweetheart?" she asked.

Lacey didn't know where to start, so she blurted it out. "I'm rich, Mom. Lucas never changed the will."

Her mother tipped her head. "You don't seem too happy about that."

Her stomach cramped. "I'm not," Lacey replied. "When I left Lucas, I left it all behind for a reason. I didn't want *anything* to do with him, or *anything* that was his. And now that he's dead, I *still* can't get away from it."

"So use it," her mother said. She wrapped her fingers around Lacey's and gave her hand a reassuring squeeze. "Lucas used his power and money to hurt people. You can use it to help people, maybe even people like yourself. Y'know, I was readin' an article the other day about domestic violence. It said the main reason women don't leave their abusive husbands is they have nowhere to go, and no resources." She kissed Lacey's cheek and got to her feet, smiling warmly. "You could change that, sweetheart, for some of them at least."

Lacey watched her mother leave the room, the scent of her perfume lingering after she'd gone. She stretched out on her bed and pulled her favorite stuffed penguin to her chest, contemplating her mother's words. Ideas began to swirl in her head and when she fell asleep, she was actually smiling.

***

Lacey walked toward the BMW as Frank loaded his suitcase into the backseat. He turned, paused when he saw her, and closed the door.

"I didn't expect to see you this morning," he said. "Come to say goodbye?"

She scuffed the toe of her boot against the sidewalk, feeling uncertain. "You said I could come with you."

"Of course you can," he assured her with a nod. "I thought you'd want to spend a few more days with your folks."

"I do, but I need to get this over with." A stray curl fell into her eyes and she tucked it behind her ear. "Once the details of Lucas's estate are settled, I can start the rest of my life."

Frank put a hand on her shoulder and squeezed it. "That's my girl." He picked up her duffel bag and opened the back, putting it beside his suitcase. "Let's go."

***

Lacey pushed the microphone out of her face, the cacophony of reporters' questions ringing in her ears. Frank tried to make a way for her, but they were thicker than flies, and it took them nearly ten minutes to reach the lobby of the office building. Flashbulbs blinded her and she shielded her eyes, wishing it would all go away. Once inside the lobby, the doorman closed the doors in the reporters' faces and barred the way. Lacey gave him a grateful smile and he tipped his hat.

"I hate the press," she said, running a hand over her hair. "It's been three weeks. You'd think they'd have gotten the whole story by now."

Frank grinned as he escorted her into the elevator and pushed the button for the top floor. "What you're doing with your late husband's estate is an entirely new story, Lacey. It's not often an heiress gives away the majority of her fortune."

"Yeah, well it's mine to do with as I please, right? Since when is that *their* business?"

"Since *you* became *big* business," he replied with a chuckle.

Lacey rolled her eyes and watched the numbers over the door. When the elevator finally opened, she stepped into Lucas's old domain and her demeanor changed. She wore a red linen power suit, her hair and makeup perfect. Her walk was confident, her spine straight, and she met the eyes of those who chose to stare with a cool, self-assured smile. There were whispers and surprised looks, but she ignored them and made her way to the conference room. A pot of coffee and a tray of pastries awaited them.

"How much longer is this going to take?" she asked as Frank followed her and shut the door behind them. She sat in one of the plush leather chairs, opened her briefcase and pulled a sheaf of papers from inside. Frank poured himself a cup of coffee then did the same, sitting across from her. Lacey pored over the documents and mentally ticked off items.

Frank studied his papers, then retrieved his laptop and started tapping keys. "It'll be several months for the licenses to be approved, and the ranch will undergo some rigorous inspections, but I don't foresee any problems."

"And Claire is willing to run the place?"

He grinned and took a sip of his coffee. "When I told her you wanted to turn the ranch into a shelter for abused women and children, she said if I didn't let her run it, she'd divorce me and run it anyway."

Lacey smiled. "Well, good. And the trust for the ranch is all set up?"

"Set up, and drawing interest as we speak," he assured her. "Havenbrook Ranch is going to be very well funded, thanks to a very generous benefactor." He gave her a pointed look.

"Well," she drawled, "what's the point of having hundreds of millions of dollars and nothing worthwhile to spend it on?" She looked back at the papers. "Now, what about the rest?"

He shuffled the documents until he found what he was looking for. "The remaining real estate has been sold; the chateau in Aspen, the penthouse downtown, the house on Padre Island. Lucas's car collection goes to auction next week. Have you decided where the proceeds from that should go?"

"The Wounded Warriors' Project," Lacey answered automatically. "And I want an endowment arranged for them as well. Also, I want to set up a scholarship fund to help our military and their families. Our troops deserve more than yellow ribbons for the sacrifices they make."

Frank wrote that down. "That's a great idea." He looked over his list. "Okay, that leaves the house in Kauai and the Z8, which you requested be kept out of the auction, and...the cabin in Cooper's Ridge." Lacey said nothing and he looked at her. "Have you spoken to any of your friends since you left?"

Lacey swallowed hard. "No." The picture of Ross as she'd last seen him flashed in her mind and she blinked back tears. She missed him desperately, and her friends too. But every time she thought about calling, Suzanne's words came back to haunt her. Lacey shook her head. "They don't want to hear from me, not after what I've done."

Frank lit a cigar, leaned back in his chair and took a long, slow puff. "And what exactly did you do?"

She stared at him, incredulous. "I...I *lied* to them, I brought Lucas down on them, and then I . . ." she paused as her voice cracked, "and then I ran. Like a coward, I left without a word."

"I don't think you give them enough credit," Frank said as he tapped his cigar against the ashtray. "The people I spoke with were very concerned about you, one man in particular."

Lacey blinked rapidly and shuffled her papers. "Well, once they discover the depth of my deception...their feelings will change."

"Now that they know the story, I think they'll understand the *depth of your deception.*" He inhaled deeply and the end of the cigar glowed red. "But what about you?" Frank asked as he proceeded to blow smoke rings at her. "Have *your* feelings changed?"

She stood up abruptly and walked to the window. Dallas was spread out below her, and from this height the people on the ground were barely visible. She pressed her forehead to the glass and sighed as a tear slid down her cheek.

"I miss them," she said at last. She smiled as she pictured Fanny and Boomer. "I've never met a more decent, likeable group of people in all my life."

"Don't you think they at least deserve to know you're well?" Frank asked. "As you said, it's been three weeks."

"I wonder how Ross is," she said to herself. A shudder ran the length of her spine as the sound of bones snapping echoed in her head for the millionth time it seemed. "He must hate me now."

"Hate you?" Frank repeated. "Why would he hate you? You saved his life."

Lacey turned and gaped at him. "Saved his life? If not for me, he would never have needed saving."

Franks brows drew together. "Wrong, Lacey. If not for *Lucas*, he never would've needed saving."

"Lucas came looking for *me*," she said.

"Exactly," Frank agreed as he set his cigar aside. "*Lucas* came. *He* did this, *not* you."

"But..."

"No butts!" Frank glowered at her and got to his feet. "You are *not* responsible for Lucas's actions, Lacey, so stop trying to shift the blame. You did the same thing when you were married to him, and it turned my stomach. Every time he hit you, every time he hurt you, you found a way to make it *your* fault. Somehow, someway, you'd said or done something to provoke him."

"I knew what buttons to push," she said in a small voice.

"No!" Frank shouted, slamming his hands down on the table. Lacey jumped and stared at him as he continued. "*No.* There are no buttons you could *ever* push that would excuse what he did to you. Lucas was a vicious, vindictive, bitter person, and he took out his unhappiness on you. So, *stop* trying to make yourself responsible for him. He's dead, Lacey, and the responsibility died with *him.* Leave it in the grave where it belongs."

Lacey sank down in a nearby chair, completely deflated by his vehemence. He was right, of course. But knowing he was right didn't assuage her guilt. She ran a hand over her face and sighed heavily.

"You're right," she said, "as usual." She moved back to her place at the table and sat down. "Let's finish up here. My parents are coming into town this evening, and I have some other matters I must attend to before they arrive."

***

The sun turned the sky a brilliant shade of orange as it sank in the west. A smattering of late spring rain clouds drifted slowly by, glowing in shades of gold, pink and purple. Lacey stretched out on the chaise and stared up at them. A warm breeze ruffled her hair as she glanced at the cell phone in her lap. On the small glass table to her left, a half-empty glass of white wine held down a rumpled business card, and Lacey peered through the glass base at the distorted letters. After several minutes of this she sighed and slid the card out from under the goblet.

"Well," she said, "it's now or never."

With the card in one hand and the phone in the other, she got to her feet and moved to the balcony railing. Her hands shook as she dialed, and when she was done she reached for the goblet and took a long drink. The wine warmed her as it settled in her stomach. That comfortable feeling didn't last long, however; her stomach knotted as the recipient of her call picked up.

"Hello?"

Lacey swallowed hard and cleared her throat. "Hi. Fanny?"

There was a sharp intake of breath and then Fanny's words poured out in a rush. "Ohmigosh! Lacey, is that you? Of course it's you, what a silly question! Are you in Dallas? Are you all right? Why did you leave like that? Why didn't you call us? We've been worried sick about you. Boomer, honey! It's Lacey!"

There was a click. "Lacey? Where are you? Are you okay? What happened?"

"Oh, stop, Boomer," Fanny interrupted. "I've already asked her all those questions."

"And how was I supposed to know that?" he asked, sounding frustrated.

Lacey started laughing even as tears streamed down her face. She'd been so afraid of losing her friends, but their concern showed her how wrong she'd been. She only hoped she'd been wrong about Ross.

"I'm fine, you two," she interrupted them. "I'm fine. How are you?"

"Well, much better now that you've called," Fanny replied. "You could've done so before now and saved all of us a lot of worry, y'know."

"I'm sorry," Lacey replied. She paused, gathering her courage, and it took a moment before she could find her voice. "How's Ross?"

"He's recovering more quickly than the doctors expected," Boomer said. "They released him early. One of the guys from the bar installed a lift so he can get up to his apartment with his wheelchair."

"Wheelchair?" Lacey repeated in a whisper.

"It's only temporary, hon," Fanny chimed in. "When his legs are mended, he'll be back playing hockey in no time."

Lacey heaved a sigh of relief and sat down, her knees wobbling. "Oh, thank God."

"Lacey, honey, if you don't mind my asking," Fanny began, "why did you take off like that? You scared us to death."

The last words Ross had spoken to her sounded in her mind, and she took a shaky breath. "Ross...he, um...well, he sounded so...angry...with me, and hurt." She closed her eyes. "And then I ran into Suzanne..."

"Say no more," Fanny said. "I've got it, and I'll fix that little bitch."

"Fanny!" Lacey and Boomer said in unison.

"...if it's the last thing I do," Fanny finished.

The woman's show of loyalty was the last straw. "Oh, Fanny, I'm so sorry," Lacey said. "I...I bolted." Tears started again. "The whole day...I...I couldn't handle it." She choked back her tears. "I'm so sorry. Can you ever forgive me?"

"Of course, dear," Fanny said, Boomer echoing her. "Now, when are you coming home?"

Home. The thought of going back to Cooper's Ridge and seeing Ross after what she'd done filled her with dread. "I – I don't know."

"He misses you, Lace," Boomer said. "He doesn't say much, but I can tell he's hurting."

"We've seen the news reports," Fanny interjected, "and we understand you've got a lot going on right now, but he loves you."

"I don't think I can face him," she whispered, her throat clogging with tears. "Not yet."

Fanny sighed softly. "Well, I suppose I can understand that. Just... don't wait too long, honey. Love wilts if it's not properly tended."

Lacey knew that all too well. "Thanks, Fanny; you too, Boomer. I love you both; you know that, don't you?"

"Of course," Fanny answered. "What's not to love?" She paused. "We love you, too, sweetie."

Lacey smiled. "I've got to go, but I'll talk to you soon, okay?"

"Fine. Should we tell Ross you called?"

She thought about that for a second, and then decided against it. "No. I'd rather talk to him, but I want to do it face to face."

"We understand; don't we, Boomer?" Fanny's voice had a threatening tone.

"Of course, *dear*," Boomer replied. "Sheesh!"

"Thanks, guys. Love you."

"Love you, too, Lace," Boomer said; his tone solemn. "We'll be here when you get here."

"Thanks, Boomer. Bye."

She hung up the phone, feeling torn. She wanted to speak with Ross, to hear his voice, and on sudden impulse she dialed the number for Lights. A female voice answered.

"Hello?"

Suzanne.

Lacey almost lost her nerve as all sorts of sordid thoughts went through her head. It was too early for the bar to be open, so what was Suzanne doing there? Gathering her courage, she forced her vocal chords into action.

"Um, yes, is Ross Devlin there?"

There was a pregnant pause, and when Suzanne finally spoke, Lacey was surprised at the venom in her tone. "He doesn't want to speak to you."

Lacey swallowed hard. "May I ask why?"

"Why? Are you serious? You nearly get him killed, he can barely get around, which makes running this place nearly impossible, and he's going to lose the bar because of all the medical bills."

Lacey was shocked. "I...I had no idea."

Suzanne laughed harshly. "Of course you didn't. You turned tail and ran like a frightened jackrabbit." A voice said something in the background and Suzanne paused. "Look, I've already told you he doesn't want to talk to you. Don't call here again."

The phone clicked in her ear and she stared at it in disbelief. She hit the reset button and dialed another number.

"Frank? There's something I need you to do for me." She paused as he replied. "No, I want you to take care of this personally."

Chapter Twenty-Three

Ross wheeled up to a table and frowned as Suzanne strolled in, his mail in her hand. She gave him a dazzling smile and handed him the stack of envelopes.

"Don't you have anything better to do?" he asked. Ever since he'd left the hospital a month and a half ago, Suzanne had stayed close. She waited on him hand and foot despite his protests. He felt like he was married, and to someone he didn't really care for. Lacey's image flashed briefly, but he pushed it away, along with the ache in his soul. "I can take care of myself."

Suzanne gave him a dubious look. "You never minded having me around before," she pointed out.

Ross ground his teeth together. "Yeah, but you never *stayed* around before."

Her brows shot skyward. "So, what was I to you? Just a good lay?"

He scowled at her rudeness. "Were we ever anything else to each other? You gave no indication you wanted anything more than sex every now and then, and I never made you any promises."

"Did you make *her* promises?" Suzanne asked with a sneer.

She couldn't be talking about anyone but Lacey. His heart twisted, but he clamped down on the emotion before it got out of control. "Thanks for getting my mail, Suzanne," he said from between clenched teeth. "I appreciate your help, but I'd like to be alone."

"She nearly killed you, she's practically ruined you, and still you want her." Suzanne shook her head in disbelief. "You are a piece of work, Ross Devlin."

He leveled his gaze on her. "Takes one to know one, I guess."

Suzanne's spine stiffened and she gained two inches in height. Her expression turned frosty. "I'll stop by later and see if you need anything."

Turning on her heel, she strode down the hall toward the back door.

"Don't bother," Ross called after her. The door slammed shut and he sighed heavily. She'd be back. That much he knew.

He pulled his pocket knife out and opened the envelopes with deft swipes of the blade. He looked at the hospital bill first and braced himself for the shock. And what a shock it was, too. The balance read zero. Frowning, he wheeled to his office and pulled out the previous statement. The shock intensified. He wheeled to the bar, grabbed the cordless phone and called the hospital billing department.

"May I help you?" the service agent asked.

"Yes," he replied. "I just received a bill, but it must be wrong. Last month I had a balance in excess of $200,000, and the statement I received reads zero."

The clerk asked for some information, and Ross heard the clicking of the computer keyboard in the background.

"There's no mistake, sir," the woman said. "Your bill was paid in full three weeks ago."

"But...how?"

"Hmm, it says here it was paid by certified check. And you say you didn't pay this?"

Ross snorted. "Sorry, lady, but I don't have a couple hundred grand sitting around."

"Well, if you'll hold, I'll do some checking, to make sure there's no mistake."

"Fine," Ross said. "Whatever. Just find out."

He listened to the Muzak as the woman checked. Holding the phone between his jaw and shoulder he wheeled back to the table where the mail sat. In the pile was a mortgage statement from his bank, and he looked at that while he waited. Air whooshed out of him and his eyes widened in shock as he saw that, too, had a zero balance.

"Hello, sir? Sir?"

It was a moment before Ross regained his speech. "Um, yeah. What did you find?"

"I'm looking at a photocopy of the certified check. There's no mistake, sir. It was made out for the exact amount of your bill, and your name and billing account number are listed in the memo section."

A sneaking suspicion started to wiggle up his spine. "Who signed the check?" he asked.

"A Frank Milligan."

The name sounded familiar, but he couldn't place it, so he wrote it down. "What bank was it drawn on?"

"A bank in Anchorage," the woman replied. "Alaska Federal."

Ross wrote that down, too. "Thank you." He stared at the bill, then looked at his mortgage statement. A call to his bank confirmed that his mortgage had also been paid by certified check, drawn on the same bank.

"Oh, and Ross?" the teller asked as he started to hang up.

"Yeah, Mike?"

"Whoever paid off the mortgage also made a deposit to your account," the teller paused and whistled, "for $1,000,000."

Ross was floored, and it took several moments to find his voice. "What? That can't be right. Let me speak to Betsy."

Betsy, the bank manager, was on the line in seconds flat. "Yes, Ross?"

"What's this about a deposit to my account?"

"Oh, yes. I remember that. Handled it myself since it was such a large amount."

His eyes widened in disbelief. "So, it's true?"

"Yep," Betsy replied. "You didn't know? Check your most recent statement."

Ross glanced through the mail and saw the envelope from his bank. "Who made the deposit?" he asked as he opened the statement. "Tell me about them."

"Same man who paid off your mortgage. The name on the deposit slip is Frank Milligan. He's *definitely* not from around here. Real fancy dresser; Rolex, Italian leather shoes, tailored designer suit, diamond pinky ring, a *big* one. A little shorter than you, about fifty, nice looking. Oh, and he spoke with an accent."

"Accent?"

"Sounded like a southern drawl," Betsy said. "Georgia maybe, or Texas? I don't really know."

Suddenly Ross remembered. The man at the hospital. He'd been high on pain medication when the man had talked to him, but the general description and accent fit. It had to be the same man. He'd assumed the guy was some sort of investigator. He hung up the phone, called information, and then dialed Alaska Federal.

After speaking with the operator, he was transferred to one of the bank managers. He asked about the checks and was put on hold. Ross fidgeted in his seat as an orchestration of Pat Benetar's "Hit Me With Your Best Shot" played in his ear, and he almost jumped to his feet when the manager picked the line back up.

"I'm sorry, Mr. Devlin, but I really can't tell you anything more. The checks were paid for with cash via wire transfer."

Ross swallowed hard. "C – cash?"

"Yes, sir. We do have some information on the man who purchased the checks, but that's because of Federal regulations regarding the transfer of such large sums of money. Unfortunately, I can't tell you anything else without the purchaser's express permission or a court order. Is something wrong?"

"Um, no. I was trying to find out who my mysterious benefactor was, so I could thank him."

The manager laughed. "Well, I'd love to help you but I can't. That information is privileged. I'm sorry."

"No, not at all. Thanks for your help."

He hung up the phone he stared at the bills without seeing them. Instead, he saw Lacey. She had to be behind this.

***

Lacey parked the coupe in front of Fanny's and Boomer's house, and stared at the familiar dwelling wistfully. Instead of being covered in snow, the yard was a profusion of dazzling flower beds and lush green grass. The picket fence was awash in rose vines; radiant blooms perfuming the air. She got out of the car, paused at the gate, and then opened it.

Halfway up the walk, the front door opened and both Boomer and Fanny stepped out. Boomer had a duffel bag over one shoulder and a lunch box in the other, and Lacey smiled as he turned to his wife for the obligatory kiss before going to work. When he started down the porch steps they both froze, Fanny's eyes widening.

"Lacey!" she said with a gasp as she rushed forward and enveloped her in a hug. "It's you! It's really you!"

Boomer grabbed her next and nearly squeezed the life out of her. "It's great to see you, Lacey. We sure have missed you."

"I've missed you, too," she replied as happy tears filled her eyes.

"Oh, come on," Fanny said as she grabbed her arm and pulled her toward the house. "It's too hot to stand out here. Let's go inside. Boomer, you call and tell them you're going to be late while I make some iced tea." She turned to Lacey. "Thirsty?"

Lacey grinned. "Parched."

The woman bustled her into the house, which was considerably cooler than outside. After Boomer made his call and Fanny made her tea, they sat down at the kitchen table.

"We've been watching the news reports," Fanny said as she squeezed some lemon into her glass. "The media follows you like you're a movie star."

Lacey rolled her eyes. "Tell me about it. I can't even go to McDonald's without someone snapping my picture. It's beyond crazy. I keep wondering when all this uproar is going to die down and they'll leave me alone."

"When you stop being so philanthropic," Boomer said. "I think it's great, by the way; all the stuff you're doing, giving to charity and all that. And turning your husband's ranch into a safe haven for battered women and their kids, well, that's amazing."

"It certainly is," Fanny agreed. "The media keeps saying you're giving it all away."

"Just about. Want some?" Lacey asked, a teasing note in her voice.

Fanny gave Boomer a sidelong glance. "Well, I could use a new car..."

Boomer's brows drew together and he rolled his eyes. "Ignore her, Lacey. That brief stint in the summer sun has obviously fried her brains."

They laughed at that and chatted some more. They didn't question her about her ex-husband, or her past, but Lacey guessed Ross had probably filled in some of the details for them. She prepared herself for the inevitable questions about Ross, but to her surprise, they never came. At least, not until Boomer left nearly half an hour later.

As soon as the door closed behind her husband, Fanny's expression softened. "So, have you seen Ross yet?"

Lacey dropped her eyes and shook her head. Her throat tightened. "Not yet. I wanted to talk to you guys first, in case he wants nothing to do with me. That way, I can come back here and cry on your shoulder."

Fanny reached across the table and gave her hand a squeeze. "I don't think that will happen, though I was beginning to worry. I mean, it's been two months since your phone call. I figured you'd show up before now, especially after you made Ross the first millionaire in Cooper's Ridge." Lacey said nothing and Fanny leaned toward her. "You *were* responsible for that, weren't you?"

Lacey sighed. "I heard he was having financial trouble. Since it was my fault, I thought it was the least I could do. And, ironically, it *was* Lucas's money." She chanced a quick look at her friend. "How did he take it?"

"Not well," Fanny said, a small frown marring her brow. "But you made sure there was no way he could return the money. I doubt he's spent a nickel, but he's settled with it now. Besides, I told him if that son of a bitch had lived, he could've sued him and come away with ten times what he did; your ex being a Texas billionaire and all. I suppose it didn't sting as much when I put it that way."

Lacey studied her fingers. "I wanted to make sure he was okay. I owed him that much."

"No, you didn't, Lacey," Fanny said gently. "All he ever wanted was your heart. He never expected anything more from you."

"I know," Lacey replied.

"So, you going to see him?"

Lacey nodded. "I'm going to swing by Annie's first, but then, yes. I need to apologize and try to explain some things, if he'll listen to me. I'm assuming he's still at Lights?"

"Yep," Fanny said with a smile, "and you'd better get going if you want to see him before the bar opens. Since he's back on his feet, for the most part, the place has been packed."

Lacey forced herself to stand. "Wish me luck?"

Fanny came around the table and gave her a hug. "You won't need luck, hon. He loves you."

***

Suzanne was standing at the window of Ross's apartment when she saw the little red sports coupe pull up in front of the café. Her eyes widened when she recognized the woman getting out of the car. Thankfully, Lacey Jamison went into the café, but Suzanne knew she'd be coming here sooner rather than later. Her mind worked furiously.

"What do you want, Suzanne?" Ross called from the bathroom.

The shower sputtered to life and Suzanne was hit with sudden inspiration. She stripped out of her clothes and tossed them haphazardly around the room. "Um, Burke told me you might need another waitress."

"Yeah, so?"

She glanced out the window. Lacey and the redheaded waitress hugged in the doorway, the woman waving as Lacey crossed the street to the bar. "Well, I'd like the job." She left her bra in the middle of the floor, mussed up the bed, tossed the comforter in a heap on the foot of the mattress, and partially untucked the sheets. "I could use the extra money."

"I don't know," Ross said.

Suzanne wiped her lipstick off on a tissue, then ruffled her hair and sprawled on top of the bed. "Oh, don't decide right away. Think about it for a minute, and when you get out of the shower, we can talk."

"It's not that," he began.

"Please, Ross, I'm sorry for how I've been acting, but don't hold that against me." The water turned off and a feline smile curved her mouth. "All I'm asking for is a chance."

Meanwhile, downstairs, Lacey stood at the door uncertainly, the key to the bar held in shaking fingers. Annie had been ecstatic to see her, and had urged her to talk to Ross immediately, but she wasn't sure now. Her insides quivered like Jell-o and her heart pounded unmercifully. Finally, after many deep breaths, she put the key in the lock and opened the door.

The interior of the bar was dim, the mini-blinds drawn to keep the brunt of the sun's heat outside. Several ceiling fans swirled lazily, and, other than some new tables and chairs, the lift and a new banister, the place looked exactly as she remembered.

"Ross?" she called. The pipes squealed as they always did when the shower was turned on or off, and a smile lit her face. She walked to the stairs and listened for a moment before heading up. The door at the top was partially ajar and the sound of his favorite jazz recording drifted through the opening. Lacey pushed the door open and stuck her head in. "Ross?"

What she expected to see, and what she actually saw were so very different that for a moment she was unable to move. Her eyes met those of Suzanne and a dagger pierced her heart as she recognized the woman's gloating smile. It was obvious what had just gone on, the scattered clothes and Suzanne's nakedness telling her all she needed to know. Then, the bathroom door swung open.

Ross stood there in a towel and Lacey froze, her throat closing up. For a moment they stared at each other. He looked so wonderful, naked except for the towel, water glistening on his skin. He was a trifle thinner than she remembered, but that was to be expected after what he'd been through. Unbidden, heat surged through her and she closed her eyes, remembering another time when she had walked in uninvited.

Idiot, she thought. *You should've known better.*

"I...I'm sorry," she whispered. Tears gathered behind her lids and she turned, not wanting him to see her cry. "I'm sorry." With that, she bolted down the stairs.

"Lacey, wait!" he called.

She heard him call, but ignored him. She sprinted through the bar and raced across the street, almost getting hit by a truck, but she barely noticed despite the blaring horn. She hopped into the little red convertible, jammed the key into the ignition and the engine roared to life. Her vision blurred as she backed out, tires screeching, then she threw the car in drive and stomped on the gas pedal.

She squealed into the airport parking lot ten minutes later, nearly colliding with a light pole as she pulled into a spot. She retrieved her suitcase from the trunk and ran across the tarmac to the hangar. Dave Jenkins had seen her pull into the lot and sprinted toward her.

"Lacey! Wow, it's good to see you."

"Dave, I need a ride to Anchorage, right now."

His expression sobered when he saw the tears on her cheeks. "Hey, what's wrong?"

"It's an emergency. Can you take me?" She swiped angrily at her eyes, but more tears only replaced the ones she smeared away. "Please?"

"Sure," he said, taking her bag. "Sure thing. Shouldn't be a problem. Lemme gas 'er up, call the tower, and we'll be off." He looked toward the Z8. "You want me to do something with your car?"

Lacey thought about it for a moment, then tossed the keys at him. "Yeah," she said. "Keep it."

***

Ross stared at Suzanne in disbelief, anger boiling in his chest, and her smile faded. Trying to appear nonchalant, she rose and started to pick up her clothes.

"What the *hell* was that?" he asked in a low voice. He was so mad he was shaking.

Suzanne gave him a sultry look over one slender shoulder. "What was *what?*"

His hands tightened into fists and he fought the urge to strangle her. "You know damn well what I'm talking about."

"Oh, *that.*" She blushed prettily and turned to him as she slipped into her bra. "Well, I guess you could say I was protecting you."

Something hot and molten exploded in his chest, burning up his throat. He bit back a growl. "And why would I say that?" he asked in a low voice that vibrated with barely contained fury.

"Oh, come on, Ross. She's been gone nearly four months. Does she think she can simply waltz back into your life and expect to pick up where she left off?"

Ross approached her slowly, and he saw the flash of uncertainty in her eyes. He still wanted to strangle her, his fists clenched and unclenched at his sides. "I *want* to pick up where she left off, Suzanne."

Suzanne gaped at him. "She nearly got you killed, Ross, have you forgotten that? Not to mention the fact that you almost had to file bankruptcy. None of that would've happened if it wasn't for her. All of that was her fault, and I told her so."

He went still. "You did *what?*"

She yanked on her shorts. "That night outside the hospital I told her it was her fault. If it weren't for her, you wouldn't have had to go through any of this, and we—"

"We what?" Ross interrupted. Suzanne's cheeks went red and he laughed shortly. "You think if it weren't for her, you and I would be together?" He gaped at her, incredulous. "Talk about being gone for months and expecting to pick up where you left off. Where in the *hell* did you get that idea?"

"We were good together!" Suzanne shouted.

"In bed," Ross added, taking a step toward her. "That's it." He looked her up and down and his lip curled in distaste. "Get your clothes on and get out." When she didn't move he took a step toward her, and she backed away. "*Now.*"

"But—"

"No buts." He picked up the rest of her clothes and threw them at her. "Who the hell do you think you are? You knew up front there wasn't anything between us other than a physical relationship, and you said that was all you wanted. Then you moved, and I didn't see you for almost a *year*. Now that I'm in love with someone else, you show up and decide you want our relationship to be more than what it was? Not likely." His eyes raked over her and as he imagined what the whole scene had looked like from Lacey's point of view the rage in his chest expanded. "You're a manipulative bitch, Suzanne, and I wouldn't get involved with you if you were the last woman alive."

Her eyes widened. "Ross!"

"I *love* her," he said.

Suzanne threw her arms around his neck and pressed her body against his. "Oh, Ross, if you'd only give us a chance...!"

He pushed her away. "Enough!" he roared. "Like you said, you were a good lay! Period!" She gasped in outrage, her cheeks turning crimson as she gaped at him. He paused and reined in his temper, turning away as he ran a hand through his hair. "Get out, Suzanne, and don't come back. I don't want to see you in the bar. I don't want to see you, at all."

She was silent for a moment then huffed past him, pulling on her shirt as she went. She slammed the door behind her, and it wasn't until he heard her car peeling out that he let out a breath.

He dressed as quickly as he could, the desire to find Lacey spurring him to move faster than he had in weeks. Although the bones in his legs had healed, he wasn't quite up to playing hockey yet, or anything else. He was weak from the forced inactivity, and it would be months before he was back to snuff. Workouts at the gym five days a week and physical therapy on top of that were helping, and the doctors were impressed with his progress. He was stiff, and sometimes he ached, but the pain was easily managed and the doctors assured him it would disappear in time.

Once he was dressed, he opened the drawer on the nightstand and pulled the little black box out. The lid was covered with dust and he blew it off then sneezed. Tiny springs creaked softly as he opened it and looked at the diamond ring, a deep sadness welling inside of him. He'd planned to give her the ring that day at the lake, but the bear had proved to be an untimely interruption. Then he'd decided to ask her to marry him that day she was going to meet him for a late breakfast. Her ex-husband had put a stop to that, quite decisively, too.

The one-carat stone glittered, and he scowled as he snapped the lid shut. Hell, she'd probably laugh at such a tiny trinket. She'd been married to a *billionaire*, for God's sake.

You're wrong, his inner voice said. *And you know it. You're just scared she'll run again.*

"Shut up," he said to the empty room.

Do you love her or not?

"Of course I do," he whispered. "More than anything."

Then suck it up, swallow your pride, and go get her.

Ross opened the box again and sat it on the nightstand. He stared at it for several more seconds then got up and took a deep breath.

The first thing he did was call the airport, and the receptionist confirmed his fears. Lacey was gone. He was at a loss for a few seconds, unsure what to do next. The only think he could think to do was enlist Boomer's help. He left his apartment and descended the stairs, gripping the railing for support. He hated this weakness, but the pain in his legs wasn't anything compared to the pain in his heart. Seeing Lacey had only sharpened that ache, and made him realize how much he still loved her. He could only imagine what she was feeling right now, especially since it wasn't the first time she'd walked in on him with another woman. He hoped he hadn't lost her forever. When he reached the bottom of the stairs he stopped for a moment and closed his eyes, picturing her.

She was beautiful, more so than he remembered. Even in jeans and a t-shirt she looked like a million bucks, and when he'd seen her standing in the doorway to his apartment, his heart had done a somersault. Then the rest of the scene came to mind and his stomach twisted. Opening his eyes he left the bar and locked the door behind him.

He didn't blame her for running. Hell, he'd probably have done the same thing in her place. As he walked toward the sheriff's office, he lifted his face to the sun and wished his thoughts were as clear as the sky above him.

A bell sounded when he stepped into the lobby at the station and several seconds passed before Boomer appeared from a back room. His eyes widened when he saw Ross and he walked over to the counter.

"Hey, Ross, what's up, bud?"

"I need your help, Boomer."

Boomer nodded. "Sure thing, what can I do?"

"You can put those detective skills to work, and help me track down Lacey."

Boomer was taken aback, blonde brows shooting skyward. "Isn't she with...didn't she come to see you?"

Ross hung his head and explained what had happened. Boomer listened intently, his scowl deepening. When Ross was finished, the sheriff slapped his hands on top of the counter.

"Well, with these new state-of-the-art computers given to the department by an *anonymous donor* we're a few mouse clicks away from finding that girl." He rubbed his hands together gleefully. "C'mon back,

Ross. We've got work to do."

Ross came around the corner and sat down beside Boomer's desk. "Do you really think you can find her with that?"

Boomer grinned, cracked his knuckles and sat down at the laptop with a flourish. "With this baby, I can find the *launch codes*." He tapped on the keys, then pointed and clicked until Ross was lost. Boomer was much more computer literate, and within moments a picture of Lacey appeared on the screen beneath the headline "Heiress Shelters Victims of Domestic Violence."

"I already knew she was in Dallas," Ross said dryly. "What I need to find out is where she is *now*. Oh, hold up a sec." He reached into his pocket and pulled out a scrap of paper. "Look for a Frank Milligan. He's probably a private eye, or a lawyer."

"Who's he?" Boomer asked, typing at a furious pace.

"He's the guy who signed the checks that paid off all my bills," Ross replied.

Boomer's eyes swiveled his direction. "I thought you said Lacey paid off the bills."

Ross ran a hand through his hair and groaned in frustration. "I said I *thought* she did, and I still do. This guy was the middleman. He was at the hospital shortly after the incident with Lacey's ex. Remember? The suit?"

"Ah," Boomer said. He hit a few more keys and a picture of Frank Milligan appeared, Lacey at his side. "Yeah, now I remember him. He's her attorney."

"What's the name of his firm?" Ross asked, grabbing a pencil.

Boomer scanned down through the article. "Milligan & Associates. Big surprise." He looked at Ross. "What are you going to do?"

Ross scribbled down the name and stuffed the paper in his pocket. "If anyone knows where she is, it's this guy."

"And if he won't tell you?"

He paused and chewed that over for a minute. "Then, I'll have to convince him to change his mind."

Chapter Twenty-Four

Frank Milligan leaned back in his chair and took a puff of his cigar. Ross studied the man, but the lawyer's face was as expressionless as a blank slate. Ross had a feeling he wouldn't get *any* information out of the man unless Milligan *wanted* to give it up. Ross pulled in a deep, slow breath and tried to be just as straight-faced.

"So, Mr. Devlin," Milligan began, "how may I be of assistance? My secretary said you indicated there was an emergency of sorts."

Ross tempered his impatience and returned the attorney's gaze evenly. "I think you know why I'm here, Mr. Milligan, so let's not waste each other's time, shall we? And please, call me Ross."

Milligan smiled and blew a smoke ring. "Very well, Ross. You're looking for someone." He waited for Ross's nod. "What makes you think I can help you?"

"I *have* to find her," Ross replied.

"Who?"

"You know who," Ross bit out, his hands clenching into fists.

Milligan merely raised a brow. "Why?"

Ross blinked and his throat tightened. It took him several seconds to find his voice. "Because I love her." He dropped his gaze and gripped the armrest tightly. "And...because, I need to apologize. There's been a *huge* misunderstanding." He felt the attorney's intense stare.

"What makes you think I'll tell you where she is? How do I know you're not like most every other man in her life?" When Ross looked up Milligan continued, a scowl darkening his brow. "Her husband used her to gain his inheritance. Hell, even *I* used her, at first, to get revenge on her husband. What's *your* story, Ross? I find it odd that you show up *now*, now that she's worth a fortune."

Ross jumped to his feet, a surge of irritation barreling up his throat.

He braced his hands on the edge of the desk and leaned in. "I *love* her. I don't want her money."

"Good," Milligan said in a curt voice, "because she doesn't have any. She has nothing but a small stipend to sustain her until she finds work. The rest of it she gave away. Now, how do you feel about her?"

Ross didn't even hesitate, anger boiling in his chest. When he spoke he did it through clenched teeth. "The same. My feelings for her aren't based on the size of her bank account, *Mr.* Milligan. They never were."

Milligan pursed his lips and tapped out his cigar. His gaze turned assessing, and then, suddenly, the attorney smiled. "Please, sit down, Ross. And call me Frank. It's nice to finally meet you."

***

Ross sipped his beer, leaned back in his chair and watched the man across from him. Javier's was quite the place; very upscale, but Frank had walked right in as if he owned the establishment. The host had taken them immediately to a private booth. Now here they sat, sizing each other up, and Ross wondered what was going on inside the lawyer's mind.

"I know you're wondering what I'm thinking," Frank said at last, his gaze unwavering. Ross hid his surprise and Frank smiled. "Well, I'm thinking I like you, Ross Devlin."

"You don't know me," Ross said.

The lawyer shrugged and took a drink of his martini. "I know more than you think. After all, Lacey's more than a client. She's become like a daughter to me, and I intend to see she's protected."

"Protected from what?"

Frank smiled. "Protected from *whom*," he corrected. "Once news hit that she'd inherited the Davenport fortune, men started coming out of the woodwork. They still send flowers, gifts; offer declarations of undying love. She's had her phone number changed three times, but somehow they always manage to find out what the new number is." His eyes narrowed. "But she wasn't interested in any of them. No, her heart was somewhere else, and now I know where."

"Why did she pay off my bills, the mortgage?" Ross asked.

"She heard you were in financial straits and felt responsible," Frank replied. "The extra million was for any unforeseen expenses, like more medical bills."

Ross pulled a paper from his pocket and slid it across the table. "I've already told you, I don't want her money."

Frank picked up the paper and his eyes widened as he stared at the certified check for $1,000,000. He smiled, put it on the table, and pushed it back toward Ross. "It won't do any good to give it back. She's instructed me if you try to return the money, to simply make another deposit. You'd better accept it."

Ross picked up the check and ripped it into little pieces. "I don't. Want. Her money."

"What *do* you want, Ross?" Frank asked directly.

"I want *her*, the way she is," he replied. "Money or no, I *love* her. So, are you going to tell me where she is, or not?"

Frank stared at him for a moment, then a slow smile lit his face. He loosened his tie and finished his martini, then poured himself another from the shaker on the table. His eyes twinkled as he looked at Ross over the top of his glass. "So, Ross, ever been to Kauai?"

* * *

Lacey closed her eyes against the warm breeze blowing through the lanai. Sheer white curtains fluttered and a ceiling fan turned in lazy circles overhead; the sun sinking low on the horizon. This was her favorite time of day, but the ache in her heart kept her from enjoying the brilliant Hawaiian sunset.

After rising from the white, overstuffed couch she crossed the white-tiled floor and stepped outside, the lush grass soft beneath her bare feet. Thick stands of palm trees lined the property and extended to the shore, the underbrush vibrant with hibiscus and other tropical blooms. She'd always loved this place; its seclusion and romantic atmosphere, but now it seemed hollow. The servants had left for the day, and the six-bedroom house seemed awfully large for just her.

She strolled across the lawn to the beach, black sand crusted with thick, white foam where the sea lapped lazily. This was a place for lovers; lush tropical rainforest, a gorgeous private beach, a house that was a designer's dream. It all reminded her how very alone she was.

Above her, late summer rain clouds threatened, but she didn't care. Gathering her skirt in one hand she walked into the water and the warm Pacific embraced her ankles. Rain started and soft, fat drops plopped noisily onto the ocean's surface. In no time, the gauzy white skirt and matching top were soaked and clung to her like a second skin. *At least it's warm,* she thought. She pushed the hair out of her face and looked at the sky, closing her eyes against the downpour.

Ross watched her from the tree line, leaning against the trunk of a palm with his hands stuffed in his pockets. His breath caught as she simply stood there, letting the rain wash over her. Her hair hung in long, wet curls down her back, the filmy outfit she wore nearly transparent as it hugged every curve and hollow. *God, you're beautiful,* he thought. He longed to hold her, but for now he was content to watch.

She let go of her skirt and waded deeper, the material fanning out on the placid ocean. She walked parallel to shore, water swirling about her thighs. Her stride was unhurried, her movements slow and graceful, her expression pensive. Ross wished she would smile, as he remembered how her smile would light up a room and lift his spirits. Unable to be this close to her and yet still be so far away, he pushed away from the tree and walked toward her.

"Excuse me," he called when he reached the water's edge. "Is this a private beach?"

"Yes," she said, not bothering to look at him. "But it's big enough," she paused and glanced his way as she added, "to share." Her eyes widened when they met his and she froze.

He saw the pain before she turned away from him. Heedless of his clothes he waded in and stood at her side.

"That's good," he said. "It would be a crime to be in this gorgeous tropical paradise...*alone.*"

"Unless, of course, you *want* to be alone," she countered, her voice low.

"And *do* you . . ." he asked, almost afraid of the answer, "want to be alone?"

She looked at him briefly before her chin went up. "Yes." Without another word she waded to shore and walked toward the large, rambling house.

Ross followed and grabbed her arm before she'd gone ten feet, his grip gentle but firm. "Lacey, wait. Please."

She went absolutely still, her face averted. "How did you find me?" she whispered.

He released her arm and pushed a long fall of wet hair over her shoulder. "With a little help from my friends."

"*Why?*"

The pain in her voice nearly undid him, and he took a deep breath. "Well, y'know, it's really a great story, how I ended up here and all. See,

I met this fabulous girl, but then some things happened and, instead of the girl, I wound up with all this great stuff. I mean, I really hit the jackpot. All my bills were paid off, someone dumped a million bucks in my bank account, tax free I might add, *and* I got this trip to Kauai, via Dallas, Texas." He paused and put a finger under her chin then turned her face to his. "Only problem was, I didn't have the girl anymore." A tear ran down her cheek, mingling with the rain, and he wiped it away. "I'd give it all back, *every penny*, if I could just have the girl again. *She's* what I really want." Confusion shimmered in her eyes and he knew the next question before she said anything.

"But...Suzanne...?"

"There's *nothing* between me and Suzanne," he said, cupping her face. "Give me a chance to explain?"

Lacey dropped her eyes. "Ross, you...you don't have to explain anything to me."

"Yes, I do," he interrupted. "Lacey, please look at me."

She shook her head and pulled away from him. "It doesn't matter, Ross. I left. I'd say that makes you free and clear to do whatever you want, with whomever you want."

"And what if the person I want is the person who went away?" When she looked up at him he grabbed her around the waist and pulled her close. "Suzanne helped out while I was recovering so I gave her a set of keys to the bar. That day you came I was in the shower when she let herself into the apartment. Please, believe me when I say I was as shocked as you were to see her. She staged the whole scene because she thought, with you out of the picture, she and I would be together." He saw a faint glimmer in her eyes and continued before it died. "What she didn't count on was the fact that I love you, Lacey. It's *you* I want, not Suzanne, not anyone else. You, and *only* you."

Pushing out of his embrace she swiped at her eyes. "But I have nothing to give you, Ross." She gestured toward the house. "See that house? It's beautiful, isn't it?"

He glanced at the sprawling structure. "Yes."

"Well, it belongs to Frank. He's letting me stay here until I get things figured out. All the money, all the houses, everything, I sold it all and gave it away. There's nothing left."

He took her hand and pressed his lips to her palm in a lingering kiss. "That's not true. You have something left to give me, something far more valuable than all the money in the world." Pausing, he looked at her. "Give me your heart, Lace. That's all I want from you. I don't care if you're a princess or a pauper."

She shook her head slowly and backed away from him. "I...I don't..."

His heart faltered as her voice trailed off, his abdominals tightening. Had her feelings changed? He swallowed hard. "If you give me your heart, I'll give you mine," he offered with a hopeful smile. "You already have it, but let's make it official." His nerves were taut but he kept his smile firmly in place. "Speaking of making it official, I *do* have something to offer *you.*"

As he reached into his pocket, Lacey thought her heart would explode. When she'd first seen him, standing there so casually and looking so incredibly handsome, she'd nearly come out of her skin. Fear, longing, desire, joy and sorrow had coursed through her all at once, and her body still trembled in response to the tumult. Her eyes welled with tears when she saw the little black box. He lifted the lid almost reluctantly, and gave her a sheepish look before holding it out to her.

"I know it's probably nothing like the ring Lucas gave you," he said, his voice low, "but I bought it for a waitress, not an heiress."

Lacey stared at the ring. He pulled the solitaire from the velvet covered foam and held it out to her again, but she took a step back. She shook her head, unable to believe what was happening. Her life had never even remotely resembled a fairy tale, but here was the man of her dreams offering her a chance at a happy ending. She was almost afraid to reach for it, so she gave him an out. "Ross, you don't have to do this."

He took her hand. "I know I don't *have* to do this. I *want* to do this." He held up the ring between them. "I've been sitting on this little baby for months now. I was going to propose that day at the lake, but we were interrupted by the local wildlife." He sighed and laced his fingers through hers. "And that day we were supposed to meet for breakfast, I was going to do it then, but...you know what happened."

Lacey's heart did a flip-flop. She looked down at the ring, twinkling in the twilight, and when he knelt before her, her breath caught. His brilliant blue eyes held hers, and she saw the love reflected there. It filled her and warmed her, and the tears started in earnest.

"Lacey Jamison, you would make me the happiest man alive if you would do me the honor of becoming my wife."

Suddenly the rain stopped and an unnatural hush descended, as if all nature waited for her answer. Lacey couldn't speak, her vocal chords frozen, and when Ross saw her hesitation he stood up slowly.

"I know I'm asking a lot, Lace," he said, his voice barely above a whisper. "You've just left one marriage, and to ask you to jump right back into another is a *huge* request, but..." His voice died and he pressed a hand to her cheek, his thumb lightly stroking her skin. "The thought of spending another day without you...I can't do it. I love you, Lace. I *need* you."

He kissed her then, and time stood still, the world unmoving. His arms enfolded her, warm and strong, his lips moving with lazy intent over hers. The flame she thought she'd put out flared again and heat surged through her like a drug. Her limbs were languid and heavy as her hands slid into his hair. He pressed her close, the friction of their bodies making her gasp. Seizing the opportunity, his tongue met hers and Lacey knew she was lost.

She was barely aware they were moving until she felt the sand beneath her back. Her senses launched into overdrive as he covered her body with his, leaning on his elbows as he plundered her mouth. Her breasts tingled as they brushed his chest, and a low moan escaped her.

"Marry me, Lacey," he whispered against her mouth. "I can't live without you."

His lips trailed down her neck and over her collarbone, searing her flesh. He cupped her breast in his hand and lifted it to his mouth, suckling her through her clothing. Lacey gasped and arched her back, her hands twined his hair.

"Marry me," he repeated.

When he took the sensitive tip into his mouth again, Lacey could stand no more.

"Yes..."

***

The sheer netting hung in graceful folds over the bed and rippled gently as a cool breeze blew through the open windows. Silver moonlight gave the white furnishings an eerie, fog-like glow, the ocean a soft whisper in the background. Ross leaned up on his elbow, watching her as she stared at the ring on her hand.

"I know it's not much—"

"It's beautiful," she said, a smile curving her mouth.

He ran one finger along her collarbone. "No," he said, *"you're* beautiful." Her smile deepened and he kissed her shoulder. "God, I've missed that smile. It seems like forever since I've seen it."

She dropped her eyes and fingered the sheet self-consciously. "Ross, I'm so sorry..." Her voice died and when he ran a finger over her cheek she looked up at him.

"Why did you leave, Lacey?" he asked in a whisper.

Lacey rolled onto her side and faced him, bringing the sheet with her. "I...I guess it was too much for me," she replied in a low voice. "I was *so* scared, and I felt *so* guilty. When you woke up in the hospital... the way you looked at me, so hurt and confused. And when you said you thought I was going to shoot you, I—"

"Wait, hold on a minute," he interrupted, nudging her chin up. "When did this happen? I don't remember seeing you after the emergency room."

Tears gathered in her eyes and she lowered her lashes. "It was after they put you in a room. Boomer took me to see you, and...and..."

"Lacey." He framed her face and forced her to look at him. "I was in pain, half out of my head, and pumped full of narcotics. Whatever I said, it was gibberish." He sighed when two tears spilled down her cheeks. "Babe, you saved my life. I was surprised you shot *anybody*. I wasn't sure if you had it in you. Shooting at paper targets is one thing, but shooting at human targets? That's something else entirely."

"So...so you weren't angry with me?" she asked, sniffling.

Ross chuckled and kissed her soundly. "Not even for a second. I was mad as hell at your ex, but you? Not a chance. And you can forget the guilt too. I lay the blame for this whole incident squarely on your ex-husband's shoulders."

"Frank said the same thing," she whispered.

"Well," Ross drawled, "he's your attorney for a reason. You should listen to him, because he's right."

"Frank's always right." She gave him a small smile. "He must like you, or he never would've told you how to find me."

He laughed softly and shook his head. "At first I couldn't tell, he's got a killer poker face. But after he took me to lunch at Javier's—"

Her head snapped up. "He took you to Javier's?" She blinked when he nodded. "He *definitely* likes you."

"What's not to like?" Ross asked with a devilish grin, lowering his head to capture her mouth.

Lacey surrendered to him, her lips pliant beneath his. He pulled her close as his hands roved up her back, his kiss slow but insistent. His skin was warm and smooth against hers, muscles rippling as she caressed the width of his shoulders. Throbbing heat settled between her thighs when he touched his tongue to hers. He took his time, exploring her mouth, savoring her with deliberate, unhurried purpose. When he finally pulled away, she was dazed, breathless, and left wanting.

"You are so beautiful," he whispered, brushing the hair from her face.

She traced the outline of his mouth with a tentative hand and giggled when he nipped at one of her fingers. She stared into those eyes, captivated by their depths. "So are you."

He smiled. "Men aren't beautiful. We're handsome or rugged or *manly*, but not beautiful." He pressed his lips to her brow. "You on the other hand . . ." he kissed her cheek, "are ravishing…" a kiss to her throat, "gorgeous…" he pulled the sheet down, exposing her breasts. He paused and exhaled slowly as he stared at them then lifted his gaze to hers. "Absolutely amazing." He trailed one finger from her collarbone over her breast, stopping to tease the taut peak. "So, when do you want to get married?"

She inhaled sharply when his tongue replaced his fingers, and she closed her eyes as her body responded. "Is...tomorrow too soon?"

His soft laugh was the only reply.

***

The hammock swung gently back and forth as the rising sun painted the sky. Ross and Lacey lay entangled, her head on his chest, legs entwined, fingers laced. He played with a long, golden curl as they enjoyed the early morning quiet, waves lapping softly only a few feet away.

"This place is great," Ross said softly. "Do you think Frank would let us come back here, say, for our honeymoon?"

Lacey bit her lip and kept her eyes on the sky as a tingle of uncertainty shivered up her spine. "Um, yeah. I think he might go for that."

"Cool. Now all we have to do is plan the wedding."

"Something small," she said. "I've already had the huge wedding with all the proverbial trimmings." She pressed her face into the crook of his neck and snuggled closer. "How about family and close friends? My parents, your parents, Fanny and Boomer, Annie and Dave, and I know Frank and Claire will want to come, too."

Ross pressed a kiss to her hair. "Sounds good. Where do you want to have it? It'll have to be someplace inexpensive, that's for sure. You're broke, and I spent the majority of my cash store on plane tickets."

Leaning up on her elbow she looked at him and frowned. "What about the money I gave you?"

"Yeah," he said with a sigh, "now that I look back, what I did seems kind of stupid."

"What did you do?"

"I tried to give it back," he said with a rueful shake of the head. "When I went to see Frank, I handed him a check for the whole million. He wouldn't take it, so I tore it up."

She rolled her eyes and giggled. "Oh, is *that* all?" she asked. "Trust me. Frank still has that check, and it's probably taped back together. But even if it isn't, that's okay too." She settled back against him. "I say we have the wedding here in the gardens. Fly all the guests out, and they can stay with us in the house."

He tapped his knuckles lightly against her forehead. "Helloooo! Fly everyone out here? Did you not hear me when I said I had no money?"

She shrugged and tried to look nonchalant as that tingle of uncertainty intensified. "That's okay. See, I may have...*fibbed* a bit when I said I gave it *all* away. I didn't really give it all away. I did keep a little bit for myself."

He pulled back and looked down his nose at her. "And exactly how much is a 'little bit'?"

A guilty flush warmed her cheeks and she chewed her lip. "Um... well...and this is just a ball park figure, but somewhere in the range of...$25 million."

Ross's jaw dropped. "Twen - say that again?"

She rolled over and drew lazy circles on his chest with one finger, unable to meet his eyes. "$25 million. It's a figure Frank came up with. He calculated how much Lucas would've spent if he'd hired someone to do everything I did; run the household, play the dutiful spouse, plan and host all those lavish parties, et cetera. Throw in some extra for pain, suffering and emotional distress, and that's what you end up with." She dared a glance and quickly lowered her eyes. "At least, that's what *Frank* ended up with."

Air whistled from between Ross's teeth. "You call that a 'little bit'?"

"Considering what the original estate was worth, it's less than 1%."

She shrugged. "In comparative terms, that *is* a little bit."

"And the house?"

Her heart thumped uncomfortably. "Mine."

He put a finger under her chin and tipped her face up. His eyes searched hers and she wanted to look away, but he wouldn't let her. "Why didn't you tell me?" he asked softly. "Don't you trust me?"

Remorse squeezed her heart with hard, cold fingers. "Of course I trust you. I...I mean I..." Her voice trailed off and she lowered her gaze. "I was afraid to tell you. I wasn't sure if you'd like me more or less if you knew I was rich, and I wasn't willing to risk it. It was..."

"A reaction," he finished for her. His fingers slid into her hair and he turned her face to his. Lacey bit her lip and waited for the scolding, but it never came. He studied her intently. "Is there anything else you haven't told me?"

A great sadness welled up in her and she scooted as far away from him as the hammock would allow. With a heavy sigh, she ran a hand over her eyes. "Yes."

Ross waited, and when she didn't say anything, he leaned forward. "What is it, Lace? You can tell me anything, you know that, right?"

She nodded and bit her lip, and when she spoke, her voice was low. "I...I can't have children." Pain roiled through her and she fought against the memory that wanted to surface as she waited for him to speak. When he didn't respond she dared a glance at him. His expression was unfathomable and she dropped her gaze. "Lucas didn't want any children." She took a shuddering breath and squeezed her eyes shut. "When he found out I was pregnant, he, um...he..." Her throat tightened and she swallowed hard as tears stung. "I tried to get away, but by the time he was finished with me..." Her voice died and she felt the warm trickle of tears on her cheeks. Shame and regret savaged her insides, adding to the anguish that threatened to drown her. She took several deep breaths and clawed her way back to the surface. "By the time he was finished with me I had to have an emergency hysterectomy."

Ross was quiet for several seconds, and then he exhaled slowly. "Jesus." He grabbed her and pulled her to his chest. He held her tightly, his lips pressed to her brow, his body taut and trembling. "If he weren't already dead, I'd kill him all over again for what he did to you."

He continued to hold her and as the minutes ticked off his anger seemed to gradually drain out of him.

"It's okay, Lace," he whispered. "It doesn't matter to me. If we come to that point and decide we want some rug-rats, we can always adopt."

Lacey sat up quickly and the sudden movement toppled them out of the hammock. Ross cushioned her fall with his body, and then rolled her onto her back. She stared at him as if nothing had happened. "Really?"

Her voice was hushed and Ross smiled. "Of course." He kissed her softly, then pulled back and looked into her eyes. "You're not getting rid of me that easily. Besides, I think Fanny and Boomer and my parents would love a trip to Hawaii, don't you?"

Lacey nodded, then her eyes widened. "I've never met your parents. Do you think they'll like me?"

Ross laughed and started planting soft, feathery kisses on her face. "My mother was beginning to think I'd never get married," he said. "Trust me. They're going to *love* you."

Epilogue

Lacey planted her foot on the bottom slat of the pasture fence and smiled contentedly. Horses grazed, tails swishing lazily in the afternoon air as the crickets started their buzzing song. The sun was beginning its descent into the West and a faint breeze feathered through the leaves of the trees. She inhaled deeply.

The ranch had changed a lot since becoming Havenbrook. A number of dormitory style buildings stood on the land behind the main house, and the house itself had been remodeled to accommodate more people. A gigantic covered porch had been added along one side of the building, outside the newly expanded kitchen, and this was where most of the meals were served. Tonight, however, the porch was empty.

The broad lawn between the dormitories and the main house was filled with tables and chairs, children ran to and fro, clusters of people gathered to chat. Three full size barbecue pits sent the mouth-watering aroma of roasting meat into the air, and a band warmed up inside the tent where the dance floor had been set up. Servers dressed in jeans, boots, and cowboy hats meandered through the area, serving soft drinks and other non-alcoholic beverages. Lacey smiled. Havenbrook's third anniversary celebration was in full swing.

"You look like a proud king surveying his kingdom," Ross said in her ear. He placed his hands on the fence and effectively pinned her in as she leaned back against him.

"Queen," she corrected.

"Does that make *me* the king?" he asked.

She gave him a sidelong glance. "Only if you remember the power *behind* the throne."

He laughed heartily and rested his chin on her shoulder. "Of course, your majesty." Midnight galloped by and he took a deep breath. "It's quite a realm you have here."

"It is beautiful, isn't it?" she said. "To think I used to be so miserable here, and now it's a place of help and healing."

"I'm so proud of you," he said softly, nibbling her ear. "My wife, the philanthropist."

Lacey turned and draped her arms over his shoulders. "You helped a lot with that, you know."

"And how did I do that?"

She fingered the buttons on his shirt, suddenly very aware of the hands massaging her back. "You made me stand up for myself, from the very beginning." A smile tugged at her mouth. "If not for you, I'd still be the same frightened, timid woman who lived under Lucas's thumb for all those years."

He traced the curve of her jaw. "I think you shed your frightened, timid self when you found the courage to leave him in the first place."

"Maybe," she said, looking up at him. "But you kept me from putting that self back on. You and Fanny and Boomer, and everyone else."

"Fine, keep believing I had some great influence on your newfound independence," he said with a teasing grin. "If it makes you feel indebted to me, by all means, continue."

"I *am* indebted to you—"

"No," he interrupted with a frown. "You're not. When we got married we became partners. There are no debts between us."

Lacey gave him a look filled with hidden meaning. "Then...I *can't* repay you for all the wonderful things you do for me?"

Ross narrowed his eyes on her. "Well, it's not necessary, but...what did you have in mind?" She leaned forward and whispered in his ear, grinning when he flushed slightly and cleared his throat. "Well, um, that's very...*interesting.*"

"And *that's* just for starters." She nibbled his earlobe. "After all, it would be a shame to waste that enormous, sturdy four-poster bed. Especially since I brought those furry handcuffs you got me last Valentine's Day."

His eyes widened and stared at her for a moment. "Yes, well, I suppose maybe you *do* owe me *something.* I'll take your suggestions into consideration."

She laughed softly as he lowered his head, his mouth a welcome pressure on hers. He kissed her slowly, deeply, curling her toes as he pressed her body against his.

"Um, excuse me."

Lacey and Ross parted quickly and turned toward the sound of the voice. A young girl of about ten stood there, blonde hair hanging in two neat plaits over her shoulders. She was a trifle thin, and her brown eyes looked huge in her piquant face. Her hands were clasped in front of her and she rocked back and forth on sandal-clad feet as she chewed her lip nervously.

Lacey smiled and crouched in front of her. "Yes? What can I do for you, sweetheart?"

The girl picked up one of her braids and twirled it around her finger. "Miss Claire asked me to come get you. She says it's almost time to eat."

"Why thank you...what's your name, hon?"

"Jennifer."

"Well, Jennifer, I'm Lacey, and this is my husband, Ross."

Jennifer turned narrowed eyes to Ross and her chin tipped up. "Does he hit you, Miss Lacey? My daddy hit my mommy, that's why we're here."

Lacey looked helplessly at Ross. With a gentle smile, he knelt in front of the little girl.

"I would never raise my hand to Lacey." His voice was low and soothing voice. "I would never raise my hand to anybody, unless I had to defend myself. It's wrong to hurt people, especially the ones you love."

Tears welled in the girl's eyes. "Daddy hurt Mommy, a lot. I wanted to go away, but Mommy said we didn't have anywhere to go." Jennifer looked at Lacey with a wisdom far beyond her years. "The last time we went to the shelter, the lady told us about this place."

"And now you have somewhere to go," Lacey said gently, fighting her own tears. "And you can stay here with your mommy as long as it takes for her to get back on her feet. Then, she'll find a real home for the two of you."

"Miss Claire says this used to be your home," Jennifer said, running a freckled arm over her eyes. "Is that true?"

"Yes, it is," Lacey replied with a nod.

"Then why don't you live here?" the little girl asked.

"Because she lives with me," Ross answered, "in a place called Alaska."

"That's right. Since I didn't live here anymore, I decided to let other people live here." Lacey's heart went out to the girl and tears threatened again. When Jennifer threw her arms around her neck, Lacey looked at Ross in stunned surprise.

"Thank you," Jennifer whispered. "Thank you very much."

The little girl relinquished her hold and scampered back to the party, and Lacey stood up, her eyes stinging. Ross rose and turned to her. They looked at each other for a moment. He pulled her to his chest, his arms enfolding her as the tears slid down her face.

"Ssh, Lacey, don't cry," he whispered. "You should be proud of yourself." He pulled back and framed her face, kissing her tears away. "You did good, Lace. You did real good."

She sniffed. "I couldn't have done it without you."

He smiled and kissed her mouth. "Hey, I'm just glad I was along for the ride." His eyes twinkled. "And what a ride it's been, too. Hopefully, there are more where those came from."

Lacey frowned and punched him lightly in the stomach. "Watch it buster, or you won't be *going* on any more rides."

Ross laughed and draped an arm over her shoulder. "C'mon, *Miss Lacey*, they're waiting for you." Arm in arm they walked over to the party, and the celebration of life began.

The end

About the author

Leslie McKelvey has been writing since she learned to write, and her mother still stores boxes of handwritten stories in the attic. Her debut novel, Accidental Affair, was published in 2012.

Leslie is a veteran of the Gulf War who served with the U.S. Navy, and she was among the first groups of women to work the flight deck of an aircraft carrier.

Leslie lives in California with her husband and has three sons.

Also by Leslie McKelvey

Accidental Affair
Right Place, Right Time
Her Sister's Keeper

Coming soon from Leslie Mckelvey

Final Kill